# THE BUTTERFLY AND THE BEAR

GARY MILSOM

LITTLE BEAR PUBLICATIONS

*For Mollie and Harry*

This novel's story and its characters are fictitious and, with the exception of public figures, any resemblance to persons living or dead is coincidental. Any opinions expressed are those of the characters and should not be confused with those of the author. Descriptions of places and buildings, institutions or agencies, and any references to culture, history or events, are similarly fictitious and created from the author's imagination.

ISBN 978-1-9161281-1-8
Little Bear Publications
Sudbury, Suffolk, England.
www.littlebearpublications.co.uk

Cover illustration by Cara Thurlbourn

# FOREWORD

I was on a beach in Majorca when I first started writing this novel. Three chapters in two days. Then I stopped. Two years later I picked it up again and wrote every day for a couple of months with only a vague idea of the story I wanted to tell. I was surprised how the plot developed but don't doubt I was guided by the personalities of the characters I'd created. It's funny how you get to know them. Those first three original chapters bear little resemblance to those in the book now.

I had visited Majorca many times, but never Söller. Studying a map of the Island I saw the coastline there had a little peninsular – 'just the right place to build a villa' I thought. By the time I decided I should visit the town, I had written the first draft.

I searched for some accommodation and was amazed to discover that a hotel with the same name as the one in the book, the 'Söller Grand', actually existed! I stayed there of course and spent several days in the spring rain 'editing'. I was a little disappointed that the peninsula wasn't quite as I imagined (it had a sheer drop to the sea and certainly wasn't suitable to build on), but so many aspects of the town were as I imagined, and I immediately felt at home.

This is a fictional tale of love, relationships and fate, and the way we can impact, for the most part so positively, on one another. It is those human traits of kindness and compassion that provide happiness and I wonder sometimes if we become too embroiled in everyday living to really appreciate them.

They say love takes many forms, but all love encompasses care, kindness, understanding and a desire to see those we love happy. Sharing these wonderful aspects of our humanity brings joy. I feel blessed to have shared my life with so many people I love – people who have enriched my own existence and who I hold so very dear. Without that love, that friendship, life would be a lonely place and I dedicate this book to all of you. I hope you enjoy it.

Gary Milsom

*She said he was born a butterfly*
*To roam where the Buddleia grows*
*And so nurtured and nourished, with tenderness flourished*
*In the sweet fragrant love of the Rose.*
*His world was a meadow of ranunculus fields*
*Of orange and crimson and gold*
*One in which he'd flutter quite freely*
*One in which he need never grow old.*

# I

# HENRY AND MALISSA

*"May I?" he asked and dipping a paw*
*Fed on honey that tasted so sweet.*
*It was different to the nectar the butterfly loved*
*But he smiled and got to his feet.*

# THEIR FIRST ENCOUNTER

## GOODWOOD RACECOURSE, MAY 1983

"You know, I'm sure it's not that bad." The voice came from behind and belonged to a man standing by one of the phone booths.

"Sorry?" she offered, suddenly back in the present.

"I'm sure your troubles aren't as unsolvable as you think." His voice had an uncommon tenderness.

"Oh," she said, "I was just waiting to use the phone."

"I did wonder," he continued. "But when the phone is in demand it's probably best to make it a little more obvious that you're waiting and that you are next in the queue."

She noticed that another man had entered the booth and was busy dialling. She was a little disarmed at the intrusion and wondered just how long this stranger had been observing her, but the sudden appearance of her colleague saved her from any possible embarrassment. "Ah, there you are Malissa," he said. "We were beginning to think you'd got lost."

"Oh, sorry Malcolm. I've finished now. I was just coming." And, stealing a glance at the phone man added, "There was a queue."

Then she turned and headed back towards the restaurant.

"Enjoy your afternoon, Malissa."

She looked back. He had such a wonderful smile.

1

# GOODWOOD RACECOURSE, MAY 1983

## HENRY

She had turned when he called her name. Her eyes were a soft and dreamy shade of hazel and the tilt of her head promised playful mischief. She had clearly taken great care in preparing herself for the day. So lovely in a floral dress of pink and orange and green, with hair painstakingly arranged beneath a little matching hat. As she resumed her walk back to the restaurant, loose blonde curls bouncing off her shoulders, he found her draw magnetic.

He made his way outside and to the Owners Bar to meet Bobby Anderson.

"All good, Hip?"

"Yeah, fine Bobby."

"You look like you've just seen a feckin' ghost. All okay at the office?"

"Yeah, all okay. I was just thinking."

"Dangerous when you think, Henry. Anyway, she looks great. Real spark in her eyes this morning. Bit flustered when she got here, but that's the occasion. She'll settle down. She's a good'un, Hip. I know it. Gorgeous."

Bobby was enthusing about the horse, but the sentiments could so easily have fitted the image in Henry's head. "Was she biting her lip and blowing up her nose in contemplation?"

The trainer shot him a quizzical glance and handed him a beer.

Henry smiled. "I'm sure you're right. I'll be in the restaurant if you need me. Brad said I should call in on the charity ladies." He took a couple of swigs, placed the glass on the bar, beamed broadly at Bobby, and left.

## 2

# GOODWOOD RACES, MAY 1983

## MALISSA AND HENRY

Returning to the restaurant she was immediately reclaimed by the obnoxious Mr Clark, and her hopes for a more pleasant afternoon seemed well and truly scuppered. Of some consolation was the fact that Malcolm and two other guests were now sharing the conversation so at least the burden of *'Mr Been-There-Done-That'* was diluted.

Her morning had been hectic. Pondering what to wear for the occasion initiated her first crisis and she spent some time deciding whether the fascinator really did go with her outfit. Then she had to ask the driver, a nice man who seemed to approve of her appearance, to turn back because she had left her ticket behind. Then the A3 closure.

She hated being late and felt uncomfortable as soon as she arrived. Almost immediately, Mr Clark had pounced on her. Her boss, Brian Fenner, had warned her he could be a bit full of himself – "up his own arse" – he'd said, but he was an important associate so "try and give him some slack." Malissa had given him plenty, but, straight after lunch, and in response to his outrageous invitation to dinner that evening, she had got up pretending she needed to make a phone call. She needed that time to compose herself.

Now, back at their table and conjuring up as much humour and enthusiasm as she could, she noticed Phone Man was sitting at another table talking with two middle-aged women. He was a kind looking man and Malissa didn't doubt the conversation he was enjoying was much more convivial than the one she was engaged in.

Phone Man looked over at her and, despite the distance between them, their eyes met. She smiled at him. Then, remembering their earlier encounter, felt herself blush. He obviously recognised her and was probably wondering why she had been standing outside the phone booth like that. She upped her involvement in the conversation, though having no knowledge of horseracing was sure her contributions were scarcely relevant. Phone Man was looking again. And then he was getting up. Maybe he was going. God, he was coming her way!

As bold as brass, he approached them. "Malissa, how wonderful to see you again. Excuse the interruption sir, Malcolm, ladies, but there's someone I simply must introduce Malissa to. I won't keep her long."

With a flash of a smile, and before she could contemplate what was going on, he took her hand. Within seconds they were out of the restaurant and into the sunshine. "Hello again," he smiled.

She was gathering her thoughts, dazed by what had just happened. Who the hell did he think he was? And more than that, why had she just allowed herself to be hijacked? "Excuse me, but…?" She searched for appropriate words. "Well… do I know you? I mean, apart from seeing you by the telephones?"

Funny, once outside and on the lawn she wasn't entirely sure she was pleased he had let go of her hand. He smiled again. His eyes deep brown and fizzing with energy. "No, Malissa. Not yet anyway. But I really thought you could do with some air. I hope you're not angry."

A little awkwardness as she reached in her jacket pocket for her sunglasses.

"I'm sorry if I misread the situation," he continued. "I'm Henry, Henry Ovmeister."

"Like the beer?" She shocked herself with the remark. She should have been expressing her exasperation at this sudden assault on her liberty, not responding to his introduction.

"Ah yes, like the beer. But with a vee, not an eff. It's sort of German."

Malissa nodded curtly. "Keats," she replied, "Malissa Keats. Malissa with an 'a', though it's invariably abbreviated to Mel." What was she doing? She shouldn't be humouring him.

"Well, Miss Keats, I promise you that I am, despite what you may think, completely harmless and quite sane. I was watching you and thought you might need some respite from your hospitality duties. Drink?"

They were already heading towards the little Pimm's kiosk.

"Mr Ovmeister..." She realised she had taken the glass he offered.

"Henry, please."

"Mr Ovmeister, I think you should know that I'm here on business and that those people you have torn me away from just happen to be very important clients."

"I guessed as much."

"What I mean, Mr Ovmeister," - she really should make her point, - "is that I am here on business. I've only just started the job and I really shouldn't have left like that. In fact, I shouldn't have left at all and I was under quite strict orders not to drink. Well, not too much anyway, and..." Her protest faded and somewhere deep inside she realised she didn't mean a single word. She held out her glass as Henry poured.

He smiled again. That bloody smile. "Well, technically, Miss Keats, you didn't leave, you were sort of..."

"Kidnapped!" she interjected. The word seemed only to broaden his smile.

"I'm sure they'll be fine without you for a while. Anyway, if I know Brian, he'll be only too pleased that I stepped in to assist one of his newest recruits."

"You know my boss?"

"Some," he said. "I like him." And, without further elaboration, he clinked his glass against hers and carried on the conversation as though the way they had met was nothing out of the ordinary. "Do you like racing?" he asked.

"To be honest, Mr Ovmeister, it's the first time I've been." She mentally kicked herself, realising she was indulging him again.

"Well, this a perfect venue for your first day at the races. Plenty of colour, lovely surroundings, no queues at the little lawn bars, and lots of sunshine. You're dressed perfectly by the way."

God, was he always this confident, this easy? It was more like a statement of fact than anything overtly complimentary.

"Thank you," she responded. But before she could form her next question or try to mount another protest, they were interrupted.

"Henry, how the devil are you? I was only just discussing Delores a minute ago. How is she? In good form I hope."

In his sixties, with pointed features and wearing a red velvet jacket and matching bow tie, he reminded Malissa of a more dapper version of Fagin from the musical 'Oliver Twist.'

"I'm fine thank you, Stuart. And Delores is well too. Very well. Stuart, this is Malissa Keats. Malissa this is Stuart Campbell."

"Pleased to meet you," she said, shaking his hand.

"Likewise, my dear," he replied, glancing quickly at Henry to seek clarification as to their relationship. His curiosity was simply greeted with another smile.

Sensing he wasn't going to receive an answer, they exchanged perfunctory pleasantries. They agreed lunch was fine, though Stuart would have preferred the beef Malissa had chosen. "Watching the weight, so salmon for me," he said. Five minutes later, after another mention of Delores and unanimous agreement about the wonderful weather, Stuart was off, apparently to lose some money on the good thing in the opener.

Smiling as if he was relieved to have her to himself once more, Henry asked, "So, Malissa, did you sort out your problem?"

"Problem?"

"Your urgent phone call that wasn't. I trust you managed to resolve whatever was bothering you?"

She hoped her sunglasses disguised the little flush of embarrassment. "Oh, that. Well, no I didn't need to in the end. Make the phone call I mean."

Skirting around how uncomfortable and out of her depth she had felt since arriving, Malissa outlined the circumstances which led to her being at the phone booth.

Henry nodded sympathetically and topped up their Pimm's. "So, you work at Fenner's and it's your first-time racing. What else keeps you busy Miss Keats? How did you come to be here?"

Malissa suddenly and unexpectedly felt relaxed. She found herself telling Henry about her job at Fenner's and the manner of their conversation quickly became one of two people who were already acquainted. She told him about her ideas. He seemed impressed by her ambition, especially her plans to develop the firm beyond the literary agency it was mostly known as. At times she felt like she was a candidate at an interview who had limited time to make a good impression and wondered why she felt compelled to try and do so. As they talked, she warmed to him and she was sure the feeling was mutual.

"So, these guests of yours are all writers?" he asked. "That's interesting. Any I may have read? Not that I could be described as an avid reader."

She smiled. "Well, if you'd call '*Doctor Derek Harper*', who advises the readers of 'Teenage Kicks' whether to kiss with or without tongues, an author, then I guess so. But no, most of our guests here are from the printing or design industry, suppliers rather than clients. Brian Fenner seems to have set up quite a broad selection of contacts."

"And Mister Bombastic?"

She knew who he referred to. "You mean Mr Clark. No, he'd struggle to write a postcard let alone a novel. He has a printing business and a rubber stamp company called Plonkers."

"How apt!" He laughed out loud, and she nodded and smiled her agreement. He poured the last of the Pimm's. "So, you love books. What about the theatre, are you leaving that altogether now?"

"Well, the West End didn't quite work. The job I applied for at Fenner's was Assistant Editor, on the book side as it were. But Mr

Fenner seemed more interested in my time in the theatre, especially how actors and dancers got their jobs. He said it was about time he looked at other things and out of the blue offered me the PR Manager's job. Bit of a surprise, not the job I went for, but he was very enthusiastic. To tell the truth, I don't think there ever was a PR Manager's vacancy. I think he just made it up! He really is keen to get into the theatre. So no, it doesn't feel as if I'm leaving the theatre at all. And that's absolutely fine by me of course."

Henry smiled. "That would be typical of Brian. Sounds as though he has grand plans for you."

The small ensemble previously gathered around the kiosk had mostly departed by this time, gone to watch the first race, but Malissa and Henry stayed.

"And you, Mister Ovmeister. What do you do to earn a living and pay for such expensive suits?" Something told her he wouldn't be as keen to answer too many questions about himself.

"Me, Miss Keats? Now that is nowhere near as interesting. I'm just one of those people who wished he'd followed his heart instead of winding up in an office. And as for the suit, don't tell anyone but it's actually one of only two I own and was an impromptu purchase from M&S."

It was warm and sunny, a beautiful day and, in that moment, Malissa could think of nowhere else she would rather be, and no other person she would rather be with. Amazing, considering the circumstances of their meeting.

Henry was an attractive man. His handsome face exuded strength, and though chiselled in that manly way it was somehow softened by its animation and the mystery that lurked behind those deep, dark eyes. About ten years older than her, undeniably charming, confident, and easy to talk to, she found herself drawn to him. On any other occasion she would have made her interest in him more obvious, but, somehow, she didn't feel it was the right thing to do just now. The runners were at the start for the second race. She wanted to know him more.

"And Delores," she ventured, "is your wife?"

As soon as the words left her lips she felt a little foolish. Was she assessing his availability? Did he think so?

He laughed. "I am not married, Miss Keats. Delores is, however, one very attractive young lady, but she happens to have two too many legs to be considered a serious candidate for marriage. She runs in the 3:45, and if you've never placed a bet before you could do much worse than putting a little faith in her."

"Excuse me, Mr Ovmeister..." Another interruption, this time from a boy displaying the urgency of a soldier who had been tasked to deliver an important change of orders. "Mr Banks has asked me to tell you that your party has arrived."

"Ah, right, thank you. Could you tell Mr Banks I'll be there shortly?"

The boy turned and departed briskly, and Malissa realised they were nearing the end of their encounter. In Henry's eyes, she detected the same disappointment she herself felt.

"Well, Miss Keats," he said, placing his empty glass on the kiosk counter, "it seems I am being summoned."

"You're in demand, Mr Ovmeister."

"Sometimes business disrupts even the most pleasant of meetings," he said thoughtfully. Then he hesitated, and she wondered if he was about to ask to see her again.

"Well, business comes first," she said.

"Hmm." For the first time she detected something other than total self-confidence. "And a summer in the States. Sometimes, Miss Keats, a business commitment can scupper those more wonderous desires we feel in our heart."

It was a considered statement, a question to himself she thought, but his manner soon reverted to that of the man who had abducted her. "I wish you well at Fenner's. They obviously have an excellent recruitment policy." He took her empty glass and placed it next to his. "Better get you back."

He slipped an arm unthreateningly around her waist and gently manoeuvred her through the small crowd and up the pavilion steps. In less than a minute they found themselves back in the restaurant.

"Please forgive me for detaining Miss Keats for so long," he said to her guests who appeared to be in the same position as when they left. "And please, Malissa, do pass on my regards to Mr Fenner." He took her hand and kissed it. "It was a pleasure to meet you again."

"It was a pleasure to meet you too, Henry."

On hearing her use his first name, she was sure he wanted to say something else, but instead he turned to the others. "Ladies, gentlemen, enjoy the rest of your afternoon."

A last smile at her then he zig-zagged his way through the tables and disappeared through the doors at the far end of the restaurant. He did not look back.

Malissa resumed her duties, not needing to elaborate on the reason for her absence. She suddenly felt so much more comfortable and Mr Clark seemed to have realised she was not there solely for *his* amusement. Conversation flowed convivially and the three Fenner's employees and their guests flitted between their two tables and the balcony that overlooked the racecourse.

Mr Fenner appeared briefly to ensure all was running smoothly. She could tell from the warmth of his glances towards her that he was satisfied his business associates were in good hands.

Before the fourth race, he invited Mr Clark and two others to accompany him to the paddock for a close-up view of proceedings. Mr Clark looked at her as if to say, 'I told you I was important'. Several more guests also ventured outside for the race and she found herself sitting alone at the table, enjoying the privacy of her own thoughts.

The encounter with Henry Ovmeister, 45 minutes that had flown by, had changed her afternoon. Since his departure she had been keeping an eye on the doors just in case he reappeared. When she recalled his image, she found herself smiling. What she found more difficult to understand was the same reaction whenever she thought about the sheer audacity of the man, just imposing on her space like that. She wished he was a member of their party, so she could talk to him more.

"Who do you fancy, Mel?"

*Henry Ovmeister. I fancy Henry Ovmeister.* She was surprised by this sudden silent but frank admission but, turning to Malcolm and picking up a race card, she said, "Number three, I've been told she's a good thing."

Malcolm who, like Malissa, was a relatively recent recruit to their firm had made it perfectly clear, that he fancied her. He looked at his paper. "Delores Delahay. Well, that'll do for me. I haven't had a sniff in the first three apart from the odds on shot in the opener."

Malissa smiled and stood up. They made small talk as they approached the Tote booth to place their bet. From there they made their way to the balcony. Looking down, she was surprised how busy the area in front of the grandstand was and by the colourfulness of the people either waiting for the off or busying themselves placing a bet. Was she looking for Henry? Maybe, but there'd be little chance of picking him out, even if he was there.

Malcolm stood close to her. She noticed a few of their guests were at the far end of the balcony. She smiled at them. The others, she assumed, would have found satisfactory vantage points elsewhere. The commentator announced the runners were, 'Going behind for this afternoon's feature race', and shortly afterwards they were off. The milling around below stopped as the racegoers paid attention to the race.

The horses started some way from the grandstand and looked like one multi-coloured entity as they moved along the far side of the track against the backdrop of the South Downs. *How picturesque,* she thought.

A few spectators used binoculars to follow the horses, but most took advantage of the televised images on the giant screen. She found number three, the jockey sporting pink with purple stars, in about third or fourth place as they started coming down the hill to the sweeping bend which would lead to the finishing straight.

"She's doing okay Mel." Malcolm was closer to her than he needed to be. "Nice position – every chance from there." She hoped he was talking about the horse.

She smiled, and saw the filly manoeuvring to the outside as the horses rounded the bend. She was surprised how the excitement started to build in her. The commentator upped the tempo but as the horses entered the straight, his words struggled against the crescendo of encouragement coming from the crowd. Looking up at the screen, she could see Delores travelling sweetly, her jockey, unlike several others, relatively still in the saddle as his mount moved steadily toward the front. The crowd were now in full voice, shouting their fancy home and under her breath she whispered, "Come on Delores. You can do it."

"She's got it Mel, she's got it. She's gonna win!"

Malcolm had his arm around her waist and was obviously excited, but even as a novice Malissa could see that Delores was far too good for them. "She's won," she muttered and, by way of celebration, turned to her colleague and gave him a friendly hug.

"Yes, Mel, and how she won. Come on, let's get a drink."

Malissa was pleased that several of their party had also returned to the table. It wasn't that she didn't get along with Malcolm, she just didn't want him to get the wrong idea and the presence of their guests would ensure their exchanges remained on a professional basis.

Malcolm was keen to share the news of their win and ordered champagne. Apparently, the win dividend paid five pounds something for a pound, turning Malissa's investment into twenty-five and Malcolm's more hefty wager into a week's wages. No wonder he was pleased.

The next race came and went, afternoon tea was served, and conversation flowed as freely as the wine. Mr Fenner returned to the restaurant, accompanied by a very 'well-oiled' Mr Clark and several other quite high-spirited acquaintances. They too had seemingly bet on Delores Delahay and more champagne was ordered.

The afternoon had gone well, a great day courtesy of The Fenner Agency. Malissa hadn't drunk as much as the others and ensured everything continued to run smoothly. More than once Mr Fenner shot her a smile of appreciation as he took centre stage amongst his guests.

She could see he was liked and held in high esteem and was glad she had accepted the job with him. Always encroaching upon her thoughts though, was her meeting with Henry Ovmeister. Maybe, when they were back in the office, she would ask her boss about him.

Another man joined the party. "That filly of Henry's looks something special, Brian," he said causing Malissa to look up.

"Geoffrey, how are you? Yes, Henry certainly thinks a lot of her," replied Mr Fenner.

"He knows Malissa," Malcolm butted in excitedly. "He told her to back her at lunch time. A tip straight from the horse's mouth."

Malissa received another warm smile from her boss. Maybe he watched the race with Henry?

"And when Henry likes one," Brian Fenner continued, laughing, "then you got to follow the bear."

So, Delores was Henry's horse. Of course. And 'follow the bear' was from the Hofmeister beer advert. Malissa found a little smile creeping up on her as she reached for the race card for confirmation. Delores Delahay. Two-year-old filly. Owner: Henry Ovmeister. Sponsor: OC Transport Ltd.

Henry Ovmeister. The Bear. She remembered their encounter on the lawn. "How interesting" he had remarked when she told him her name in Greek meant honeybee - bears loved honey. She smiled. How she wished right now that she could congratulate him personally, how she wished they could continue their conversation. A summer in the States, he had said. Surely, she would see him again?

3

## MAJORCA, MAY 2007

## LEWIS LEARNS ABOUT A WEDDING

The softness of the tune and the fact that she didn't recognise it suggested it was one of their son's own compositions. Melancholy, romantic, troubled even, his music was akin to so much of his father's more solemn narrative.

She really should get up and do something more productive, but she laid a little longer, her eyes closed as she enjoyed the warmth of the morning sun. *Five more minutes,* she thought as she allowed the gentle invasion of the notes to gradually stir her.

Lewis had arrived late last night, and during the journey from the airport Malissa had told him that she would be marrying Robert in September. As expected, he wasn't entirely thrilled at the news, but once she had convinced him it was what she wanted he said he was pleased for her. That news out of the way, she would have him to herself for a couple of days and that made her smile. It had been too long since she'd last seen him.

A sudden surge in tempo as Lewis switched to some rock number from the eighties brushed aside the remnants of any drowsiness. She put on her shawl and headed inside. Ouch, the paving was hot on her bare feet. Maybe it was later than she thought. She looked at the clock as she entered the villa. It had just gone midday.

Lewis smiled as she walked in, switching tune to Here Comes the Bride. She waltzed happily towards him, throwing her arms around his neck. He stopped playing.

"Good morning, Love, did you sleep well?" she asked.

"I did, thanks Mum." He closed the lid on the grand and they walked into the kitchen. "I forget how beautiful it is out here," he said looking down over the plateau and out to the sea.

"Yes, it is lovely. But I want to hear all about you and what you've been doing. Tea or beer?"

Malissa spent the next half hour questioning him about his life in New York. She didn't know why she was always surprised to hear of the things he had done, how he earned a living doing what he loved, making music and videos. So creative. He played sometimes at Mikes Too, but no longer in the restaurant on 7th Avenue where Malissa had first introduced him to Robert. He was purposely vague in response to her questions about the girlfriend Henry had mentioned, but Lewis was happy and that's what counted.

"And you, Mum? What's keeping you busy? And how is Mister Politics?"

"You mean Robert? He's in Paris at the moment discussing fishing quotas." She knew that would make him smile. "And we're very happy," she added.

He shot her that look, just like his father's, and she fell into the familiar trap of justifying her response. "Lewis, these things are serious business and someone has to do them. Robert is an important man."

A wrinkled eyebrow and a cheeky grin, and then that smile. God, he reminded her of Henry sometimes. She threw the tea towel at him. "He is, in fact, a very lovely man who I'm very much looking forward to marrying. Now, stop making me laugh. You want another beer?"

Malissa had known Robert for more than three years and although she agreed to marry him before his secondment to the Seychelles, they had decided to wait until he was settled back in France to formally announce it.

He travelled a lot and that suited Malissa. In truth, she believed their life together had been fine as it was. Robert understood and whilst he had mentioned marriage several times he never really pushed the point or questioned her commitment when she hesitated. But Malissa was aware of the awkwardness he felt when introducing her at some of the more formal gatherings they attended. She knew he longed to say; 'And this *my wife,* Malissa.' So, eventually, they set a date.

Funny, on all the occasions she had met people with Henry, she could never remember him using those words. It was simply, 'this is Malissa.' Labels. Henry never liked labels, just names. Perhaps she had picked up on his dislike for them.

Ever since she and Robert had agreed on a date, she found she was thinking a bit more about Henry than usual. Perhaps the scheduling of the marriage had driven home the fact that they were finally over and that didn't sit quite as comfortably with her as it should.

They moved outside. "And Dad's okay about you marrying at the villa?" Lewis asked. It was a legitimate question.

A simple ceremony with a few close friends on the lawn here would be perfect. It was what she wanted. And if it was too close to a past life and didn't sit easy with Henry, he hadn't said so.

"Of course. Why shouldn't he be?" In her heart she could think of a million reasons.

"Just asking."

"Anyway, when you come out in the summer, why don't you bring Anna? Dad and Millie will be here, Brad too. And Vanessa and Fifi. It'll be like old times."

Lewis took off his t-shirt. "Nice," he said shooting her a quizzical glance before diving into the pool.

Malissa watched her son swim a few lengths then went inside. She opened the fridge and thought about what she could cook for dinner, but found her mind was on Henry. She went upstairs and entered the small bedroom. The wooden chest was on the floor as it had been for some time, its contents securely locked away. She looked under the bed. She smiled to herself and wondered if she should move the instruments to the farmhouse.

Then she checked her phone. There was a missed call from Vanessa and a text announcing she would be arriving Wednesday, two days earlier than planned but she hoped that was okay. Of course, it was. An early arrival meant Malissa would have more time to seek her valuable counsel. She thought about Lewis's comments about marrying Robert at the villa. Maybe Henry did mind. She would seek Vanessa's input.

## 4

# SADLER'S WELLS THEATRE, LONDON, APRIL 1989

## HENRY AND VANESSA MEET

"Excuse me, Richard," Malissa said, "but I need to borrow my husband. Henry this is Vanessa."

Henry turned and, for a brief moment, was sure he recognised the woman to who his wife was introducing him. "Miss Cozzette. How wonderful to meet you at last. Malissa mentioned you were a picture of radiance and if she has similarly undersold your ability as a dancer then I very much look forward to seeing you on the stage."

"Henry, why can't you simply say, 'Pleased to meet to you' like everyone else? I apologise for my husband Vanessa, but I did warn you. You'll get used to him."

Vanessa smiled at them both and shook Henry's hand. "Pleased to meet you, Henry."

Malissa wished she could conjure up Vanessa's silky French accent at times.

"If I can just leave you in Henry's capable hands for a minute, Ness? Henry, look after her and don't go rubbishing the ballet." Malissa was hosting the event and occasions like this necessitated her mingling with all of her guests.

"You don't like ballet, Henry?" asked Vanessa.

"I love ballet. Well, I certainly appreciate it. I'll admit I'm not quite the enthusiast my wife is and that can provoke discussion. But it's okay. Now tap dancing." He paused, then satisfied this was not a form of dancing close to Vanessa's heart continued, "Now that, I certainly would rubbish."

Vanessa smiled. "Tap dancing and ballet are, of course, compulsory elements of a dancer's portfolio but I agree they are not quite as exciting as the more contemporary facets of our trade."

"Quite," smiled Henry, impressed with her structured reply. Perfect English.

Maybe it was her accent that stirred his memory. He ignored it. "Malissa tells me you have an injury that's keeping you from dancing. I'm sorry to hear that."

Vanessa explained that she had always had a weakness in her left ankle. She was assisting with the choreography here and was also tending bar when required but there was no immediate prospect of a return to performing. Henry was sympathetic and interested but admitted his experience of troublesome limbs was limited to those who had four of them. The bell rang, announcing the end of the interval and their brief encounter.

Vanessa was pleased that Henry was as charming as she'd always imagined.

Considering she had known Malissa for more than two years, it was amazing that tonight was the first time she had met her husband.

As she cleared the plates, she thought about Henry and how he would have been when he was younger. She smiled to herself, realising she had warmed to him immediately. Perhaps it shouldn't have been that surprising.

She thought about Malissa's invitation to dinner. "So, you will come tonight Ness?" she had repeated when she collected Henry, adding an elongated, "pleeaasse..." when she sensed her hesitation. It would be difficult to refuse.

She was still putting the glasses away when the applause from the auditorium filtered into the bar signalling the end of the performance. Not being a classical ballet and interspersed with a little comedy and more contemporary dance, and certainly no tap dancing, she imagined Henry would have enjoyed it. Soon the dancers would be getting changed, happy that they had delivered. She missed that camaraderie.

A couple appeared at the door.

"I'm afraid this bar's closed, madam," she informed them and redirected them to the downstairs bar before locking the door and returning to her duties. Twenty minutes later she was finished and as she buttoned her coat at the theatre's door thought again about Malissa's invitation.

For some weeks now, Malissa had been asking her to come to Majorca for the summer. No doubt, she would ask again tonight. She paused and considered her options. Left to the tube station then home? Or right to the restaurant? It was cold for April but thankfully not raining as it seemed to have done every day since Christmas. She smiled to herself. She hadn't been out for ages, Malissa was lovely and always fun and she would like to know more about Henry. She turned right.

Fenner's had hired the whole of the restaurant for the evening. Rather than the usually intimate layout, the tables had been arranged in two long rows. A few people had already taken their seats, but most stood in groups enjoying canapés and a pre-dinner drink. She smiled at one or two who noticed her arrival and walked towards the bar, looking for Malissa.

Henry saw her and beckoned her over. "Bonsoir, Vanessa. Je suis très heureux que vous venez." It was a little formal, but she appreciated his greeting and complimented him on his accent.

He introduced her to the group of people he was talking to before ushering her aside a little. "I'm afraid I'm out of my depth," he whispered. "I thought I followed the story. She didn't want to marry him, but she had to for the good of the pompous King and the Kingdom, a couple of murders and everything seemed okay." He helped her off with her coat and with a smile swapped it for the last two glasses of champagne that the waiter had on his tray.

"They're talking about A Midsummer Night's Dream. The ballet is a parody and they were comparing it to the original. It helps if you've seen the play."

Henry hadn't. "Shakespeare," he said. "Well, I enjoyed it. Quite ironic really, tomorrow being the first day of spring."

Vanessa wasn't convinced it was the first day of spring tomorrow but was thankful that he had made her feel welcome and wondered if he, despite his air of overwhelming ease and confidence, actually enjoyed these occasions.

"An unusual name – Ovmeister," she said.

"Well, in England I guess it is. Think there's a few more in Germany. I understand you're going to Majorca with Malissa?"

Vanessa smiled. "Well, she has mentioned it, but I haven't said yes yet." It wasn't difficult for her to imagine Malissa had told Henry it was a done deal.

"Oh," he said. "That's Malissa for you. She can be very persuasive, but you should consider it. You'll enjoy it out there, I'm sure. And there's something very French about Söller."

"Well, I won't be dancing for some time, that's for sure. Have you always lived in London, Henry?"

She sensed the question surprised him and for some seconds he looked into her eyes.

"Vanessa, so glad you made it." Malissa had saved him from answering. "Sit next to me at dinner," she whispered and then smiled at Henry. "Well, I guess I better get them seated."

"Another time, Miss Cozzette," Henry said when Malissa had gone.

"Another time, Henry. À votre santé." She raised her glass. Henry smiled.

Vanessa watched as Malissa made her way round the various groups suggesting where they sit. She did so with a smile and an underlying authority until only she and Henry remained standing. Sure enough, there was an empty seat next to Malissa and Henry escorted her to it before taking his position several chairs up on the opposite side of the table.

A few introductions whilst the waiters tended to the wine and soon everyone was busy in little conversations. Henry was seated next to Mr Fenner and they were seemingly discussing racehorses.

"He's probably tapping him up for a tip," Malissa whispered to her. "Why he doesn't buy a horse of his own is beyond me. Still, each to their own. So, what do you think? You interested? Go on, say yes, it'll be fun and so much warmer than here. And it'll do wonders for your ankle. Who knows, by the time you get back you could be ready to dance again."

The offer was appealing. Malissa and Henry were building a villa near the farmhouse where they had honeymooned several years ago. On the face of it, she would simply be company for Malissa and babysitter for Lewis on the occasions when Malissa would have to work or if she needed to come back to London. They had become great friends over the last couple of years and the time they spent together was always enjoyable.

"I don't want to leave him here," Malissa continued, referring to her son. "And Henry has such a busy schedule for the next few months that he could hardly play stay-at-home-dad. And do you know, Ness? I've missed out on so much mother and son time. I can't believe he's nearly three. But this gives me an excuse to just get away and have time with him. And my best friend."

There was a sudden spout of laughter from those listening to Henry. Brian Fenner looked confused and confessed he had no idea whether Henry was serious or not. Henry just smiled, leaving him to wonder more.

"Henry, I hope you're not leading poor Brian astray," Malissa called across the table and then, to Vanessa, "Henry will visit too, and I can always persuade him to bring Brad."

Malissa had always suggested that Vanessa had been single for long enough and had told her on numerous occasions that Brad, Henry's right-hand man, was the perfect candidate for her.

More laughter and a loud Brian Fenner stood up. "Henry here has just sold me a horse, the son of an Oaks winner who will be aimed at next year's Derby. And how appropriate we've all just been to Sadler's Wells. It's an omen he says. Sadler's Wells has a great blood line. Isn't that right, Henry?"

Henry smiled.

"But, and you may disagree," continued Brian, "I am not so drunk as to overlook a good deal when I see one. And I'm not saying this horse was expensive but if you, Tom, and you, Denise, could hurry along those best sellers, it would be most appreciated! Now, we need champagne." He motioned to the waiter. "And we need a name for him. Fenner's Fancy, I am told, is not suitable for such a well-bred individual. Oh, and a few other shareholders please. It's got to be a good thing. Remember, I've always said that when Henry really fancies one... *then you gotta follow the bear!"*

As the laughter and banter continued, and as appropriate and inappropriate suggestions for a name and bids for a 10% share in the horse were thrown Brian's way, Malissa smiled at Henry. He smiled back and for a second it was just the two of them in the room. Even after five years she could still, like some love-struck teenager, feel herself melt when his eyes had that look.

He had promised her the son of Delores Delahay would go to a good owner and she could think of no one better he could have sold him to, no doubt at 50% of his real value, than her business partner.

She looked around the room. Happy faces, happy clients many of whom she counted as friends. She watched as Brian took out his cheque book, complaining how broke he would be as he wrote, and she thought about the day he first offered her a job – a job that didn't exist but which proved such an opportunity. She smiled again and blew Henry a kiss as he put Brian's cheque in his pocket and then she turned to Vanessa. "Looks like I spoke too soon," she said.

# 5

## MAY 1989

## VANESSA ARRIVES IN MAJORCA

*Casa de la Colina,* a farmhouse originally built of flint and stone, still oozed the charm of its 16th century origins. Built into the hillside at the top of the peninsular, rear windows would have been superfluous but the view from the little front garden was truly spectacular.

To her left, heather-clad scrubland, crossed by the coastal road which led up here, stepped its way gently down 150 metres before dropping over the cliff that formed this side's boundary of Söller Bay. The bay was protected on the far side by the Tramuntana Mountains. 50 metres of square cut rock stretched across the mouth of the bay at that side, forming a harbour wall behind which two dozen fishing boats and several yachts sat colourfully in the calm water.

An arcade of shops, cafes, and small hotels lined the semi-circular shoreline of the bay, standing on relatively flat land behind the road which separated them from the shingly beach. Behind the buildings the land rose gently, and small white houses stepped up the wooded hillside to the foothills of the mountains that overlooked them.

To her right, the coastline, like that side of the peninsular, was rugged and steep and extended a kilometre or two before bending out of sight. And in front of her a flatter expanse of land sloped more gently through a grove of orange and olive trees and to a cove which cushioned the impact of the azure blue waves that rolled into the shore.

Vanessa could understand why it was on this plateau, this little finger of sanctuary, that Malissa and Henry had chosen to build their dream. Having decided she had done enough for the day, it was here, in the front garden of the farmhouse, that she sat and watched the sun go down as she waited for Malissa.

Since her arrival that morning, Vanessa had been trying to make the house that would be their home for the next six months suitable to live in. Their major concern last night as they talked at the hotel, was whether the generator would fire up. It did, first go, and the soft thudding coming from the outhouse told her all was still well.

She had left Malissa after breakfast, collected the car, picked up some provisions, and headed up the hill. Three times she had to negotiate the steep make-shift path that led up from the clearing that served as a car park, and she smiled to herself as she recalled Malissa's assurances that the holiday would also be good for her ankle.

She sipped her wine. Below her, 50 metres down the slope, the skeleton of the villa and the plot it would occupy stood awaiting further attention. Malissa had shown her the artist's impression and she tried to imagine the finished dwelling.

She wondered how Malissa's meeting with the building company had gone. "They hate the idea of an English architect" she'd said. "And as for dealing with a woman, Ness…". Vanessa smiled, imagining the conversation and wondered how long the builders' protestations would have lasted.

Although only May, the evening was warm. She closed her eyes, content to succumb to the effects of the wine, the air, the distant whoosh of the waves, and the soporific rhythm of the old generator.

The scrunch of gravel announcing the arrival of a taxi woke her. She heard Malissa thanking the driver, the clank of a closing door, more gravel crunching as the car reversed, and a minute later Malissa appeared at the garden gate. She was panting. "Why we didn't have a proper path built first, I don't know. How's you?"

Vanessa kissed her friend, confirmed she was well and rubbing her ankle agreed a friendlier approach to the garden gate would be desirable. She took Lewis from her and they went inside.

"Not bad at all," said Malissa as she wandered around. "You have been busy."

Vanessa carried the sleeping Lewis upstairs whilst Malissa found a wine glass and returned to the garden. She was pleased to be there, and though the half-built grey construction in front of her looked a bit of an eye sore she smiled, satisfied that this place remained as beautiful as she remembered.

Vanessa joined her. "It truly is lovely up here, Malissa," she said, sitting down.

Malissa had little doubt her friend was as captivated by the place as she was, and they spent the next hour or so exchanging details of their respective days.

Malissa, as expected, had met a deal of *unjustified* resistance from the builders. "We hadn't budgeted for that, Mrs Ovmeister." And, "Those slates will have to come from the mainland, Mrs Ovmeister." Her exaggerated Spanish accent made Vanessa laugh.

"Honestly, Ness, it was like listening to a mechanic saying 'hmm' and 'ah' when all you want is an oil change. Anyone would think I was asking for the moon!"

Vanessa looked out across the bay. The moon was rising beautifully bright. "Seems nothing out of the ordinary to me," she said, and both laughed appreciating Malissa's strive for perfection could easily intimidate those who didn't know her.

Anyway, the builders would start next week, devote their best men to the job, and do their utmost to meet Malissa's impossible deadlines.

"So, what do you think of Henry?" asked Malissa, alone with Vanessa properly for the first time since she had introduced her to her husband.

"He's exactly how I expected."

"I think that's good. He told me he thinks you're wonderful. I better watch out. Or get Brad out here, seriously, Ness, you'd love him…"

"Malissa, I'm just not interested in men at the moment, no matter how handsome."

"You're never interested. A beautiful woman like you. You could have your pick."

Vanessa changed the subject. "The theatre went well I think. Everyone seemed to enjoy themselves and Mr Fenner seemed really pleased about the horse."

"Yes, the son of Delores Delahay. Henry might come across as the big businessman Ness, but Bobby told me he was offered twice what Brian paid. Wants him in a good home. Typical Henry."

"He has a good heart."

"Yes, I can't fault him there. It'll be great when he comes out here. Brad too."

Vanessa looked at her.

"Well, Brad's a good-looking man. Anyway, Henry's in New York for a couple of weeks so it's just you and me 'til then. And Lewis."

"You'll miss him."

"Yes, I will. But I have you."

Vanessa smiled.

Malissa poured more wine. "It's funny Ness. It's almost six years to the day since I first met Henry. You mention Delores, and Henry's in the States. Did I tell you we didn't see each other for six months after we first met because he went to New York?"

"Yes Malissa, several times, you said it was fate."

"Or love."

"Both."

"Six months, Ness. Then bang. How time flies."

## 6

# BURLINGTON HOTEL, LONDON, DECEMBER 1983

## MALISSA AND HENRY'S SECOND MEETING

Brian Fenner loved hosting these charitable balls and this year, the 25$^{th}$ anniversary of The Fenner Agency, he had yielded to Malissa's suggestion that this one be something special. Now, approaching 50 with his company employing 40 plus staff, he was entitled to feel justly proud of his achievements. A charming man, he would modestly point out that his success owed as much to being in the right place at the right time, and employing the right people, as to the hard graft and sacrifices he had made.

He started his working life in a second-hand book shop. It was there he met the talented but humble Bob Norris, who under Brian's stewardship became one of the world's most popular novelists. Following that success, many more writers quickly sought Brian's assistance and Fenner Publications was formed. Today, although his company's roots could be traced back to publishing, the Fenner Agency also represented and promoted painters and musicians in addition to the good number of writers they had on their books.

Hiring a room in The Burlington was expensive but it was the perfect venue for a get together such as this and he was pleased Malissa had persuaded him. "It's investing in the future", she had said. And who was he to argue? Employed as PR Manager 18 months ago, she was as adept as he at spotting talent. As well as being responsible for the most successful publication in the company's history - the bonus for which paid the deposit on her house - she had successfully managed the company's expansion into the theatre industry. Her enthusiasm was infectious, her work ethic faultless, and she had given Brian and the company a new lease of life. With his own children following careers outside the business, he regarded her as his natural successor and was already talking to his accountants to establish the theatre side of the agency as a separate entity so he could offer her a deserved shareholding.

He watched with a great deal of pride as she talked to the hotel manager, making sure everything was in place and ready for their guests. He hoped she knew how much he thought of her.

Out of the corner of her eye, Malissa caught Brian looking at her. He was standing at the bar enjoying an early gin and tonic and smiled. She smiled back. Tonight was a special night and she wanted everything to run smoothly. The band had arrived and were setting up. The tables were laid and the wine uncorked and waiting. She was pleased.

She looked at the table plan one last time and for a second considered altering it so that Mr Henry Ovmeister, instead of being seated opposite, would be sitting next to her. Too obvious, and anyway, it would mean reprinting.

Apparently, Henry had been invited to several Fenner functions over the years but had always politely declined. Until now. That, of course, set her mind racing. Had she detected a quizzical look from her boss as he cast an eye over the final table plans in the boardroom last week? Maybe she did, though typically he didn't comment.

A week after Goodwood, during one of their meetings, Malissa had casually asked Brian about the man who owned the horse. "He said you knew each other", she said.

"Well it's difficult to entirely know Henry," he had replied," but we are quite well acquainted."

They had met at a race meeting ten years ago, at a time when Fenner's was looking to expand and Henry had lent him money when the banks wouldn't. "I couldn't say we are close friends, but I will always be grateful. I see him at some race meetings and I follow his horses".

That conversation took place seven months ago and though she had wanted to ask more, something inside told her she was sure to find out more about Henry herself at some later date. Perhaps she would this evening.

Malissa joined her boss at the bar. It was 6.30pm, just under an hour until their guests were due.

"Fantastic, Malissa," was his greeting. "You drinking?"

"Orange juice, please."

The barman acknowledged.

"What would I do without you?" They clinked glasses.

"Hopefully stay sober and be in control," she laughed.

Brian liked a drink; socialising was his forte, but both knew he was always aware of what was going on.

"Vera showed me her dress. She's going to do you proud," Malissa continued. "And you're looking a bit dapper yourself."

"Five hours to choose it and the shoes. She should be down soon." He looked around the room. "Thank you, Malissa." And then, reiterating the genuine appreciation, he thanked her again and kissed her forehead.

Malcolm joined them and ordered a beer. "Hello, Mr Fenner. Looks great, Mel..."

"Thank you, Malcolm. Now Brian, I must get changed. And Malcolm, I haven't laid out all the place cards so if you wouldn't mind please..."

She handed him the remaining bundle and as she left turned to him saying, "You'll be pleased to know you're on the same table as Linda. But remember, this is an evening for looking after our guests, not those we fancy from accounts."

Malcolm smiled his acknowledgement. He had quickly appreciated Malissa was beyond his grasp and it was hardly a secret that Malcolm had been asking Linda for a date for several weeks.

As she left them to go to her room, the string quartet was warming up. They sounded good and Malissa made a mental note to ask them later if they had an agent.

She had spent more time than intended ensuring everything was to her satisfaction in the ballroom, so back in her room she showered quickly, relieved she'd her hair done at lunchtime. Like Vera Fenner, she too had invested in a new outfit for the evening. She was pleased with it.

As she applied her makeup, she remembered that afternoon at Goodwood, when she had felt so out of her depth and had sought the refuge of the ladies' loo and a telephone kiosk to escape unwanted attention. Then she was hiding, evading the limelight, but now the face in the mirror looking back at her was that of a confident businesswoman and all, seemingly, because of a racehorse named Delores Delahay.

The week following Goodwood, Malissa had received a manuscript, couriered to the company for her specific attention. It was a novel about love in the First World War and Malissa knew upon reading it that it was something special. Brian Fenner took Malissa's advice, immediately published it and it became a bestseller. The author was Jack Dexter, but it was sent to her by a middle-aged woman named Barbara who had been at Goodwood, heard Malissa talking, and hoped she was the person to bring it to life. Malissa had never met Dexter and only once did she ask Barbara to admit that the novel was her own work. She denied it emphatically, but its success certainly added to Malissa's growing reputation and she wasn't going to argue. Yes, that day at Goodwood was certainly one she would remember.

She smiled at the prospect of meeting Mrs John Clark, deciding any sarcastic remarks she might direct her husband's way would be subtle. Well, subtle enough to go over his head. She looked forward to meeting all the guests, many of whom she already knew to some extent and several, especially those from the theatre, she knew well.

Networking was what she did best. She would be both professional and charming in cementing her firm's growing reputation and was confident of a successful evening. But, as she left her room and descended the stairs, she wondered why the thought of meeting Henry Ovmeister again made her nervous.

# 7

## MAJORCA, JUNE 1989

### VANESSA AND MALISSA

Scrambling out of the water and onto the little pebble beach, Vanessa checked her watch. Two minutes fifteen seconds. Figuring it would have taken her 20 seconds to get from the rock, she was satisfied she had broken the two-minute barrier.

She checked on Lewis; still fast asleep in his pushchair. He was strapped in, of course, but she wasn't entirely convinced it was wise to leave him there while she went for a swim. Perhaps that was the incentive she needed to sprint back. Her time would be unofficial, but she looked forward to telling Malissa that her record was in imminent danger. It was 1pm and hot. She gently moved Lewis further into the shade and laid her towel on the shingle.

Since they had arrived last month, she and Malissa had spent many days here on the beach. Both were accomplished swimmers and sharing a love of the sea had devised a challenge which, at first, had started out as a bit of fun but quickly took on a degree of seriousness. Starting from the rock that stood proud of the water 20 metres from the beach, they would swim about 40 metres along the shoreline to another protruding rock, round it, and swim back. They had christened the first rock Blackpool and the second one Brighton. The official record for the Blackpool–Brighton Challenge was Malissa's, at two minutes three seconds. Hence Vanessa's delight at *unofficially* breaking it.

Malissa was in London. It was her third return home since they had been here. With any luck her visit would coincide with Henry's planned return from New York and allow them to spend some time together. Business commitments had kept Henry away for over a month. He hadn't been home nor had he yet been able to come to Majorca as he envisaged.

According to the builders, construction of the villa was on schedule. This was, they said, despite Malissa's ongoing interventions and requests to construct something impromptu, the first of which had been the pushchair-friendly pathway that Vanessa now navigated on her return to the farmhouse.

The builders rarely worked at the hottest part of the day, but as she passed the villa she noticed the roof tiles had been delivered that morning as promised. She woke Lewis and carried him inside. She would feed him, shower, and then they'd go into town for an ice cream and to check with the hotel for any messages from Malissa who was due into Palma on 6pm flight that evening. They also needed more wine.

The town was busy and the car park at the Söller Grand full, so she headed directly for the supermarket. She had no reason to believe Malissa would not be back as planned so gathered enough provisions for the next few days. As ever, the staff there were helpful and only too happy to carry the boxes to the car.

That done, she headed up to the hotel. Sergio, the hotel manager, was his usual exuberant self. "Hello, Miss Vanessa and how more beautiful you look today." And, "Just look at the little Lewis, how he grows each day, such a handsome little boy." He confirmed Mrs Ovmeister had indeed left a message and would be back that evening.

Vanessa exchanged pleasantries, thanked him, and agreed they would come for dinner soon, maybe even to sample Friday's 'Special Spanish menu in the garden with special wines and special Spanish dancing show'. She left smiling thinking just how wonderful this little town was.

"Now, Lewis, it's ice cream time," she said, and as they made their way to the harbour, they talked about Mummy coming home and about the pretty boats in the sea.

Malissa's flight had arrived ten minutes ahead of schedule, and a swift exit through customs meant she was in the car and heading north earlier than anticipated. It was still warm, some ten degrees warmer than in London, and the road to Söller clear. She should arrive at the house by seven, a whole hour or so before Lewis's bedtime. She was pleased to be back.

Exiting the car, she heard her son shouting, "Mummy, Mummy". As she made her way up to the house, she called out to him, "Is that my little Lewis I can hear?"

On reaching the garden gate, upon which Lewis had perched himself, she lifted him over, gathering him in her arms and smothering him with the affection he loved. She smiled an acknowledgment to Vanessa, but the moment belonged to Lewis and the next 15 minutes were spent helping him water the garden as he told her about everything that had happened while she was away.

It was 9pm when Malissa came downstairs and appeared in the kitchen. She sidled up to Vanessa, who was adding the finishing touches to the salad bowl and put her arms around her waist. Nestling into her neck, she kissed her gently. "I've missed this place, Ness. Have I time for a quick shower?"

She entered the little tiled alcove that was once the larder but now served as a convenient downstairs wet room and turned on the tap. "Oh, Ness, it's so good to be back."

"It's good to have you back. Lewis has missed you so much. Big prawns and salad. Shall we eat outside?"

"My fave, and dinner in the garden would be lovely." She stepped under the shower, revelling in the cascade of warm water droplets which washed away all the niggling worries she had brought back with her.

Refreshed and wearing just a baggy t-shirt, she joined her friend in the garden. She kissed her again, repeating how good it was to be back and they sat down to dinner.

The sun had disappeared, but it was still light enough to admire the view. The shell of the villa was practically complete and sat commandingly in front of them. Although grey in the twilight and surrounded by evidence of work in progress, it was not difficult to picture how wonderful a home it would become.

They talked for a while about Malissa's work. Fenner's was still expanding and recruiting suitable people was proving difficult, so she had been shuffling staff from one department to another.

To help with the backlog of manuscripts that had been submitted, she had brought several back with her. Although not strictly her responsibility, it was an aspect of her work she quite enjoyed and suggested she and Vanessa could read through them while sitting in the sun.

"Well, Mrs Ovmeister," said Vanessa as they finished dinner, "I have to tell you I broke your record today. One minute fifty-five."

"You broke the two minutes?"

"Yep."

"Unofficial," snapped Malissa with a smile. "Unless, of course, you got Samuel or Juan to time you? Even then I wouldn't believe you. That Juan would lie through his eye teeth for the love of his life."

Juan was one of the builders. Younger than Vanessa and handsome, with jet black hair and stubble, he took every possible opportunity to gain her attention. He would often bring oranges from the trees explaining that, although usually harvested earlier in the year, these early summer ones were the best. Two weeks ago, he had spent an entire afternoon telling them how this whole area was once an orange grove and recited the story of the young and beautiful farmer's daughter who once lived here and who captured the heart of a merchant's son who, against his father's wishes, whisked her away to the mainland.

Juan was besotted with Vanessa, and insistent she should teach him better English so he could "Find better job and meet more lovely woman like you." Vanessa was always polite but told Malissa there was absolutely no chemistry between them. He was not her type. No one was Vanessa's type!

Vanessa smiled. "It may not be official, and I haven't written it in the record book, but maybe tomorrow I'll do it again and be the champion. How was Henry?"

"I didn't see him." Malissa's expression was a little more serious. "Apparently he had to stay in New York." She paused. "Something to do with remote telephones and important business meetings he couldn't get out of. God, Ness, I haven't seen him for weeks and I miss him. And as for this telephone business, you'd think the first thing he'd want to do is get one installed here!" She smiled. She was showing a vulnerability which she'd believed was a thing of the past. "Sometimes...well, I don't know, sometimes I wonder if he loves me anymore?"

"Malissa," said Vanessa. "You are the most beautiful, caring, and interesting woman I have ever met. Furthermore, you and Henry are the most wonderful couple I have ever known and are loved by so many people. And look at Lewis. And look at your dream." She pointed to the villa. "No, Malissa, if Henry says it's important then it's important. You've had too much wine."

"Rubbish," Malissa replied emptying the bottle into their glasses. "I shall have more wine. In fact, I shall make a famous Malissa Keats sangria and we shall drink it under the stars and talk about dancing, and the theatre, and who you should marry."

She got up from the table and entered the kitchen, turning as she reached the door. "You don't think he's having an affair then?"

Vanessa retorted in French and at speed, and whilst Malissa didn't understand it word for word she accepted it meant something along the lines of, "Stop being such a stupid cow and make that effing sangria."

While she did, Vanessa checked on Lewis. When she came back down, she mischievously added a little more brandy to Malissa's concoction before sitting back down at the patio table.

"*Voila. Sangria a la Malissa.* Avec a little more brandy than there should be," Malissa said and poured two glasses.

The night was warm and calm; the gentle hum of the generator, the distant whisper of the waves, and the chirp of the crickets adding to the tranquillity.

"*Un moment mademoiselle,*" Malissa said.

She went back inside and a moment later returned with a packet of Vogue slim menthols. "Let's drink and talk and smoke."

Neither could be classed as smokers but from time to time, like naughty teenagers, they would share a packet of cigarettes.

"I guess..." continued Malissa, picking up from their earlier conversation, "that if you are nearing my record..."

"Beating it," Vanessa interrupted.

"If you're starting to challenge my Blackpool to Brighton time, then your ankle must be feeling a little better?"

They laughed. Malissa was aware Vanessa had not seen a physio since she had arrived here, but she was pleased her injury seemed to be on the mend. Funny, she didn't seem to miss dancing so much these days.

"I think so," Vanessa confirmed stroking her calf. "Though I would not be tempted to *en pointe* just yet. But if I keep drinking with you and don't start dancing soon, then this belly..." she patted it, "will grow even more."

Malissa raised her eyebrows and stood up. She lifted her t-shirt. "Now this, my dear friend... This! This is what you call a belly. This is what happens after you have a baby." She pinched the flesh of her stomach. "Yours, my darling Nessy, is as flat as a pancake, untainted by stretching and shrinking, and the envy of every woman around here. I love your belly and wish it were mine."

She was suddenly aware she was wearing no underwear and promptly pulled down her top. "I should have put knickers on," she whispered.

They both laughed again and Malissa sat down. "Now, tell me all that has been going on since I left. And you'll know I'll want a detailed account."

Vanessa relayed the events of the last three days. Firstly, about Lewis and how she expected he'll be swimming without his armbands soon. About the new words he had discovered, and that chocolate now appeared to be his favourite ice cream.

She updated her on the progress of the villa, denying Malissa's insistence that the builders must have thought they were on holiday with her in charge. She confirmed the delivery of the roof tiles and told her the landscaping company had eventually turned up, suggesting Malissa was crazy if she believed the garden she envisaged could be constructed up here. An inspector from the planning department had also called by to check on things – twice.

"Anybody from the telephone company?"

"Nope."

"Electricity?"

"Nope."

"What do you have to do to get things done around here?"

"And how was London?" asked Vanessa. "And Dawn and Jenny, are they well? Are they working?"

Dawn and Jenny were dancers who shared lodgings with Vanessa in London. They were well and working, as were the other actors and dancers she knew. They discussed the prospects of Vanessa's return to dancing but agreed there was no urgent need to do so; there would always be a job for her somewhere.

They discussed Henry, who had promised to spend a considerable amount of the summer here, (mobile phone development permitting), and if Malissa aired any doubts concerning her relationship with her husband she was grateful of Vanessa's steadfast reassurance.

They talked about the town and the people who lived there and of their own plans for the coming weeks. And sometimes they didn't talk at all, just drank the sangria and smoked their menthols in the pleasure of each other's company.

They had been talking for over two hours. The night sky was a deep dark blue and studded with stars. Since their first week here they had threatened to sleep outside and tonight seemed the perfect opportunity.

After checking on Lewis, Malissa gathered together some cushions and blankets and arranged them on the lawn. She fetched some snacks and the remainder of the brandy from the kitchen and made herself comfortable on the makeshift bed.

She lit a cigarette, exhaling a silver stream of smoke into the darkness. "Me and Henry must have spent a week sleeping out here when they were doing the bedrooms," she said. "Though we did resort to a tent and a blow-up mattress after a couple of nights."

"That must have been so romantic. It's so peaceful," Venessa replied joining her friend on the improvised bedding.

"Apart from the crickets. And the generator was a lot louder then," Malissa added thoughtfully.

Both women were feeling the effects of the alcohol and their conversation was tired and a little slurred. "I wonder why they chirp?" questioned Vanessa. "And I wonder if they chirp during the day? Crickets I mean, not generators. In fact, who named them crickets? And why is cricket that you play in England called cricket?"

Malissa regarded Vanessa's questions as profound ones. "Now that, my most dearest beautiful friend, is something I know. In fact, I learned all about crickets from Henry. The chirpers, not the game, though you know Henry was apparently rather good at that."

"Tell me more..."

Malissa lit another cigarette - it would aid her concentration while she explained the finer points of the cricket kingdom. More plumes of silver into the night sky. "I think they do chirp in the day. A bit – hic! But more at night. They rub their legs together or something. It's their call for a mate."

"They rub their legs together?" Vanessa lifted hers high and vigorously rubbed them together, but the rustling sound produced did not, in the least, resemble a chirp.

Laughing, Malissa did the same with a similar result and as a finale they rubbed their legs against one another's until the sudden burst of exercise took its toll. Retrieving their discarded cigarettes, they resumed their original positions.

"We should be careful not to start a fire," said Vanessa as earnestly as she could. "Go on."

"Well maybe they rub something else. It might not be their legs."

"I'm not rubbing that!" Vanessa interrupted. "And I can assure you if I did, it'd be more than a chirping you'd hear."

"Ness you are disgusting. Remember, there's a young child asleep indoors."

More laughter as they both mocked the sounds of a woman climaxing, before frantically shh-ing each other for fear of waking up Lewis.

A few moments to catch their breath and Malissa resumed her explanation. "As I was saying." She adopted a more serious tone. "It's a mating call. They only chirp when it's warm. And maybe they chirp during the day but the other daytime sounds drown them out? It's why there's none in England; it's too cold. In fact, Henry says you can tell the temperature by the frequency of their chirps. Now, let me see if I can remember. Yep. You count how many chirps one cricket makes in 14 seconds and then add 40. Or is it 30? No, I'm sure it's 40. And then you get the air temperature. In degrees Fahrenheit, of course," she added with authority. She sipped her brandy.

She could see her friend was impressed by the science and they spent the next 15 minutes or so testing the theory, estimating the ambient temperature to be between 63° and 81°.

It was way past midnight and brandy and sangria exhausted. Maybe it was time to sleep. Vanessa slipped her dress over her head and, snuggling down beside Malissa, pulled the blanket up over them. The scattering of cushions beneath provided surprising comfort. They lay on their backs, like teenagers having a sleepover, enveloped in the sounds of the outdoors and looking up at the stars.

The night had cooled a little but not so much to warrant another blanket, which was just as well as neither would have volunteered to go and get one. They lay quietly for some minutes reflecting on their day.

Malissa broke the silence and returned the topic to her husband. "I know he loves me, Ness. I think Henry loves everyone and everyone loves him." Her words were soft and earnest. "But sometimes, I don't know. It's like he loved me so much more when I was finding my way. Do you know what I mean?"

Vanessa smiled softly. Malissa knew her friend would always listen and, rolling over to face her, she changed her tone. "Well, if he's sleeping with another woman then so am I, and I can tell you, Ness, whoever he's sleeping with won't be a patch on you."

She kissed her friend. She intended to plant a kiss squarely onto Vanessa's lips and break away, but for some reason the kiss lasted longer. She pulled away a little, surprised at what she was feeling. For a moment nothing was said as the pair gazed questionably into each other's eyes.

A thought shot through Malissa's mind. Such great friends yet she was completely unaware of Vanessa's sexuality. Almost unbelievably they had never discussed such things. Right now, with Vanessa's beautiful face just inches away, she felt compelled to kiss her again and she wondered what Vanessa was thinking. Was she waiting for Malissa to make a move?

Through her skimpy cotton top, Malissa could feel Vanessa's breasts touching her own. She slowly moved her face closer until the sweetness of their breath mingled. She was aware of her quickened heartbeat, heard and felt her breath catch as their chests pressed together. Vanessa's eyes seemed to reflect her own sweet confusion.

They lay silently like that for many seconds, enjoying the closeness but perhaps neither of them sure what to do with it. Then Malissa kissed Vanessa quickly, unravelled herself from the embrace they had found themselves in, and, as she rolled back onto her back, repeated, "No sir, not a patch on the woman I'm sleeping with tonight. Night, Ness."

Vanessa let out a little laugh. "Sleep tight you drunken ol' whore."

They said goodnight again and lay quietly. Whatever their thoughts, they did not air them.

Malissa was aware of the ambivalence her friend had felt towards men when she was younger and wondered whether that feeling had remained. If her preference was for women, it would change nothing between them. All she knew was that they shared a special bond. She found Vanessa's hand underneath the blanket and closed her fingers around it. "Love takes so many wonderful forms, Ness. Thank you for coming to Majorca with me."

She felt the squeeze of Vanessa's hand and, before she closed her eyes and submitted to the beautiful weariness enveloping her, she scanned the night sky for The Great Bear. She thought about Henry and the evening they met in London.

## 8

# BURLINGTON HOTEL, LONDON, DECEMBER 1983

## MALISSA AND HENRY'S SECOND MEETING

The melody from the string quartet could just be heard from the corridor. *Perfect,* she thought as she entered the room. Several guests had already arrived and Malissa made her way to the bar.

Brian Fenner was in the same place as when she left him. "Malissa, this is Mark Cartwright and his wife, Amanda. Mark, Amanda, this is Malissa Keats who would be the best chief editor in the business if she wasn't so preoccupied with the theatre."

Malissa suggested her boss's introduction may have been a little over the top: "Whilst Brian might well say I spend more time with actors and dancers these days, I do still read. And when I have children, I'll be introducing them to Harry, Roger, and that naughty badger at the earliest opportunity."

Malissa hadn't met Mark Cartwright before but he was a long-standing client of the company and she had familiarised herself with the children's books he wrote. "And Amanda, I love your illustrations," she added.

Amanda told her she and her husband shared a love of literature. They met at college and working together on their books led to marriage, and children, and so on. It was a romantic story.

Malissa spent the next hour greeting guests, making small talk and ensuring all felt welcome. She was surprised how brash and bullish Mrs Clark was. She certainly wore the trousers and Malissa could appreciate why her husband felt the need to blow his own trumpet when out of her sight. Malissa didn't embarrass him but was sure any subsequent lunchtime conversations they had would be different to the one they engaged in at Goodwood.

In total, they expected almost 200 guests arriving from 7pm onwards. Brian would take the stage around 815 and officially welcome everybody before inviting them to sit down for dinner.

Malissa was talking to a group of friends from the theatre when Henry appeared at the door. He was accompanied by a very attractive woman wearing a demure black satin dress. She oozed sophistication and confidence. Malissa realised she had been checking the door, waiting for his arrival and felt her stomach lurch when she saw the two of them walk in. This must be his wife or girlfriend, though she had been certain he was coming alone. They looked good together with Henry dressed in a grey suit, pale shirt and a dark tie with splashes of pink. Malissa mentally compared her own dress, pastel and smart but nowhere near as classy, and suddenly wished she had dressed more boldly.

"So, what do you think, Malissa?" The question came from Simon, one of the theatre friends with whom she had been speaking. "Mel?" he repeated.

"Sorry, Simon?"

"What do you think? Should we tell her?"

Malissa regained her composure and remembered what they had been talking about. "It's difficult. You've got to be sure, I guess. Now, I really must get everyone seated. Speak later."

She turned, not exactly sure of where she was going but feeling she had to do something positive. She found Brian making his way to the stage.

"Ah, my favourite lady," he said with a broad grin. "If you're reminding me to welcome everybody – I'm on it. Shouldn't you have a glass of champagne in your hand?" He beckoned the waiter. "Going to be a great night, Mel," and with that he made his way up onto the stage amidst the polite applause for the string quartet whose session had come to an end.

Malissa smiled at those around her, mouthing, "hello," before focussing on her boss who had taken up the microphone.

"Your attention if I may, ladies and gentlemen." The gathering became respectfully silent.

Brian was his usual entertaining self as he welcomed the guests, said a few thank you's and outlined the order of events which, according to his understanding, was pre-dinner drinks, dinner, drinks, presentation, drinks, and then a live band and disco intermingled with drinks. His speeches were always appreciated, and he was warmly applauded off stage.

"Some just have the gift I guess." An interruption from behind. *Henry*.

"Mr Ovmeister…" Her voice was a little too enthusiastic.

"How lovely of you to remember," he said.

Malissa was floating straight back to the lawn at Goodwood. *What do you mean, 'remember'? Don't you realise I've been thinking about you every day for the last six months?* She suppressed her natural response. "Of course, I remember," she said. "How are you? How's Delores? Would you like a drink?"

"I'm fine, thank you, Miss Keats. And as for Delores she is grubbing very well, which I understand is a good thing. And you? How are you? I hear you are excelling at Fenner's."

How did he know? Why would he care? "Yes, things are going very well, thank you." People were taking their seats.

"Shall we?" He took her arm and led her to the table. "I love your dress," he whispered as he attended her chair and then sat himself down next to her.

He picked up the place card. "Hope you don't mind," he said, before shrugging his shoulders and showing it to Wayne, the freelance illustrator who seemed momentarily confused that his own designated seat didn't match the position on the table plan in the foyer.

Malissa's normal reaction may have been to ask if they were okay with their positions but of course she didn't mind and smiled at Wayne. Henry introduced himself to Diane, editor-in-chief of a women's magazine who sat the other side of him and Malissa made the remainder of the introductions.

Diane seemed very interested in Henry. As they waited for their main course Malissa heard her ask Henry if he was a writer. He laughed. "No, I'm afraid not." Then, glancing at Malissa, "But I do write a mean postcard." She recognised his reference to their Goodwood conversation and smiled.

Henry explained that he was in the transport industry and that his relationship with Brian Fenner was more as a friend than anything professional. Diane was tipsy and continued to flirt with Henry. When she asked why he had never married, Malissa found herself leaning closer to their conversation. Henry, however, deflected the question with a smile, did not allude to any current or past relationships and made no mention of Audrey Hepburn who he had walked in with.

During coffee, Brian took to the stage again to announce the winners of the annual 'Fenner's'. Although a tongue in cheek ceremony, the awards recognised those clients of the company who had excelled during the last year and the accolades were always well received. Malissa accepted the award for Best First Novel on behalf of the absent and, as far as she was concerned, non-existent Jack Dexter for 'his' novel, My English Rose, and she and Henry shared another private moment when Mr Clark accepted the Innovation in Printing Award on behalf of his company.

By the end of the presentation, people were ready to leave their tables and mingle, and several took to the dance floor as soon as the band started playing. Half of the guests on Malissa and Henry's table had departed but Little Miss Editor-In-Chief, was still hitting on Henry, who continued to politely deflect her advances.

"Malcolm!" shouted Malissa, catching her colleague's attention as he passed by their table. He turned and stepped towards her. "Malcolm – this is Henry Ovmeister."

She knew Malcolm would welcome the opportunity to meet the

racehorse owner he so enthused about at Goodwood, but more importantly she knew he would also succumb to Diane's obvious charm. "Mr Ovmeister," he said, "it's a pleasure to meet you. I always follow your horses. How are you and how is Delores Delahay? I see she's second favourite for the Oaks."

Henry thanked him for his interest.

"You own racehorses?" Diane interjected.

For a moment, Malissa felt her plan had backfired. She had just unintentionally upped Henry's appeal. But she quickly regathered her wits. "And this is Diane," she said to Malcolm. "Diane owns the magazine I was telling you about. You may be working very closely together over the coming months."

Malcolm shot Malissa a quizzical glance, to which she smiled. He had nothing to do with the publicity side of the agency and Malissa knew he would be assuming he must be in line for promotion. He sat down. "Lovely to meet you, Diane."

"Now, Henry," said Malissa, "if you have a moment, I'd like to introduce you to somebody."

Henry needed no second invitation. "Well, duty calls. Lovely to talk to you Diane and good luck with the magazine. Nice to see you again, Malcolm." He bade them farewell and accompanied Malissa towards the bar. Out of earshot, he turned to her and said, "Thank you."

"You're welcome. Returning the favour from Goodwood and, I think you'll agree, it was a little more subtle than kidnapping."

"Indeed. Can I buy you a drink?"

"It's a free bar but I'd love a gin and tonic." She looked back to the table, pleased to see that Malcolm had managed to engage Diane in conversation.

Accepting her gin and tonic from the bartender and trying to sound as though she was merely curious, Malissa finally asked, "Who was that you walked in with? I didn't see a plus-one for you on the guest list."

"Oh, um, Margot Someone-or-Other. I believe she's a book critic."

Then, perhaps seeing Malissa's eyebrows arch questioningly added, "We met at reception and took the lift together."

"Margret Annabelle Simpson," Malissa muttered under her breath. They had never met but she knew of her and recalled the name on the guest list.

"So, you work in transport and own a racehorse. Or more than one." Malissa annoyed herself sometimes but she had always felt compelled to gather as many facts about people as possible. It was just her way.

Henry smiled, and his brown eyes smiled too. "Yes, Miss Keats. I work in transport and own, or at least have a share in, several racehorses. Delores is one of the best."

"H.O. Transport?" She remembered the race card. "So, you own it?"

"Most of it."

"And you know Brian from...?" She was aware that this sounded more like an interrogation than a casual conversation. The band were gradually ramping up the tempo.

"I met Brian ten years ago, at Newmarket I think. We got talking and later we did a little business together. We bump into each other from time to time, mainly at racecourses, and we get on well. He's a good man with a good company. I'm glad he's making a success of it."

"He said he was pleased you'd accepted his invitation tonight. He said you would usually politely decline."

"I wanted to see you." There it was again. So matter of fact. So embarrassingly direct but, as Malissa stumbled for a reply, he relieved her awkwardness.

"Enough about me. When we met at Goodwood you'd only recently started at Fenner's but I see you have blossomed. You obviously enjoy your work but what else do you like to do?"

She liked his response and sensed his warmth. "I like dancing." It was a good reply and she smiled coquettishly, thinking she was just possibly edging him out of his comfort zone.

"Of course, you do." He finished his drink. "Shall we?"

Henry Ovmeister could dance, which surprised Malissa a little and in this environment, their relationship quickly became akin to a couple who had just met at a disco. He even loosened his tie and did a passable impression of John Travolta when the band went into a Night Fever medley just before their break.

They came off the floor hand in hand and laughing. It was comfortable, and they spent the next hour or so talking with people who probably regarded them as a couple. When he answered a question Malissa found herself listening to his response as keenly as those who had asked it.

They were saying goodbye to a couple of guests who were leaving early when the band slowed down the tempo. Malcolm was dancing with Diane, and Malissa didn't doubt he would be seeking clarification regarding his new role come Monday morning.

"Could we dance again, Miss Keats?" asked Henry.

"I'd love to Mr Ovmeister..."

They danced to Billy Preston's 'With You I'm Born Again' and said little. He held her close and she felt as though she was melting into him. They broke away slowly and kissed gently before applauding the band and leaving the dance floor. It was just a few minutes but Malissa couldn't help feeling it was a moment where she had always belonged.

The evening had passed quickly. The Fenner's Ball had been a great a success but Malissa's thoughts were far from anything work related. She wanted to take Henry back to her room and extend that moment on the dance floor, but somehow knew that wouldn't be part of the journey mapped out for her.

Just a few guests remained. Malissa and Henry were talking at the bar when Brian and his wife joined them.

"Henry, I'm so delighted you came," he said. "Let me get you a night cap and, if you have time, please tell me all that's going on with those horses of yours."

As the four of them talked about the evening's success, Mrs Fenner smiled and said to Malissa, "You know, you and Henry make a wonderful couple."

Although the remark was premature, neither she nor Henry corrected it.

"A wonderful couple indeed," Brian said. "The saviour of the business ten years ago," and slotting an arm around Malissa's shoulder, "and the propeller of the business today. If indeed 'propeller' is the right word. All this time around writers, you'd think I'd have extended my vocabulary by now. Cheers!" His enthusiasm was infectious, and they felt compelled to down their brandy in one. "Now, Henry, tell me what I need to know and, as ever, I promise to buy one of your yearlings when that boat comes well and truly in."

Henry and Brian, like old friends, discussed his horses and racing in general, and Brian suggested they next meet up at Kempton on Boxing Day. Malissa, whose only previous meeting with her boss's wife had been a fleeting one, warmed to her immediately. She was the epitome of the adage, 'behind every good man, there's an even greater woman.' Malissa was surprised how much Brian must have told his wife about her role at Fenner's and was somewhat embarrassed by the obvious high esteem in which he held her.

At 1am a middle-aged man in a grey suit and leather gloves appeared at the door. Henry acknowledged him and, looking at his watch, indicated to the man he would be ready in five minutes.

"I guess it's time to go," Henry said. The Fenners, who both thought one more brandy was called for, stayed at the bar while he and Malissa departed. She had so much more to ask him.

As they waited for the elevator, he kissed her goodnight. "It's been a wonderful evening, Malissa." It was the first time since the phone box incident that she had heard him say her name. "We should see one another again." It was the sentence she was sure he had wanted to say at Goodwood.

"I'd like that very much, Henry. Maybe racing? I'd like to know more about that."

"Now, there's an idea. I usually go racing more in the summer, but I am planning to go to the stables next weekend, if you fancy that?"

The lift arrived with a ping. He stepped in but held an arm against one of the doors so they wouldn't close.

"Yes, I'd love that. I'd love to see Delores."

"Would you now?" A glint appeared in his deep brown eyes on top of that smile. "Then that's a deal. I'm sure Delores would like to meet you too. I'll pick you up next Saturday at nine."

She smiled and gave him her address, repeating it to ensure he had understood. He kissed her again, still more reserved than she would have liked, and still with an arm against the elevator door. He smiled again. "Until Saturday then..." And as he allowed the doors to close, he added, "You'll need your wellies and your passport."

He was gone. Malissa returned to the bar and Brian smiled as she approached. Once more they agreed what a wonderful evening it had been, and in response to the inevitable question Malissa confirmed she had arranged to see Henry again. "Yes, I'm going to his stables next weekend. Told Henry I'd like to meet Delores Delahay. She's sort of became special. Good night, Brian. Night, Vera."

But as she headed for the door, Brian called after her. "Then I'll book you the week off Malissa. You'll have a wonderful time."

She turned. "Week off?"

"At least! If you're going to see Delores next week, then I expect you'll be going to Dubai."

# 9

## DECEMBER 1983, BERKSHIRE

## A VISIT TO THE STABLES

Malissa's Monday morning meetings with her boss usually consisted of her enthusing about the continued expansion of the theatre agency and the visions she had for the future, and Brian vainly trying to rein her in. At this one, however, they talked about Friday's dinner party and, of course, about Henry Ovmeister's apparent invitation for Malissa to accompany him to Dubai.

"Well, he did say don't forget your passport Mel..."

Malissa was sure she had heard him correctly and, while the comment should have rung alarm bells, maybe she just assumed it was a security requirement. Maybe she had drunk a little too much or was simply too caught up in the moment for it to have made the impact it should. Brian rather annoyingly thought the whole thing quite amusing, even suggesting it was typical of Henry.

"What? To take women he barely knows to strange countries?" she had interjected.

"No, Malissa, for him to surprise."

On appreciating her predicament, he did, however, become the fatherly figure she loved and assured her that Henry would have nothing but honourable intentions. Truth was, she could think of nothing better than spending a week alone with him, but surely, he would have expected her to seek reassurance. As it turned out, he did, and after she had phoned him for clarification, she felt more relaxed.

She spent the week researching Dubai, buying appropriate clothing and telling all those who needed to know, in particular her parents, that she was going on a business trip. As she sat in her front room, awaiting Henry's arrival, she was nervous and excited and felt that if the last six months had been a wonderful journey of self-discovery, the next six were going to be an expedition into the unknown. She heard a car pull up and knew it was him.

Any anxiety she felt melted as soon as Henry got out of the car to greet her. Putting her suitcase in the boot, and ensuring she hadn't forgotten anything, their conversation resumed just as they had left it a week ago. Soon, she was wallowing in the familiar, yet still remarkable, feeling that she had known him forever.

Paul, the driver, was the same man who had collected Henry from the party. After asking if she was comfortable, he informed her that, although it had been snowing, he expected the roads to be okay.

Their flight was not until 7pm. Henry's plan was for them to visit the stable near Newbury and head for the airport after lunch. Henry talked about the stable and horse racing, telling her Bobby Anderson, Delores's trainer, cared far more for horses than for any of the owners who paid the bills, including him.

Malissa listened, keen to learn more about horse racing, but was amazed Henry's only reference to their imminent trip to Dubai, hardly standard procedure for a first date, was a mention, when it started snowing again, of the difference she would find in the weather. She wanted to ask more. Shouldn't she, for example, be concerned about their sleeping arrangements?

They crossed the city, awash with Christmas shoppers, without much fuss and headed west along the M4. Leaving the motorway at the Newbury turn off, they were soon negotiating smaller roads and the snow-covered uphill lane towards the stables at Wickham Heath. It was a good job they had a four-wheel drive.

Driving through the gates, and past two large barns, they pulled up outside a small cottage with a snow-covered roof and smoking chimney. Save a few footprints, human not equine, the cottage was surrounded by a carpet of white which stretched to the foothills in the distance; a stitch-work of black fencing breaking what otherwise would have been a perfectly flat canvass. There had evidently been no procession of horses on the gallops that morning and the scene, Malissa thought, belonged on a Christmas card.

"It's beautiful," she said.

"Yes, it is," agreed Henry. "I've never seen it like this before."

As they got out of the car, a woman appeared at the door of the cottage, cigarette hanging from her mouth as she pulled on boots and grabbed a jacket from the hallway. "Henry, you old buggar, you could have picked a better day to tow your arse up here." An Alsatian and a smaller dog pushed passed her to greet their visitors.

Henry smiled. "Bobby, this is Malissa Keats."

"Lovely," she said, discarding the cigarette and extending her hand.

"Nice to meet you, Bobby." Malissa hadn't for one moment considered the trainer would have been a woman.

"Now," continued Bobby. "Henry tells me you're interested in seeing some horses. Well, you can see some inside but even these rugged darlings don't like coming out in this weather. Henry, I couldn't be arsed to cook so I've booked us a table at The Vine. Fanny – in!" she shouted at the smaller dog who was seeking Malissa's attention. Both dogs obeyed and went back in the house. Bobby retrieved another pair of boots from the hallway. "You'll need these," she said, handing them to Malissa.

"Thank you, Bobby." Malissa had brought her own change of footwear but thought it more polite to accept Bobby's.

Henry smiled as Malissa balanced herself against the car to put on the boots. She could tell how fond he was of Bobby Anderson, who was not one to stand on ceremony. "The Alsatian's called Dick" he whispered, which made Malissa chuckle.

"Yeah, couldn't be arsed to cook." Bobby mumbled. "And them there meat puddings are something to die for. We can have a look round then mosey on down." She lit another cigarette, closed the front door and complained about the price of winter feed as they made their way to the nearest of the barns.

Malissa couldn't imagine Bobby Anderson cooking for dinner guests. She wondered if she lived alone with just the dogs and her horses for company. If she was married, her husband would need some very special qualities indeed. Malissa smiled at the thought.

The stables were surprisingly warm and Bobby introduced each horse as if it were a friend. Her love for them was obvious and her brash tones invariably softened when she whispered reassurances to each of the animals they visited.

Occasionally, she would examine one a little closer, lifting a leg or pulling back a blanket. One she actually crawled beneath and, flipping on her back, ran an expert eye and caring hands over its belly. "Barbed wire," she said simply as she dusted herself down.

They lingered longer at each of Henry's horses, where Bobby would elucidate on the programme she envisaged for them. Henry would suggest this race or that and an ideal distance, and sometimes Bobby would agree with him in a 'yeah, that's a possibility' manner. But most of the time Bobby would outline the plans and Henry knew not to argue. He clearly respected his trainer's expertise and love for what she did, and Malissa instinctively knew that his respect was totally justified.

The second barn housed fewer horses. "She won't be missing this weather," said Bobby as they passed the stall that Delores usually occupied.

Bobby was in regular contact with the facility in Dubai, and Malissa had no doubt she was ensuring the horse was receiving the utmost care. From their conversation, it was obvious that Delores was the stable star and her racing plan had been agreed some time ago.

"She'll like you," Bobby said. "Blow up her nose when you see her. And, Henry, make sure Pinto ain't riding. He don't squeeze right." Henry's reaction suggested it wasn't the first time he had heard the instruction.

They toured the stable for almost an hour, and as they washed their hands Malissa asked how the stables were heated. There was no evident heat source and, of course, the whole environment would be susceptible to a naked flame. Even Bobby refrained from lighting up in there. "Keep 'em dry and use the best blankets. Give 'em plenty of hay and they can warm up this place like a toaster. Now, you wanna come in for a cuppa before we eat?"

Seemingly, Henry knew the answer was to go straight to lunch and suggested as much.

"Good. I could do with a beer. You mosey on down, Hip and I'll meet you there in two shakes. Better let the Chuckle Brothers know I'm out for the afternoon." With that, she left, reaching in the pocket of her waistcoat for a cigarette.

"She's…." Malissa searched for the appropriate words. Henry smiled, eyes bright in the half light of the barn. "Lovely."

"Well, I've never actually heard anyone describe Bobby Anderson as 'lovely', but I agree. And I can tell she thinks you are too. She'd probably be happy to give you a stall in here, should you ever become homeless."

They laughed and he took her hand as they left the building and headed back to the car. They settled into the warmth of the back seats for the short journey to The Grapevine and a meat pudding lunch and a couple of beers.

# 10

## DUBAI DECEMBER 1983

The first thing to hit Malissa was the heat. Although it was early morning the sun was already intense, and as they crossed the concourse to Arrivals, she wondered how the airport staff, all seemingly of Indian origin and in too many clothes, could possibly work in it.

They were met courteously by an Arab man, dressed in much cooler white, who escorted them past the queueing people and handed their passports over for stamping. Customs formalities seemingly completed in record time; she was grateful to be inside the air-conditioned building.

Informed that their suitcases would be delivered to the hotel later, they made their way out of the airport and within twenty minutes of touching down were being driven to their hotel by Ramesh, an employee of Henry's company there.

Malissa had read much about the customs and culture of the country. On the plane she asked Henry many questions, especially regarding how women were expected to behave. She was no feminist, but what she had read made her a little apprehensive.

Henry assured her there was nothing to worry about, and unless she planned to *'run drunken and naked down the high street kissing every man in a tunic and shouting Emily Pankhurst for President',* their trip would be like any other holiday. It was obvious from the manner of their greeting at the airport that Henry was an esteemed and welcome visitor, and she had no reason to believe that the warmth and respect shown to him would not be extended to her.

The road from the airport resembled a motorway back home. It was busy but flowed well in both directions, traffic consisting primarily of trucks and Mercedes and large petrol guzzling four by fours.

Evidence of structural transformation was all around. One minute an expanse of desert, the next a cluster of impressive buildings stretching skywards. New modern offices, apartments and hotels in varying stages of construction were springing up everywhere as were the first stretches of new roads that would connect them more efficiently.

The big road into the city effectively dissected a gigantic building site. It ran parallel to the coast, offering glimpses of the sea and Malissa smiled, appreciating it was as blue as it appeared from the air.

On the outskirts of the city, new shops and cafes stood alongside more traditional and modest buildings, and more were under construction. Dubai's charm surely, however, lay in the ancient narrow streets of the old city they now crossed to reach their hotel.

Little avenues of white and sand-coloured buildings, many without windows and built hundreds of years ago, served as shops with their merchandise displayed outside. Colourful silks and cottons draped the walls, clothing and leather goods hung on rails, pottery and ceramics stood on anything that provided a surface, and grocers displayed an array of fruits, vegetables and pulses in baskets that sat amongst the rolled-up carpets on the cobbled pavement.

Men with beards smoked and drank coffee while they chatted at little tables. Malissa could imagine a time when the merchants visited on their camels and wondered just how long this little part of the city could remain untouched.

As she expected she saw men in Kaftans and women in burqas, and workers dressed more humbly. But she was surprised to see just how many people went about their business dressed in the fashions you'd see in any hot European city.

The whole place, she thought, was a vibrant mixture of old and new, of Arabic and Western culture. She could sense the upheaval the city was about to experience, and she wondered how it would affect the ordinary people who lived there.

Any concerns she had about the sleeping arrangements were quickly dispelled when they checked into the hotel. Separate rooms.

She was aware of the country's rules on pre-marital contact but realised she was secretly hoping Henry had found a way round them. For a moment she couldn't help feeling she was unattractive to him. But those feelings quickly dissipated because everything else he did and said told her otherwise.

The hotel manager greeted them warmly on arrival, but unlike Ramesh who addressed Henry as Mr Henry, Hussain, addressed him more formally. "Welcome back, Mr Ovmeister. If there is anything we can do for you or your companion, please do not hesitate to ask."

Henry made a phone call from the lobby. Malissa overheard snippets of, "Yes, Brad," and "of course, Brad," and "you worry too much, Brad."

When he returned he rolled his eyes. "Don't ever appoint your best friend as your legal advisor."

Something told her Brad was very important to Henry and she made a mental note to ask about him later.

Without going to their rooms, Henry left with Ramesh. He had already told her he would need to attend a meeting as soon as they arrived, but he apologised again, hoped he wouldn't be too long and looked forward to seeing her later.

When he had gone, Hussain showed her around the hotel.

Speaking perfect English, he introduced her to several of the staff who all appeared to be of either Indian or Philippine origin.

Hussain didn't drink alcohol himself, but informed Malissa that the bar was always well stocked, and the experienced staff could make every cocktail including the refreshing non-alcoholic ones for which the hotel was renowned. She said she'd be sure to try one. If she had any questions or requirements, including a guide who would happily show her the city, she need only ask.

Her room, like the rest of the hotel, was truly impressive. Her suitcase had been delivered as promised and was on the bed. She changed into the new swimming costume she had bought and wore it beneath a loose-fitting dress. She would spend the rest of the day relaxing by the pool and reading a book. Funny. Nowadays, with her more trained and critical eye, she couldn't quite lose herself in a story as she once did.

More suitably attired, and cooled by the breeze coming off the sea, it was good to feel the warmth of the sun on her skin. Just twelve hours earlier she had been wrapped up against the bitterness of a cold English day.

Lunch with Bobby Anderson had been as much fun as she imagined it would be, and she took the opportunity to discover more about Henry. Bobby explained they met when he was 15 and she 18, and that he quickly came to appreciate horse racing. There were stories of gambles when he had won serious money, and a tale of one particular horse who her then-boss had been cheating with before 'running him proper and landing Henry a right old touch', something that would not happen these days. 'And rightly so,' said Bobby.

Bobby painted a picture of Henry as a young man who seized every opportunity to make money, and when he did, to invest it in 'good causes'. The most sensible of these, as far as she was concerned, was of course, the purchase of Wickham Heath.

Perhaps the most unexpected thing Malissa learned about Henry was that he was an orphan. He was brought up by an aunt who passed away a year before Bobby and Henry met and who had, by all accounts, left Henry a substantial inheritance; effectively the means to launch his business.

Malissa had warmed to Bobby and could completely understand why Henry placed so much faith in her. She even imagined that only Bobby Anderson, indifferent to the high regard in which Henry was held, could challenge him the way she did. "Cos I know horses, girl, and Hip knows that, and for all his understanding for things I know cack all about, I know he loves me."

Bobby didn't seem to call anyone by their real name. 'Hip' was somehow derived from Hooray Henry and Hip Hip Hooray. She obviously knew Henry very well, but many of Malissa's questions intended to enlighten her about his true nature, were lost amongst his and Bobby's shared passion for horse racing to which the subject would invariably return.

Bobby wasn't married and had no desire for children. As for Henry, she remarked, "Who'd ever put up with him?", adding, "He's far too romantic for all that." Then downing her pint and pausing looked at Malissa in a rare serious moment and said, "You know. You're the only woman he's brought up here to see his horses."

Possibly recognising the implications of her statement and not wishing to elaborate, she poured the last drop of wine, ordered another bottle and quickly changed the subject. The comment, however, was not lost on Malissa and she mentally added it to the 'why has Henry never got married?' questionnaire.

Husain appeared, disrupting her thoughts. He told her Henry had phoned, saying he would be a little later than expected but could she be dressed and ready by 7pm. "'I think you are going to dinner with some very important people," he informed her.

He then asked her where she would like to take lunch, and before departing added, “Oh, and Mr Ovmeister asked me to tell you that tomorrow he has no meetings whatsoever.”

Malissa smiled. Henry brought excitement and intrigue, and she looked forward to the week ahead. But as she lay in the shade and closed her eyes, she reflected on all she had learned about Henry and thought about the 15-year-old boy in grey cotton shorts and braces that Bobby first met 16 years ago.

11

# JUNE 1967 BERKSHIRE DOWNS

## WATCHING RACEHORSES

Henry loved these early mornings. He had been here most weeks since discovering the place a couple of months ago. Just an hour to himself, in secret.

It was quite cool as he walked through the wood and he welcomed the warmth of the rising sun as he perched himself on the fence. He pulled down his cap and opened his can of Coke.

About 100 metres away, in another field, half a dozen horses were finishing their morning exercises and gathering for their return to the stables. Even from this distance, Henry appreciated the spectacle, and if he had arrived ten minutes earlier he would have heard the thunder of their hooves as they pounded up and down on the firm summer ground.

The trainer who used the field immediately in front of him didn't have as many horses as some of the others, but Henry loved being up close to them and watching them work. At first, he had hidden as though spying on proceedings, but the riders had often noticed him, and since they didn't object to his presence he now sat in full view, taking it all in.

Right on cue, three horses appeared, cantering side by side. They looked small in the distance and grew as they got nearer, the familiar drum of their feet growing louder as they approached. As they passed him, the rhythmic hiss of their panting, like a downward push on a foot pump, told him just how hard they were working.

It always amazed Henry that, despite the number of horses, the tempo of their galloping feet and the rhythm of their breathing seemed to be in unison. Only on cold mornings, when you could see the individual vapours of expelled hot air, could you appreciate that each animal was working independently. They faded into the distance. He knew they would come back down soon, this time possibly at full gallop, a process that would be repeated several times.

When he first came here, he could only recognise individual horses by their size or any distinguishing marks, but with time he noticed other characteristics like their head carriage or stride pattern. As they came back into view he observed a new recruit, a brute of a horse who, despite his rider's efforts to restrain him behind the other two, was pulling for his head and wanting to run faster. As they passed him, Henry was treated to the sight of a horse being given full rein and surging by the others. When they came back at a canter, the horse was still pulling, like a giant petulant four-legged child, resisting his rider's efforts to settle him between the other two.

This went on for some 20 minutes or so before the two other horses returned to the stable. Henry had never seen a horse working alone before. His rider was asking him to gallop in both directions now, hunching down over his neck, balanced behind a loose rein which cut any restraint on the animal's power. It was thrilling to watch horse and rider in harmony. Henry had never seen a horse run so fast.

Gradually the horse tired, but when his rider tried to pull him up almost directly in front of Henry, he swerved sharply, catapulting the jockey sideways out of the saddle before cantering off. Instinctively, Henry jumped down from the fence, running the 30 metres to where the rider lay prone on the ground.

"You okay?" He was genuinely concerned.

"Feckin' dumb arsehole." It was a girl, older than Henry with an Irish accent, and he assumed she was talking about the horse and not him. "Yeah, I'm okay," she said, taking Henry's hand as she got to her feet. "Think I'll have some feckin' bruises." Then, removing her helmet, patting herself, and stretching her limbs, confirmed - "Nothing broken."

"I was worried," said Henry. "That's some horse you've got there."

"Yeah, if the fecker would listen to me we might even be able to race him. I'm Bobby. I see you here a lot. Guess you like horses?"

They were walking towards the horse who seemed to have a touch of guilt and was returning slowly to the scene of the incident before standing still sheepishly, a little way away.

"I've never really met one. I'm Henry." They shook hands.

"Meet Dick," said Bobby.

Henry gingerly placed a hand on the horse's neck, surprised just how wet and oily it felt. White sweat oozed between his fingers and, for the first time, Henry looked into a horse's mirror-like deep, dark eyes which studied him back with either indifference or curiosity. He couldn't tell which.

"Hi Dick," he said.

Bobby chuckled. "Funny hearing *you* say that. That's what I call him. It's short for Dick Head. His real name's Reynard's Way."

"Dick Head sounds more appropriate." Henry smiled.

Bobby checked over the horse. Her voice was reassuringly soothing as she comforted the brute that had thrown her. The sudden change in her manner surprised Henry and he immediately warmed to her.

She was by no means a typical girl. Her auburn hair was wavy and framed a face that, rather than being femininely pretty, was alluringly natural. Her tanned skin and sun-tinted eyebrows and lashes created the impression of a much younger person, and her bright blue eyes promised adventure.

"Well, he seems alright. Think I'll walk him back though. You wanna come?"

"To the stable?" Henry asked.

"Yeah. I thought, seeing's you like hanging about on the fence watching 'em work, you might want to come and meet 'em."

Henry thought for a moment. He had promised himself that he'd go into school, but this invitation was too good to turn down. He fetched his bike from the woods and soon they were walking back down the gallop.

As they walked they talked. Henry loved hearing about the horses and the finer points of training them. To him, she lived in another world, an exciting one full of dreams with incredible highs and bitter disappointments. She was her own person with scant regard for small talk. It seemed that life beyond horses just didn't interest her.

Henry loved Bobby's passion and sensed she was more profound than she chose to portray. By the time they reached the stable gates he knew this was the beginning of a wonderful friendship.

12

# DUBAI, DECEMBER 1983

Henry was waiting in the hotel foyer when they met, as planned, at 7pm. His meeting had apparently gone well.

It was short drive to the restaurant, where they would be meeting some of the dignitaries responsible for building the new airport and launching a new airline. Henry's company acted as a procurement consultancy for much of the materials and expertise they would need.

It all sounded so grand, yet to Henry it was just another piece of business and, after telling Malissa how wonderful she looked, he said he expected to say little because those they were meeting would be captivated by her beauty. She did feel good; she had slept by the pool for much of the afternoon and was amazed that Henry wasn't tired.

Malissa was the only woman at the dinner table. There was Sheikh Somebody-or-Other, a British man from the Embassy and two other gentlemen: David, an ex-pat, and Mr Ranjet. Conversation was easy and courteous and Malissa became caught up in the enthusiastic visions they shared. As well as the airport and the airline, they talked about commerce, tourism, hotels, and theme parks. Everything seemed to be so extravagant, as if they were taking everything they had learned, the good and the bad, and applying it to the blank canvass that was Dubai.

She couldn't talk much to Henry, not how she would have wished to, but found herself falling easily into the role of his… his what? Secretary? Partner? Wife? Certainly not mistress or casual acquaintance. It was hard to believe they had only just started to get to know each other and she was certain those gathered there regarded them as a couple.

At times, the situation seemed utterly surreal but mostly so natural. She loved it when Henry secretly squeezed her hand under the table and read his coded message as something like, 'Hey I'm sorry to spring this on you, but thank you for coming'. She squeezed back and wondered if he understood her reply 'I'm enjoying myself Henry and am happy, but I can't wait to get you alone and really get to know what goes on in that head of yours'.

When Henry, Mr Ranjet and David discussed the merits of companies bidding to build the airport's transit system, the Sheikh talked to Malissa. He often visited London, had been educated there and his family owned several properties in England. He loved the West End theatre and seemed enthralled of her knowledge of the industry. She assured him she and Henry would be delighted to show him around when he next visited.

David drank wine, but Henry, like the Sheikh and Mr Ranjet, drank fruit juice. Malissa did the same. Dinner that evening reinforced Malissa's understanding of how things were changing in Dubai and she appreciated the challenges the country would face in mixing their traditional way of life with the culture of the so-called modern world.

David was staying at the same hotel that evening and shared a lift back with them. He was pleasant enough but Malissa was glad he went straight to his room, leaving her and Henry alone for the first time since they had arrived. Henry suggested a night cap and soon they were sitting on the veranda that overlooked the pool. The evening was hot and the breeze very welcome.

"Did it go well, Mr Ovmeister?" Malissa asked, seeking confirmation of her belief that it appeared to be a very successful meeting.

"Yes, Malissa. I believe it did." He took off his tie and loosened his shirt. "I would even say it could not have gone any better and I should put you on the payroll, though I think the Sheikh would demand first choice and no doubt pay you so much more than I could afford."

She smiled. She just wanted to take him to her room and nestle into his chest. "So, you're building an airport?"

Henry smiled. "Well, *I'm* not building it. The Sheikh, well, his family, effectively the Government is. Their own airline too and God knows what else. They're very aware that their oil supplies won't last forever, so they're determined to put Dubai on the map as a centre of excellence for tourism and the like. Little expense will be spared. This is a very rich country and they have ambition."

"So, what's your involvement exactly?"

"Exactly? I don't know exactly, but for some reason, they trust me to oversee certain aspects of the development. My company has been doing business here for many years and it's just a matter of knowing them, respecting their way of life and appreciating their culture and desires."

"Because you're a man they can trust. And they want to do business with you because they like you."

"You think business is conducted on the basis of people liking one and other?"

"Where you're concerned, Henry, yes I do. I see it wherever you go. I see it in Bobby Anderson and in Mr Fenner, so why not a sheikh? I think you're probably very good at what you do and can build the best airport ever, even if it is in a desert, but I think you only do the business you do because people like you."

"Hmm." He looked at her quizzically. Had she had rained on his parade? "That's quite profound. Useless at business but a nice man. You sound like Braddon."

They both laughed.

"Braddon. That's your friend Brad? I thought he would be a Bradley; I've never heard of a Braddon."

Henry asked the waiter for two more drinks.

"Braddon Carmichael. Met him when I was 14 years old. Now he *does* have a business brain. And he's nice too."

"Tell me about your relationship with Braddon Carmichael..."

"Brad... Brad is a wonderful man. Very intelligent and perceptive and I trust him implicitly. He is the son of a man who was very close to my aunt. As kids we would play together but he was always destined for great things, businesswise I mean. He had the best education, is the most proficient accountant in the world, and is also a brilliant lawyer." He paused.

Malissa felt him opening up to her, telling her things close to his heart; she imagined he didn't do that easily and she loved the feeling.

"He could have worked anywhere," Henry continued, "for anyone. Or, of course, himself. Unfortunately for him, his words not mine, he decided to work with me. He tells me every day that he regrets his decision and is *always* going to leave. Secretly, though, I think he loves what he does, and I love him to bits."

It was a speech and, for one moment, Malissa thought she had found her answer to why Henry had never married: he was gay. It was the first time she had heard him mention the word 'love' and it was in relation to another man. Just her luck! But, looking into Henry's eyes, something told her Brad was just a fellow human being who he held close to his heart.

Nonetheless, she sensed Henry was tired and relaxed. His guard was down and she wanted to know him; she wasn't the kind of girl to let an opportunity slip.

"So, you love Brad?" her comment was deliberately mischievous.

"Hmm."

She knew there would be a 'hmm' and smiled.

He took a sip of his drink. "I think I said that wrong. My relationship with, or fondness for Brad is not one of a sexual or intimate nature."

"But you do love him?" Malissa was enjoying the moment.

"Love takes many forms, Miss Keats. If love is care, respect, and a genuine concern for another's welfare then yes, I would say I love him. Now, a love for a woman – that is different. It's all that, plus something else."

"Sex, you mean."

"Sex, or intimacy, is something very special and, I guess, the expression of love in a more..." he was struggling, "in a more private or special way. I have absolutely no desire to have sex with Brad."

Malissa laughed. This man who ran a big business, owned race-horses and God knows what else, and who had formed close ties with sheikhs and Kings was, when it came down to the basics of love and sex, seemingly shy. For once, she had the upper hand. On a warm night with a cool breeze, with light music filtering out to where they were sitting, where they seemed so far from any trouble in the world, where it was just the two of them, she had the power.

"And Mr Ovmeister." She took a provocative sip of her brandy, placed the glass delicately upon the table and ran her fingers slowly around its rim. "Do you harbour any desires of having sex with me?"

Their eyes met and for a moment, one which could have been awkward but wasn't, there was silence. Then Malissa burst out laughing and, taking Henry's hand and leaning across the table to kiss him, simply said, "I love being with you."

"Me too," Henry replied. "We shall go and see Delores tomorrow."

"And make sure she's being looked after, 'proper,'" Malissa said, in her best Bobby Anderson accent.

"Quite," replied Henry.

They spent the next half-hour talking about Henry's plans for Delores, Malissa finding herself caught up in the enthusiasm he displayed for her tilt at the Epsom Oaks in six months' time. As they talked Malissa realised they were making plans for the future and she wondered why it felt so natural to be doing so.

It was 2am when Henry escorted her to her room.

"I was wondering about the sleeping arrangements," she whispered as they stood outside the door. "I don't know if I'm flattered or sorry we are not sleeping together."

Henry took a little time to answer but didn't 'Hmm'. "Malissa, for the first time in many years you've stirred feelings in me that I thought were extinct. But as much as I would love to walk in here with you it would, in this country, only be appropriate if your name was *Mrs* Ovmeister."

Malissa suddenly, desperately, wanted to tell him she loved him. "Is that a proposal, Henry?"

"Miss Keats, if there was a minister here I would not hesitate."

Malissa looked up and down the corridor. "Lucky for you, it would appear they've all gone to bed." She turned the key to her room. "Until tomorrow. Breakfast at eight..."

Henry smiled. That wonderful smile. "Until tomorrow, Miss Keats."

The journey to Al Wiseman Ranch could have been completed in 30 minutes but Henry wanted to show her the coastline so they stopped several times. The beaches were expansive and sandy and the sea beautifully blue. Save a few sunbathers on sunbeds clustered directly outside the hotels spaced along the shore, the beach was largely devoid of people. "What a waste of a beach," Malissa said.

Evidence of development abounded, and Henry's commentary left Malissa in no doubt that the whole stretch of land would soon be transformed beyond recognition. He somehow painted pictures with his words, going into greater detail than she would ever have expected as he pointed out the intended location for this building, the plans for that piece of land, and how each construction would rival any built anywhere in the world.

She also sensed Henry's struggle between his appreciation for the natural beauty of the place and the impact so called progress would have. She liked that, it showed he cared, and she wondered how he balanced his business ambitions with his obvious empathy for the environment.

Leaving the coast road, they headed inland and within ten minutes, turned off the tarmac onto the sandy track that led to the ranch. "And this is where they'll build the new racecourse eventually," he informed her.

"I thought gambling was illegal here?"

He smiled. "It is. But horseracing isn't."

Al Wiseman was smaller than Malissa had imagined and nothing like Wickham Heath. There was no grass and the fenced off area would perhaps have been just about big enough to accommodate two football pitches. There was the main building, towards which they headed, a large barn, and 20 individual stables that stretched around one corner of the establishment. There were two horse boxes and three cars in the car park as they drew up.

"You're not impressed," said Henry as they got out of the car.

"Well, it's different to what I expected. I mean, the rest of the modern buildings here seem so 'with it'. Don't you worry someone will steal her? They don't seem that hot on security."

Henry chuckled. "I guess you have a point, but I imagine the penalties for horse stealing are deterrent enough."

"Mr Ovmeister – good morning." A small Indian man had appeared at the door to greet them.

"Mostafa, good morning. May I introduce you to Miss Keats…"

Mostafa welcomed Malissa to the ranch and they went inside, taking a few steps along the hallway before finding themselves in the sitting-room-cum-office. They sat on one of the two sofas that flanked a glass coffee table. At the other end of the room, two desks and chairs, a filing cabinet, and a few shelves supporting foolscap folders formed the office. It was not an elaborate set up by any means.

"Tea?" Mostafa asked.

They accepted, and while he was out of the room Henry told her the ranch belonged to an American businessman named Bill Wiseman who owned many racehorses and was convinced that keeping them warm in the winter was beneficial. He had enjoyed great success with those he had sent here so who was Henry to argue?

Wiseman was also involved in the development of the racecourse, but when Malissa asked Henry why he himself wasn't involved in what, on the face of it, would appear such an appealing project, she sensed the only reason was that he hadn't warmed to Mr Wiseman. Henry obviously didn't do business with people he didn't like. She liked that too.

The large barn-like building housed an equine swimming pool and two state-of-the-art horse walkers. It was air conditioned and provided an additional exercising area. Malissa quickly realised that unlike a training establishment designed to get horses to a peak of fitness this place was an equine holiday home intended to keep them healthy and ticking over.

Pinto, the man Bobby Anderson had mentioned, met them at the stables and immediately enthused about Delores. "She's fast, Mr Henry, very fast, and if you push her out she's bound to stay. Miss Bobby will be pleased." Henry raised an eyebrow and Pinto qualified his remark as he opened the stable door. "I mean, we watch her and we're confident she'll stay. Jamel's very careful with her. Very careful indeed."

Henry followed him in, placing a hand on Delores' cheek. "Hello my girl. How are you doing?" and then, satisfied she was perfectly okay, made the formal introduction. "Malissa meet Delores, the most beautiful lady on four legs. Delores meet Malissa, the most beautiful lady on two."

Malissa shot him a smile which suggested his comment was about a tenth as clever as he thought it was. Placing a hand on the horse's cheek, she remembered what Bobby Anderson had said and moved her face closer, gently blowing up Delores' nostrils. That close, she could sense the horse's power, but she also felt her gentleness and the instant bond she believed she would. "Hi, Delores," she whispered, "you won't remember me, but I saw you at Goodwood and I think you are very special."

Delores nodded enthusiastically and Malissa had to take swift and evasive action to avoid being headbutted.

"I think she likes you," laughed Henry.

"Does she recognise you?" Malissa asked as the horse was led outside.

"I like to think so, but Bobby's adamant that the horses only recognise her and those who spend a lot of time with them. Mind you, even if Delores held out a hoof and whinnied, 'Hello, Henry so nice of you to visit', Bobby wouldn't have it. I know a bit about horses and I see different characteristics in them. Not in the Bobby Anderson league, but I can tell she is well."

Pinto was parading the horse up and down. "She's doing very well, Mr Henry. Put on thirty kilos, just like Miss Bobby wanted. We'll just keep her ticking over and happy. And she's growing fast."

Even to Malissa's untrained eye she could tell Delores was something special. Her bay coat glowed and the white foot and blaze on her nose gave her additional distinction. Her gait was smooth too; just as you thought there'd be a jolt in her movement, her body would tilt ever-so-slightly, making the whole transition effortless.

"Rounded," Henry remarked, reading Malissa's thoughts.

"How old is she?"

"Technically she'll be three on the first of January. All thoroughbreds share the same official birthday. But she was actually born in March. I'm sure you've heard of the Derby?"

Malissa nodded.

"Well, that's for three-year-old colts. The Oaks is really the girls' Derby, contested by three-year-old fillies."

"So, she's really just a baby." There was a little concern in her voice.

"I guess she is, but it has long been decreed that three is the pinnacle age."

"We'll canter her in the morning," interjected Pinto, "just after sun-up. You want to come see?"

"Maybe," said Henry. "Or maybe later in the week."

"Do you ride her every day?" asked Malissa.

"No, Miss. I have others to ride. Jamel takes this one. But don't worry, Jamel is a perfect jockey for her and she's so well behaved – she never gives any trouble."

Henry gave her an approving glance. Bobby's concerns answered and no injured pride.

They spent a further 15 minutes with Delores, and on returning to the office Henry was handed a piece of paper and informed he had received a phone call. "Miss Keats, Delores, and a mysterious phone call," Henry said, dialling the number. "Remind you of anything, Malissa?"

Remembering their very first encounter, she shot him one of her sarcastic smiles. "You are so funny, Henry, excuse me while I try so desperately hard not to split my sides."

Henry chuckled and Malissa truly believed he thought himself funny, which really amused her.

He was a little more serious on the phone and after a brief exchange turned to Malissa, "Dinner at the golf club?"

She knew what dinner was and what a golf club was. She assumed too that it would be this evening and would involve the person on the other end of the phone. Armed with this information, she said, "sure," and Henry relayed the confirmation to whoever he was speaking.

A few further details and words about Delores passed between Henry and the caller before he turned to Malissa, his eyes smiling. "Yes, she's absolutely wonderful, looks a picture – I think bringing her out here was the best thing I could have ever done. See you tonight, Rod."

13

## DUBAI, DECEMBER 1983

They left the ranch just before 1pm and after returning the car to the hotel went for lunch in a small coffee shop within walking distance.

Their dinner engagement that evening was with Rod North, an Englishman who had settled in Dubai after a period in the armed forces and who headed Henry's storage and distribution operation. The golf club was the centre of his social life and he took great pride in taking people there. Meeting that night would save Henry a visit to Rod's offices later in the week.

Somehow, it bothered Malissa that she felt so at ease with Henry and she had to keep reminding herself they were still comparative strangers. Her more sceptical mind just couldn't understand why she already felt so comfortable with him. It didn't, however, seem to worry Henry in the slightest. She had no doubts she was on a one-way ticket to falling in love with him, if she hadn't already – she'd come so close to saying so last night- but what was he thinking? She found it so hard to tell.

Sometimes she was overwhelmed by his apparent feelings for her and at other times she felt she was living some surreal fantasy and that he was simply being gentlemanly. She would love to show him how she felt. To tell him right now. To shower him with affection so he knew. Yet somehow, she felt he was already aware.

He had asked nothing of her except her company and she felt sure that what she was feeling from him was love; a love for who she was, a love that didn't need words or verification. This seemingly powerful, influential man, so sure and so confident in everything and with everyone. Practical, intelligent, witty, and yet so… so… something. Something she couldn't fathom but something she instinctively knew had no malice; just something kind, soft, and even vulnerable.

"You think a lot, Miss Keats." He had interrupted her thoughts.

"Yes, I do. It's a habit of mine I'm afraid."

"Well, we all think to some extent," he smiled. "Sometimes too much."

She took a sip of her tea. "What are you thinking now, Henry? Right now. About us I mean. What do you think about us? Me and you?"

It was a direct question delivered softly, but the substance of it could hardly be misunderstood.

"Hmm…" The pause, then, "Malissa, when I *think* I weigh up various scenarios and possibilities and things do not necessarily become clearer. Now when I *feel,* that's different. Feelings don't need further exploration. Feelings come from somewhere else."

"Your heart?"

"Yes, your heart. Maybe to be truly happy we should listen only to our hearts because that's where feelings come from and feelings can't lie."

"Alright, then what do you *feel,* Mr Ovmeister? What do you *feel* about us?"

"Now, that I can answer. I feel attracted to you, more than any woman I've ever met. I feel happy when I'm with you and a little empty when I'm not. I feel your warmth and your kindness and your fondness for me. I feel an overwhelming desire to lay next to you, naked, to kiss you, taste you, touch you, and pull you close to me, real close, and hold you there so that you can share what I am feeling. So that you can experience my joy and realise the depth of my feelings, so deep they supersede any other feelings I have about anything else."

There it was again, the directness that always surprised her. She bit her lip and searched for an appropriate reply. "That's a lot of feelings," she said. "And I love your feelings. And they're akin to mine, though I'm not sure I could have expressed them in that way. Have you been in love before, Henry?"

"Yes, I have."

"And were those feelings similar?"

"Yes, I believe they were." A pause. His gaze was direct, his eyes serious and thoughtful. "And?" he asked.

"Do you think you love me?"

"I feel I love you." Another pause. "And you, Malissa, what do you feel?"

It was her turn to deliberate. "I feel totally gob-smacked and a little scared. Taken aback. Yes, I believe I love you. I think I have from the start, but it seemed so impossible. I feel I've known you forever, but I haven't. I feel I know you, but how could I? And you don't know me, not that there are any skeletons, but you're not to know that, you've never asked."

"People never stop getting to know one another, Malissa, that's the wonder. In fact, how many of us can say we even know ourselves? Knowing someone is a life-long journey and we change along the way. But if it concerns you, why not ask? My life is not that complicated."

Malissa mentally kicked herself for probing. He had said he loved her, something she realised she had wanted to hear ever since they met, but she couldn't forgo this opportunity.

"Well, what do I know about you?" She continued. "I know you're an orphan, or were I should say…"

"Technically, still am," he corrected.

"I know you were brought up by your aunt. Is she still alive?"

"No, she died when I was 14."

"Oh yes, I remember, I'm sorry. How did you live then? Who brought you up after? I mean, you were only young."

Henry shrugged. "Nobody really. My aunt was quite rich and had always had a housekeeper, she would have been in her twenties then, so I guess she took care of many things. I had money left to me and more in trust. A great friend of my aunt's was Charles Carmichael, Brad's father, who remained trustee of my aunt's estate and was often on the scene. So, I guess I just got on with things. I was quite an independent young man really, though I imagine both Alice and Mr Carmichael kept a wary eye."

"Where did you live?"

"Our house was in Berkshire."

"And how did you become successful? I mean, you're not just well off – you're filthy rich."

He smiled. "'Well off is more apt. The filthy rich build airports in the desert. I guess I was lucky with a few investments, though I have from time to time worked quite hard."

"What did you invest in?"

"Not *what,* rather who. You'll hear people say I have an eye for an opportunity but secretly it's a feeling about people. As for the types of industry I'm involved in, they're quite varied. Brad, I'm sure, could give you a run down if you really wanted to know."

She smiled. Why did the past matter anyway? Why, like Henry, couldn't she just trust her feelings? If he asked her to sleep with him tonight she would, no matter what the outcome. She wasn't some prized possession or vestal virgin so why continue the interrogation? He wasn't asking anything of her. But she had one more question and she knew that he knew it was coming.

"And finally, Mr Ovmeister," she smiled. "This great love of yours. When was this and what was her name?"

He smiled back. His face happy and very handsome. "I was about 14, Malissa and her name was Emma. She broke my heart so much I vowed never to love again. Until now, until I saw you at Goodwood." He held up his coffee cup and they both laughed.

Inquisition out of the way and with the mood so much lighter Malissa thought it only fair she invited him to ask her some questions.

"I have just one," he said.

"Fire away..." she replied.

They were alone in the corner of the cafe. He reached across the table and clasped her hand. "Will you marry me, Miss Keats?"

14

## MAJORCA, MAY 2007

### MALISSA AND LEWIS

"I think this is the most wonderful room in the world," Lewis said as his mother entered the room.

She looked out of the window. Below her, the farmhouse garden was awash with blooming lupins, phlox, aquilegia and roses which cascaded colourfully over the old stone wall. Behind the wall the mauves and yellows of the heathers tumbled gently down the hillside, around the villa, then through the orange grove to the little beach. And beyond the shore the deep blue Mediterranean sparkled in the sunshine.

"And, you know, Lewis, I think this is the most wonderful little house in the world too." She handed him a mug of tea. "May I?" she asked, picking up the note paper from the desk. "Oh, The Ballad of Juan and Theresa. You still believe the old story?"

He smiled, "I'm trying to fit it to an adaption of Oranges and Lemons."

"How appropriate! I look forward to hearing it. I'm just popping into town with Vanessa. You coming?"

"No, Mum. I think I'll pack and spend the afternoon on the beach. Long journey tomorrow."

"Okay. You need anything?"

"Flippers?"

She chuckled, kissed him and walked into the room Henry had slept in last week. She picked up a pillow and held it to her chest for a few seconds. She opened the shutters and went downstairs, trying to recall the last time she set foot in there.

She paused at the garden gate. She heard Lewis playing his new song and thought about the farm girl who lived here 300 years ago and found love with her prince. She thought about Lewis's comments regarding marrying Robert here. If Henry did attend and stay at the farmhouse, Malissa and Robert had planned to leave for their honeymoon immediately after the ceremony. They rarely stayed at the villa together anyway and never had when Henry was visiting; it was *her* home.

She looked at the shed. She missed the sound of that old generator and as she closed the gate saw Vanessa coming out of the villa with a basket of washing. She would talk to her tomorrow when Lewis had left. Right now, they were going into town. She would find something special for dinner tonight. She was going to miss her son.

Lewis was just reaching the rock as Malissa stepped onto the beach. Reaching up, he squeezed the rubber bulb on the old bicycle horn that still sent out its brassy oink after all these years. She saw him check his watch before he gave her a wave and waded back to shore. He kissed her and reached for his towel.

"Well?" she asked.

"One fortyish. You sure Dad did one thirty-seven?"

"That's what the record book shows."

She handed him a beer and they sat at the table.

"I need a calmer day," he said. "Unless you bought the flippers?"

"I think Dad would love you to break his record. It's stood for 17 years give or take. Red Snapper Delight for dinner."

He smiled and sipped his beer. "Mum, I still see how you look at

Dad and how he looks at you. You're sure you're doing the right thing?"

"Lewis, how many times are you going to ask me the same question?"

"Do you still love him, Mum?"

The answer to that question resided deep in her heart and was so emphatically 'yes' that she didn't need to think about it.

"I will always love your father Lewis. Always have, always will. You know that."

"And do you think he loves you?"

"Yes."

"I don't think I'll ever understand why you broke up."

She thought for a moment. She had asked herself the same question a million times and somewhere deep inside she knew their marriage could have been saved, if only... If only what? She wished she had the answer.

"You know, Lewis, sometimes things make no sense. Maybe we still love each other because we *did* break up. Who knows? Love is shown by a million people in a million different ways. There are no rights and wrongs or rules, or any guidebook for that matter. Love is... well, love is just love. It's either there or it isn't."

"You sound like Dad."

She thought maybe she did.

"And marrying Robert doesn't worry you? I mean, it's what you truly want?"

"Yes, it's what I want."

"And you're not rushing in?"

Malissa laughed. "Lewis. Have you ever known me to rush into anything?"

She knew he'd empathise with that statement. Malissa had always preferred to weigh things up. Some would even call her calculating.

"Lewis," she continued, "it took me six months to accept Robert's proposal and then 18 months for us to agree a date and announce it. I'm not rushing in at all."

"Okay. I'll say no more. Knowing you, Mother, it will be the best organised wedding ever and you never know, I may even get to like Monsieur Goody Goody Diplomat Man eventually. Funny, next time I come out here it'll be for your wedding. I'm gonna grab a shower. See you later." He kissed her and sprang up the steps.

Malissa sat and thought about the wedding. She thought about the marquee on the lawn, the band, the catering, the number of guests and the logistics of accommodating them. She thought about how she had harboured doubts about marrying again and she thought about the plans she and Robert had made since announcing the date.

Then she thought about another wedding. A wedding in a strange and wonderful land, that from proposal to matrimony took less than 48 hours.

15

# DUBAI, DECEMBER 1983

## PLANING A WEDDING

The whole hotel seemed captivated by Henry's enthusiasm. He spoke rapidly with excitement, firing questions which preceded his own immediate answers. Hussain would acknowledge each request, signalling his understanding while he paged through this ledger or that, issuing instructions to, or seeking clarification from, the staff he had summoned.

Malissa watched from some yards away, wondering how these people were keeping up with Henry who was like a child at Christmas yet still retained an air of authority, drawing them in so they too shared and believed in the picture he was painting. A picture that anything was possible if you just put your mind to it.

If she had been stunned by Henry's sudden proposal of marriage, she was totally floored when she realised he meant here and now in Dubai. Her 'yes' was emphatic but since then she had been in some kind of suspension, unable to glue together the thoughts in her head which refused to settle or find sanctuary.

Her heart, though, sang. Its music carefree, loud, and joyous - music that drowned out any sensible lyrics being written by her brain. She had boarded a roller coaster that had just been freed, its speed determined by gravity, its direction by tracks she hadn't laid and all she could do was close her eyes and hold on.

Suddenly all was calm. Just Hussain, Henry, and Malissa, in a reception area devoid of anything but its architectural elegance. "It is most unusual, Mr Ovmeister," said Hussain, "but, as you say, not impossible. And, if I may say so Sir, rather wonderful too. It will be our pleasure to assist in any way we can." He turned to Malissa. "May I offer my warmest congratulations, Madam."

"Thank you, Hussain."

"Now, if you'll allow me."

Hussain ushered them through the restaurant and out of the doors at the far end which opened onto a shaded terrace. On the patio stood an ornate white table and chairs, and on the table a cream lace cloth covered with a scattering of rose petals and a bottle of champagne. A secret garden surrounded by plants that shouldn't grow there and through the flora you could see the ocean. An unexpected and surreal oasis of colour to match the unbelievable events of the last few hours.

Hussain invited them to sit down and, like the best trained English butler, took the bottle from the ice bucket, opened it and poured. "Mr Ovmeister, Madam, the hotel and I are at your disposal," and with obvious pride, and possible relief that his staff had managed to prepare this special place at such short notice, he turned and disappeared back through the door.

Henry was grinning and obviously pleased with his afternoon's work. This was a new side of Henry. Childlike, excited, infectious, and she wondered how many people had witnessed it.

"To us." Henry raised his glass.

"To us, Henry," she replied. "Henry. Henry, you just asked me to marry you."

She hated to infringe, but she had always been a little nervous of roller coasters.

"Yes, Malissa, I have. And you said yes, and for the first time in more years than you would know, I feel truly happy."

"You don't think it's sudden? I mean, are you sure?"

He took her hand and perhaps aware that people did not always immediately share his enthusiasm for his spontaneity said, "Malissa, from the moment I first saw you biting your lip I have not been able to shake off your image. I am not sure there has been a single day since then that I haven't thought about you, and I have imagined how wonderful it would be to see that image every day. The you I have come to know is even more lovely than that image and it's something I never want to lose. Yes, Malissa, I am sure."

"You're saying I bite my lip a lot?"

Henry laughed. "You've done it a lot in the last couple of hours."

She thought about it and didn't doubt Henry was right.

"Henry?" She was being serious again.

"Yes, Malissa?"

"Henry. I too have thought about you every day since we met. It's possible also that I have dreamed of being with you, like, well, like we are now, of being your girlfriend or, yes, even your wife." She knew this was absolutely true and couldn't believe she was alluding to it as being a mere possibility. "You've just taken me so completely by surprise. I am absolutely stunned and…" she paused. "Flattered." It wasn't the word she intended.

"Flattered, Miss Keats? Flattered that I love you? Don't be. I am a man and you are a woman. If you feel half the love I feel for you, then I, Henry Bartholomew Ovmeister am a happy man indeed."

"Bartholomew?" she questioned trying to suppress a laugh.

"I know, I tend not to broadcast it. Malissa, sometimes I appear impetuous, but sometimes I just know. I just feel. And in those times, I *feel,* I am sure.

"You are right we have known each other for what many may consider a relatively short period, but we have a lifetime ahead of us to get to know each other more, and I have no doubt the more I discover, the more I will love. I am sure Malissa, and unafraid by what lies ahead. Maybe these events are a little unconventional, but I never believed that I would find what I have found with you and my very being tells me you are the one. I need no more time.

"You are you. You are now, a product of your life to date and I love you because of who you are, the woman I'd love to spend the rest of my life with. I don't expect you to be as captured by the moment as I am I just ask you to look into your heart."

"My heart overflows for you, Henry."

"Then listen to it, Malissa, and believe what it says."

"And if it all goes wrong?"

"Wrong? "He paused. "Well, if it does, if you discover your feelings are something other than love, then I guess you'll become a very rich divorcee." He smiled broadly.

It suddenly dawned on Malissa just who was taking the risk here. His motive could not be anything other than love. Why on earth would she question things? Why on earth did he allow her to?

"Oh, Henry, please never think that my questions or considerations or whatever you call them override my love. It's just me. I have never felt for anyone what I feel for you, nowhere near, not even remotely close. Yes, I have dreamed of being Mrs Ovmeister, of course I have. To have your children and live together as a family and..." she paused, she just couldn't help herself. "You do want children?"

For the briefest of moments, she thought she detected horror in his eyes as if the thought of children appalled him, but with even wider eyes and a broad grin he said, "Of course, loads, as many as you want."

They still held hands.

"So, what now?" she continued.

"Well, I think we can get married Thursday. The honeymoon suite is available, and I could squeeze in everything else I need to do here tomorrow, leaving the rest of the week free for us to get to know each other even more. It's bad luck to see each other on the eve of the wedding anyway."

Malissa had already gathered this was going to be the shortest engagement in history.

"Henry, I have heard many stories about a man trying to get a woman into bed. I know many women who have fallen for a silver tongue or a proclamation of love never ending but bringing a woman to a foreign country, where pre-marital sex is frowned upon, romancing her and *actually marrying* her to get his wicked way really does take the biscuit. I hope you'll believe I was worth it."

He laughed. "Tomorrow you can buy a dress and Hussain will put the hotel at your disposal. I can conclude any business and the rest of the arrangements will just fall into place."

Malissa took that last comment as he would move heaven and earth to ensure the job got done.

All girls, she thought, dream of a fairy tale. Of being whisked away by a handsome prince, taken to his castle and living happily ever after. Here and now she was in the midst of such a dream and she hated her hesitation. She had always believed she would have a traditional wedding, in England, surrounded by her family and friends. She had found her prince and he loved her, and she loved him. What the hell was her problem?

"Shall I wear white, Mr Ovmeister?"

Henry was still grinning when they arrived at the golf club. During the afternoon Malissa had assured him her hesitation had nothing to do with marrying him. She was sure if she asked, he would postpone things until they got home, where they would get engaged and follow a more conventional path to matrimony. Life with Henry was not, however, going to be conventional, and though her head whispered a sonnet of wisdom her heart sang a melody of romance.

Henry understood. They needn't tell anyone they had married in Dubai, he said, and once back in England could announce simply that they had got engaged. They could then plan the wedding she had always dreamed of.

"Wouldn't that be bigamy?" she'd asked.

"It'd be big of me too." He laughed at his own silly joke before explaining they could have a blessing ceremony which would be indiscernible from the real thing.

As ludicrous as everything sounded, there was an undeniable logic to Henry's thinking. He saw obstacles as challenges and the impossible as a maybe. Bridges would be crossed as they approached them.

She was wearing the same dress that she had worn at Goodwood. But no hat. She was pleased Henry noticed.

Rod was about 50, lean, with longish grey hair and grey twinkling eyes which he intermittently framed with the silver-rimmed half-moon spectacles that lived on his head. He wore a light blue cotton shirt and beige linen trousers, and Malissa could not imagine him dressed any other way. Rod of Arabia, she thought.

He was talking to the barman when they arrived and his greeting to Henry was warm and enthusiastic, with hugs accompanying the more conventional handshakes. "And Malissa, you are even more lovely than Henry has said. And he said you were *very* lovely."

"Thank you, Rod." It was good to know that Henry spoke to people about her.

The restaurant was about half full, with six or seven tables occupied. Mostly men and mostly English as far as she could tell. Henry and Rod talked a little about business, all of which, as far as Malissa could tell, was functioning perfectly.

Rod, or 'Sticks' as Henry called him, used to be a drummer in the Marines, settling in Dubai after the second world war and setting up a trucking business. He was obviously one of Henry's 'investments' and the relationship between them wasn't that far removed from a father and his son. Malissa wondered if Henry secretly searched for a father figure. Did Brian Fenner represent that too?

The mutual respect and love between them was obvious and Malissa was beginning to appreciate the expertise of Henry's eye - or was it his heart, in choosing those with whom to do business. And she thought that same expertise had chosen her, not that she was an investment but because he had an instinct for good people.

Once seated, they talked about Delores and her tilt for the Oaks next June. Rod it seemed had made a considerable ante post investment, but apparently not at the 100-1 Henry had got before Delores had ever even seen a racecourse. It was during their main course that Henry dropped the bombshell.

"Sticks," he said matter-of-factly. "Malissa and I would like to get married here."

Rod stopped eating. He thought for a second or two. "Well, congratulations. You do, if I may say, make a wonderful couple. It's about time, Henry." Then turning to Malissa, "It's not a bad place to say 'I do'. When are you planning?"

He seemed a little shocked at the news but appeared genuinely pleased at the announcement.

"Thursday," added Henry

Rod forked a piece of fish into his mouth, considering his response while he chewed. "Thursday? You're getting married Thursday? This Thursday? The day after tomorrow? Why didn't you tell me?"

Another forkful while Henry answered. "Because we only decided today. Besides the hotel, you're the only person we've told, and I was wondering whether you'd have a word with Reverend Roberts so he could organise things?"

Rod just about managed not to choke, and as he chewed he cast alternating glances between his two guests, seemingly waiting for the punchline. It didn't come.

"Ah ha," he eventually said. "That's funny. Had me there for a moment."

Henry smiled at him.

Rod read his face. "You're serious, aren't you?" he said after a few seconds.

Henry nodded and added, "Yes, it's quite short notice and probably a little unusual for how things work out here, hence why I was asking if you could do us a favour. You know Bill well. Any time Thursday's okay, even out of hours. And also, I was wondering if you'd be my Best Man?"

Malissa was getting a little more used to Henry's ways of portraying the most absurd situations as totally normal. She watched, almost wanting to laugh as Rod struggled to find a suitable response.

"You are joking, "he smiled and looked at Malissa, who's raised eyebrow and nod of the head suggested he wasn't. "Tell me you're joking." and, to Malissa; "Not about marrying *you,* Malissa, but about

Thursday and Bill Roberts. Very funny." He laughed and repeated how funny under his breath.

He stabbed another piece of fish but made no attempt to put it in his mouth. His thoughts were almost audible in the silence. Then it sank in. Henry wasn't joking.

"For fuck's sake, Henry. Excuse my French, Malissa. You *are* serious. You actually do want me to see if Billy Roberts will marry you the day after tomorrow?"

"Well, not marry me," Henry interrupted, "I'm not that way inclined and, anyway, that would be a ludicrous thing to ask out here. No, just ask him to perform the ceremony. Malissa and I have fallen in love and would like to get married. That all seems quite normal to me."

An exasperated Rod stared open mouthed at Henry. Malissa could imagine the two of them had discussed many difficult strategies and issues over the years and she had no doubt a good proportion of them would have incorporated one or two of Henry's more bizarre suggestions, but she thought this one had possibly trumped them all.

"For fuck's sake Henry!" Much louder this time, accompanied by the clutter of dumped cutlery but no apology for his French. "Normal? Normal Henry, this is Dubai." The other diners took heed. "God, you're not even Muslim. You're a Christian. Well, you're not even Christian. People just don't get married because they..." he was stumbling. "Because they..."

"Fall in love?" smiled Henry.

"Love!" Rod's face had reddened somewhat. "Love? Henry, you know what I mean, you just don't get married like that."

"But I know many westerners come here to get married. Others too."

"Yes, Henry, they do. They plan it for months. They get a licence. Bring their families over. Book nice hotels and pleasure trips and get a suntan, say 'I do', have a wonderful time, and then go home.

"They don't come here to finalise details about building a fuckin' airport and then say, 'well that's done now, how about we get married?' Fuck, I'm surprised you haven't asked me to talk to the captain of the Alia. She's in port tomorrow. That'd be much easier. I'm sure Captain Phillips would oblige."

"Sticks, you know Captain's don't really do marriage ceremonies."

"Henry. These things take time and thought and planning. You can't just do things like this overnight. I don't know why I'm even having this conversation."

"I understand that, that's why I've said Thursday. That gives us the whole of tomorrow to plan things. That and the fact it's unlucky to see the bride the day before."

Rod ignored the overnight quip and tried to calm himself down. He took a swig of his wine and adopted a very serious, even fatherly voice. Malissa noticed the other diners were making no longer making a secret of their interest in the exchange between the two men on her table.

"Henry, I love you." Rod said seriously. "I have absolutely no doubt of your intelligence or integrity. I know you can achieve things when the odds seem stacked against you. But sometimes…"

"So, you'll ring him?" Henry interrupted. "We would really appreciate it. I'll get the licence."

Malissa was laughing now and apologised to Rod, who did not see any humour whatsoever in the conversation.

His calmness was short lived. "Ring him? Ring him now? Go over to the phone dial his fuckin' number and ring him? Hi Bill, how's tricks? Listen mate, you busy this week only I've some lunatic here, you know that Henry Ovmeister chap. Anyway, he thinks you could marry him Thursday. He would do tomorrow, but that's unlucky and he obviously appreciates these things can't be done overnight, so Thursdays absolutely fine. He's not Muslim or engaged or anything like that, but he is in love. Really head over heels. He's free at four o' clock but if that's inconvenient he could do five.

"What Bill? License, blessing from the authorities? How long as he held residence? No, Bill, none of that but don't worry, he's real good mates with the Sheikh, and you know how *he* loves a wedding and a knees-up."

He finished his parody and, more softly, added, "Henry, he'll probably be drunk this time of night."

"That may be better." Henry could always see a positive.

"For fuck's sake!" Louder still, instigating an apology to all patrons present. He stood up. "Henry." A pause. "Henry."

He couldn't think of anything to say and, apologising again to the other diners, stormed off to the office behind the bar saying, "They want to get married. Can you believe that? Un-bloody-believable."

Henry wore a wry smile. Malissa a broad grin. "You know Miss Keats?" he said, "with people like Sticks in this world is it no wonder they say romance is dead."

It was 20 minutes before Rod returned to the table. He said nothing and took his seat. He took a forkful of the remnants of his dinner, placed the cutlery squarely and deliberately on his plate, and sat there chewing. Malissa wanted to ask if his fish was cold but thought better of it.

When he had swallowed, he patted his mouth with the serviette, ensuring they waited further to learn the outcome of his conversation with the Reverend Bill Roberts. He took a sip of his wine and studied their faces in turn. When he decided to break the silence, he reached for both their hands.

"Henry," he said solemnly. "You are amongst the most wonderful of human beings I have had the pleasure to have known. Malissa, I can see how happy you make him, and even an old cynic like me can see the love in each of your eyes. Henry, I know if Brad was here I'd be Chief Usher at best, but in the circumstances I will be absolutely honoured to be your Best Man."

And right on cue the waiter appeared with a bottle of champagne and three glasses.

They got back to the hotel at 11pm. Somehow, marrying Henry here, the day after tomorrow no longer shocked Malissa. She seemed to regard it more as a grand gesture of their developing love than the legally binding contract they would be entering. More akin to an engagement, which would of course go hand in hand with Henry's idea of doing it all over again when back in England.

When she had mentioned Henry to her mother last week, she'd surprised herself when she said they had met six months ago. This generated the inevitable 'it's serious then Malissa' assumption which, of course, got her mother thinking. She didn't, however, tell her she was travelling to Dubai with him.

They sat at the same table they had last night, beside the pool. One of the hotel staff brought over a telephone and plugged it into a nearby socket.

"I have to call Brad." Henry checked his watch. "He should be in the office" and as he dialled the number added, with that mischievous grin, "Maybe I'll give him the good news."

Malissa smiled. She could just about hear the ringing on the other end of the line and Brad answering. They exchanged greetings and a few niceties and then Henry listened, saying, "Hmm," and, "uh uh," and smirking as Brad updated him on affairs back home.

"Well, it all sounds fine," said Henry when Brad had completed his rundown. A pause and then, "Oh, by the way. I'm getting married Thursday." A moment's silence then Brad's muffled voice, seemingly seeking clarification.

"Yes, married. Married to Miss Keats." Another moment's silence and then Henry held the phone from his ear as a barrage of apparent disbelief, abuse and concern streamed from the receiver. Henry shrugged his shoulders and, cupping the mouthpiece with his hand, whispered, "I think it surprised him."

The bombardment from the other end of the line continued. There'd be a pause and Henry would venture to say something, but Brad seemed determined not to be interrupted and would resume his volley. Malissa didn't know whether to laugh or be concerned, but Henry's face suggested this was the reaction he may have expected.

Rant seemingly over, Brad must have asked who he had appointed as Best Man. "Rod," said Henry, which initiated a further barrage of abuse. "And the plan is," said Henry, trying to interrupt, "when we get back to the UK, we'd like to have a proper wedding and I would be honoured if you would be my Best Man."

More exasperation from the other end of the line but Henry was smiling now and reverted to his, "Yes, Brad," and, "I agree, Brad," and, "Uh uh," responses. Then silence as neither said anything for several seconds before Henry said, "He would like to speak to you," and handed the phone to Malissa.

"Me?" She was a little apprehensive as she took the receiver. "Hello, Braddon, this is Malissa."

"Braddon?" his voice was soft. "It's Brad."

"Oh, hello, Brad, it's nice to speak to you."

"Yes, you too, Malissa… Malissa… Malissa, I understand you and Henry are getting married."

"Yes, Brad."

"Now, I'm sure you've got to know Henry a little…"

"Yes, Brad, I have. As much as you *can* get to know Henry." She took Henry's hand across the table, looking into his eyes as she spoke.

"Hmm," said Brad. He must have picked that up from Henry. "Malissa, Henry has talked about you a lot since you met in May. It's been a long time since I have heard him talk so much about a woman. Malissa, do you love him?"

"Yes, Brad, I do." She squeezed Henry's hand.

A moment's reflection from the other end of the line. "I mean *really* love him? He's a little different to most as I'm sure you are aware, but I love him too. He can sometimes be impetuous but often his sense of things is spot on. I do believe he loves you very much."

"I hope so."

"And you don't think you're rushing in?"

"Yes, I do think we are rushing in, but…" she paused. "It feels so right, it's like we've known one and other for so much longer and Henry seems absolutely certain that now is the right time. Maybe it's wiser to wait, but here with him, now, there seems no need to do so and Henry, well, Henry seems so," she searched for an appropriate word but couldn't find one, "so sure."

"That's Henry, Miss Keats, but I think you know that. Henry

Bloody Ovmeister. Will he ever cease to surprise me? Well, Malissa. I offer my congratulations and look forward to meeting you."

"Me too, Brad."

"Now, if you'd be so kind and hand me back to Mr I'll-Never-Do-Anything- Conventionally Ovmeister, it would be appreciated."

She smiled. "Bye, Brad," and handed over the receiver.

Brad's softer tones continued as he talked to Henry.

"Yes Brad. Sure, Brad. Okay, Brad. That's fantastic, Brad."

And then a sudden change in his tone, which Henry met with raised eyebrows.

"Oh, I'm sorry about that. But she knows my middle name too," and then a series of, "Bye, Brad's" as he gradually replaced the receiver, the voice at the other end continuing to the point of hanging up.

They smiled across the table. "Quite a day, Miss Keats."

"Indeed. I think it's one for the diary. Do you think he approves? I mean, he seemed quite shocked and a little upset at times."

"Malissa," said Henry, that grin returning to his face, "I think he was more upset that I told you his name was Braddon. For some reason he doesn't like people to know that. Strange fellow."

# 16

## DUBAI, DECEMBER 1983

### WEDDING DAY

Malissa had half expected Henry to have arranged for a camel to take her to the church. On balance, she was relieved to learn Husain was taking her in the hotel's limousine.

She wore a pale pink dress and hat and looked more like a wedding *guest* than the actual bride, but she was happy. She was one half of a surreal romantic adventure where her heart called all the shots.

The chapel was a white building, no bigger than a bungalow, with walls of large irregularly shaped stones and an overhanging tin roof. It stood alone in the desert with no churchyard and Malissa wondered what on earth its original purpose was. It did have a cross on the roof and even though it was leaning over it did, she conceded, indicate it was a place of worship. For a minute she hoped Hussain had driven to the wrong place, but as they pulled up she saw Henry emerge from the door.

He was dressed in a morning suit and he looked a little hot and bothered. He approached the car with a smile. Malissa wound down the window.

"Hello, my love," he said. "What a beautiful day."

As far as Malissa was concerned every day in Dubai was like this one. Hot and sunny and she detected something wasn't quite right.

"Shouldn't you be inside waiting for me, Henry?" she said, the heat of the day suddenly hitting her.

"Hmm," he said. "You look beautiful. You are beautiful. Aren't you early?" She wasn't, it was 4:05pm.

Rod appeared at the chapel door. He was also dressed in a morning suit, but his collar was undone and he wasn't wearing his jacket. Malissa noticed him. Henry looked around.

"Five minutes," Rod whispered and disappeared back inside.

"What did he say?" asked Malissa.

"Who?"

"Rod."

"Oh, Rod. He said everything's okay and you should drive around the block a couple of times, you know to be a little late, make the Groom worry. You know what a stickler for tradition he is." He kissed her through the open window, smiled, and turned his attention to Hussain. "Yes, Hussain, just round the block, five minutes. Fantastic. See you soon my love."

He turned and went back inside.

Malissa closed her window and caught Hussain's questioning face in the rear-view mirror.

"Well, I believe, Miss Keats, we are perhaps a little early." He pulled off and commenced a circle of the church.

Reverend Roberts had stopped singing, which was significant progress. The fact he was now standing, albeit still in his underpants was a minor miracle.

"I can't find his trousers," said Rod.

"What do you mean you can't find his trousers? Bill, where are your trousers?"

"I'm sorry, Henry." The Reverend had been apologising all morning.

As Rod attended to the last few buttons of the Reverend's cassock, Henry removed a cloth from a table and draped it over the pulpit stand. "There," he said, "he can stand behind that and she'll never know."

Rod shot Henry a questioning glance, probably doubting that the Reverend could even stand unaided, let alone position himself to hide the fact he would be conducting a wedding ceremony in his y-fronts. "You remember Fawlty Towers, Henry?" he said.

"Kurt," acknowledged Henry, remembering the episode with the drunken chef. He wished he thought it was funny. "Okay. I think we're ready. Now, you can remember the words Bill, right?"

Reverend Roberts apologised again but assured him the words of the ceremony were deeply etched in his memory. A last look around and Henry was satisfied things were as right as they possibly could be. He rolled the empty whisky bottle under one of the pews, reminded Rod to do up his tie, checked himself, and went outside to inform his wife-to-be that they were ready.

Although Hussain had driven very slowly, ten circuits of the church had made her feel quite dizzy. Henry was standing at the far end of the church, and as she entered he pushed the button on the cassette player which played 'Here Comes the Bride' as she walked up to him.

She was pleasantly surprised. The inside of the building did bear a resemblance to a Christian church, though she couldn't understand why a pair of black trousers dangled from their braces on the candle stand in the corner. Henry caught her look at them and smiled. She noticed too that Rod, the Best Man, instead of standing next to Henry as was customary, was behind the pulpit, facing out with an arm around the Reverend's waist.

Henry kissed her, smothering any question she may have wanted to ask, and the Reverend began. "Dearly beloved, we are gathered here..." and as he spoke, his words a little slurred, Henry held her hand and indicated they should be still and give due credence to the Reverend and to the solemnness of the occasion.

They left the church with papers signed and as Mr and Mrs Ovmeister. A simple affair indeed that was concluded within 20 minutes. Henry assured her their wedding in the UK would be much more akin to what she would expect and she shouldn't be too disheartened. "Look upon it as an engagement ceremony," he said, "a bonus."

Malissa sensed a degree of relief on Henry's face and she vowed she would ask any questions later.

Back at the hotel, they were welcomed by a guard of honour as the staff lined up to greet them. The restaurant had been transformed for the occasion, decorated with balloons and ribbons and a sumptuous buffet adorned one of the tables. There were many well-wishers of several nationalities. A few were those she had recently met, and all offered sincere and warm congratulations. She felt at ease, she felt special. She felt like Henry's wife. She was Henry's wife.

Halfway through lunch the dancers arrived. A first dance in England would be a smooch, with the newlyweds taking the floor just before inviting their guests to join them. On this occasion it was a belly dance they were expected to perform. Henry was not a natural, but much to the delight of their guests, and to Henry's chagrin, Malissa with her musical theatre training enthralled the audience with her performance.

Rod did not let the relative unusualness of the reception deter him from a best man's traditional duties. He talked about Henry and Dubai and about their evening at the golf club, and read messages including a telegram from Brad. The Sheik said a few words and as a gift offered them the use of his yacht for the remainder of their stay.

Henry thanked the people for the kindness they had shown and paid tribute to the country he had come to regard as a second home. He read a poem which he entitled 'Marriage, Malissa and Dubai'. She was impressed to discover he had a flair for the written word, perhaps not constructed as it should have been, but it flowed with an abundance of warmth and humour and love.

He had remembered the first song they had danced to and they rounded of the evening with a discreet smooch on the patio. By the time they decided to go to bed, only Rod and the Reverend Bill Roberts remained. Henry thanked them for their assistance and, as they stood up to say goodnight, Malissa was sure she had seen the trousers the Reverend was wearing somewhere before.

# 17

# JULY 1989

## A SUMMER IN MAJORCA

"*And you don't see udders loik this every day I can tell you.* Honestly, Ness, this is like Benny from Crossroads." This time Malissa's imitation of Bert, the West Country dairy farmer, was too much and Vanessa rolled onto her back in fits of laughter.

"I feel guilty taking the piss like that, Ness, but I think this one's a 'no'," she eventually added, trying to inject some compassion and seriousness. Instead she instigated another burst of the giggles as the two women exchanged lines they thought more appropriate than those written by the wannabe author.

They had spent many days on the beach like this, reading through manuscripts Malissa had brought with her from London, but it was fair to say that this one represented the worst novel ever written. It had either slipped through the first submission process or been forwarded as a bit of light entertainment. She would ask the office to write back, thanking the author for considering Fenner's and leave it to their imagination to try and find something positive to say.

Their frivolities had long since distracted Lewis, who wondered what was going on. "Guess who's coming today, Lewis?" his mother said, picking him up from the sand.

He thought for a few seconds before excitedly shouting, "Daddy!"

She hoped Henry would arrive before Lewis' bedtime. "Well, Ness, I guess we'd better get back and get ready."

They gathered their belongings and headed back to the farmhouse.

"I think Henry will be surprised," remarked Vanessa as they passed the villa. Malissa agreed the builders had made fantastic progress over the past few weeks.

Malissa hadn't seen Henry for nearly two months, and since she learned he would be here this weekend time had passed slowly. She missed him. With no telephone, communication wasn't easy, and it had been several days since they had spoken.

She had told him she was having problems getting electricity and telephone lines installed so he was meeting with the town's council to see if he could hurry things along. He was probably with them now, in The Grand, having stopped there en route from the airport.

The farmhouse had always been a charming building, but with the benefit of being lived in for a few months it was now a home. Malissa and Lewis tended the garden whilst Vanessa showered.

"Soon we will be living down there, Lewis," she said, peering over the garden gate. "You're a very lucky young man."

She picked him up and took him inside. "Daddy will be here soon," she repeated, feeling those familiar butterflies.

Henry arrived shortly before 8pm and, coming through the gate, Lewis ran up to him. "How are you my little man?" Henry said, picking him up and holding him above his head to get a good look. "I've missed you so much."

He lifted him up and down delivering a volley of raspberries onto his belly and sending him into fits of laughter. Malissa stood at the kitchen door, wishing she wasn't too big to be greeted in the same way. She felt his gaze. She felt his longing and was sure it matched hers.

"And guess what, Lewis? Guess who else I've missed?" he said.

Lewis pondered, looking fleetingly between his parents. "Mummy!" he shouted and Malissa joined them, nuzzling into Henry, absorbing that familiar fragrance as he slipped an arm around her.

"Beautiful," said Henry, looking at the farmhouse. "Beautiful," he repeated, finding Malissa's eyes. "Everything is beautiful," he exclaimed, lifting his son up high again, this time whirling him around before they all went inside.

Vanessa stood in the kitchen towelling her hair. "Miss Cozzette. How lovely to see you again."

He released one arm from his son to greet her. Malissa thought he was about to say something more but he switched his gaze to her. "Now, I've so much to catch up on. You've done wonders to this place. But first my little boy, I think you should tell me all about what you've been doing."

He sat down and Lewis enthused about the beach and the boats while wearing the *I love New York* cap that Henry had placed on his head.

When Lewis was tired, Henry took him upstairs. Malissa joined them shortly after, bringing a beer, and listened to the story he read. When Lewis fell asleep, Malissa wanted to take her husband into the next room and show him just how much she had missed him. She sensed it was his wish too, but they would have to wait. Creeping quietly out of the bedroom they went downstairs and out into the garden.

The sun had set but it wasn't dark yet. "I can't believe what you've done here," said Henry and then, looking down at the villa, put his arm around his wife. "And Malissa, I am, as ever, amazed by what you can achieve." He raised his glass. "To Casa de Luna de Miel."

Vanessa had been preparing dinner. Malissa took hold of her hand as she sat down to join them. "And this, my darling husband, is not only the most beautiful woman on the Island, she is an inspiration and the most wonderful companion in the world."

"I see that. And I've yet to see you dance," he smiled.

That instigated a little exchange about Vanessa's injury, which was clearly on the mend. She had no immediate plans to recommence her career. In truth, Vanessa too had fallen in love with the place and the people of the town, and had already talked to Malissa about opening a dance school in Söller.

"So," said Malissa, tossing the salad. "How did the meeting go?"

"As well as could be expected, I guess. They will run electricity and phone lines up here. They understand they are needed."

"And?" Malissa knew it wouldn't have been that simple.

"And, my darling, I think they will start straight away."

"And?"

"And?" he smiled, his eyes mimicking surprise at her question.

"Well, from my conversations with them I'm just surprised they agreed so easily."

"Hmm." He shuffled in his chair and said something to Vanessa about how nice the wine was but could not escape Malissa's enquiring gaze and smile.

"And they'd like the Grand refurbished a bit," he casually conceded.

Malissa's smile broadened. She raised her eyebrows and cocked her head. Henry frowned. "And they'd like a new, but not too big, hotel built on the old storage yard. I can see why they believe it would be a fantastic investment."

Ever since Henry had purchased The Grand to save it from the banks when they honeymooned here five years ago, the town's authorities had regarded him as some kind of benevolent investor. They correctly believed that any economic misgivings he might have about investing in Söller would be softened by his love for the place and in this instance his desire to build their dream home here.

"And you agreed?" smiled Malissa. His look told her he had.

"They thought rebuilding the harbour wall would be a good idea too."

"Did they really? And Brad's happy with it?" She knew he would not have consulted his business partner.

"Well, I haven't exactly spoken to him yet. I have to go over the figures again. I'll run it past him soon. He's not so keen on hotels and things, he prefers other investments."

"Like viable ones, Henry?" she teased a broad grin on her face.

She had witnessed many spats between Henry and Brad but never once felt anything could infringe on their great friendship and respect for one another. In the grand scheme of things, the money Henry would have promised would be a drop in the ocean and she knew too he would not have agreed unless there was potential for some sort of return – even a modest one.

"I can't wait for Brad to hear about the new arrangement," she continued. "I guess he's still coming?"

"Yes, he'll be arriving on Monday and I have told him this is all pleasure and no business – absolutely no talk about work. So maybe I'll talk to him at a later date. It's been a while since we have spent good times together. He likes this place and I bet he falls in love with it by the time he has to go back. I'll tell him the details another time."

Malissa smiled. She loved Henry and the way he would put his neck on the line for her.

"You'll love Brad," Malissa said to Vanessa. "And he'll certainly love you. And Henry, Vanessa is not part of the Brad softening up inventory."

Henry changed the subject. "Such a beautiful place. Such a beautiful evening. Such beautiful company." He raised his glass. "To holidaying with friends and to the villa, and its completion by Christmas."

"Christmas here would be wonderful," said Vanessa.

"Let's hope it's finished by then," Malissa responded.

They usually spent Christmas in England, but Christmas out here? Yes, she thought, she would like that. She loved Christmas. "Well, I guess Brad will know all about promises made by then, Henry," she added. "You can't have secrets at Christmas, can you?"

He smiled and she knew that he'd picked up on her reference to the first Christmas they spent together. Brad would be fine.

## 18

# CHRISTMAS EVE 1983, WEST KENT

## WITH MALISSA'S PARENTS

She stopped the car at the bus stop 200 metres from her parents' home. She had been back in England for a week and while she still felt as if she was on a rollercoaster, the familiarity of the surroundings in which she was brought up comforted her, reminding her she did at least have a hand on the brake.

Mrs Drake looked out of her front room window. Malissa hoped she didn't recognise her and come out for a chat. She needed these five minutes to get herself together and go over, again, just what she would say to her parents.

Henry was everything she could have ever wanted and soon she would be introducing him to them. But what exactly would she say?

*"Hi Mum, hi Dad. This is Henry. We met at the races in May. He's rich and a bit different but we've fallen in love and – would you believe it – we've just got married. Funny, eh? In Dubai! We wanted to consummate our love, you see, and obviously in a place like that you can't just sleep with someone, so it made sense to get married.*

*Sorry you missed it and all that, but we're planning to do it all over again in the summer. You know, more in the way we'd think of a traditional wedding. And when we do, you're most welcome to be there. Now, can I help you with the turkey or peel some carrots?"*

She shivered at the thought but then smiled to herself as she remembered their wedding night. No swinging from the chandeliers or awkwardness, just love. A natural desire for one another and a tenderness she had never known before. Apart from last night, when she'd stayed at her own house, they had spent their time in a little love nest just outside Newbury doing much the same thing.

She had asked him about his plans for Christmas, explaining she always spent it with her parents. "Fine," he'd said. "That sounds great, it's about time I met them."

She was surprised and pleased by her new husband's response. She had expected him to say they should spend Christmas in Mauritius or somewhere similarly exotic. Visiting parents, she thought, would just seem too normal for him. And then she remembered he was an orphan and realised he would never have spent Christmas with *his* parents. They had much to learn about each other.

Malissa had telephoned her mother last week and talked about Henry. She knew she would be desperate to meet him and wasn't surprised by her suggestion that he should come for Christmas dinner. She would even make up the spare bedroom in case he wanted to stay. That did make Malissa smile.

"It sounds serious, Malissa. I'm so pleased for you," she had said with undisguised delight. Her mother never understood why, at the age of 21 her daughter wasn't engaged.

"Yes, I think so, Mum. We really like each other."

A bombardment of questions followed but Malissa staved off most, telling her she would meet him soon. She was a little nervous about how Henry would react to the undoubted inquisition that would come his way but knew he would rise to the occasion and simply charm them. She was sure he would warm to them too.

As part of their plan, she and Henry had decided to use this opportunity to tell her parents of their intentions to marry that summer. When and how to tell them, said Henry, would become apparent. No need to worry. Malissa could then spend the next few months arranging the event, embracing her mother's input, and as far as everybody was concerned they would simply be witnessing two people getting engaged and planning to marry in the traditional manner.

Brad was the only English resident who knew they were already married and sleeping together. A sudden, shocking thought made her make a mental note to talk to Henry in respect of family planning. Up until now, their contraception philosophy had been far from thorough and Malissa did not relish the idea of walking down the aisle six-months pregnant.

She quickly dismissed the thought. They would stay one or two days with her parents and possibly go to Kempton Park Races on Boxing Day which was something Henry often did.

They would play this by ear, as the day after Christmas in the Keats household was usually devoted to TV, cold turkey sandwiches, boiled bacon, and pickle. These were just details, Malissa thought as she put the car into gear to complete her journey.

She felt quite at ease when she pulled up onto the drive. She would have several hours with her parents before Henry arrived. This would be an interesting Christmas.

## 19

# LONDON CHRISTMAS EVE, 1983

## OVMEISTER CARMICHAEL OFFICES

"You ready?" asked Brad.

Henry turned, holding the photograph. "Guess this belongs somewhere else now."

Brad came in, closing the door behind him. "I guess so. Malissa is a wonderful woman Henry and I think you'll have a fantastic Christmas."

"I know, my friend. Just a little reminiscing. Come on, it's party time and you can do the speech this year!"

"I did it last year."

"No, I did. I'm sure I did. Anyway, Paul's picking me up at five and I've got in-laws to meet, remember!"

"I hate speeches."

"You're great at them."

"Bob can do it."

"Needs to be the boss."

"You're the boss."

"Then I delegate you."

"Fuck off."

They left his office, Henry still holding the photograph that no longer belonged there. The image would always remain in his heart.

## 20

## CHRISTMAS DAY, 1983

## THE KEATS HOUSEHOLD

Henry, as expected, had charmed her parents from the moment he arrived last night.

"Where did you meet, Mr Ovmeister?" her mother asked.

"Henry, please. At Goodwood, Mrs Keats. I know Brian Fenner."

"Oh, Doris, please."

A little talk about the wonderful Brian Fenner and how well Malissa seemed to be doing at his company.

"She did want to be a dancer, you know," her mother said proudly.

"And an actress," said Henry. "And I believe she would have excelled at either."

Good answer.

"So, you've known each other six months?" her father asked, trying not to show his concern.

"Yes, though it seems so much longer. I think in Dubai we realised just how much we had in common."

"I thought you were on a business trip in Dubai, Malissa?" Her mother asked, arching her right eyebrow the way she did when she felt her daughter had been hiding something.

Henry quickly clarified, "Fate, maybe, Mrs Keats. Although we knew we would both be there on business, and at the same time, and thought how nice it would be if, by chance, we happened to meet, our *coming together* wasn't planned, it just happened so naturally one evening."

Malissa felt herself wince. She knew he was being covertly mischievous and referring to their lovemaking in Dubai, but the innuendo passed completely over her parents' heads. Of course, it did.

Henry elaborated, his smile melting her mother as it melted so many. "We both had spare time and it was my honour to show Malissa around. And while she fell in love with the city…" he took her hand, "I fell in love with your daughter."

This, Malissa thought, was perhaps a little over the top, but her mother returned his smile so Malissa kissed him on the cheek.

"Another drink, Henry?" her father asked, closing proceedings and signalling his approval.

The evening passed quickly. Her parents clearly surmised Henry was a relatively successful businessman, kind and caring, with sufficient prospects to ensure their daughter would be adequately cared for. By the end of it all, Malissa just wanted to take him somewhere and show him again just how much she loved him, and she appreciated him taking so much time to placate her parents' natural concerns.

This, however, was neither the time nor place to do that. When Henry was shown to his bedroom, the one her brother occupied when they lived there, he marvelled at the collection of Dandy and Beano annuals on the shelf. He would love to read them, if of course, it was okay with her parents. Henry certainly played his part.

Henry was cooking breakfast with her father when she got up Christmas morning. Her dad was smiling, and her mother paraded about the house with a grin that would make the most euphoric Cheshire Cat seem glum.

Her brother, Simon, and his wife arrived at midday. Henry was again his charming self, perhaps a little too much as far as Simon was concerned, but Malissa recognised that Henry's interaction with Simon's wife, Carol, was not the flirtatious one that somebody less familiar with him may have thought.

They had dinner and opened presents. Her mother beamed and her attentiveness to Henry bordered on embarrassment. "You okay, Mum?" Malissa had asked on several occasions.

It was after dinner, when attending to the dishes, that her mother, no longer able to suppress the reasons for her constant grinning, grabbed her daughter. "We love him Mel," and, following Malissa's obvious reply of 'Well I'm glad you do', added, "Don't you dare say no."

"Sorry?"

"He's going to ask you to marry him," she whispered. "Tomorrow at the racing. We're not meant to tell you, but he asked your father's permission when they were cooking the bacon this morning. Such a gentleman. Henry, I mean, not your father."

Malissa was genuinely surprised that Henry had chosen this morning to implement the first stage of their plan.

"It's a bit of a shock, Mel, I know. That's why I thought it best to tell you." Her mother was still whispering. "You will say yes?"

Malissa smiled inwardly. Her mother was suddenly concerned. "Mel." The whisper was a little more urgent. "He's going to ask you to marry him and, as your mother, I'm just saying I think you should accept."

Malissa wanted to burst out laughing. She guessed this would have been the way the proposal may have come if it were made here in England anyway. Or would that have been too normal? In fact, she felt that excitement all over again, almost caught up in the parody and believing it herself.

A little part of her wanted to clear the air and say, 'Mum, we are *already* married,' but she trusted herself to go along with the plan. "Oh Mum, I do so love him. And I'm so glad you and Dad do, too. Of course, I'll say yes."

Her mother smiled and hugged her. "Remember to act surprised, darling. You don't want to hurt his feelings. Men like to think they have the upper hand you know, and you should play along. It'll be our little secret."

So, they were going to Kempton Races. No turkey sandwiches or Wizard of Oz this year. All had been arranged and attending too would be her boss, Brian Fenner, with his family and friends. How romantic, her mother had enthused.

They played their traditional game of Monopoly in the afternoon. Her mother was still smiling constantly and Malissa thought if Henry asked if he could buy Mayfair from her for five pounds, she would have willingly sold it to him – with a hotel!

They played charades, and a new game Henry introduced which he called 'In the Bucket'. They had a late tea consisting of the sandwiches they would have usually had on Boxing Day. It was as joyous a Christmas Day as Malissa could remember.

Her parents suggested Henry should stay another night, but he said that as much as he would love to, he must go. He had preparations to make.

"Yes, Henry, preparations, we understand," said her mother, nodding to the rest of the family. She even winked at Malissa. Henry pretended he didn't see.

Malissa saw Henry to the door. Like teenagers they kissed good night. "Take me with you," she whispered, knowing that couldn't be part of their plan.

"Miss Keats, that would not be appropriate. We have a big day tomorrow."

"So I gather, Mr Ovmeister." Even at this stage, although she knew Henry would have known her mother would have told her, she wanted to play along. "It's an important meeting. The King George Chase I believe?"

"Quite so, Miss Keats, quite so," he replied possibly impressed that she had done some homework.

Stepping out onto the porch she pulled the door behind her to screen off any prying eyes and kissed him passionately. "I love you, Henry."

"And Mrs Ovmeister," it was the first time she had heard him say it, "I love you too. And have had a wonderful Christmas. Until tomorrow."

He kissed her again and walked to the car, turning and smiling as he slipped into the passenger seat.

She stood there for a minute enjoying the memory of the moment. She knew on returning indoors that conversation would be about her and Henry. About love, and marriage, and family and she wondered if she would have to continue to pretend she was the only one unaware of the impending proposal. That would be hard work.

She went back into the sitting room to be greeted by smiling and expectant eyes. Carol stood up and gave her a hug, "We're so happy for you, Mel."

Malissa smiled and looked to her mother.

"Well, we all know, and I thought it best I told them I told you. Otherwise we'd be walking on eggshells afraid of saying something wrong. You know how difficult it is for me to keep secrets."

Yes, Mother, she thought, keeping secrets is not your forte.

"Kensington, Henry?" asked Paul as they pulled onto the main road.

Henry studied the photograph. "Yes, Paul. But Notting Hill first, please."

## 21

# BERKSHIRE, APRIL 1966

## AUNT ROSE'S FUNERAL

He held her hand tightly. Perhaps this was the first time he realised his feelings for her were something more than the incredibly deep affection that had been there forever. He had grown to be her protector, her strength, her eyes, but was becoming increasingly aware that it was her strength, her insight, and her loveliness that made it so natural for him to be so. Aunt Rose was gone but Henry could not imagine ever being apart from Emma.

The vicar talked of life and of 'love everlasting', his words intended to comfort those in mourning, but Henry couldn't help relating them to his feelings for Emma. He didn't quite understand what he felt but the emotion was strong, a new wave of feelings initiated, perhaps, by the loss of someone he loved.

Mr Saunders and Mrs Brown from the village were there as was Stephen, Emma's music teacher. Alice was crying. Unlike Henry and Emma, she was blood-related, the daughter of Aunt Rose's late sister. Ten years Henry's senior, he wondered what she would do now. Come to think of it, what would become of him and Emma? He was 14, Emma the same age and both had only ever known Aunt Rose as their mother and her wonderful house as home.

He recognised the man in the grey suit, Mr Carmichael. They hadn't talked much but he had visited the house often over the years. He wasn't entirely sure of Mr Carmichael's relationship with Aunt Rose but his appearance here and the sincere nature of his condolences earlier suggested it was a close one. Henry didn't believe this would be the last time he saw him.

Henry was saddened that so few people had come. How could a lady, so kind and so full of love, have so few people present at her funeral? Then again, other than the company of him, Alice, and Emma, she did lead a somewhat reclusive life. She loved painting, and reading, and sitting quietly in the garden and rarely ventured further than home.

Henry reflected on the last conversation they had. She knew she was dying and so did he. "Henry, always try to be kind. Often, people may not be kind back, but always give them the chance to be."

He remembered how she had told him that she looked forward to this day. He remembered her stories of the young love between her and Arthur who she lost so long ago. She would often ask him to read the letters he had sent to her during the War because, she said, he had such a wonderful way of reading them. He remembered how she would ask him to write poems to match her paintings. "You can paint with words," she would say.

Aunt Rose insisted he mustn't be sad when she was gone because she believed she would be reunited with Arthur. But, most of all, Henry remembered her kindness and love, and would be eternally grateful that she treated him like her own son.

These thoughts ran through his mind with the words of the Minister in the background and Emma at his side. When the sermon finished, he passed Emma one of the roses he was holding. "You've got the white rose, Em," he said, leading her to the graveside. He cast the red one.

She turned to him, burying her head into his shoulder and wept softly. He cradled her and that feeling rose again, the one he was struggling to understand. He whispered to her. "I can't imagine ever being without you Emily-Jane and I swear on Rose's grave I'll be your friend forever. I will never, ever leave you."

He felt her arms tighten around him. He felt safe, and strong, and loved, and he knew everything would be okay.

# II

# THE BUTTERFLY AND THE BEAR

*Taking a chance, he asked her to dance*
*In the silvery light of the dawn,*
*The meadow as sweet as the honey she made*
*And love and its meaning reborn.*

*With her he took to the skies again*
*His heart as light as the air,*
*Reliving the life of that butterfly*
*But not straying too far from the bear.*

## 22

# MAJORCA, SUMMER, 1989

## BRAD ARRIVES

"I do believe, Henry," Malissa said, popping her head into the bedroom. "That you are fretting about telling Brad."

"About the hotel? Of course not, my love, I believe he'll think it a wonderful idea."

"And the harbour?"

Henry shot her a knowing look. He loved her intuition but she knew he wasn't so comfortable when it recognised his own misgivings. "Hmm," he said, fastening the last button of his shirt. "Yes, and the harbour too."

There was not a great deal of conviction in his answer.

She smiled, kissed him, and left to give last-minute instructions to Maria, who had been seconded to look after Lewis.

"Whatever you say, my love," she sang as she descended the stairs, a broad grin erupting on her face when she heard another, but louder, 'Hmm,' from the bedroom.

She knew his suggestion that Vanessa should accompany them to dinner was to lend a little distraction, to soften the impact should Brad question the wisdom of his partner's newest investment. Brad would surely avoid making a scene in front of a relative stranger; it wouldn't be polite.

Malissa was okay with that and knew the four of them would have an enjoyable evening. She did, however, reject his idea of bringing Lewis along.

Satisfied Lewis was okay, she grabbed the car keys and called out to Henry before joining Vanessa in the garden who looked even more gorgeous than usual. They hadn't, up until today, had occasion to dress up. Henry was wearing shorts and a smart shirt and would probably don his flip-flops. She wondered if Brad would dispense with his tie.

The Grand was situated almost exactly mid-way along the boulevard overlooking the beach. Although it had only 30 rooms, it was the biggest and most established hotel in the town, and once home to the family who ran this part of Majorca. And it had a pool. Not a big one, in fact the pool at the villa would be bigger, but it nestled in a little garden at the back where the grounds of the hotel extended to the foothills offering scope for expansion should the need arise.

Three of the eight outside tables were occupied. The strip of red carpet that greeted visitors could be construed a little pretentious, but it was a quaint touch guiding them neatly into the small foyer where they were greeted warmly and informed that Mr Carmichael was waiting for them in the bar.

In dark blue trousers, no doubt the bottom half of a suit, and open neck shirt but no tie, Brad was the only patron there. He was talking to the barman, who looked up as they entered, causing Brad to do the same.

"Henry." Brad walked over, genuinely pleased to see his friend. They shook hands like businessmen, a ritual that always preceded their more affectionate hug.

"Malissa." He kissed her and then extended his hand to Vanessa. "And you must be Vanessa, it's a pleasure to meet you."

They ordered a drink and ventured outside to take up one of the tables.

"I can certainly understand why you love this place." Brad's comment was directed to each of them and they added their own opinion of what made it just that little bit special. "And the villa, Malissa. How's the building going? I can't wait to see it."

"I was hoping Brad, that you could spend some time up there with us. We've plenty of room. Well, sort of, in the farmhouse and I think you'll love it. And we insist this is a holiday, I'm sure business can just about survive without the two of you for a couple of weeks."

The glance Brad shot Henry was one of momentary horror and she imagined he wanted to reply, *Two weeks! Fourteen days! Are you kidding? Two days would give me a heart attack*. But, being the gentleman he was, he informed them it would be lovely to stay for as long as he could.

They ordered dinner and Brad updated Henry on some business matters. They talked about Söller, the villa, the theatre, and some of the scripts they had been reading.

Sergio, the manager, was not there and while the staff of the hotel knew Malissa and Vanessa, who were regular patrons, they did not appear to be aware of Henry's connection to the hotel. If they had seen Henry on Friday, they certainly didn't acknowledge it.

She could imagine Henry's reaction if one had said, *Nice to see you again Mr Ovmeister, we think your plans for the town are wonderful*. She doubted, in fact, whether the staff were even aware they were serving their employer. This would have suited Henry.

"Do you swim, Brad?" asked Vanessa. Malissa wondered if her friend knew just how sexy she could make a simple question sound.

"Yes, I do, I love swimming. And the sea here looks so inviting."

"And even better up at the villa," added Malissa. "Not such a sandy beach, of course, but a beautiful private little cove with such clear water. We should swim tomorrow when you come up."

"Yes," interjected Vanessa. "We will have to see how these two fine young men stand up to the Blackpool–Brighton test."

The two women shared a giggle and then elaborated on the swimming challenge they had devised.

"Good names," said Brad. Henry agreed.

"You'll have to try it, I'm sure we can think of suitable prizes." Malissa was flirting on behalf of Vanessa.

As the sun set, the lights around the harbour came on. There were quite a few people enjoying dinner or an evening drink in the handful of bars and restaurants that surrounded it.

"Lovely," said Brad. "Reminds me a little of Mevagissey in Cornwall. Though much warmer, of course. The barman tells me they're going to rebuild the wall. Seems a shame. Looks quite nice where the rocks have fallen in."

"Yes," replied Malissa. "And they're knocking the old warehouse down too, it was where they stored the citrus before the cold store was built. And they're building a new harbour station. And maybe a yacht club I guess."

"Really?"

"Yes. Apparently Söller is getting more popular. Might be the next Magaluf they say. Though, of course, more upmarket. Isn't that right, Henry?"

She sensed that Henry, who had been relatively quiet, was not entirely appreciative of his wife's attempts to steer the subject towards the very topic he was planning to avoid for as long as possible.

He took a sip of his beer. "So I understand. I think the place has potential."

It was a tentative reply, a feeler perhaps, and certainly an attempt to end the subject. The way he looked at her, though, told her that he knew it was nowhere near enough to deter his wife from her mischief making.

"Yes," continued Malissa. "They want to attract more of the jet set, the big yachts, and obviously that calls for proper and adequate facilities."

Then, with what she was sure Henry would regard as complete and unabated joy, she finished her drink and with exaggerated enthusiasm added, "and they are building a new hotel. They'll refurbish this one too, but 'The Söller Harbour Hotel,' built into the mountainside with 100 rooms of five-star luxury. They certainly have grand plans."

"Well, they'd need more visitors to make it pay," Brad replied. "I mean, this hotel struggles to break even as it is. Anyway, its charm is probably in its modesty. Perhaps Söller's a place that would do better without being discovered. That's a lot of investment."

Malissa smiled broadly, looking forward to hearing Henry's revelation about the most recent commitment he'd made on behalf of the company. "Yes, I guess it would be a speculative investment to say the least and almost certainly they would need outside money."

She lay her hand gently upon her husband's. "Still, that's business and speculation, I guess. Right, Henry?"

A thoughtful frown erupted on Brad's face and Malissa knew he was beginning to wonder whether there was something more to her comments.

Brad looked at Henry, who smiled and ordered another bottle of wine. "You must try the Majorcan my friend. Not the most renowned in the world, admittedly, but you'll be surprised. We'll have the white first."

Brad brought the subject back to the plans for the town. "Think they'll need a few more people, more evidence, to prove such an investment worthwhile. Sure, it's a pretty place, but competition for holiday makers these days is rife, and this is probably the wrong side of the island to attract passing cruisers. The southern ports are surely more ideally located?"

The waiter invited Henry to taste the wine. Henry immediately enthused about it, asking him to explain its origins and generally enlighten them on their wonderful local produce. Where was the estate? How many bottles did they produce? Did they export? Was it the island's favourite? Do they make a lower case? Brad seemed a little doubtful that the wine warranted the sumptuous praise Henry heaped upon it, but Malissa conceded that Henry had succeeded in changing the subject. He smiled at her.

It was 10pm by the time they had finished dinner. Malissa thought she and Vanessa should be getting back. They would leave the men to discuss business and look forward to swimming together tomorrow.

They concluded their goodbyes. Malissa sensed Henry was a little smug at having deflected Brad's attention away from the direction she had tried to steer it but knew he would have to tell him soon. She would have liked to have been there to witness it; it would have been fun. But there would be many more similar occasions.

As the two women started walking away, however, Brad unwittingly threw Malissa an unexpected opportunity.

"Is there a telephone at the farmhouse, Mel?" he asked.

She stopped and turned around. "Telephone, Brad? Telephone! There's not even a reliable source of electricity up there. But Henry has got things under control and I'm sure he'll be delighted to tell you all about it.

"In fact, I understand he sorted out the very same just last week when he had a meeting here. He's a clever man, knows how important communication is, and knows just how to get things done around here and knows a good investment when he sees one. Night-night boys, enjoy yourselves, we won't wait up."

The look on Henry's face was one she loved. That mixture of a sarcastic 'thanks very much, Malissa' underpinned with an admiration that he would always afford to those who had beaten him fair and square. "Love you," she mouthed and, as she turned around, she heard his customary, "Hmm".

As they got into the car both she and Vanessa could discern the difference in tone and volume as a very concerned friend and business partner enquired, "What plans, Henry? What investment? What's she talking about? Henry, I know that look. What have you done?"

Lewis was sound asleep when they got back to the farmhouse and when Maria left the women had a glass of wine on the patio and looked forward to the next two weeks. It had been a while since Malissa and Henry had spent time together and while part of her may have preferred to be alone with him she was sure the dynamic between the four of them would be wonderful.

Vanessa agreed that Brad was handsome. Maybe a little less fun than she'd have liked, but certainly a perfectly adequate companion. "Are you match making, Malissa?"

"I'm just saying Brad is probably the second most wonderful man I know." Qualifying her statement, she added that her father, and indeed her business partner Brian Fenner, were up there too, but obviously not in the same way.

In bed that night, Malissa had a tinge of guilt about forcing Henry's hand. But she knew her husband, she knew Brad, and knew the revelation was best aired now to save it festering and encroaching upon their holiday.

She could picture them arguing. Brad with his calculator and projections, Henry countering with romance and a sense of adventure. It would take several more bottles for them to reach a compromise, especially as Henry himself knew his decision wasn't based on the soundest of financial principles. But they would reach one; they always did.

She thought about the first time she met Brad. He had picked them up from the airport and, while constantly apologising to her, interrogated them regarding the impulsiveness of their marriage in Dubai.

Once he appreciated he was dealing with two people in love, however, his warmth towards her became as genuine as that for his business partner. Brad was as solid as they come and a natural check on Henry's often unbridled enthusiasm.

## 23

# VALENTINE'S DAY,1984

## MALISSA TALKS TO BRAD

Brad arrived about half an hour ago with the news that Henry had been delayed and would not be able to make dinner as planned. She was disappointed. It was Valentine's Day and they hadn't spoken since Saturday.

"I checked the schedule and, providing there's was no delay in Amsterdam, he should be here before the bar closes," Brad said. "Oh, and I have to give you this." He passed her a gift-wrapped rose. "But I told him I won't relay the message. He can do that himself."

She smiled. "Was it a nice message, Brad?"

"It was a 'Henry' message"

They laughed. She appreciated that Henry had been trying desperately to conclude his business to be back for Valentine's Day but she was grateful Brad had taken time out of his busy schedule to ensure she wasn't alone.

"So, you had no plans this evening?" she asked. "I mean, I haven't put you out or anything?"

"Of a romantic nature? No, still single I'm afraid. I guess I would have worked late, but a free meal with a beautiful woman? Now that did sound a better idea, and perhaps I'll pick up some tips, so this time next year... Well, you never know."

"Thanks, Brad."

They ordered drinks.

"I guess, seeing as I have you all to myself for a while," Malissa continued, "and I'm guessing that West End musicals and the finer points of editing novels probably don't float your boat, I should take this opportunity to learn a little more about the wonderful man I am to marry soon..."

Brad raised an eyebrow. She'd forgotten that, outside those in Dubai, Brad was the only person who knew Malissa and Henry were already married.

She smiled. "You know what I mean. Tell me how you met."

She knew Brad wasn't much of a man for small talk, but she was right that talking about their prospective professions would probably fail to enthral either of them. They were not on a date and Brad certainly wouldn't want to talk about his or, for that matter, anybody else's love life, so recounting a little history seemed a perfectly sensible way to pass a couple of hours.

"Well," he commenced, seemingly gathering his thoughts to ensure his account would be in some tangible and logical order. "We met in 1966, in August, a couple of weeks after England won the World Cup, not that Henry would have been the least bit interested in that..."

"I thought he liked sport?" Malissa interjected.

"Well, some, and yes he was a reasonable cricketer, but back then he wasn't that interested. The first thing I asked when we met was what he thought of the match and I couldn't believe he didn't see it. Anyway, my father was guardian of the estate, or of his Aunt Rose's estate to be more precise... You know about Aunt Rose?"

"Some. Go on..."

"Well, I was with my father on one of those visits when we met. My dad would often go there and since we seemed to get along so well, we sort of hitched up. I lived in town and the bus passed right by the house, so it was easy to visit and we spent the rest of that summer holiday together. Just hanging out I guess."

"But what was he like back then? He is a little different to most people and I can't imagine he was your typical teenager, if you know what I mean?"

"Yes, Malissa, I do know what you mean. Was he different then? You know, even then he could charm his way out of a paper bag. No malice, nothing like that, it was just his sense of adventure.

"I'd been a little more sheltered than him. Brought up to be an accountant or a solicitor, to follow in my father's footsteps as it were. It was numbers and facts I knew, and I'd spend ages on homework, reading this and writing that. Henry was genuinely interested in what I was learning. I think he found the syllabus at his school a little too easy. But he would always use facts and figures in a different way.

"Maths for example he'd simply see as a language. In fact, he'd often assign numbers to your wellbeing, so instead of being simply 'alright' or 'fine' he'd want a number. One hundred – ecstatic, and zero – dead I guess."

"Sounds like Henry."

"Yeah, funny really, I had the privilege of private education and studied hard, yet he just seemed to pick things up easily. He could take school or leave it."

"So, what about business, how did that start?"

Brad laughed. "What a good question. I'm not sure I could even tell you really. There was the greengrocers, what were they called? It doesn't matter, but the shop burned down and Henry, he would have been 15 or 16 then, lent the owner the money to rebuild it. You know he inherited quite a sum when he was young?"

"Aunt Rose," she nodded.

"I think that was just to help out a friend really. No, I guess *our* first business venture was the record shop..."

Brad then took her on an 18 year journey, starting with two teenagers who would spend hours exploring ways of making a million. Henry had the imagination, enthusing about the potential of an idea, and Brad would counter with its viability. They would look at stocks and shares and invest, keeping a careful eye on the fluctuations and deciding when to pull out or to reinvest.

The record shop coincided with the advent of cassette tapes and a general boom in music sales. Henry used almost all his money to relocate a local businessman, almost three times their age, into a more prestigious London property. One shop became two, two became three, the business was sold, and the money reinvested in more property and so on.

At the outset of 'containerisation', which was to revolutionise shipping, Henry took his biggest gamble when using his money, and for the first time that of several outside investors, to purchase containers that were subsequently leased to shipping lines. Henry had told her himself that he liked shipping, it was the movement, the travel, the going somewhere, which appealed. Of course, now, his and Brad's company had vested interests in many aspects of the freight and travel industry.

Malissa was sure it was not as simple or as smooth as Brad was telling her, and he did throw in one or two of the more bizarre ideas and some of the failures. But today the Ovmeister empire was a diverse one, comprising shipping, storage, property and stock broking companies, and investments in many other and varied businesses around the world.

These days, Henry was more of a facilitator or consultant, the face of the company but, according to Brad, still the same teenager motivated by spotting the next opportunity. The stables and the stud farm run by Bobby Anderson were outside the business but, by all accounts, successful.

"You've married well," he smiled when he finished his account.

"It seems so. Mummy will be pleased," she said, smiling back.

Tomorrow, she and Henry were off to Hatton Garden to choose their wedding rings. She was wearing her Dubai one now, on top of her engagement ring, but only ever wore the two when she was with Henry or, sometimes, when she was alone.

She had, until this point, been unaware of the pianist playing in the corner, so engrossed she must have been in Brad's story, but the unobtrusive and gentle rhythm caressed the restaurant air perfectly. The maître d' came over and whispered in Brad's ear; they had received a message, and Mr Ovmeister should be here within the hour.

"Brad?" Malissa asked. "Henry never talks about his past relationships. In fact, I can't recall he has ever asked about mine. But with him, well he's a rich, great looking guy, you'd think they'd be no shortage of women after him. I mean, I'm surprised, if anything about Henry surprises me, that he never married."

Brad's face was a little more serious this time. This type of conversation was perhaps beyond his comfort zone but surely not his knowledge.

"I mean it just seems strange…" she added.

"I guess, I've never really thought about it. Never thought it strange. Both of us have, to some extent or another, devoted our energies to business."

"The two of you together at a function? Now that would be some serious pulling power!" she joked.

Brad laughed and turned the subject to his own love life. "Well, I nearly married a Suzanne once, but we split up several years ago, usual thing, and one or two acquaintances since but nothing serious. Guess I'm waiting for Miss Right."

"And Henry?"

"Do you know, Malissa? I can honestly tell you I can't recall Henry having ever talked about getting married until he met you. In fact, he didn't really talk about it then, he just did it! I do recall him going on about this girl he met at Goodwood though. Wouldn't stop and bored me to death." He smiled cheekily at her. "You certainly distracted him from business. Maybe it was work, maybe until now he hadn't felt he had the time. Who knows? And who would I be to pass an opinion anyway?" Another smile. "No, when I think about it, I guess there must have been the casual acquaintance, but you were the first girl I heard him talk about for years. That was some broom you swept him up with…"

Malissa smiled. "What about Emma?"

"Emma? "

"Yes, in Dubai, when he was talking about love he said he'd only had that *love feeling* once before and that was when he was 14. She broke his heart. Perhaps you knew of her, when you first met?"

Brad looked at her before looking down at the table circling a finger around the rim of his wine glass. "When he was 14 you say?" He took a sip, obviously searching his memory.

"Emma, yes there was a girl called Emma. Sweet young thing with ribbons in her hair." His words were slow and considered, teasing almost. "Perhaps that was it. Scared him off at an early age so he thought he'd give it another 20 years."

Then he stood up and finished his wine. "Now, how about a best-man, bride-to-be dance before your husband appears?"

The pianist was now singing gentle love songs, and across the room, three couples were smooching. "Not as intimate as that of course," he smiled.

Malissa sensed he'd had enough of talking about relationships. "Well, Mr Carmichael, I don't usually dance before dessert but I know you are a gentleman and so I'd be honoured."

Brad escorted Malissa to the small dance floor. He looked at his watch. Henry should be here within forty minutes. Over the years, Henry had put him in many awkward situations but these past ten minutes or so could have easily precipitated the most difficult predicament of all.

## 24

# ASHBOURNE HOUSE, MAY 1966

## AUNT ROSE'S WILL

"Well, what do you think? Tasty?"

Henry couldn't answer, his mouth was full, but Emma, who was much more delicate in her eating habits, told Alice it was the best bread pudding she had ever eaten.

"He'll be really impressed with these, Al," Henry confirmed when he finished chewing, but received a slap on his wrist when he tried to take another slice.

"Wait for our guest to arrive, Henry."

Content with their verdicts, Alice returned to the kitchen. It was 3.45pm and a fine spring day.

Henry sat at the table, Emma at his side. He looked out onto the lawn and imagined Aunt Rose sitting in her favourite chair. It was nearly a month since she had passed away and today the man from the funeral, Mr Carmichael, was visiting as arranged. He would be here at 4pm.

Alice, who for the past ten years had kept house, had quickly assumed the role of custodian of the estate and self-appointed guardian to Emma and Henry. His aunt wasn't there, and he missed her, but their routine continued much as it had before her death. The gardener still turned up, the food cupboard remained full, Henry attended school, and Emma's tutors still came. Aunt Rose's love, kindness, and provision for them remained.

Emma was quiet and Henry reached for her hand. "You okay, Em?"

"Yes, Henry, I'm fine. I was just wondering what will become of us and what Mr Carmichael wants to say. I guess we'll know soon."

Henry looked at her face. Sometimes he felt he was intruding, staring even when he did so, but even though her eyes did not see in the same way his did they were still the window to her soul. So big and brown and sparkling.

"You're staring, Henry."

"Emma, I stare in wonder. Every day you get more beautiful and I'm a young man who appreciates beauty, so you shouldn't really blame me..."

She reached up, gently caressing the contours of his face. "And you, Henry, will break many hearts."

Her smile was magical. He clasped her hand and kissed it, holding it against his cheek for some seconds before she gently drew it away.

Alice reappeared with a plate of sandwiches. "He's late," she said.

She was a little panicky, she liked things to run smoothly. Satisfied Henry hadn't taken another slice of the bread pudding, she placed the sandwiches carefully down on the table, adjusting the plates and straightening the cutlery before returning to the kitchen to answer the call of the whistling kettle.

"Poor Alice," said Emma quietly. "I think she has been flustered about today ever since the funeral. She's been cleaning since six this morning."

The doorbell rang and before Henry could get up Alice dashed from the kitchen. Pausing at the door to straighten her dress, she opened it with the grace of somebody greeting royalty. "Ah, Mr Carmichael," she said. "You're early. Please come in."

She escorted him towards the table, apologising for the mess, and told him she had just made some cake and he was most welcome to join them for afternoon tea.

Charles Carmichael was a tall, thin man in his mid-forties, with dark Brylcreem'd hair and glasses. He wore a blue suit, blue shirt and blue tie, and carried a brown leather briefcase. His face was serious but kind and Henry wondered if he ever laughed.

"Henry, good to see you."

Henry stood up, shook his hand, and invited him to sit down.

Alice poured the tea and offered sandwiches which Mr Carmichael accepted enthusiastically, complementing her on the spread and saying he couldn't wait to try the bread pudding. He talked a little about how wonderful the place looked and just how proud Aunt Rose would have been to see how well they were coping. Alice sat down, pride evident amongst the blushes that greeted his kind words.

At the funeral, Mr Carmichael had introduced himself, explaining he had known Gertrude Ovmeister (this was Aunt Rose's real name) for many years. Their family's history stretched back not only to the time when she lived in Germany but to America before the outbreak of the First World War. His firm had been entrusted to look after her interests after her death and, while this was the legal position, Henry sensed the arrangement was much more personal. The meeting today had been planned so that Mr Carmichael could inform them of Aunt Rose's wishes and discuss her legacy.

During the second cup of tea and the first sampling of the bread pudding, Mr Carmichael lifted a wad of papers from his briefcase, handing Henry and Alice a copy. Then he looked at Henry, awkwardly, clearly wondering what to do with the copy he had prepared for Emma.

"Emma," Henry said smiling. "Mr Carmichael has given us some papers about Aunt Rose." Then, redirecting his attention to their visitor assured him that Emma was a good listener with an amazing memory and that written words weren't necessary.

"You didn't think of bringing a copy in brail, Mr Carmichael? I guess at least I won't get misled by the small print," Emma teased. The smile that accompanied her words left no doubt that they were intended to make light of an otherwise possibly embarrassing situation.

"That was remiss of me, Emma, I'm sorry. I just didn't think."

He gave them some background of Aunt Rose's family history. Much of what he said, Henry already knew, but he was clearly a man of empathy and honour and Henry could see why his aunt had warmed to him. With his preamble completed, he invited them to inspect the more relevant pages of the documents they held.

"Henry, this, you will see, is your official certificate of adoption. This is what we call a closed adoption. Your aunt was insistent that you all legally became her children to avoid any ambiguity in respect of your inheritance..."

"Closed?" Henry interrupted.

"Yes, this means that the identity of the mother and or, indeed, if known or disclosed, the father, is not recorded. There are other sealed envelopes addressed to you, at least one of which I understand contains more information in relation to your adoption and, quite possibly, the identity of your biological parents. I have not seen the contents of these envelopes but they are under my firm's care. My instructions are to hand these to you whenever you request." He paused. Maybe he expected Henry to seek further clarification.

"Aunt Rose is my mother," Henry said, defiantly. "Sorry I interrupted you, please go on."

"Please understand that I may come across as a little direct or abrupt, but this is in my professional capacity as trustee of your aunt's legacy. You should know I was very fond of Mrs Ovmeister. She was a wonderful woman and I am aware of the love she had for the three of you."

He turned to Emma. "Emma, your official adoption papers are here too." Emma smiled, but he didn't talk about any sealed letters that may have identified her birth parents. "Now, if you turn to page four..."

Henry and Alice found the pages to which he referred. Aunt Rose was indeed a wealthy woman. The house was bequeathed to the three of them jointly and money had been set aside for its upkeep. Alice being so much older than the other two, had been appointed as guardian and, as such, would receive a generous allowance until Emma reached the age of 18. This caused a chuckle as Alice had already assumed the position but making it official clearly appealed to her.

Henry was left an immediate sum of £10,000 and more when he reached the age of 21. Emma had been bequeathed an inheritance sufficient to ensure she could be cared for, for the rest of her life.

Other details included the continued patronage of the charities she supported and the distribution of her personal treasures. The three of them could regard themselves as being financially secure for a considerable time to come and they were humbled by the love Aunt Rose continued to show them through her legacy. Neither Emma nor Henry had known the joy of natural parents but recognised how fortunate they were to have been adopted by such a wonderful lady.

Mr Carmichael informed them that he was at their disposal and would keep in touch. A few more papers would need to be signed and they were most welcome to visit him at his offices to discuss appropriate investment opportunities.

When he left, the three of them talked for some time. When Alice went to bed Emma and Henry sat together on the sofa as they had done on so many occasions over the years.

They talked about their younger days, remembering how they played in the garden. They talked about what they hoped to achieve in the world. They talked about Aunt Rose's kindness and told each other stories they both already knew. They talked about music and whether she would teach him to play the piano, or the violin, or both, and they talked about their dreams.

And then Emma talked about Lucy Johnson, who would always give Henry an apple when he passed by the greengrocers on his paper round. "I think she loves you Henry," she giggled.

But when Henry thought about love he thought only about the wonderful girl sitting next to him. And they talked until they were too tired to talk and joked that they were rich. And that's when Henry wondered whether £10,000 was enough to enable the most beautiful girl he would ever know, to see again.

## 25

# MAJORCA, SUMMER 1989

## THE BLACKPOOL TO BRIGHTON CHALLENGE

Vanessa was making coffee when a dishevelled Henry returned to the farmhouse at 7am.

"Good morning, Henry, I didn't hear you coming."

Henry stood in the doorway, momentarily stunned. She was wearing just a pale cotton shirt that barely covered her thighs and he wasn't sure where to look. Her shoulder-length auburn hair was shorter at the front and curled into her cheeks, loose strands falling across her face as she turned to him.

Her eyes were deep and bright and knowing, beneath eyebrows that were never trimmed. She wore no makeup and her complexion was soft and lightly bronzed, accentuating the paleness of her lips. She was a naturally beautiful woman, and standing there with one hand on the work surface and the other on her hip, he saw a woman he once knew.

"Good morning, Vanessa." His voice was tired and gruff and hid his alarm. "I walked up from town."

"Did it work?" She grabbed her dressing gown from the shower room door. "The walk. Did it clear your head?"

He frowned. Obviously not.

"I'll get you some coffee. I think Malissa is dressing Lewis."

"Thank you," he said, wondering if it would be possible to ignore everybody and creep upstairs and climb into bed.

"Possibly no swimming this morning." Vanessa smiled, handing him his drink.

He sipped it gratefully and sat down at the kitchen table. He knew Malissa would not be as sympathetic. He needed some sleep and knew this was going to be a long day. One of those you'd rather skip and start again tomorrow.

Malissa came down. As expected, she showed little empathy for Henry's morbid state. Neither did Lewis, who was insistent that his father should amuse him. Henry answered his wife's questions regarding how it went with Brad with a series of 'ums' and 'ahs', promising to give her the full rundown later. How could she always be so chirpy? He was grateful when Vanessa took Lewis off his hands.

Brad would be coming up later, but the swimming was probably best left until tomorrow. Henry politely declined their invitation to accompany them into town, and when they left at 9am he surrendered to his weariness and fell asleep on the sofa.

Outside, the roofers were fixing the tiles to the villa. The rhythmic hammering was audible but not intrusive and, as he drifted off, he hoped Vanessa could persuade his wife to stay out a little longer than she may have otherwise intended, giving him the best chance of a quick regeneration.

Brad arrived at 5pm saying he would stay at the hotel rather than the farmhouse, which might be a bit crowded with the four of them and Lewis. He was, to Malissa's surprise, in high spirits. If there was any disagreement over the plans to build a harbour and a hotel they had obviously been ironed out last night over several bottles of Valcanto.

He had spent the afternoon walking around the town, taking lunch at one of the harbour restaurants. Like the other three, he seemed to be falling in love with the place, though of course could not yet admit it.

They were going to eat lobster salad that evening in the garden and, while Vanessa prepared it, Brad was given a tour of the peninsular. The orange grove on the way to the beach offered welcome shade from the sun. Malissa explained that though they had come out too late to pick the best oranges, they did witness the subsequent blossoming of the orchard which filled the air with the most delicious fragrance.

Brad said he loved the beach and both men were introduced to Blackpool and Brighton. 'Rock Stars', they called them. On the way back up to the farmhouse they stopped at the villa. Malissa confirmed the installation of running water, electricity, and phone lines was being accelerated which meant completion could be within three months. "So I understand," said Brad. Henry just nodded.

Tour over, they returned to the farmhouse. Malissa checked on Vanessa, wondering whether she needed help with dinner, and Henry read to Lewis, making up for the attention denied him during the day.

Brad sat on the patio and looked at his watch. It was gone 7pm, just after 5pm in London, and Malissa wondered if he was thinking about ringing the office. She brought him a beer. "It's a beautiful place, Malissa," he said.

"Maybe phone calls can wait?" she said handing him the bottle.

"Well, I guess you'll soon have a phone up here". He smiled. He had obviously forgiven Henry.

"Vanessa's making sangria."

"You know, Mel, I'll probably give that a miss tonight. Big day tomorrow."

Brad arrived just after breakfast the next morning to learn the Blackpool-Brighton Challenge had been postponed for the foreseeable future while the contractors worked round the clock to get the cables laid. Instead they would spend the next two days in Palma.

"We can go on the old railway. You'll love it, Brad," said Malissa. He had been to Palma once before, ten years ago.

"Holiday?" she asked.

"Not quite," he replied, and glancing Henry's way added, "more of a business trip really."

Below them, the diggers sent out the first deafening echoes as steel clattered rock vindicating their decision to abandon the farmhouse for a couple of days while the work was done.

They spent two nights in Palma and a third in town. As promised the diggers had done their job and were gone. Even the outline of the garden, including the area which would accommodate the pool, had been sculptured. Malissa smiled to herself. It was amazing what could be achieved in three days given the right incentives.

In Palma, Brad had hired a car with a phone and Vanessa travelled back with him instead of taking the train. Malissa would not have been surprised if they shared a room in The Grand last night but, no, neither showed any inclination towards romance. Funny, both so good looking, both single, you would have thought it the most natural thing. If Vanessa did not want a relationship or did, indeed, prefer women, it was okay by her.

Malissa and Lewis were already on the on the beach when the others arrived at midday.

"Soon," said Henry, "there will be a whole new generation of car phones. Well, not even car phones, they'll be more mobile. 'Cell phones' they call them in the States. You'll carry them with you. It will revolutionise communication and the potential is endless..."

"You'll be in heaven, Brad," said Malissa. "Imagine, constant contact with the office. So, we could have a phone, not plugged into anywhere, no wires, just powered by a battery and it would work up here?"

"Like radio", Henry confirmed. "You hear the radio but there are no wires, no evidence of a connection, but it's there. It's simply taking advantage of what we already know exists."

Brad agreed their investment in the potential of mobile communications was likely to prove more lucrative than their most recent one in the Söller tourist industry.

Vanessa interrupted the conversation. "Now, gentleman. I have familiarised you with the rules and perhaps Malissa and I may now give you a practical demonstration."

She lifted her sweatshirt over her head and unbuttoned her shorts. It was, of course, necessary for Vanessa to strip down to her bikini but Malissa wondered if she knew just how provocative her undressing like that appeared. "One minute fifty-five is the record," Vanessa shouted as she ran into the sea.

"Unofficial," Malissa called after her, explaining to the men there was no witness and two minutes three seconds, her time, was the one in the record book.

Vanessa reached the rock and when given the signal, pushed off and headed towards the other. She moved rhythmically, breathing every third stroke, occasionally looking up to check her position. She disappeared behind Brighton, and Malissa checked her watch. "Forty-eight seconds. That's good," she said.

Henry and Brad watched, seemingly with growing interest. "Is that the best way around the rock?" Brad asked.

"It's debatable. Ness says it is because you round the rock with the tide." She spoke her last six words in an exaggerated sexy French accent, "But then, of course, you swim against it when you come back. It's calm today so she should do a good time. Maybe she will break that two minutes?"

"Go Vanessa," Brad shouted, then looked a bit sheepish, possibly thinking he was perceived as being biased.

Halfway back you could see Vanessa was tiring, losing a little rhythm and breathing every stroke. Lap completed, she touched the rock and in an exhausted breath shouted "Stop!"

They compared times, agreeing two minutes one second would be official. Malissa conceded it was a new record and would be recorded as such. "Two O-one" she called to her friend as Vanessa made her way to shore.

Back on dry land and breathing hard she towelled her hair. "Too many croissants," she puffed, flopping down on the sand next to Lewis.

"I'm impressed," said Henry. "And, to tell the truth, now a little nervous. That looked exhausting."

Malissa stood up stretched and then shook her arms and legs. "Well, if that's the best you can do Ness," she quipped as she made her way out to Blackpool.

Henry watched his wife wade out to the rock, suddenly feeling a degree of concern. Vanessa joined him and Brad by the table, her short, wet auburn hair clinging to her face. "That's some challenge you've set," he said to her.

He returned his attention to Malissa. They confirmed they were ready with their watches and Malissa set off.

She was not as smooth as Vanessa in the water, her strokes were more aggressive, but her feet certainly kicked more. She too rounded Brighton on the far side and in a similar time to Vanessa's. Henry had swum with her on many occasions but at a much more leisurely pace and he felt his heart warming as he witnessed his wife's effort to get inside the target time.

In a way it was symbolic of just how far she had come over the last six years and he could feel her determination. He willed her on, feeling that familiar sense of wanting to help but he needn't, she was doing fine.

"Go, Mel," shouted Brad.

"She going to do it," said Vanessa and, sure enough, as Malissa shouted stop, so the stopwatch Vanessa was holding recorded one fifty-nine.

Henry looked at his wristwatch and then at Vanessa. His less official recording would have suggested a time some three seconds slower. He wondered but said nothing and greeted his wife as she came onto the beach by wrapping both himself and the towel around her.

It had been a surreal five minutes or so. What Henry had regarded as a bit of fun suddenly became something more and it was difficult to explain why. Was it the challenge? The rivalry, or in its own relative modesty, just the appreciation of human endeavour? Or was it simply the wonderful bond between them? They sat back at the table deciding to have lunch before the men took their turn.

Brad and Vanessa denied any romantic connotations but said they enjoyed the drive back from Palma, which because of the winding mountain roads was more than twice the straight-line distance. Brad had heard of plans to build a road tunnel, two miles in length which would take traffic from the main road out of Palma directly into Söller. He liked the idea as it would make the town more accessible and therefore easier for tourists to visit.

"But if you have a hotel surely you would want them to be stuck here Monsieur Carmichael?" There was a certain logic in Vanessa's comment. Almost Henry-esque.

Brad decided that Blackpool was flat enough and the water sufficiently deep, to accommodate a diving start. "The start of a race, and your diving ability, are integral to any swimming event," he said, and for the 'men's challenge' they would be starting with a dive.

They also suggested they would race against each other as this was normal practice in any swimming race. The women were open to the suggestion of the dive but seemingly set against the duel swim, but because this was their first attempt they could understand if they were 'scared of doing it alone'.

They did dive off the rock. They rounded Brighton from different sides and Henry was about a length up when Brad grabbed hold of his ankles. Henry retaliated and the whole thing turned into a farce as, like a couple of kids, they ducked each other under the water, deciding a handstand competition was more appropriate. The initial men's challenge was therefore declared void. They would try again tomorrow with proper regard to the rules.

Brad arrived at 10am the following morning and informed them he would be returning to London tomorrow. Henry had been teaching Lewis to swim but came out of the water when he saw Brad.

They talked a little about the issue Brad needed to sort out and Henry conceded it made sense for him to go back. Maybe he could return later.

At times like this, Henry wondered if Brad ever regretted not following the career in finance mapped out for him. He was paid more than any London accountant, but business was insistently intertwined with his life. He hoped he knew how appreciated he was, and he hoped he was happy.

"Now," said Brad. "I've bought this."

From his bag he produced an old-fashioned car hooter, its curly golden trumpet sparkling in the morning sun. He squeezed the rubber and the honk was deep and brassy and surprisingly loud. He squeezed it several more times much to the delight of a mesmerised Lewis.

"This," Brad said, "shall be activated by the swimmer upon completion of the lap, thus removing any ambiguity in respect of the swimmer shouting stop too early." He had also procured a fixing bracket, some rather serious looking masonry nails, and a hammer.

"Hmm," said Henry, twiddling the nails between his fingers and looking at the rock. "Okay, let's do it."

The two men waded out. They argued about the best place to fix it and once agreed attempted to attach it to the rock. Mighty nails they may have been but banging them into the rock was not possible and after several attempts they returned to the beach, somewhat disappointed.

"I've got an idea," said Henry and bounded up the slope saying he wouldn't be long.

When he returned, he was followed by Juan, one of the builders, dressed in shorts and sleeveless vest and carrying a pneumatic drill over his shoulder like one of the marines out of the film Aliens. He smiled at Vanessa. "Miss Cozzette. How nice to see you."

Henry introduced him to Brad.

The three men waded out to the rock. Juan suggested it was safer for Henry and Brad stand back a little, and with a look back at Vanessa he pulled down his goggles, fired up the drill and bored into the rock. Like assistants in an operating theatre, Henry and Brad handed him first the bracket and then the expansion bolts.

Job done, Juan gave the rubber a squeeze. Vanessa acknowledged it was perfectly audible. Henry and Brad ensured it worked too, then Juan joined them for a beer on the beach. Before returning to his duties he explained to Vanessa just how the expansion bolts gripped the rock and reassured her the hooter would not budge.

"There," said Brad when Juan had gone. "Now we are ready."

They tossed a coin and Henry was to go first. He stood on the rock preparing for the swim. As he stretched up he caught Malissa looking at him and smiled.

"Take you marks. Go."

He dived in. He headed out to Brighton pausing halfway to check his bearings. He rounded the rock from the far side. Twice on the way back he corrected his direction and upon reaching Blackpool reached up and squeezed the hooter.

Vanessa pressed the stopwatch and showed it to the others. One minute forty-four, an inaugural men's record and a very challenging time for Brad to beat.

Henry made his way back to shore, his heaving chest just starting to show the first signs of grey. His advice to Brad was to check his direction often. "You wouldn't believe how difficult it is to keep straight," he said.

Brad completed the lap slower than Henry and during the afternoon they made several more attempts. The women swam too, for the first time diving in and sounding the wonderful old-fashioned hooter to announce their finish.

The rules of the challenge had been cast. There would be a trophy presented at the end of September each year. The official record book read:

***MEN'S***

*Henry Ovmeister 1 min 41*

*Brad Carmichael 1 min 50*
***WOMEN'S***
*Vanessa Cozzette 1 min 56*
*Malissa Ovmeister 1 min 59*
***UNDER 5'S***
*Lewis Ovmeister (with armbands) 7 min 20*

Malissa and Vanessa suggested Juan might like to have a go. He did fix the hooter, after all, and it seemed only fair to include him. He was ten years younger than Brad and Henry and fit from a life of manual work. Henry hoped he couldn't swim.

"No, I think, it should be confined to the English," Henry suggested.

Malissa smiled and put her arm around him. "And by invitation only Henry?"

"Quite. It's a special thing."

Vanessa looked at him. "And the French, of course surely?" she enquired raising her eyebrows.

"Indeed Vanessa. Et Les Français," smiled Henry.

## 26

# MAJORCA, SUMMER 1989

## HENRY AND MALISSA

The day after Brad returned to London, Vanessa went to France for a few days and up until she returned yesterday it had been just Henry, Malissa and Lewis at the farmhouse. It wasn't often the three of them could enjoy such an uninterrupted schedule and they had wallowed in the joy of each other's company.

Henry knew Malissa was the face of Fenner's these days. It wasn't just the result of the work she had put in over the years; it was her personality and her ability to capture people's imaginations. Add to that her subtle persuasiveness and charm, and even her attractiveness, and he could understand why Brian was desperate for her to attend the meeting. Henry knew he was being unfair in suggesting she stay, but right here, right now, he just wanted the romance to continue.

"I'll be gone two days darling, three at the most," Malissa whispered. "Think how much we'll miss each other and the fun we can have when I get back." They still cuddled at night, even after five years of marriage. "And think of the father-son time you can have with Lewis. Now that, I know, will appeal to you."

"In that case, Miss Keats, I shall teach our son to swim. I shall take him around this wonderful island. To Alcúdia, to Magaluf, and up in the mountains where we shall camp out, and when you come back you will witness him swimming Blackpool to Brighton unaided."

His change in tone was welcomed. She chuckled. "He's not yet three Henry." She kissed him. "When I get back, Mr Ovmeister, I wonder if you will do me the honour of sleeping with me in the garden."

He remembered their honeymoon. He drew her close, all misgivings melting. He knew he would miss her.

Malissa's flight was on time and there was nobody seated next to her which would make going through the copious faxed notes she'd picked up from The Grand easier. The meeting Brian had requested she attend was an important one, concerning the acquisition of a competitor. Her job was to provide them with the reassurance they sought. Brian was picking her up from Gatwick and business may well be concluded during dinner tonight.

She thought about Henry and the last two weeks they had spent together, especially the last few days and smiled to herself. Other than in the new mobile phones, he had shown less enthusiasm for business over recent months. The Ovmeister empire had long since outgrown him and she doubted even he knew the full extent of its reach these days. Perhaps that was it. He had achieved what he set out to do and now longed for something else.

He was driven but by no means ruthless in business, and it was certainly something other than money that motivated him. He could be passionate and protective, kind and generous to a fault, loving to everyone he met, and so tender towards her.

Even when she was so obviously content with life he would ask if she was happy. He could be deep and serious, on occasion displaying great insight and empathy, and at other times, like in the last two weeks, so carefree and light-hearted.

She loved watching him with Lewis. When their son was born, she detected a nervousness, a sadness even, mixed in with his obvious joy.

She guessed that being an orphan and becoming a father stirred his subconsciousness, pricking emotions she would not necessarily understand, and she wondered how often he thought about *his* parents.

But he rarely talked about the past, saying life was best lived in the present. Maybe they should have another child? She found herself smiling again. Yes, she'd like that.

27

# MAJORCA, SUMMER 1989

## VANESSA AND HENRY

The feeling of disappointment on realising Henry was not there surprised Vanessa. Before they left for the airport he had been chatting with Lewis and considering what they could do for the day. Perhaps he had taken him out somewhere, maybe into town. But the car was still there. She filled the kettle.

Several faint honks interrupted her thoughts. Henry and his son were at the beach. She smiled, this time disturbed by the sudden relief she felt on realising he *was* there after all.

She undressed and put on her bikini and one of her long t-shirts. She grabbed some provisions, a bottle of wine and a towel, and put them in a bag. She would take them lunch.

The inside of the villa was being plastered. She smiled at the workmen saying *mañana* as she passed, knowing they would be ogling her from behind as she made her way down the slope. She didn't mind. Since the age of 14 she'd known she possessed something men craved and she would have no hesitation in exploiting their pathetic weakness for a pretty girl if it served a purpose.

She stood at the edge of the ridge with its little drop onto the beach. There would be wooden steps there soon. She watched Henry with Lewis. They were building sandcastles, Henry constantly speaking to him as if he was older. He certainly was a striking man. Not as cute as Brad, not as pretty, but certainly handsome.

His eyes were knowing and kind, possessing the wisdom of both happiness and great despair. On several occasions she had wondered just what they were seeing when they looked at her. What questions they required her to answer and if asked should she answer them all?

She skipped down the bank, confident her observations had not been noticed. Henry looked up, pleased to see her. "It's Vanessa," he told his son and, picking him up, came over to the table to greet her.

"He'll need this," she said, pulling out the sun cream.

"Of course he will," said Henry, taking it from her. "Now Lewis, don't forget this anymore," and he tickled his son as he applied the cream, unconcerned how much sand got mixed with it, before sitting him on the chair next to him.

"*Et vin blanc. Très bien,*" said Henry, helping unload the provisions. "I assume Malissa got away okay?"

"Yes, flight exactly on time."

They had lunch and discussed where to go for the afternoon, deciding on Söller Port where Vanessa would introduce Henry to orange flavoured ice cream. They could take the tram into old Söller too and, dependent upon Lewis, either eat in town or when they got back to the farmhouse.

Henry told her he first came to Söller many years ago, spending the best part of two months touring the area. He stayed in an old farmhouse just outside town.

"I thought you would have stayed at The Grand," she said.

"No, that wasn't until later. No, when I first came here it was the old town I fell in love with," he replied.

Vanessa showed him the building she and Malissa thought would make a great dance studio. It was originally the schoolhouse, and when the new school was built the council had considered relocating the museum there. Those plans, however, never materialised and word was that it would soon be up for auction. It needed a degree of modernisation, but Henry enthused about its suitability.

They talked much about the town and a little about their lives. At times she detected he wanted to say more and once or twice she caught him looking at her with that same questioning look in his eyes. She would have loved to have talked more intimately but realised it was so much more than her great friendship with Malissa that prevented her from doing so. She was adamant, however, that his reason for first coming here, was more than the walking holiday he described.

Henry was not surprised Vanessa had taken such a liking to Söller. This part of the Island had strong historical links with France and many street names, especially those here in the old town, would not have been out of place in Paris.

Lewis was hungry at 5pm and back at the harbour he and Vanessa shared a pizza while Henry popped into The Grand to make a few phone calls and check for messages. He could not get hold of Malissa.

They returned to the farmhouse at 7pm. Vanessa went upstairs to shower, and, after a little play time, Henry took his son up to bed. As she passed the bedroom on her way downstairs, she paused as Henry started his bedtime story. "Once upon a time, long ago, this house was surrounded by orange trees which produced the most juicy, delicious, sweet oranges you had ever, ever tasted..."

His voice was soothing and full of enthusiasm for the tale he was telling. She wanted to stay and listen, but she felt she was intruding upon something precious and carried on downstairs to cook the bolognaise she had promised him.

She laid the patio table. She thought about dressing for dinner, about reapplying her makeup, about tending her hair, and she hated the thoughts that crept into her mind about why she was considering doing so.

She only met Henry three months ago but had previously gleaned much about him from Malissa. She knew he was an intelligent and very successful man, but anyone would appreciate that from a 30 second conversation with him. What she saw was the tenderness and care he exuded and she smiled, believing this must have always been with him and bestowed upon those he loved. She opened a bottle of white and a bottle of red but wouldn't put the pasta on until he came down.

"Smells good," he said when he appeared in the kitchen and, picking up the bottle of red, "ah mainland rioja, I take it you think this better than the local produce?"

She smiled. "Did you finish the story?"

He chuckled. "Not really, I was just getting to some good bits when I realised he had probably been asleep for 20 minutes. Still, gives me the chance to refine it tomorrow."

"Was it the story of Juan and Theresa?"

"Oh, the local love story… yes sort of. Call me an old softy but those stories always have mileage in them."

How lovely you would take such romance to heart and instil the same belief in your son, she thought, but instead said, "I hope you like garlic." He said he did.

Henry went outside and sat down. The sun had disappeared but there was no need to light the lantern just yet. Vanessa joined him, pouring herself a glass of white. "Just waiting on the pasta," she said.

They said nothing for a few moments. There was only the sound of the crickets disturbing the stillness.

"Malissa has told me you can tell the temperature from a cricket's chirp." Vanessa topped up their glasses.

"She told you that did she? Well, it happens to be true, tried and tested. It will be warm and sunny tomorrow."

She got up and went back into the kitchen, continuing the conversation by saying it's always warm and sunny here in July and asking whether he wanted parmesan.

Henry watched, chatting idly as Vanessa prepared the meal, wondering exactly what it was about her that conjured up images of Emma. Not entirely alike to look at, but not so different. Similarly built, but so were many women. The hair, its movement to be precise, but there must be something else.

The way she moved, perhaps? Or, more likely, it was just his imagination. It no longer impacted on him in the same way it did that morning when he walked back from Söller, but it was still there. She was just a very beautiful woman and so was Emma. And so, of course, was Malissa, and she was the most beautiful of all he reminded himself.

As they ate, they talked about Malissa's rise to success at Fenner's. They talked about Vanessa's curtailed dancing career in London and the viability of opening a dance school in town. They talked about mobile phones and even the Blackpool-Brighton challenge that they may well attempt tomorrow. They talked about many things but, like earlier in the day, Henry felt they were skirting around what they really wanted to talk about, if, indeed, either knew exactly what that was.

They finished dinner and both cleared the plates. They had also finished the wine. Henry suggested another bottle might be in order.

"Or something stronger," Vanessa suggested. "Sangria. Perhaps a 'Malissa Special'?" Henry had heard all about it. "That would loosen our tongues," she added looking at him.

Their eyes met. Her gaze penetrated him. It wasn't the first time she had unnerved him like that. Henry did want to talk to her more intimately, and though unsure why he felt that way, he felt she wanted to too.

He felt a connection. Malissa could pre-empt and even formulate replies for him, she could read his moods. This woman, however, seemed to look inside him. He was sure her mention of more alcohol was to facilitate mental rather than physical seduction; to weaken the barrier that may have hindered them talking deeper during the day.

"Loosen our tongues? Now, that would be something," he said. "Well, it's a fine evening and since you've mentioned it, perhaps we won't need the sangria. This bottle should be sufficient stimulus." He uncorked the wine and they returned to the table.

They sat in the stillness for a minute or two. "Ladies first," he said.

More thoughtful silence. "You are a wonderful man, Henry," Vanessa said earnestly.

"Less accent, please." He was more relaxed now and happy to tell her he loved the way she spoke, so seductive. "Or this could go completely Pete Tong."

"Pete Tong?"

"It's an expression for something going wrong. Never mind, I interrupted. Please continue."

Vanessa visibly digested the Pete Tong - wrong conundrum, understood, smiled, and carried on.

"You do much for people and people love you. You do much because you believe this brings great happiness to them and therefore to you. You wish the world was a kinder and gentler place. You see the good in people and find it hard to imagine them otherwise. You fear loss, especially the loss of love, and you do so because you have loved so deeply and lost. And you know that that love, the love you had, made you so happy and the world a better place. You see few people who have known such love."

She stopped.

He was taken back 15 years and wondered whether to change the subject. How much did he trust this woman? He needn't divulge details, but the connection was strong. He looked into her eyes knowing she would not turn away whilst he spoke.

"You are very beautiful and ooze sexuality. You know it, but often resent it. It hindered your childhood and it bothers you now. You believe no man sees beyond your physical beauty. You, too, yearn for a love but find it hard to believe in. It takes you a long time to trust another human being, but you have rightly come to terms with the secrets you keep."

She looked at him, deeply, her eyes fixed on his but her face expressionless. She nodded, very slightly, and replied.

"Malissa rarely talks about your past love affairs, I guess because you don't. She knows about one or two casual acquaintances but it's difficult to believe a man like you has had so few lovers. She has joked about a girl who broke your heart when you were young. My guess is she must have been soft and kind and more important to you than you let on. A girl whose love was pure and made you feel worthwhile, a love that gave you purpose, and the loss of that love is the one you have sought to replace."

A thousand images flashed through his mind. He couldn't reply and didn't believe she expected him to. She was very beautiful and, in another life, they may have found a great love together. They were holding hands across the table, but he couldn't remember either of them initiating that.

He kissed the back of her hand and broke the physical contact.

"And you, Vanessa," he said, shaking off the images that had invaded. "You will live up here. And you will change your name to Theresa and you will plant orange trees, and they will bear fruit, and you will be known throughout the land as the woman with the juiciest, most gorgeous, ripe and beautiful pair of..."

By the time he got to this point they were laughing, unsure if the previous conversation was wise but both seemingly pleased, they had found an appropriate exit.

From now on they may have a deeper understanding of one another. Brought about by an exchange of a few intense and cryptic sentences while looking into each other's eyes. Whether they would talk so intimately again he wasn't sure, but this woman moved him and somewhere in his mind he knew she would always be special.

It was nearly midnight. Tomorrow they could go to the beach or into town and there was every possibility that Malissa would be back by night fall. He hoped so.

Henry would not sleep well tonight. She had roused too many memories.

## 28

# ASHBOURNE HOUSE, MAY 1969

## EMMA AND HENRY

It had been uncharacteristically hot for the time of year and today felt particularly muggy, heralding an inevitable break in the weather. The clouds rolled in from the south and a five-minute downpour preceded the lighter rain that now fell. He hadn't taken the car and was on the bus during the worst of the rain, and a quick sprint to the front door meant he wasn't as wet as he may have been.

The temperature had dropped somewhat but it was still warm. Henry went inside, eager to tell Emma the outcome of his latest meeting with Charles Carmichael.

She was in the garden. She stood, arms outstretched, palms upwards catching the rain. She held her head back, curls of wet auburn hair clinging to her cheeks. Her eyes were closed, and her lovely face wore a smile as she enjoyed the gentle massage of the falling water droplets.

Her t-shirt hugged her, and the little white threads of the unstitched hem of her denim shorts stuck to her lightly tanned thighs. It wasn't unusual for Emma to delight in the feel of the rain and, as she spun, he realised the most wonderful girl he had ever known had blossomed into the most beautiful woman in the world.

He had been on a few dates. To the cinema, to a dance, and to the local pub where the landlord would serve him even though he knew he was 17. He had been out with, and kissed, Lucy the greengrocer's daughter, Karen and Janice who he had known since school, and he was constantly being harassed by Beverley who was three years older and not very subtle; "And, to be honest Em," he'd say, "frightens the life out of me." But there was always something missing.

Emma and Henry talked about everything and anything. They had grown up together, naturally learning each other's strengths and weaknesses, and it was a privilege and a source of joy, pride, and love for Henry to paint pictures of the things that Emma couldn't physically see. He did not see her blindness and she never need be blind whilst he was with her. As he opened the back door to join her in the garden he realised exactly what would always be missing. No other girl was Emma.

"Hey," he called.

She turned to him smiling. "Hey. How did it go?"

He put his arm around her, her head falling onto his shoulder as he led her back inside.

"One day, Em, you'll catch pneumonia being out in the rain like this."

"I'm not sure the rain gives you pneumonia, Henry," she replied. "In fact, it's a common misconception that the cold actually gives you a cold. Eskimos, for example, don't get colds because the cold actually kills the germs. I love the scent of the garden when it rains in summer. Can you smell the philadelphus?"

"Philly-who?"

"Mock Orange, they have white flowers."

Henry looked around, spotting the shrub she referred to and suddenly become aware of the faint aroma of oranges. "Yes, I can now you mention it."

"Now, tell me about your meeting."

"Em, everything looks great. One or two finer points to take care of but it's really exciting."

He watched as Emma crossed the kitchen to the old pantry, which now housed the boiler and served as a downstairs cloak room. She stored some of her clothes there, and Alice would always arrange them so Emma would know which ones hung where.

So familiar was she with the layout of the house you would never believe she couldn't see. She grabbed a towel from the shelf and started drying her hair. "No peeking," she said as she reached for one of her dresses.

Henry found it difficult to look away, but he did and continued to relay the details of his meeting with Charles Carmichael.

Brad and he had, for some time, been assessing the viability of setting up Bobby Anderson as a racehorse trainer. Henry, who was developing a keen interest in racing, was obviously enthusiastic, but this was a substantial investment and would involve several young people upping roots and starting a new life. Bobby was keen on the idea from the start. She'd more or less run the establishment in which she had been employed for the last eight years, anyway, and neither Henry nor Brad doubted her ability to train racehorses. Horses were her life. She didn't even regard looking after them as work.

Brad suggested Bobby would need help in respect of the accountancy but agreed the real estate investment was sound. The overriding factor was they had every confidence that Bobby was capable of making a success of the thing she loved doing best. All Henry had needed to do was persuade Brad's father to release a sizeable proportion of Aunt Rose's money. Carmichael's remit was to do this if he felt it would be put to good use.

Charles Carmichael had always been impressed by Henry's maturity, energy and approach to a challenge. He was also somewhat in awe of his investment prowess.

Though Carmichael recognised Henry's natural flair, when it came to providing career advice, he would instinctively promote prudence and job security. When Henry left school, for example, he found him a position with a London stock broking firm. He questioned him earnestly when after a month Henry told him he wished to leave but, in his heart, Carmichael knew Henry harboured greater ambition than to follow the well-trodden path of a career in finance. That would be more suitable for his own son.

Carmichael could always hear Aunt Rose in his ear; "He's very special to me, Charles, and has something to offer this world. I trust your judgement and intuition, that's why I pay you so much. Promise me never to stand in the way of his creativity. Always hear him out".

Henry was very persuasive when sure about something and his enthusiasm was infectious. Two years ago, when working part time for Bob Buttery, he used his money to help the greengrocer relocate following a fire which destroyed his small shop. While Bob mourned the loss of a family business, Henry re-established it; firstly with a market stall in town, then another in Bracknell, then by offering deliveries to customers doors.

Within a year, the shop reopened and when it did it was the fifth 'Buttery's' establishment which, along with the traditional fare of a greengrocers, supplied an ever-growing range of food products. Henry had a 51% share in the business, and a re-enthused Bob Buttery a new lease of life. Carmichael's firm was currently handling the sale of the business for a sum equal to 30 times the original turnover of that burned-down shop.

A racing stable was another step. So convincing was the written presentation, (Carmichael was unsure whether he was delighted or horrified when Henry told him it was largely his son's work), the requested amount of £40,000 to supplement the £10,000 Henry was eager to put in would have seemed reasonable even to the most conservative of bankers. Charles agreed to make the funds available with no caveat other than that he would like the odd tip or two.

As Henry left his office, he made a further request for £25,000 for a property in Cornwall that had the potential to be developed into a stud farm. He was happy to repay much of that from the sale of the Buttery business.

"Where was the business plan for that?" Carmichael had asked, almost throwing him out of the door for his cheek.

"Here," said Henry, putting his hand over his heart and looking him directly in the eye. Carmichael couldn't refuse.

Henry had left Charles Carmichael's office eager to tell Bobby Anderson and Brad the good news. But first, of course, he needed to tell Emma.

"Bobby will be over the moon," Emma said when Henry finished recounting the details.

"Yep, I think she will. I'll tell her first thing in the morning."

They were seated on the sofa. He could sense her warmth and feel her joy, her joy for him. She let her head fall onto his shoulder. "You never know," she said, "one day *you* could have horses trained by her. I could buy you one for your birthday. You could name her So Nature after the most wonderful woman we ever knew."

Henry realised the suggested name was an anagram of Aunt Rose. Amongst Emma's many talents was her ability to see such things so quickly.

Henry chuckled. He loved the idea of owning a racehorse. "But if I was using that criteria then I would have to call the horse 'Em' or 'My Emma'."

She squeezed his hand. "Charmer."

Alice came in. She had been shopping and hadn't avoided the rain. She told them she'd bought steak and kidney pie for tea and that later she was going to the cinema with David from the art club. Henry smiled and Alice blushed, denying any romantic connections. "We just like painting trees," she said. "In water colours."

The rain was steady and they sat there listening to its pat against the window. Henry had his arm around her and Emma could feel the beat of his heart. She sensed there was something on his mind. Something other than Bobby's new business they had discussed earlier.

"I think she's quite fond of David," Emma said after a while.

Henry pulled her closer. "Emma," he said. "I love you."

"Me too." This was her standard reply. It was not unusual for the two of them to say they loved each other. It was obvious they did.

"No, Em, I mean I really love you."

Perhaps her usual reply would have been, "And I *really* love you too Henry", but she said nothing, detecting an uncharacteristic solemnness in his words.

He turned to her and put his hand on the side of her head gently sweeping back her hair. She could feel his breath on her face. How, at that moment, she wished she could see him.

"Em, I've always loved you." He was whispering. "But now it's even more. You are the most beautiful woman I have ever known. Every day I long to hold you and to kiss you. Everything you are is everything I feel life should be. I thought it was just a phase, you know, because we're older now, but it's not, Em.

"I think about you all the time, about you and me loving, sharing, touching, and while I know we could never imagine being out of one another's lives, I can't imagine ever needing anyone else in mine."

"Henry," she whispered, almost protesting as his words whirred through her mind.

"Shh," he continued. "Emma, I want to marry you and grow old with you and have children with you. Build a life with you, talk to you every day, and share every adventure with you."

"Henry…" She wasn't sure what she wanted to say and struggled to hold back the tears she felt welling. She had both longed for and dreaded this moment since she'd realised the depths of her feelings for him.

"Emma. You're going to say you cannot see. But you do, Em, you see more in this world than anyone I have ever known. It is me who would be blind without you, me who would be unable to see the magic and love in this world if it wasn't for you. I feel you love me too but have just never surrendered to it. Maybe I haven't until recently, but it feels so right, Em. Surely you feel it too? I love you, Emma. I have always loved you and always will. We were destined, Em, can't you feel that?"

As his lips found hers, she surrendered. She knew Henry, she knew him so well and had known and feared, for the last couple of years, that this moment was inevitable.

## 29

# DELAHAY HOUSE, OCTOBER 1989

## MALISSA

It wasn't often that they sat down together and enjoyed a traditional Sunday roast, and Malissa certainly couldn't recall ever inviting her parents to join them. Since returning home, however, she and Henry seemed to have fallen into a more comfortable routine.

They still spent time at the Kensington apartment, which provided more conducive accommodation should they ever work late, but this house, the one they shared in England, was their home now. They were man and wife, with a child, and while business kept them both busy, and Henry still travelled to the States, it no longer seemed the priority it had once been. She liked their new life. It was almost normal.

Save one or two interruptions they had spent a great deal of the summer together in Majorca. Vanessa had remained there after they left, and she kept them updated on the development of the villa. It was, for all intents and purposes, finished, and if furniture was installed perfectly habitable. It had electricity and a phone, but because of the terrain around it the garden was always going to take some time to build. If they didn't quite manage to get out before, they would certainly be there for Christmas.

They had bought this house shortly after Delores won the Oaks five years ago. Since it cost approximately the amount she had won for her owner, it seemed appropriate to name it Delahay House. Henry liked that. Its proximity to the scene of her victory also seemed apt. Malissa's mother was overjoyed. The house represented the country dwelling she always hoped her daughter would have, and it wasn't too far away.

Asked to arrive by 1pm it was now 11:30am and Malissa expected them any minute. It had been three months since that wonderfully romantic night, sleeping under the stars outside the farmhouse and, having been told everything was perfectly okay, Malissa could now tell them she was expecting their second grandchild.

## 30

# MAJORCA

## MALISSA – FOUR DAYS BEFORE THE WEDDING

The rain stopped as suddenly as it had begun. Exposed to the late afternoon sun the flowers and shrubs, their foliage freshened by the downpour, now released an aromatic steam into the air. The dark clouds which had rolled in from the sea melted into a lighter grey as they passed over the mountain behind her. Rain was unusual at this time of year, but when it did come it would be short and sharp and accompanied by a sudden and welcome drop in temperature.

The gardens of the villa and the farmhouse always yielded colour thanks to their watering systems, but Malissa knew that for the next few days even the relatively barren slope down to the orchard would pay homage to the rain and reveal its collection of tiny white and yellow rock roses and pink catchfly. She stood at the kitchen doorway knowing the view from here tomorrow would be one of an artist's dream. Perfect timing for the wedding, she thought.

Lewis had driven to the airport to pick up his sister; they should be back soon. Malissa had spent the morning in town, visiting Vanessa in the dance school and her brother and his family who had checked into the hotel. She hadn't changed her name following the divorce and Simon would be sure to make most of the fact that he was related to the owner of the rather exclusive Ovmeister Harbour Hotel.

They were staying for free, of course, as were all the wedding guests who would be accommodated there or at The Grand. Usually upwards of 200 euros a night she wondered if Brad would be questioning the legitimacy of such an arrangement and discussing with Henry whether this should be a personal expense as opposed to one borne by the company.

She could picture the scene as he requested clarification. "But you married her years ago, Henry, twice really, and Malissa's hardly destitute. Not that I begrudge it of course, but business is business."

She imagined Henry's reply. "Brad," he would say, "I believe I recall a certain very sceptical gentleman who was adamant that investing in Söller was the surest waste of company finances there would ever be. I think you'll agree that Malissa's persistence in persuading you otherwise has proved rather lucrative and that she has earned a little gratitude. That and the fact that she, theoretically, owns upwards of 50 million in shares."

Although they were divorced, no settlement was ever agreed. None had been sought and none had been awarded. They simply agreed there was no need to argue about money.

She didn't want to think about the divorce now. Soon she would have both her children with her, and many friends, and Henry. She still missed him when he wasn't there. Her phone rang – it was Lewis.

"Hold on darling," she said and made her way out onto the patio and to the higher ground behind the villa towards the farmhouse where reception was better. "I'm here," she said after twenty seconds but he had gone. She hit redial and was immediately reconnected.

"You really should get a better phone, Mum. We'll be about 45 minutes."

"Hi, Mum!" She heard Millie's voice in the background.

"Hi, darling. How are you?" More crackling and the line went dead.

She could climb up to the farmhouse and call back, but they would be here soon, so she could wait. Maybe she'd ask Henry if he wouldn't mind arranging for the installation of a radio mast when he got here. The thought amused her as she returned to the villa but then she imagined the horror of some ugly steel construction here in the garden and dismissed the idea. She called Vanessa from the landline to ask how the final rehearsal went.

~

Millie jumped out of the car and ran up to the villa to meet her mother, leaving Lewis and Joe, mainly Joe, to tend to her luggage.

"You're too thin, Millie," said Malissa as she reached the kitchen door, much to her daughter's delight.

Joe appeared lugging two suitcases and a holdall which he dumped on the patio, followed by Lewis. Malissa liked Joe. Handsome with kind eyes, designer hair, and a face feathered with stubble to match. He was not complicated and could appear naïve to those who didn't know him, but his laid-back attitude complimented her daughter's deeper nature perfectly.

He and Lewis had become firm friends, no doubt much assisted by Lewis's ability to translate some of his sister's more unfathomable comments into a language he could understand. Joe was tall and athletic. A keen sportsman, he seemed to admire Lewis's more artistic talent, and Lewis was intrigued by his friend's love for all things sport. Ironically, Joe was not quite the swimmer Lewis was and couldn't understand why he lagged a full ten seconds behind him whenever they took part in the Blackpool-Brighton Challenge. "You've got to feel the water," Lewis would tell him.

Millie loved the villa but like Lewis had told her mother that she would prefer to stay in the old farmhouse. They passed the marquee laying on the ground awaiting erection as they walked up to the old house that would be their home for the next week or so.

Malissa held open the gate for the burdened Joe to enter. She suggested to Millie that she should help him but Joe said, "I'm fine," and smiled. Did he ever complain?

"What a wonderful place to be made," Millie sang as she waltzed around the farmhouse garden. "Was it here?" she enquired. "Or here?" pausing in the middle of the lawn.

Her mother smiled. Millie would always play this game when she came here.

"Yes Millie, we know, and I'm sure Joe does too," said Lewis. "You were going to be called *Millie Estrellas Noche Ovmeister.*"

"Just Millie Estrellas," his sister replied.

"Whatever," said Lewis sarcastically. "The night of a thousand stars."

They laughed, but Millie was clearly a little frustrated she hadn't been able to tell her story again.

It was perfectly possible that she was the result of a wonderful night Malissa and Henry had spent sleeping in the garden, and she loved reminding people of it. Henry hadn't gotten his way with the choice of Millie's middle name, though he would often call her 'Millie Estrellas', but 'Rose', of which there was a plethora in the garden, was a decent alternative.

"Better than Lewis *Late Night London Apartment Leg Over.*" Millie had the last word, as usual, and they went inside.

"Any news from Bobby, Mum?" asked Lewis. "About the chances of Aligatrix I mean."

The trainer had a runner in the big filly's race at Ascot on Friday.

"I talked to her yesterday," Malissa replied. "She's booked on the 7pm flight that night so I don't think she's expecting any celebrations."

"No Delores then?"

"I think you'll find there will only ever be one Delores Delahay, Lewis. The Oaks and Royal Ascot."

"And a wedding in between," he smiled.

"Indeed." She looked down at the plateau that would stage the celebrations in four days' time and wished the marquee was pink.

"Delores was a special lady," she said. "A real fighter. Now help Joe with those suitcases."

31

# THE OAKS, JUNE 1984

## DELORES DELAHAY

Henry had two houses in London. This one in Kensington and another in Notting Hill. His company owned many more.

Although not much bigger than her own three-bedroomed semi in South London, the Kensington house was much older and full of character. It had high ceilings and a rear garden enclosed by a red brick wall. It was situated in a surprisingly leafy street, one of a whole terrace of colourful and individual properties with flowery facades and wisteria-covered walls. Malissa didn't understand why he called it an apartment. It was a house.

They had only ever stayed at Notting Hill once, following a night out with Mr and Mrs Fenner. Occasionally, Henry stayed at Malissa's house and they had also spent several weekends in the cottage near Newbury.

Henry travelled a lot and Malissa would accompany him whenever she could, but her own responsibilities at Fenner's took up an increasing amount of her time. They had discussed where they should live once they were officially, or was that unofficially, married and they had looked at a few properties, but there was no urgency.

The 'wedding' had been booked for the 28th July in a small church near Maidstone. Finding a suitable venue had proved challenging, and although the vicar there was unable to accommodate their request for the ceremony to be indiscernible from the real thing, Henry had found just the man who could.

She had told her mother that, although Henry was as Christian as they were, he followed a slightly different philosophy. She wasn't wrong there. Like most people, her parents only attended church to celebrate weddings or christenings or to show their respects at a funeral. If, therefore, her marriage ceremony appeared slightly different, they shouldn't be concerned.

They understood of course. After all, who were they to question a man who had obviously spent considerable time exploring his ecclesiastical conscience?

Malissa had, on more than one occasion, considered telling her parents the truth - that they were already married and that the ceremony they were planning was purely a blessing - but she'd managed to resist. Strangely, since the announcement of the date, both she and Henry had also become engulfed in the charade and they themselves now regarded the 28th as their big day.

Today, however, was all about a racehorse. A three-year-old filly who would remain etched in Malissa's memory for ever. A horse whose appearance at a racecourse changed the direction of her life. Delores Delahay wouldn't know she was running in the biggest race of her life today, but her owner and trainer certainly did.

Delores had returned from Dubai at the beginning of March. She ran at Lingfield in a recognised trial and won easily by ten lengths. She had won all four of her races to date. Three weeks ago, a serious challenger emerged; a horse called Snow Angel from a powerful French stable who was very impressive when crossing the channel and winning another recognised trial at Goodwood. Since then, the two had vied for favouritism and those in the know were split almost exactly down the middle as to which horse was the better.

It was 9am and Henry had gone to get a paper. She had never seen him this anxious. Last night he got up several times to phone Bobby Anderson, who 30 minutes after telling him not to worry and go to sleep, would phone him back to tell him Delores was still okay. She had set up a camp bed just outside Delores' stall. She wasn't leaving anything to chance. "We don't want another feckin' Shergar," she'd said.

The media's interest in Delores had been constant since she won at Lingfield, and Bobby, who could never be described as a publicity seeker, was relieved when half the attention was transferred to Snow Angel. But then it became England versus France and the interest increased. Now, the day had come, and having such a high-profile runner in such a prestigious race the spotlight was unavoidable.

Malissa realised Henry's anxiousness was not because of his desire for Delores to win the race for him, but that she should do herself justice for the many well-wishers and supporters who followed her. With so much expectation, she wondered if he would actually be able to enjoy the day and, for the first time since they had met, she detected a vulnerability in him. She felt it was her job to be at his side, to support him, and the feeling gave her a great sense of being needed.

Her boss, Brian Fenner, would be there too. He had planned on taking his own table, like at Goodwood, but this time he and his wife and a few select clients were guests of Henry's. Guests of Henry and Malissa.

Life is strange in the way it works out. Brian owned the company she worked for and paid her wages but she now regarded him as a partner in business and was pretty sure he regarded her the same. Was it really less than two years since she accepted his offer of employment? Was it only just over a year ago that she attended another race meeting which altered the course of her life? Yes, Delores Delahay would forever be engraved in Malissa's memory.

In the box with Henry and Malissa were her mum and dad, Alice and Charlie, Mr and Mrs Fenner, Brad, his parents, a dozen business associates and Rod who had flown over from Dubai and been warned not to mention weddings.

Bobby had not appeared. She would, as Henry predicted, forego lunch, adamant her duty was to be with Delores until the race. To everybody else, except maybe Brad, Henry was his charming self, though quieter. Brian Fenner could, however, keep a crowd entertained and this relieved much of the pressure on Henry.

Several times, Henry reached for Malissa's hand, seeking a reassuring squeeze and she was pleased to provide it. Two races had passed, and in an hour's time twelve horses would be lining up for the race that would crown the best three-year-old filly in training. It would be a long 60 minutes.

At 3:15pm Henry stood up. "Ladies and gentlemen. I thank you for coming here today. Delores has already taken me on an incredible journey and owes me nothing. I know several of you have looked forward to this moment as much as I, and I know several of you have backed her at much greater odds than she will be at today. She is fit and well and I sincerely hope she does herself justice. Now, if you would excuse Malissa and I for the time being, we really should go and check on our girl. And, Brad, no skimping on the champagne."

Brad would not skimp on the champagne and she saw him mouth something like, "Good luck, my friend."

Brad didn't share Henry's passion for horseracing but knew how much this moment meant to him. They left to a chorus of best wishes and, "ooh isn't it exciting," from her mother. Malissa wondered why Henry hadn't invited some of the others to accompany them to the parade ring as he usually did.

Once outside, she stopped him. She looked into his eyes. "Henry Ovmeister. I love you. I don't profess to know that much about horses, but I do know you, and I think I'm sharing what you are feeling. Have faith in her as you have faith in so many good things and don't feel responsible, because whatever happens you should know so many people love you and on this journey you've travelled with Delores so many have travelled with you."

Her words weren't planned and she wasn't even sure they made sense, but they came from the heart. For a moment, she sensed he wanted to cry, to be anywhere but there, to be a little boy and to be cradled in her arms. And how she would have loved that.

"Thank you." His voice was soft and humble, taken by surprise.

Then, quickly regaining composure, he smiled and kissed her gently. "Miss Keats, this is just another race. There will be a winner who will go down in history and other heroines who time will regrettably forget. Win, lose, or draw Delores is as good a horse as I have ever seen. Certainly, the best I have been directly associated with. If she gets beaten - well, that's racing, that's life. It's just another race."

"She's going to *win*, Henry, I know it," Malissa suddenly beamed.

A bigger smile from Henry and they continued their journey to the paddock.

The preceding race had just started and as they passed the Tote booth she broke free from Henry. "One minute..." she said, and on returning, "my second bet. Five pounds win, number three, same as Goodwood. "

"Was she number three at Goodwood?"

"She most certainly was."

They reached the parade ring. Many onlookers were already there but many more would come once the horses entered. Bobby hated the parade ring. She'd told Malissa that the horses would much prefer just to get on with things rather than, 'Fanny about for people in ridiculous hats.'

Major races like this called for lengthy preliminaries, and although Delores had shown no adversity to the pre-race hype before, Bobby did worry. At breakfast last week she'd said, "I want her as relaxed as Hippy in the ring and as bolshie as me when she's running."

There were several owners and their parties in the enclosure but not yet any horses. Representatives from the press and TV were waiting to interview co-operative trainers. Bobby had told Michael, her assistant, to dress up in a suit and tie and to intervene should anybody from the media approach her.

They entered the ring, Henry shaking hands with several of the other owners and wishing them well. It was an overcast day but by no means cold. The going was good which suited most of the runners. It certainly wouldn't inconvenience Delores.

The horses filed in, all of them looking magnificent. Delores was the last to appear, led in by Cheryl with Bobby at her side. Bobby walked half a circuit with the horse before spotting Henry and Malissa.

Malissa smiled. She had only ever seen Bobby in jeans, jumper, and waist coat, but today, wearing a lilac trouser suit, white blouse, and even a hat, she had dressed for the occasion. Her red hair bounced rhythmically on her shoulders as she strode towards them.

She was stopped en route and a microphone unsubtly thrust under her chin. She looked around. Where was Michael? They could just hear her comments. "She's well and has earned her place," and, "Yes, the ground will be fine," and "I think you'll find it would mean the world to any trainer, male or female. Now if you'll excuse me..."

"Feckin' press," was her greeting as she reached them. "Malissa, how lovely to see you. Hip..."

"You okay?" asked Henry.

"Think I'll be better after the race." She lit a cigarette.

"You look gorgeous," said Malissa, then wished she hadn't, but Bobby smiled.

"Well, sometimes yer gotta, ain't yer. You're not looking too bad yourself. Henry, she's much too pretty for you."

He laughed. "All good?"

"I think so." It was the first time Malissa had heard Bobby express anything that resembled a doubt. "Don't like that feckin' French horse. 'Ell of a beast and they call her a feckin' angel," she added. "I'm seriously worried about her."

"Thanks for getting her here," said Henry and leaned over to kiss her.

"Ah, go shag yourself, yer soppy date."

Henry smiled.

Their jockey Niall joined them and shook hands.

"Look after her, Niall," said Henry.

"What yer feckin' talking about. Go win the damn race," interrupted Bobby. Then in softer tones, "But don't take the French bitch on, she'll out stay you. You'll have one burst. Hold her 'til yer round the corner."

They had discussed tactics many times, the repetition was just habitual. Niall shook hands again and left to find his mount.

"Where are we watching?" asked Henry.

"You really wanna watch, Hip?"

He smiled. He too just wanted this moment over.

"Follow me, I know just the place."

They left the parade ring and three minutes later stood at a spot on the rails about a hundred yards beyond the finishing line. There were several spectators there, but it was away from bustle of the grandstand.

They could hear the commentary clearly which Malissa considered a good thing because their view would be restricted to a head on one as the horses came up the home straight. She sensed the closeness of Henry and Bobby. It was their dream, their journey she was sharing, but she did not feel she was intruding. Her thoughts were with Henry, theirs with the racehorse they had procured to run in this very race.

Bobby turned to Malissa. "Sometimes girl, feeling a race - listening to the crowd and the commentary and the pound of thundering hooves - gives you a greater picture than if you just watch. Ain't that right, Henry?"

Malissa was surprised by Bobby's almost poetic statement. Henry took both women's hands as the commentator announced 'one to go'. "Come on, Delores," he whispered. "You deserve this."

A cheer went up. They were off.

Epsom is a turning, undulating racecourse, similar to Goodwood and Lingfield where Delores had proved her athleticism and balance. The only reservation they had was her ability to stay one and a half miles in a truly run race. Her breeding suggested she would be better suited to shorter distances, but as Malissa had learned, and indeed witnessed, Delores had courage and an ability to quicken; to change gear and surge by the opposition. It was up to Niall to time her challenge right.

Delores was midfield as they rounded Tattenham Corner, which was okay; the French filly having just taken up the running. Neither Henry nor Bobby had said a word up to this point, which was unusual but strangely appropriate. The noise from the crowd was growing and Malissa expected it soon to drown the official commentary. She heard, *'And now Niall Murphy is bringing Delores Delahay to the outside...'* and then the commentary lost distinction as it merged with the noise of the crowd.

"Not yet, Niall," whispered Bobby under her breath. "Not yet..." and a few second later, a louder, "Now Niall, now!"

They were at the rail, leaning over it and looking to their left. They knew Snow Angel, her jockey in white, and against the far-side rail was leading, but their head on position gave them little indication of by how far. To Snow Angel's outside, the pink and purple stars worn by Niall came into view as he manoeuvred Delores diagonally right and then straightened her up as if just having moved to the outside lane of a dual carriageway.

Head down, driving the filly for all he was worth, Delores responded to Niall's urgings and headed straight towards them. The French jockey went for his whip to encourage his mount who was coming under increased pressure, to maintain concentration. But Niall just kept on pushing and Delores just kept on galloping, keeping to a true line down the centre of the track. Malissa felt Henry squeeze her hand, holding it tighter and tighter.

Only two names came out of the loudspeaker as the horses duelled passing the furlong pole, and then only one. By the time they passed them, Delores was five lengths in front of the French filly. The winning margin, however, was less than half that distance.

The last two and a half minutes had been a strange mixture of excitement, concern and suppressed expectation and the few seconds following the realisation that Delores had won the Oaks, surreal. They just looked at one another as if to say, 'What now?'

Henry's eyes were moist with relief, with pride, with joy, with what? Bobby and Malissa were almost sobbing. But as the horses filed onto the bridleway that would lead them back to the Winners' Enclosure, and as the crowd and the reporters rushed towards them, reality set in.

Bobby wiped away her involuntary tears. Henry hugged and kissed them both, and Malissa kissed Bobby. As they set off to greet Delores, Bobby turned to Henry. "There you go, Hip, told you. Nothing to worry about."

A microphone was thrust Bobby's way. She looked around for Michael. Henry smiled at her. "Your first Classic, Bobby. Enjoy the limelight." And as he and Malissa slipped off to the Winners' Enclosure they wondered if what she was about to say would be suitable for a live afternoon transmission.

Life is made up of special moments. That moment after Delores won the Oaks was poignant and difficult to describe, but when moments pile on top of one another they turn into a momentous occasion and that was the case with that celebratory afternoon and evening. So many people shared in Delores's success; so many people were happy because of a racehorse, because of a journey, because of Henry.

It was 2am when Paul dropped them off. They were exhausted but wondered if they would be able to sleep. She lay with her head on his chest. "Do you know, Henry…" Her voice was soft and tired. "I always wondered if Delores was named after an old girlfriend of yours, but Bobby told me she was named after a friend of your Aunt Rose. You'll have to tell me about her one day."

She felt the familiar tightening of his arm around her shoulder and he kissed the top of her head. Weariness and contentment overwhelmed her. "Thank you for today Henry," she whispered.

# III

# THE BUTTERFLY

*Sometimes he'd need to shed gossamer wings*
*Discard colour and float down from on high,*
*Grow fur to stay warm, and accept in a storm*
*That it's far from conducive to fly.*

*He'd reminisce Rose and cradle the Sage*
*And gather those under his care,*
*Accepting the role of protector,*
*Assuming the guise of the bear.*

32

# LONDON, SPRING 1973

## HENRY

He was seriously considering growing a beard. A beard would make him look older and he wouldn't have to spend so much time overcoming prejudices against his age.

That's why he was late today. His facts, his figures, his projections were solid, based on six months of hard evidence. It wasn't until he knew he was going to be seriously late, or not even get home at all, that he upped the ante. Patience exhausted, he interrupted the chit-chat.

"Look, gentlemen. I can appreciate I'm young and that in your eyes I'm just a whippersnapper. I understand your reservations. In front of you is the proposal evidencing the potential of this investment.

"Mr Jackson. You say you need *another* six months of trials before your company commits and that's fine, except that in six months someone else will have beaten us to it. Mr Jones, you say you're nervous because the figures look too good.

"I need nearly half-a-million and I only have 50% of that. That's me, that's my investment. At 21, a whippersnapper, I will be putting up as much as you gentlemen combined. Effectively, I shall be risking everything.

"I can invest in Fairway and their model, but we are further ahead than them, and it would mean trusting another company. I trust me, and I trust my company. This is a young industry and I am a young man, but the most important thing to me right now is another young person, the most beautiful woman you could ever imagine. I have not seen her or held her in my arms for nearly a week and I miss her desperately.

"I love business but, believe me, gentlemen, nowhere near as much as I love Emma. I'm packing up now and driving home. If you want in, I'd be delighted. If you don't, I'll be disappointed but will understand. Either way, I shall be cuddled up contented and happy tonight with the woman of my dreams because I know, even at my tender age, that love is the most important thing you can ever invest in. Thank you."

They looked at him and then at each other. It was John Mathews, 6'3"and 20 stone, a truck driver who had made good, who broke the silence. "Good on you, Henry," he said, standing up and clapping slowly for a few seconds. "I have a wife and we have been married 20 years. She has given me three children and stood by me through thick and thin."

He turned to the others. "I trust this man. I like his attitude and I am in. And, like Henry, I'm going to drive home now and I'm going to tell my wife that I love her. I can't recall the last time I told her that."

Another moment's silence before Mr Jones stood up and started clapping, then Mr Everett and within seconds the applause was unanimous. It appeared the deal was done.

Henry had a warm glow in his heart as he drove back to Ashbourne House. He had seemingly closed a deal with something other than hard facts or the promise of a monetary return.

He thought about Reynard's Way and the coup he had instigated a few years ago when, despite the admiration he earned, the so-called success left him with a feeling of emptiness. He remembered Emma's words that evening as they sat on the sofa. "You only feel bad, Henry, because you believe the success came out of cheating. But you've really only played them at their own game and beaten them. You've cheated the cheaters and made a lot of people happy. Don't be sad, Henry, no one was hurt. Just learn."

Maybe he had. What would he do without her?

It was gone 11pm when he arrived home. Alice was still up playing mother. He kissed her. "Emma waited up but she's in bed now," she said. "How did it go?"

Henry smiled. "It went okay, thanks Alice," and he reached beyond her to grab one of the cakes she had baked that afternoon.

"They're for the church fete," she said, slapping his wrists. She let him have one.

He loved Alice and hoped one day she would find a man deserving of her. Maybe he could help. Right now, he just wanted to feel the warmth of Emma. He bade Alice goodnight and went upstairs.

She was sleeping. He wanted to turn the light on to look at her but didn't. He wished he had arrived a couple of hours earlier to tell her about their latest success, but it could wait until the morning.

He undressed and gently slipped in behind her. She stirred and her feet hooked around his. He kissed the nape of her neck, breathing her in, and felt the muscles of her legs tighten as she welcomed him. She took his hand and circled it on her belly before drawing it upwards. Her other hand reached behind, exploring, sending images to her brain that her eyes never could. He melted into her more sensitive world where feel, and taste, and scent, and whispered reassurances of love completely negated the need to see.

33

# LONDON, LATE SUMMER 1973

## THE BIRTH OF OVMEISTER-CARMICHAEL

Henry couldn't believe Brad had never been to London to see a play. Tonight, however, they would introduce him to the delights of the theatre. He was bringing his new girlfriend, Suzanne, who they hadn't met. Emma made it clear to Henry that he should be on his best behaviour because he could easily destabilise Brad who was far less comfortable around women than him. Henry wasn't quite sure what she meant, but experience told him she was rarely wrong about these things.

He loved their visits to the theatre. If they were attending a play and something happened on stage which he thought he should relay to Emma, he would whisper quietly. Often Emma would thank him for the enlightenment. Occasionally she would whisper back something like, "I am aware of that Henry, I may be blind but I'm not stupid." No offence was taken either way; they had grown up in much the same vein.

Last year they saw The Mousetrap. Despite his obvious intelligence and uncanny ability to read a situation, Henry's gift did not easily translate to an Agatha Christie 'whodunit' which was specifically designed to mislead. Henry had whispered a plethora of scenarios to Emma, probably more for his benefit than hers, to which a lady behind took exception.

A small contretemps erupted, and while the lady was absolutely mortified upon appreciating Emma's blindness, it brought a piece of reality to the situation. Since then, instead of sitting in the stalls they would take their own private box whenever they could.

A musical was a different proposition. Emma had a talent for all things musical and she would be the one relaying information to Henry, who would get his own back by retorting, "Okay no need to shout, Em, I'm not deaf."

They were celebrating tonight. In fact, it was a double celebration. Brad, following his fantastic exam results, had been offered a prime position at London's top accountancy firm and Emma had been chosen to play solo violin at a forthcoming concert at the Royal Albert Hall. Henry had already purchased 40 tickets.

They were sitting in their favourite restaurant, a little Italian bistro in Notting Hill, where Henry thought he and Emma should buy a second home. Property in London was a sound investment and as soon as he concluded the deal on the South Kensington offices, they should buy a place of their own here. It would be handy for work. It was just gone 5pm and Brad was late.

"Do you remember when we bought the stables, Em?" He would always say 'we'. "It's just gone five by the way."

"Of course I do," she said. "It was the first time you told me you loved me."

He smiled and continued. "Well, you know I said it came with the stud farm?"

"Yes, and Bobby's using it for the yearlings."

"Well, did I tell you it came with a house? An old house in need of restoration, on the top of a cliff overlooking the sea, where you can feel the wind in your hair and taste the sea, and on a summer's evening feel the setting sun on your shoulders?"

"And the winter rain, and the gales, and the howling wind. Yes, Henry, you told me."

"You love feeling the rain." He frowned, detecting a hint of negativity and touched her arm. She gave him her hand.

"Well, they're doing it up now and Bobby says it'll look wonderful. I'm not saying we should move there, much too far away, but what a fantastic place to spend a holiday. It could be our second home."

"I thought you wanted one round here? In one of the mews. One of those with ivy growing over the doors."

"Well, that too, but that's for London or if we ever move out of Ashbourne."

"Henry, do you ever think your ambitions may be just a little too grand?"

Henry did not see Emma's blindness, he just saw the woman he loved. He would often seek her opinion or even approval believing she possessed so much more wisdom than him. In fact it wasn't that unusual for her to quip he was the one who was blind.

"Hmm." He gently let go of her hand, put his elbows on the table and clasped his hands under his chin.

"You're thinking, Henry."

"Well, Cornwall's lovely. I thought you'd like to live there."

She smiled. "Henry, I'm sure I'd love Cornwall and London. In fact, I'd love anywhere with you."

"Bora Bora?"

"Yes Henry, Bora Bora too."

He smiled and squeezed her hand. "I'd love to go there Em."

"I notice, Henry, you say *hmm* as opposed to *hmph* these days. That shows you are listening and considering the possibility that sometimes people may not immediately find your suggestions as credible as you instinctively do."

He saw Brad coming up the street. "Well, perhaps we should go there soon. Cornwall, I mean. We can do Bora Bora later. Brad's here."

The door opened with a ping and then Brad's familiar voice. "Thank you, George."

George always tended door if not serving tables. Although Saturday, it was relatively early, and only three of the twelve tables, including theirs, were occupied.

"Sorry we're late," said Brad. "Suzanne, this is Henry, and this is Emma who's much too good for him."

Suzanne had been briefed on Emma's blindness and was a little awkward as she took her hand, "It's lovely to meet you, Emma, I've heard so much about you."

"Then you have a better boyfriend than me, Suzanne, because Henry tells me nothing."

Henry knew this wasn't true and was just one of Emma's clever ways to help people she first met feel comfortable.

Suzanne was clearly surprised by Emma's beauty. The condition that caused her blindness left no obvious evidence. They were sitting at the table, Henry opposite Emma and Brad opposite Suzanne. George gave them three menus.

They talked about how Brad and Suzanne met and about the musical they were about to see. Emma informed Suzanne that she hadn't always been blind and could often visualise things by calling upon images stored in her memory. Suzanne welcomed her request to touch her face and was impressed when she described her, even the colour of her eyes (lucky guess), and her hair. Like everybody else, Suzanne soon fell in love with Emma and her blindness became a fact rather than the avoidable subject it may have otherwise remained.

"So, when are you starting?" Henry asked Brad halfway through their meal.

Brad laid down his cutlery. He assumed that earnest manner he always did when considering one of Henry's business proposals.

"I turned it down," he said.

"You didn't take the job?" Henry was surprised. "Why not? It's what you've worked for, what you've always wanted. You'll do great and become a rich man."

Brad paused and looked thoughtful. Henry sensed he wished to impart something serious and was searching for the appropriate words.

"Because," he continued, "I cannot see anything wrong with your ludicrous suggestion to sell the most profitable and promising business you have ever started and invest the proceeds in an even more absurd fantasy in the desert." He let the comment hang in the air before he picked up his cutlery. "And because the guy from Hollis didn't even know where Dubai was."

This was an unexpected revelation. Henry was unsure where it was leading but sensed the importance of the moment. Brad's statement warranted a considered reply from Henry. This time Henry laid down his cutlery and studied his friend. Emma and Suzanne listened.

"And your father?"

"You know him as well as me, Henry."

He did know Charles Carmichael well, hence the question.

"So, what will you do?"

"I'd like to work for Ovmeister Holdings," he said. "To join you in business as we've always discussed."

Henry often enthused about the two of them working together. He had, however, long since accepted that Brad would be best served by following the career path mapped out for him.

"Ovmeister Holdings?"

This time Brad not only put down his cutlery, he pushed the plate aside. "Yes Henry. I feel it's time we brought things together. They're too spread. Consolidating would give us more clout. In fact, you don't have to sell the leasing business, well, not all of it, you just need to restructure, sort of mortgage it. I've talked to the investors and they're keen, and the bank will at least match our investment. We can put the money directly in UBAC, instead of the agency you thought of, in direct partnership with them, possibly even raise enough to take the majority share.

"We open our own office there, mainly as a consolidation base and distribution centre, and we open another division here, effectively the procurement arm, and if you can persuade..."

He continued for some time, adding economic credibility and know-how to Henry's vision. When he finished, Henry sat quietly digesting his friend's synopsis.

"So, we supply, ship, and effectively benefit from *everything* that develops?" Henry loved the ambition of the plan.

"Yep."

"And you said we, *we* invest. That's quite a lot if we're going 50-50."

"Only in the holding company. The other businesses would be outside that. But I could raise more if needed."

"And the numbers match up?" Henry knew Brad's numbers always added up.

"Henry, if we can pull this off, I feel it could be bigger than even you imagined. The numbers *you* talked about would be chicken feed."

Another thoughtful pause.

"I already have an accountant," Henry said, "two if you include Brenda."

"I know that."

Another pause.

"You said feel..."

"Feel?"

"Yes, you said, I *feel*. You usually say, I *think*."

Brad rolled his eyes. "I feel it, I believe it, and I know it."

Henry wanted to shout for joy, stand up, shake his best friend's hand and tell him everything would be wonderful, but Brad could be risking everything for...for what? They had been talking for ten minutes but the sound of their silence spoke louder. Henry's eyes were fixed on Brad's as his brain made a million calculations. He possibly held Brad's destiny in his hands.

Suddenly, Henry stood up, beamed and walked around the table to hug his friend. "Then I guess we should call this new company Ovmeister–Carmichael Holdings."

"Not Carmichael–Ovmeister?" Brad replied

"Now you're taking the piss."

He sat back down and ordered champagne, and keeping any concerns he harboured about his friend's welfare to himself said, "Now, forget little bits of business in the desert. Did I tell you about Emma and the Royal Albert Hall?"

He had. Several times.

# 34

## SUMMER 1974

## EMMA, A CONCERT AND FEELVIEW BAY

From an early age, Emma was given the best private tuition money could buy. Music was no exception and in recognising her natural aptitude, Aunt Rose ensured she received as much encouragement as possible. "Sight stifles your feel for a melody anyway", she said, believing becoming an accomplished musician would offer Emma the best route to a satisfying and independent career.

By the age of twelve she had learned to play every instrument put in front of her. She was an extremely competent pianist, but her greatest gift was her ability to play the violin.

She had been selected to play at the Royal Albert Hall because of her talent and not her blindness, and Henry was fuming that the programme dared make mention of her condition. He would not on this occasion, however, challenge the organisers of the event. He, Brad, Suzanne, Alice and Brad's mother and father were in a box centre right of the stage.

Henry had many things to be proud of. At 22 he was quite possibly already a millionaire, but any pride he may have felt for his own achievements melted into insignificance that evening as he listened to Emma play.

"The Albert Hall, Em," he had reminded her every day since they learned she would be playing, no, starring in the concert. *"Royal,"* she would retort, *"Royal* Albert Hall, Henry," but she had spent the last few weeks trying to reel in his exuberance.

They were spending the night in London, in the house they had recently bought in Notting Hill. Tomorrow they would drive to Cornwall to visit the stud farm and the cottage by the sea that Henry was so keen to show her.

For the early part of the concert she played as part of the orchestra but her solo performances of the concertos by Mozart and Vivaldi received rapturous applause. Standing ovations greeted her interpretations of Lennon and McCartney's 'Yesterday' and 'Something' – a song which always reminded Henry of her.

It was one of the happiest days of his life, and his heart overflowed after the concert as people flocked backstage to congratulate her. He loved her and knew she loved him and was so thankful for the happiness fate had bestowed on them.

Their love making that night was playful, with Emma evaluating his performance with a succession of screeches or more melodic emanations from her violin. They were great friends as well as lovers. So many, earlier that evening, had fallen under her spell but that night he alone was the recipient of her magic. He knew her, she knew him, they were entwined.

The Cornwall estate that would eventually become a stud farm was run by Charlie Taylor. The son of an old-fashioned bookies' runner, it was Bobby who recommended him for the job. Charlie had been integral to the success of the gamble on Reynard's Way some years ago and, remembering his integrity and diligence, Henry had no reservations in sanctioning Bobby's recommendation.

He had taken up residence on the estate last year, living in one of the old cottages which was relatively easy to make habitable. Many of the other buildings, including the impressive 17th - century farmhouse, needed much more attention. His priority, however, was to make the whole estate suitable for breeding racehorses and looking after those who required a period of convalescence.

The cottage which Henry was so keen to show to Emma would, when the lane was completed, be a ten-minute stroll from the main farmhouse. For the moment access to it was only via a lane leading off the main road which ran by the estate.

He parked. "Well, Em, this is as far as we can take the car. It's just a short walk to the house."

Henry was pleased to see the pathway had been widened, flattened, and bordered by brick as requested. He took her hand. In the other she held Bart – her white stick.

"It's a bit uphill, but not that bad. This is the gate."

He was guiding her as he always did when introducing her to a new environment and they walked slowly so she could assign the route to memory.

"Elder," she said. "Reminds me of rhubarb and custard."

Henry could smell the sweet fragrance. "They're in flower, Em, cream coloured. Never noticed how sweet they smelled before. There's a lot of them. Brambles too, think we'll get some blackberries later in the year. It opens up just here."

She turned her face sunward as they reached the open space of the garden.

"Another gate, Em."

They went through.

"Now, the house is on the right down this path through the garden. It's a small lawn with flower beds. We can decide what to plant later. But the great thing, Em, is the sea. The garden opens up onto an old meadow and leads straight to it. About a hundred yards from the house. It's got its own little beach. Bit rocky, but not too bad and the sun shines on it from first thing in the morning to last thing at night."

Emma smiled. "And a stream?"

Henry suddenly heard the running water.

"Yes, Em. It's behind the house and the flow's really strong when it rains. The water's so pure you could drink it. It's got a water wheel too, but it was stuck last time I saw it. I think the stream used to be much bigger. Maybe it worked once, I don't know. You wait 'til I show you the waterfall."

"Waterfall? I'm beginning to like this place, Henry."

"Let's do the house first, Em, then I'll show you the garden and the beach."

She kissed him, and they went inside.

Downstairs, doors had been removed and the ground floor accommodation flowed like a smaller version of Ashbourne House. Even the kitchen housed a cloakroom large enough to store some of her clothes.

The upstairs was a little more difficult to replicate being more built into the roof and offering far less space, but the stairs had been moved so from them the main bedroom was easily located. Like at home, a door led from it directly into their bathroom. He led her to the window and opened it.

"Shh," he whispered. A shriek from a gull and then the faint but unmistakeable whoosh of a wave breaking.

"A sea view, Henry. I'm impressed."

He smiled. "It's calm today with small waves, but when the wind blows, Em I think they'll crash against the rocks. And smell that air."

"And I can stand here on a stormy day and feel the freezing rain, and try listening for a wave only for it to be drowned out by the howling wind that rushes through the window, blowing the pictures off the wall and soaking the bed spread."

"Hmm." Surely she was impressed? "You wait 'til you see it from the garden."

She smiled and took his arm. "It's beautiful, Henry."

Double doors led from the lounge to a patio. A gravelled walkway had been laid so you could walk all the way round the cottage, and at the back a seating area adorned a little grass verge which sloped down to the stream which bubbled over moss-covered pebbles and small rocks. "Great place for barbeques, Em," he suggested when they sat there.

Beyond the patio at the front of the house was a lawn big enough for Emma to spin round in when it rained. It was bordered by flower beds and white picket fencing. The garden gate opened onto the meadow which, with its tall grasses, ferns and wildflowers, nestled at the bottom of the hillside which protected it landside.

A path from the garden gate bisected the meadow, leading gently down to the sea and the newly constructed zig zag steps to the beach. Either side of the steps sturdy wooden fencing stretched along the cliff edge.

The waterfall tumbled onto the beach just to the right of the steps. Over the centuries, it had carved out a hollow, forming a pool that was about a metre deep where it landed, gradually shallowing out seawards over and between smooth weathered rocks. A high tide would cover the pool, mixing saltwater with fresh, but right now with the tide out and a steady supply of fresh water from the stream above, it was very clear and glistened in the sunshine.

"'Our own private spa, Em," Henry enthused

"Not a little cold, Henry?"

"Hmm."

In the driest of summers the fall could reduce to a trickle, but nobody could remember it ever being completely dry.

The beach was stony with too many small rocks to enable comfortable access to the sea and they agreed clearing a space to make a flat sandy area would be a good idea. They talked about building a mooring for a boat too.

Leaning on the fence between the steps and the waterfall they looked out over the sea. Henry described the bay as he had described the garden and the house, as he had described so many things to her before, painting a picture she would commit to her memory. Often she would seek clarification: how many rocks? How high is that peak? What colour? How far does the headland stretch? And Henry would answer in detail, elaborating enthusiastically, and creating the most vivid image he could.

"It's every bit as beautiful as you told me, Henry," she said. Then cuddling into him, added, "I feel the view. I feel the bay."

He smiled and pulled her close. He knew what he would name this place.

## 35

# MAJORCA, NOVEMBER 1989

## THE COMPLETION OF THE VILLA

Vanessa had collected Malissa, Henry, and Lewis from the airport, and from the moment she stepped into the passenger seat Malissa had been insistent that Vanessa gave her more details about the villa.

"Just wait and see," Vanessa repeated for the umpteenth time, stopping the car just before the driveway that led onto the plateau.

"Now, if I said close your eyes I know you'd peek," Vanessa said, retrieving a silk scarf from the glove compartment.

She wrapped it around Malissa's head. Malissa protested but seemed to appreciate her friend's intention of making the surprise even more special.

Vanessa turned to Henry and Lewis. "You two are boys. You don't appreciate surprises, so no letting on until we're there." As she finished the sentence, she witnessed a look of horror creep over Henry's face.

"Is that necessary, Vanessa?" His voice was shaky, desperate even, and the look in his eyes unnerved her as she considered the impact of what she had just done.

She was about to reply when Malissa butted in, "Oh let her play her games, Henry. Come on, let's look."

Vanessa tried to shake off the image of Henry as he she engaged first gear and pulled onto the drive. By the time she parked she was relieved to see he had regained much of his composure.

Malissa's questions continued as Vanessa helped her out of the car and guided her to a position directly in front of the villa. Henry, carrying Lewis, followed. Vanessa looked at Henry. She was desperate to remove the blindfold but Henry, appreciating his wife's accumulating excitement, indicated not yet. He smiled.

Beneath its red tiled roof, the villa stood majestically white overlooking the pool and the patio laid in a mosaic of colour. The garden extended to all sides, comprising small grass lawns, stepped flower beds and pathways, and a plethora of shrubs and trees. Though the flora was young it already displayed colour, and you could imagine how much more picturesque the scene would be when they matured.

Considering the terrain, the whole of the gardened area was a construction marvel and Henry knew it would surpass even his wife's wildest expectations.

"Well, Henry. What do you think? Will I be happy?" Malissa asked excitedly.

Henry had won the struggle to bring his mind back to the present. He let Lewis down and moved close behind his wife, circling his arms around her swollen tummy. "Do you think Mummy will like our new home, Lewis?"

Their son was aware something was going on and clearly shared his mother's excitement.

"Right, I've had enough," exclaimed Malissa. "Stop teasing and let me see."

"I think it might meet with your approval my love, but you do take a lot of pleasing." He removed the blindfold. Malissa opened her eyes.

The villa represented a dream they had shared since they discovered this place on their honeymoon. Negotiations to buy the land, to obtain the permission to build there, and to overcome all the obstacles they had encountered, had been a five-year journey. To see their dream standing there as beautiful as she could ever have imagined almost overwhelmed her.

She grinned at Vanessa and then flung her arms around her husband. "Honeymoon House!" She smiled and kissed him repeatedly before they headed inside.

Henry thought about the blindfold and its impact on him. There would be many happy times ahead and the invasion of those memories would surely fade.

On the kitchen worktop, he noticed a painting of Delores Delahay and So Nature enjoying their retirement at Feelview Bay - a gift from Bobby Anderson. The horses looked happy. He thought about where he should hang it. He thought about Bobby and he thought about racing long ago.

36

# ASCOT, 1975

## BOBBY ANDERSON, RACEHORSE TRAINER

So Nature was the best horse Bobby Anderson had ever trained. She bought her at the Ascot sales as a yearling, Henry's instruction to her simply being, "Find me a horse worthy of Aunt Rose's name".

As a two-year-old she had won three of her four races, and a tilt at the classics had looked on the cards. Unfortunately, she suffered a tendon injury which prevented her from running as a three-year-old and instead she spent the best part of 18 months convalescing at Feelview Bay.

She would always have delicate legs and Bobby would have to select races for her carefully. In May she won her first race as a four-year-old, easily brushing aside the filly that finished third in last year's Oaks, leaving Bobby with the question of 'What if?'

Following her impressive return, she was installed as second favourite for the top fillies' race at Royal Ascot. She drifted when it looked as if the ground would be unsuitable and Bobby Anderson was one of very few people to delight in last week's rain. The ground wasn't ideal, but it was safe enough for her to run.

Bobby had been training in her own right for six years. She had attracted other owners besides Henry and her business was just about self-sufficient. Today witnessed her first runner at the Royal meeting, and a win in such a high-profile race would be a serious feather in her cap.

Emma and Henry had spent the night at their London home and were waiting for Brad and Suzanne and the limousine that would take them racing. Tradition dictated formal dress for the meeting, gentlemen sporting morning suits and ladies their finest dresses. You did not have a runner at Royal Ascot every day and they would be attending in style.

Emma wore emerald green that added elegance to her natural beauty. Henry reminded himself that beneath the finery was his childhood sweetheart, the girl who loved wearing shorts and dancing in the rain.

"Why, Emma, do you never cease to amaze me?" he said, assuring her everything she was wearing was perfect.

"And you, Henry, look so handsome in your tails," she replied with a smile. "I wonder if Bobby will be dispensing with her wellies?"

Henry laughed.

As far as Bobby Anderson was concerned, racing was about horses and not dressing up 'poncey'. Henry had, however, convinced her she should dress suitably for the occasion and sit at the table with them. She had done her part and her presence with the horse would add no more, but her presence in the restaurant with so many prospective new owners certainly could. Charlie was perfectly capable of looking after the horse. Henry was sure she would not be wearing wellies.

The car pulled up outside. They were on their way.

Bobby looked at her watch. It was nearly midday. She had promised Henry she would be at the table by 12:30pm, or as soon as she was satisfied that everything was okay with So Nature. It was, but she insisted on checking again, asking for her to be walked round just one more time to check those delicate legs.

Charlie had come up from Cornwall to take charge, and although

Bobby knew So Nature would be in good hands in her absence, she was still reluctant to leave her. Charlie led the horse back inside the stable. She appeared relaxed.

"Don't put her in that feckin' parade ring 'til the last minute," Bobby said as she run her hands over the horse's legs.

Charlie smiled. "I think you should put on those heels now, Bobby, so everyone can check out *your* lovely legs."

"Fuck off," she snapped but left him and started making her way to the car park to get changed.

"And be nice!" Charlie called after her.

She acknowledged his comment with two fingers over her shoulder. She heard him laugh, muttering something under his breath. She liked Charlie a lot.

She reached the horsebox and sat in the front seat, swapping her boots for her heels. In the box on the passenger seat was the hat Henry had sent. Yellow with a black feather to match her dress. In the carrier bag, her grey cardigan. She wished it was cooler, so she could justify wearing it.

Heels on, she grabbed the hat and climbed down from the cab. She had spent every evening of the past week pacing up and down her living room in the shoes, and if she wasn't too bold was quite confident she could walk in a reasonably human manner.

She was tall, and in the shoes wouldn't have stood much below six feet. She had a last practice around the car park then stopped to reconsider the cardigan before putting on her hat. Suitably attired she headed purposefully towards the restaurant to meet Henry and the gathering of so-called 'potential' which after today would be queuing up at the gates of Wickham Heath, desperate to have her train their horses.

As she went by the stables, she had a quick look. All was quiet and she forced herself to believe all was also good. Just outside the restaurant, Jack Sanders from 'The Sporting Life' whistled at her. She glared at him, more formidable than usual from the extra height.

"Bobby Anderson, *I've* always known how gorgeous you are but today everyone else will know too. Anything I can report on So Nature?"

She liked Jack, believed the compliment genuine and thought about smiling but didn't. "Off the record Jack?" she enquired.

He nodded.

"Well, off the record, I hate this feckin' dress and this hat makes me feel like a feckin' boiled egg. And this place is full of pompous, dressed-up arses who wouldn't know one end of an 'orse from the other."

He laughed. She knew he wouldn't repeat her statement.

"As for So Nature," she said, "I can't see her being beaten."

She smiled warmly, suddenly feeling comfortable in her outfit. She knew her horse had a great chance and while she appreciated a win would seriously elevate her own reputation as a trainer, she knew too it would be the biggest thank you she could ever give to Henry.

Henry spotted her as she entered the restaurant and whispered to Emma, who looked up and smiled. He got up from his seat and made his way towards her. He looked calm and his smile told her how pleased he was that she was wearing the hat.

"It's okay to take it off when we sit down," he whispered as he linked her arm to escort her back to the table.

"You know, Bobby," he continued. "You do look lovely today, but not as lovely as that first day I met you." She squeezed his arm. "And you're very tall," he added.

She kissed Emma as soon as she arrived at the table and Henry introduced her to their guests. She shook hands politely and swore only once as she did the rounds. Conversation inevitably centred around So Nature and Bobby enlightened them all on her career to date and the very realistic chance she had today.

"You think she would have won the Oaks, Bobby?" asked one of the guests.

Bobby thought. "Well, she's got legs like frigging glass."

Henry smiled. He was obviously impressed that she had substituted her more usual adjective with frigging.

"I've no doubt she could have won on a flatter track but, to be honest, I would have worried me frigging head off with them ups and downs at Epsom. In fact, Upson Downs is a more appropriate name for that frigging place."

All laughed, and a guest offered her champagne. She sent a darting look to Henry, who immediately summoned the waiter saying, "I don't know about you lot, but I could murder a beer."

Several agreed, and pints were ordered, including one for the trainer, who continued to entertain them.

Owners of racehorses are, by-and-large, dreamers. Unlike wealth alone, being associated with a famous racehorse can give you a degree of immortality. Bobby enthused about So Nature and about racing in general; always mindful that those hanging on to her words might just be looking for a dream. Henry, who had heard it all before, chipped in, adding weight to much of her account so she assumed he approved of her promotional skills.

They weren't running until the fourth race on the card, but after the first, a waiter appeared and whispered to Bobby that he had received a message that everything was fine with So Nature. *Bless Henry*, she thought, knowing he would have organised this little reassurance. She smiled across the table at him. He smiled back.

Bobby was on her third pint of Guinness when the rain came. As racegoers sought shelter, Bobby beamed. "What's detrimental to their hats is good for my girl's legs. Get your money on, gents and don't be shy!"

Being even better when the ground was soft, Bobby was growing in confidence regarding the chance of her horse.

"So Nature intervenes," said Emma

"An omen," smiled Bobby. She walked round the table and whispered in Emma's ear. "She'll do her proud, girl. Now I could do with a pee before the race. You?"

Bobby escorted Emma to the rest room. When they returned Bobby announced to the table that it was time to saddle the horse.

"Now, you should get a good view from here," she said peering through the window, "but don't expect her to be in front when she passes. We'll be leaving it very late."

They all wished her good luck. She glanced at Henry, momentarily picturing the 15-year-old boy she first met. He smiled and blew her a kiss. She left eager to ensure Charlie had tackled up So Nature as instructed.

It wasn't until after the racing had finished for the day that Bobby, accompanied by Charlie, returned to the restaurant. She did so to rapturous applause. She had no hat, no heels, and was wearing an old grey cardigan.

She politely acknowledged the reception, introduced Charlie as her most knowledgeable assistant who would be pleased to answer any of their questions, and made her way over to Henry and Emma.

She placed her 'winning trainer' trophy on the table, next to Henry's 'winning owner' one.

"You know," she said, "let's have some more champers. Let's have the best. And Henry, I insist I pay."

She summoned the waiter.

Bobby knew Henry was as proud of her as she was of the horse, and when the champagne arrived she poured just three glasses. In a rare display of unabated affection, and with an arm around Emma, she raised her glass:

"To Aunt Rose, the trainer of the two most beautiful people I have ever known."

She downed the champagne in one gulp, kissed Emma on the cheek and then turned to face the many well-wishers. Before addressing them, she stole a look back over her shoulder. "Can I say feckin' now instead of feckin' frigging?"

Henry smiled. She knew her comment hadn't surprise him.

37

# SUMMER 1976

## ALICE AND FEELVIEW BAY

"Here," said Henry, fastening the necklace. "It belonged to Aunt Rose, a present from Arthur. They're not real but…" he stepped back. "They look beautiful on you."

Alice was getting ready for a date with Charlie Taylor. Typical of this summer, the evening was warm following another day of unbroken sunshine.

Alice enjoyed staying at Feelview as much as Emma and Henry and had spent much of the summer here with them; or often just with Emma when Henry was away on business. She was worried when Henry first enthused about their summer home, concerned for Emma's welfare, but satisfied the house was the safe environment Henry had promised she had simply replicated her role as housekeeper-cum-carer. The three of them had lived there solidly since Easter.

Henry loved Alice's caring and unassuming nature. They were close and generally regarded as brother and sister. He had seen the sparks in their eyes when he first introduced Alice and Charlie, and had witnessed their relationship blossom. He was overjoyed for her.

"You don't think it's too much?" Alice asked, twiddling the necklace between her fingers.

Henry smiled. "The only thing in this room that would be too much for any man, is you Alice. You are beautiful."

She blushed and turned away, muttering how ridiculous he was.

Emma appeared. "Charlie?" she enquired. "How appropriate."

"Well, by name by nature," Alice replied, clearly not in the least bit surprised that Emma could recognise the fragrance she was wearing.

"Where you off to?" asked Emma.

"I'm not sure. Charlie said it was a surprise but said it might be appropriate to wear a dress. I hope it's not dancing; I don't think I can dance and that would be embarrassing."

There was a knock at the door and Charlie walked in. Alice gasped - he was ten minutes early.

"Charlie, good to see you," said Henry.

"Hi, Charlie," Emma said.

"Emma, Henry," Charlie acknowledged, but his eyes were fixed on Alice. Usually so casually dressed in jeans and a t-shirt he was clearly taken by the sophisticated woman with tied back hair, high heels, and the ruby necklace that hung above the neckline of her royal blue dress.

"Hi, Alice," he beamed.

"Hi, Charlie," she stammered then brushed by them and headed upstairs. "I'll just get my bag. I'm almost ready."

Charlie's eyes followed her. "Wow," he said.

"Wow, indeed," Henry replied, suddenly feeling a little protective but then comfortable because he knew Charlie so well. "How's Rosie?"

They called So Nature 'Rosie'. She franked her success at Ascot with victory at York, but subsequently broke down during training and had recently been transferred to Feelview Bay to convalesce.

"She's okay, Henry, but I'm not sure her legs will ever fully recover this time. I was talking to Bobby yesterday. She'll be out for at least a year."

"Just look after her." He knew he would.

Alice came down the stairs.

"So, Charlie, what are your plans for this evening?" asked Emma.

"The Oyster," replied Charlie.

"The Oyster?" exclaimed Alice.

The Oyster had an enviable reputation for being the best fish restaurant for miles around. Very posh.

"Yes," said Charlie, "I've only eaten there once." He looked at Henry, probably recalling the afternoon they had lunch there with Bobby Anderson, "But it's really nice and on an evening like this and an outside table, I thought it'd be lovely. Hence the tie."

Henry was glad that Charlie had thought about where to take Alice. "Obviously paying you too much, Charlie. I'll have a word with Miss Anderson. Not too many oysters, Alice," he added as they headed out the door, "You know what they say about oysters."

She frowned, she didn't but Charlie smiled.

"Have a great time," said Emma, feeling for Henry and cuddling him in the doorway.

"You know, Henry, sometimes I feel like her mum, like *her* guardian. I really hope it goes well and I really hope Charlie is as nice as he seems."

He squeezed her. "I know what you mean, Em. But Charlie is a good man and, from what I saw in his eyes, I think he believes he's punching above his weight. They're going to be fine."

"Like you?" she asked.

"Fine?"

"No, punching above your weight."

He turned and kissed her. "Emma, if I weighed 22 stone and had the talent of Mohammed Ali I'd be punching above mine."

They walked around the garden as they often did in the early evening. Henry updated her on events in Dubai, suggesting she came with him when he returned there next month.

They talked about Aunt Rose, his memory having been nudged by the earlier conversation about her equine namesake. They reached the cliff's edge and lent on the fence looking out, a warm evening breeze bringing the scent of the sea into their faces. A speed boat sped by, quite close to shore.

"Tell me what you see, Henry," Emma said, snuggling into him as the noise of the passing boat subsided.

"The sun you feel is more orange than yellow and is still nearly two hours away from setting. There are only three clouds, as far as I can see, spread out, wispy and white. If they passed in front of the sun it looks like they'd evaporate instantly. The sea is just starting to lose its reflective blue sparkle but it's calm and the waves are breaking gently on the beach."

"I hear them," she said. "And the gulls."

"Yes, they're mainly above Tregan but there are a few on the water. In the distance, probably ten miles, there's a cargo ship, a bulk carrier heading south. It looks small and dark and I couldn't tell you which line. There are two sailing boats. The one with white sails is tacking back and forth between Tregan and Gunnards - mum and dad and two kids I think - but the larger one, further out with red and blue sails, is more like one of those racing yachts and that's really skipping..."

"Which direction?"

"From Gunnards. It'll disappear in about 30 seconds. Think we should get a faster yacht, Em?"

"With you sailing it? No thank you."

They both loved the days when they took their relatively humble sailboat out, but Henry was far from the proficient sailor he would make out. He had mentioned taking more lessons.

He continued. "The tide's coming in. About three feet deep at the jetty and there's a couple of oyster catchers just landed on the third rock out."

"Bit late for cockles if the tide's this far in."

"True, probably just checking. They've flown off now. Other than that, it's all very calm. Walter's still dry," - Walter was the name they had given the waterfall - "and the pool's full of saltwater. The clifftops remain brown and there's no sheep grazing. We need some rain."

She took a deep breath. "Close your eyes, Henry."

He did.

"Can you see the school of dolphins laughing and bouncing in and out of the water, the aqua blue water, so clear you can see the coral below? Red, and blue, and pink, and yellow, and all the colourful fish.

"And the little island out there, with its coconut palms, their foliage so green and creeping over the white stand, shading the hammock where the two sand-covered lovers lay sleeping recovering from their swim? There are parrots and hummingbirds, their singing filling the air..."

"Won't that wake them?"

"Their songs are melodic and soporific, no squeaking or squalling and maybe they're not parrots but colourful song thrushes."

"Are they in love?"

"The lovers? Of course they are. They live on the island and catch their own food from the sea and eat coconuts and strawberries."

"What do they drink? I can't see any fresh water."

"When it rains they catch the water in rolled up vine leaves. Or when it's dry, they live on coconut milk."

"Piña Colada?"

She smiled and nestled closer. "No. They're teetotal."

"I see it, Em." And with a sudden but quiet excitement he whispered, "Hold on, Em, what's this I see?"

"Where?"

"To my right. Let me see. Yes, I see it now. It's right here. I feel it. It's really close."

"What is it, Henry?"

"It's the most beautiful wonderful person I have ever known and I'm the luckiest man in the world."

He pulled her to him and they kissed before making their way back up to the house wondering whether they should wait up for Alice.

38

# JULY 1984

## MALISSA AND HENRY

### TWO WEEKS BEFORE THEIR BLESSING

Sometimes Malissa regarded Henry as a genius, sometimes she thought he was crazy. The meeting with Reverend Eduardo Ambrossini that Saturday morning left her feeling he was perhaps a bit of both.

He had found a suitable venue for their blessing, a chapel in a small hamlet just outside Maidstone. "It's pink!" she'd exclaimed as they drove by it on the way to the car park. "Henry – a pink church?"

He smiled. "It's technically a chapel and yes it has a certain pink hue. Thought you liked pink?"

She did, but usually as a shade of lipstick or maybe the colour of a blouse. She shrugged her shoulders as they parked.

The chapel was the junior partner of the two places of worship within the estate. The other was a more traditional and quite impressive church and the usual venue for wedding ceremonies held there. A large converted barn was one of many historic buildings that could be found in the extensive old gardens and an ideal place for a reception.

The Diocese, which also incorporated a church in Maidstone, was overseen by the incumbent vicar, Reverend Matthew Bailey. Henry first spoke to him in March, explaining they were already married and sought a suitable place to stage a blessing but wanted the ceremony to be indistinguishable from that of a genuine Christian wedding.

When Henry relayed to Malissa the conversation he'd had with Bailey she smiled and rolled her eyes – typical Henry.

"You want a mock wedding. In my Parish?" Bailey had asked after listening to Henry's request.

"Malissa really likes weddings," replied Henry.

"You don't think your request is somewhat unusual, Mr Ovmeister? This is a house of God."

"I said to Malissa that deviating from the norm always costs so much, but God is love, and we are in love, and a man of God would obviously see that. We would simply be renting His house for an hour or so and making people happy, and happy people naturally want to contribute to the cause of their happiness. It's a good job I've been saving very hard."

Bailey couldn't quite accommodate the variations to the ceremony that Henry sought and was reluctant to use the church. He agreed, however, that the chapel, with its lesser evangelical standing and need of a new roof, would be a most suitable venue.

Bailey was sure too, that he could find appropriate staff given that they'd receive double pay and, yes, since they were breaking no laws, nor indeed bringing the institute of marriage into disrepute, Henry could, subject to the usual 'corking fee', appoint his own vicar. He, himself, would almost certainly be seconded to Maidstone that day.

All this (apart from the colour of the chapel) Malissa already knew. She hadn't been able to meet Eduardo when Henry met him in London last month, so they had arranged to meet here to get a feel for the place and each other. Eduardo's own parish was the in the West End.

"So, he's Italian?" Malissa had asked Henry who smiled, saying he guessed so, before adding, "He's a bit different."

"What do you mean 'different'?" Why did this not surprise her?

"Just a little friendlier than your usual vicar. The main thing is he's a man of God, licenced to perform all things Christian, and speaks several languages including Latin. You'll like him."

They had agreed it a fantastic idea that those parts of the traditional ceremony which could not lawfully be spoken because they were already married, could be altered a little and delivered in another tongue. She was sure neither her mother nor any of her friends from the Women's Institute spoke Latin.

Eduardo was waiting for them in the little stone building that served as an office. When they walked in, Malissa was hit by surprise number two. Like the chapel, he was pink, well, dressed in pink trousers and shoes, white shirt, pink tie, and blue blazer.

He wasn't tall and just a little overweight. In his late sixties, Malissa was expecting someone of Mediterranean origin but he was of Caribbean or even African descent. His eyes housed laughter and his tight curly hair was greying at the sides. He stood up as they entered, greeting them with a smile that lifted the two permanent dimples that accentuated his cheekbones. It was the warmest and most infectious smile Malissa had ever seen.

He clasped his hands in front of his chest before opening his arms wide to welcome them. "Oooh, look at you two love birds. Come in, come in, take a seaty boo. Oooh, you beautiful people."

If Malissa was surprised by what she saw, she was gobsmacked by what she heard. His warmth and enthusiasm were as natural as his smile but his greeting was delivered in a voice and rhythm pitched somewhere between Kenneth Williams' and Frankie Howard's. Pink church, camp vicar. Henry!

"Malissa. This is Reverend Eduardo Ambrossini. Reverend, my wife Malissa."

"Oh, you are goooorgeous, my dear. And such kind eyes. You are a very lucky man, Henry."

"Indeed, I am, sir."

Henry was smiling broadly. Malissa knew he would have warmed to the Reverend the moment he met him in London.

"Now my dears. This is a wonderbubble place. I have spoken to Matty. Oooh, I mustn't call him that. That's Reverend Bailey." He lowered his voice and took Malissa's hand. "He runs this place, and though we both share the same divine belief sometimes I think he believes I'm from another planet."

Malissa could understand why.

He continued. "Anyway, all is boom diggitty doo, and the chapel, ooh the chapel is lovely, heavenly, and perfect for you two lovely lovey young love birds. Shall we do chapel, tea, biscuits, or tea, biscuits, chapel?"

He literally beamed. Malissa deciphered his words, assuming 'boom diggitty doo' was a good thing and that he was offering them a cup of tea, either now, or after they had seen then chapel. It made sense to visit the chapel first as a knowledge of its layout would surely aid subsequent discussions regarding the arrangements.

"Well, if it's alright with you Reverend…"

"Ooh, Eduardo please. 'Reverend' is more of a stage name, you know, when I'm in *His* house." He raised his eyes upwards.

Malissa smiled. "Eduardo, I think a look around the chapel first would be a good idea."

"Exxcellenteh," that was Italian. "It's a dookie fresh morning," that was something else, "so let's click our heels tooty sweetie. Follow me," and they left the office to investigate the place where they were to be 'married'.

As they walked back down the driveway she realised she had already fallen in love with the place and reverend Eduardo. Who couldn't?

On their way in, she hadn't noticed that the chapel was round instead of square. It was also half wooden and half stone which was equally unusual, but it undoubtedly had charm with its large, leaded, arched windows and brown roof that sat atop like a gigantic sombrero. Did it really need repairing? Yes, it was unusual, but so was her marriage and so was her life these past six months. Unusual and lovely.

Three wooden steps led to the chapel's old oak doors which Eduardo swung open. He stood aside and ushered them in.

Any doubts Malissa may have had were immediately dispelled as she entered. Sunlight streamed in through the windows, which ran around the building. It looked bigger inside and was certainly larger than the chapel in Dubai. Its pews were arranged semi-circularly, facing the front where several potted plants stood on the small wooden stage.

The walls were a beautiful pale pink and decorated with hanging baskets as well as the more familiar décor you would see in a Christian place of worship. Wooden beams spanned the building at the top of the walls where a ceiling may have been, and the white plastered underbelly of the roof curved upwards to its highest point where a sparkling crystal chandelier hung majestically.

It was carpeted red throughout and a scattering of pink cushions decorated the white wooden pews. It was like a giant doll's house, so simple and yet so beautiful, so light and airy and warm; a strange mixture of old and new that somehow just blended together to make it so special.

"It's beautiful," she said breathlessly. "Perfect even."

"Isn't it just the quaintest little biddy chapel in the world, dear? A few picky flowers arranged to give you a feel but I can see a bundy of beautiful blossoms on the day. They grow them in these booootiful gardens."

"I think, Eduardo…" She paused, wondering. "I think Eduardo, this amount of flora and this amount of sunshine would be absolutely fine."

He beamed that captivating smile, touched her arm, and whispered, "I'll have a word." He glanced upwards. "About the sunshine I mean. The flowers I can guarantee."

Eduardo told her that he loved the impulsiveness of their marriage in Dubai and had a clear understanding of their requirements. He said two practice sessions would be sufficient, one now and one with the

Best Man and Maid of Honour or any others who may have a key part to play.

Positioned for the first of their rehearsals, Reverend Eduardo Ambrossini stood in front of them and, in a remarkable change of persona, adopted an entirely different posture. In authoritative, fruity tones he delivered the opening words of the ceremony. Malissa burst out laughing before apologising profusely, explaining she was not expecting the sudden transformation.

"Don't you worry, dear. As soap is to the body so laughter is to the soul. Do you really think I'd be taken seriously using this voice?"

He smiled. You could not help but be caught up in this man's zest for life. In fact, when they concluded their meeting, Malissa wasn't entirely sure she was pleased when he informed her he would not be wearing anything remotely pink on their big day.

## 39

# JULY 1984

## MALISSA AND HENRY

### A TRIP TO CORNWALL

Henry had promised to show Malissa the house he was brought up in. It was a small detour on their way to Cornwall.

Any concerns she may have had about the venue for their blessing had been dispelled following the visit to the chapel yesterday. Next Wednesday, Brad and her cousin Samantha would accompany them for their final rehearsal. She looked forward to it and couldn't wait to see Brad's reaction to the man, who as far as the rest of the world was concerned would be marrying them. It made her smile.

Malissa knew that Ashbourne House was now a children's home. It was situated a couple of miles southwest of Wokingham. They pulled up in a bus stop.

"There you are, Miss Keats. Ashbourne House," said Henry.

It stood on its own about 100 metres beyond the hedge, the estate's boundaries marked by ranch-style fencing. It was an impressive brick-built building, much larger than Malissa had imagined.

"Not bad for an orphan, Mr Ovmeister," she said, taking his hand. "Your Aunt Rose was indeed a wealthy lady."

He smiled.

"So, that lane leads to it?" she said, looking over her shoulder. "I wonder if there's anybody home. You could knock and say, 'Excuse me, I used to live here. Would you mind if we looked around?'"

Henry laughed. "I think, Malissa, it would be more polite to write to them and request such a visit. You must remember, it's now a children's home."

"And what a beautiful one it is too. Ironic, you an orphan, and this place now a children's home." She sensed an uneasiness. "It must be strange to come back here after all these years. Is it different? Looking at it from here, I mean."

"Well, I have driven past here several times over the years. It's difficult to recall after such a long time how I felt when I first saw it, but now I guess I just see it as another house. A very lovely one, but just another house."

"And you have so many," she smiled. "I thought you'd go all sentimental. I still do when I visit my parents."

~

In his rear view mirror, Henry was pleased to see a bus approaching and indicating to pull into the space they occupied.

"Here's the bus," he said pulling out. "And, yes, maybe one day I'll write to them. But the past is the past and we have so much to look forward to."

"Or, you could make them an offer they can't refuse," Malissa said in her best Marlon Brando voice. "We could buy it back and live there."

He laughed. "And turn out all the poor children? Miss Keats, I am surprised at you. No, we shall buy a house that is purely ours, one we choose together, and one that will be home for all *our* children."

"All, Henry. *All* our children? I think this talk about Delores and her brood mare duties at Feelview has gone to your head."

He was pleased the subject had reverted to the present day and to their future. The thought of visiting Ashbourne, let alone buying it, wasn't one that enthralled him. "Miss Keats, despite your obvious contempt for children and their welfare, I shall buy you lunch. I know a lovely little pub and we can talk about how your mother will react when she first meets the Reverend."

She smiled and leaned across to kiss him. "Henry, do you ever yearn for a dull moment?"

Malissa had often said their life was like a roller coaster and he momentarily considered whether she would continue to enjoy a life of twists and turns or if she would begin to long for something more ordinary. He hoped she was as happy as he believed her to be.

"Miss Keats," he said, "if it's dull I seek, I talk to my best man. With my wife it's just brightness and light."

They spent the night in Bridgewater, continuing their journey to Cornwall immediately after breakfast. They planned to arrive late morning and have a look around, and after checking in to their hotel meet up with Charlie and Alice again that evening for dinner.

Tomorrow they needed to be back in London where they had work commitments and then just ten days until their blessing. They hadn't finalised their honeymoon, but Henry had suggested two weeks in Majorca which Malissa was happy with. It would be nice to get away, just the two of them, and wallow in a more leisurely pace.

Feelview Bay Stud was about three miles beyond Polperro, the seaside town where they would be staying that night. They had turned off the main road some time ago, taking the meandering and often single-track scenic route so that Malissa could appreciate the dramatic coastline. Horse boxes had to use the main roads.

They drove past a sign saying 'Feelview Bay Stud and Riding Centre – One Mile' and another, a little further on, informing visitors it was the next turning on the left.

"So, there's a riding school too?" asked Malissa. "Would we have time?"

She told him she hadn't ridden a horse since she was ten years old and seemed excited about the possibility of doing so that afternoon.

They took the next left, which was the driveway into the estate, and were greeted by another sign, 'Welcome to Feelview Bay' and another warning of horses and requesting a ten-miles-per-hour speed limit. A hundred metres in, a lane which led to the riding school, branched off left.

They continued ahead, driving steadily up a progressive incline with fields either side with perhaps half a dozen horses in each. When they reached the brow the sea came into view. Malissa could understood why this place would be chosen for a period of recuperation; equine or human.

The old farmhouse and its surrounding barns had been sympathetically restored. Two youngsters were busily mucking out the row of stables, which were newly built and abutted the original buildings.

Behind the stables was a large building that was once the grain store and down the lane, beyond the farmhouse, she could see a terrace of adorable little stone cottages. They parked outside the farmhouse.

"Well, Miss Keats, welcome to Feelview Bay," said Henry

"I read the sign," she smiled. "Thank you."

A woman appeared at the farmhouse door, smiling and waving profusely.

"Alice?" Malissa asked.

"Indeed. The one and only Alice…"

As they got out of the car, Henry was so enthusiastically welcomed by 'the one and only Alice' that it was almost molestation. "Oh, Henry, it's so wonderful to see you." She was planting kisses on his forehead and hugging him for all she was worth.

Henry had told Malissa about Alice, Aunt Rose's legitimate niece, who he regarded as his sister, but maintained she thought she was more like his mother. They had grown up together and he cared for her deeply. She was 'odd but in a lovely way', a touch naïve, and probably vulnerable in the wrong hands.

Suddenly, Alice looked embarrassed, probably thinking she had overdone her welcoming ritual. She broke the embrace with Henry, smiled at Malissa, and skipped around the car.

Instead of the more customary handshake or polite kiss on the cheek, Alice threw her arms around her. "Malissa, I've heard so much about you. It's so lovely to meet you at last." Then, seemingly realising that her greeting may have been just a little over the top, broke away, apologised and said, "I'm Alice. I'm pleased to meet you."

"And I'm so pleased to meet you too, Alice," replied Malissa, reconnecting the embrace – a gesture which seemed to delight her new friend.

"Come in, come in both of you. I want to know all about you Malissa and I can't wait for the wedding. Charlie's at the vets but he'll be back soon."

"Nothing serious, I hope," said Henry as they went inside.

"No, not at all. One of Goodwin's. Routine really, he's just picking him up. The horse I mean, not Mr Goodwin. He's on holiday. On a safari or something. The Goodwin's obviously. Not Charlie. He's never been on holiday." She was talking excitedly.

They sat at the dining room table. "Tea?" asked Alice. She didn't wait for replies. "That's a long drive. Did you come up the coast road? Beautiful view. I made some cakes."

Her conversation with herself continued quickly and without pause. She entered the kitchen.

Henry motioned to Malissa, smiling. He had told her it would take a good 20 minutes for Alice to settle down, and meaningful conversation prior to that wouldn't be possible. It was part of her charm and her shyness. He had also bet Malissa £5 that not only would they be greeted by an offering of cake, but the offering would be either lemon drizzle or pineapple tea cakes. Any other variety or, heaven forbid, she hadn't actually made any cakes at all, would mean Malissa won the bet.

When Alice returned with the tea, she asked if they would like one of the cakes. Malissa said she loved homemade cakes but somehow could never quite master the art of baking and wondered if, one day, Alice would teach her. Alice blushed at the suggestion and assured her she'd be delighted to.

"I made scones," she said. "I thought about lemon drizzle, they're Henry's favourite, but this is the West Country and I thought a cream tea would be more appropriate." She paused and looked up at the clock. It was only just gone 11am. "I know it's not strictly teatime, but who cares? I've got homemade blackberry jam. So, its breakfast really. Maybe we'll forego lunch anyway as we're going for dinner tonight. We are we still going to dinner aren't we, Henry?"

"Alice," said Henry. "Dinner with you is a delight. I booked a table at Amelia's."

"I love Amelia's," responded Alice. "It's my second most favourite restaurant. Well, my first with you, Henry, but you know what I mean. I'll get the cakes. Strawberry or blackcurrant jam? I don't have plum. I know, we can have both. Charlie will be here soon, he's at the vets. Oh, I told you that."

She returned to the kitchen. Henry gave a £5 note to his smiling wife.

They spent the afternoon touring the facility with Charlie and Alice. Most horses there were either convalescing or enjoying a well-earned break. Only one was under close supervision, receiving treatment for a leg injury in the building that used to be the grain store.

There were three stallions, one of which, Irolin, was owned by Henry and had apparently fathered more than 40 foals. "Not a bad job being a stallion," Malissa said, teasing Henry with his talk about children yesterday.

The stud owned two of the five brood mares stabled there and four were in foal. It was a different, more tranquil environment to the racing stables at Wickham Heath and a truly beautiful place to live and work.

It was gone four by the time they finished their tour. The riding school had closed but Henry suggested they could delay their return to London and come back early in the morning so that she could ride.

Dinner was booked for 7:30pm. They would just have time visit the model village in Polperro before checking in and showering for dinner.

Alice and Charlie were already seated when Malissa and Henry arrived at the restaurant. They talked a little more about Feelview Bay and their plans. Alice was now much calmer and was asking Malissa about the wedding. She would have made a wonderful bridesmaid. Henry told them they would come back tomorrow morning and have an hour's ride if it wasn't interrupting operations. Alice was delighted and said she would accompany them.

"We stopped by Ashbourne house yesterday," said Malissa. "Just to have a look."

Alice raised her eyebrows and looked at Henry. Then back at Malissa.

"Malissa, being Malissa," Henry said, "thought we should have a look inside. We couldn't, of course, not without prior warning, but I think I might write. Be interesting to see the changes."

"At Ashbourne House?" Alice seemed confused.

"It certainly is a grand place," continued Malissa. "I was joking to Henry that it wasn't a bad pad for an orphan. It must have been a wonderful place to grow up in, Alice, apart from having to live with Henry of course..."

Charlie interrupted, taking charge of the conversation. "I remember going there with Bobby Anderson, do you remember that day Henry, just after Reynard's Way won? I must have had 2,000 quid in my pocket, a lot of money then and I was thinking *bloody hell, they live here?*

"That was when I first set eyes on you, my darling," he kissed Alice sweetly, "and I thought, *play your cards right Charlie Boy. Play 'em right cos this here woman's loaded. You never know she could even get you that farm in Cornwall you always had your eye on.* Yep, that was some gaff. Children's home now. Great steak."

Henry and Malissa laughed but Alice nudged her husband sharply with her elbow and cackled sarcastically.

Charlie continued, "How do you like our model village, Malissa? It's even better at night..."

He steered the conversation back to the present, to Cornwall, to horses, and to the forthcoming wedding. Malissa loved the bond between Henry and Alice and could see Charlie was someone he trusted implicitly. Alice was certainly not in the wrong hands.

The next morning, Alice, Malissa, and Henry rode for an hour before having breakfast together in the farmhouse. Alice was giving them some scones for the journey back when Charlie walked in, said good morning and smiled at Henry, who announced it was time they were off. Alice made a sad face and hugged them both warmly, repeating how excited she was about the wedding and saying that she couldn't wait to see them again.

They got in the car and Henry started the engine. Charlie dragged Alice, who would probably have waved to them until they passed Polperro, back inside the house and closed the door behind them.

"She's so sweet, Henry. A wonderful sister," Malissa smiled, sad to be returning home.

He switched off the engine. "Miss Keats," he said, and she wondered if he would call her that after the ceremony. "There's one other member of the family I think you should meet. She also, is a very special lady."

"I'm intrigued," she said, as he walked round the car to open her door.

They crossed the yard to the stable block and stopped at the first stall. The horse inside had its back to them, turning as Henry entered and nodding as he grabbed hold of the reins to lead the animal out.

Malissa studied the horse. Too fat to be a racehorse and probably too old too, but Henry clearly had a great affection for her. "See any resemblance?" he asked.

There was perhaps something familiar, but she had seen many horses over the last two days. "Family resemblance?" she enquired. "Well, she has a hint of grey."

"Grey? Hmm." He frowned but chose to ignore the remark.

"Rosie meet Malissa. Malissa meet Rosie. The mother of Delores Delahay."

# 40

## CHRISTMAS EVE, MAJORCA 1989

### BRAD AND HENRY

"Brought you a beer," Brad said, joining him at the water's edge.

"Thanks."

"Bit of a different proposition at this time of year." There was a fresh breeze and the waves almost reached the hooter they had attached to the rock that summer. "Smoke?"

They rarely smoked but Henry took one. Brad put his arm around his friend and led him to the table. "Brought this too," he said and retrieved a bottle of brandy from his jacket pocket as they sat down.

Henry smiled but said nothing. They sat for several minutes, just listening to the waves. Brad would speak when Henry wanted to but knew his pure presence was a comfort to him.

"We've been here before my friend." Henry said finally.

"We sure have."

"She wore a blindfold..."

Brad said nothing.

"When we came here. Last month. She likes surprises, I know that and there was no harm. Vanessa wanted to add to the suspense. Blindfold on, then off, and *voila* there it was, our beautiful villa. If only all things were that simple. I thought for one minute she was going to ask me to describe it to her. I went cold, Brad."

Very few people had witnessed Henry this morose. There was little anybody, even Brad, could do to ease the pain he felt in these moments. Over the years though, Henry had at least learned he needn't deal with these feelings alone.

"I thought I was fine," he continued. "I know I'll have days like this, I always have. I just think the people arriving today and saying, 'wow look at this' and 'wow look at that' and the kids opening their presents and feeling the wrapping, you know, normal things. It just hit me a bit this year. Christmas is always tricky. I'll be okay… This is shit brandy by the way."

Brad took a swig and agreed it wasn't the best. "Henry, I know more than anyone the love you shared with Emma. I don't think I'll ever see the likes of it again. Not that love, not that pure, not that magical, and not that young. And that's from ol' Mr Cynical himself. But life goes on. I don't have to tell you that and in Malissa… Well, you love her, and she loves you. She's not Emma, but no one's Emma. No one will ever be Emma."

Henry forced a smile. "I was thinking about that first Christmas in Feelview. Do you remember?"

Brad laughed. "The best Christmas ever. Unless you were Charlie Taylor of course."

Henry recalled the inquisition he subjected Charlie too when Charlie told him he wanted to marry Alice. "Yeah, poor fella, I was a bit hard on him. Do you know he asked my permission? Like I was her father or something."

"Yes, Henry, I do know that."

"Good times."

"Yeah."

They drank a bit more and lit another cigarette. It was dark now.

"I bought you a present," said Brad.

"A present? You? Bought me? A present?"

"Yeah, why not?"

"Cos I don't think you've ever bought me a present in your whole life."

Brad frowned. "Well, do you remember the day in the restaurant when I said I was giving up any chance of having a decent and successful career and came to work for you instead?"

"For Ovmeister-Carmichael," Henry corrected.

"Quite. Well this, my dear friend, is the pen we signed the deal with."

Henry took the pen and examined it.

"I was going to get it laid on a plaque or melted into a trinket or something, but just didn't have the time. A gift to commemorate a first Christmas at the villa. I thought it would be a great memento and something you could treasure. It wasn't, after all, such a bad decision."

A moment's pause while Henry twiddled the pen between his fingers.

"Braddon Carmichael…" he said handing the pen back to him. "We have never signed a single fucking agreement between us in our lives. Fuck me, for a moment I thought you were getting all sentimental. Fucking melted down pen, signed agreement, my arse. Good try though."

They both laughed and drank more crap brandy.

"What I did sign yesterday, however," Brad said after a few moments, "and *with* this very same pen, were the papers giving us ownership of The Maltings. It should be up and running in three months."

Henry smiled broadly. The Maltings was a property near Polperro that they wished to turn into a recreation centre for blind children. He stood up and hugged his friend. "Have I ever told you I love you?"

"Yes, Henry, many times."

"Do you ever tell me?"

"Nope, men don't say that to one another."

"Hmm. You hard bastard. Come on, its Christmas Eve and we've a villa full of wonderful people looking forward to a good time. Let's go to this party. You'll love the villa. Malissa really has worked wonders."

Brad had already enthused about their wonderful new home. "She's a great girl," he said.

"The best," Henry acknowledged. "When you getting married?"

"When you can run a business..."

"Hmm."

They had their arms around each other as they walked up the hill.

"So. Ovmeister–Carmichael. Do I still own 55%?" asked Henry.

"Yep."

"And you 45?"

"mm-hmm."

"Am I as wealthy as they say I am?"

"Wealthier."

"So, you're quite well off too?"

"Yep."

"Rich?"

"Loaded."

"Because of me?"

"Seems so."

"Then you can for pay for dinner tomorrow."

"If you pay for the drinks."

"You know, my friend... Do you know what would have really made my day with that pen?

"What's that?"

"That you used it to sign the fucking papers on the mobile phone deal!"

"No, that's just *making* money, Henry. I thought you'd prefer to give it away."

"You know me far too well, Mr Carmichael Junior. Now, where's that Brian Fenner? Bobby tells me he owes three months' training fees."

## 41

## APRIL 1977

## GRAND OPENING, FEELVIEW BAY

It was time for the official opening of Feelview Bay. They expected a 100 people and a marquee had been erected to accommodate them. Henry wanted to take a back seat during the proceedings as the day belonged to Charlie, but Emma had mentioned that he was a little apprehensive about hosting and suggested Henry be on hand to lend assistance if required. He would be.

Bobby was dressed for Ascot and going over some finer details with Charlie when he joined them. Charlie had always worried that Cornwall was just too far away for many trainers to consider sending their horses there.

"Well, Charlie," said Henry, "if you want a holiday, you travel. And I can assure you if I had horse in need of a break I'd have no hesitation in sending him here. Bobby, I'm beginning to think you like dressing up."

"Just for Charlie," she said, lifting the cellophane from one of the plates and stealing a sandwich. "And talking of horses on holiday, we've just been looking at Rosie. Can't see her running again, Hip."

It was the news he had been expecting. "Well, I guess she'll just have to become the mother of that Derby winner you keep promising me."

Bobby smiled and took another sandwich. “How’s Emma, and when you getting married?”

“She’s great, coming up with Alice in a minute. Doesn’t want to get married. Doesn’t see the point. It’s not for want of asking.”

“Probably waiting for someone decent. Don’t blame the poor lass.”

“We’re trying for a baby though,” Henry smiled.

“Well get yer frigging arse up here and learn a thing or two.” They laughed. “You set a date yet, Charlie?”

Charlie and Alice had recently got engaged.

“Not yet, Bobby. We were thinking next year but we’ve been so busy here we haven’t really talked specifics yet.”

“And what about you and Emma, Hip? You gonna move in permanently down here?” she asked.

Emma and Henry were spending more and more time in Cornwall. Alice was always on hand if Henry was away.

“Well, it’s not a bad place to live Bobby.” He looked round the marquee. “Now, it all looks great and people will love the place, I’m sure.”

Alice came in and put a tray of bread pudding on the table. She noticed several missing sandwiches.

Emma and Henry left the party early. They were sitting on the bench near the waterwheel. It was just starting to get dark.

“Alice is so happy,” said Emma.

“Yes, she is, Em. Charlie’s a good man.”

“Has he asked you to be Best Man yet?” Alice had already asked Emma to be her bridesmaid.

“No, he hasn’t.”

“Oh. Alice said he was going to ask. I think he was a bit worried you wouldn’t want to be and didn’t want to offend you.”

“Offend me? I’d be honoured. Why would he think that?”

“Sometimes, Henry, because you’re a successful businessman, people are a bit worried to ask certain things. Even those you’re close to. I think he was concerned a little about that and a little about the fact you might feel it your duty to give Alice away."

He would be honoured to be Charlie's Best Man but equally so to give Alice away. As for Charlie possibly feeling apprehensive to ask him, he couldn't understand that at all.

"Hmm. I never thought about that, about giving Alice away, I mean. I can't believe Charlie would be afraid to ask."

"Henry, there are many things you never think about."

"Could I do both?"

Emma smiled, as if she'd known that would be his solution.

"Have they set a date yet, Em?" He knew they hadn't.

"If they have, they haven't told me." She paused. "Henry – Alice has always been there for me. You know, when you're not. You don't think she's delaying things because of me, do you? Getting married would mean moving out from here and, knowing Alice, she probably thinks I wouldn't be able to cope."

He pulled her closer. He had talked several times to Charlie and Alice about the help Emma would need if Alice moved in with Charlie, which would be an obvious consequence of their marriage.

"I think she'd be more worried about how she'd cope with Charlie, Em. Or what she'd do all day if she couldn't fuss over you. No, I think with everything going on, the opening and the doing up of the house, they probably haven't had enough time to think about it."

"We might have to get somebody else in," she said.

He was trying to balance his overwhelming concern for her welfare against that of her self-belief. "And you think she would allow that?"

"But when you're away it might be appropriate. Anyway, she'd only be five minutes away and I guess I could always stay there if need be."

Henry hated the thought of Emma being left alone. "I didn't think about that Em," he lied.

"Henry, there are many things you never think about."

"I think about having a baby with you, Em," he grinned. "And I think I'm getting the hang of the Blue Danube. Come on, I'll play it for you." He squeezed her and planted a kiss on her forehead.

"But you're useless Henry, as a pianist I mean, not the other."

He smiled. "Well, practice makes perfect. On both accounts. Come on, and afterwards I'll write you a poem," and as they got up off the bench he began composing. "I wonder if she really knows, how much she means to me, I wonder if she knows I'm thinking, always, her and me, I wonder..."

He was seated at the piano and Emma joined him, his light-hearted words of love whirling through her mind. She took his left hand, ready to assist it over the keys and squeezed it. For the next hour or so they'd be laughing as he played his Les Dawson version of Strauss's masterpiece on an instrument it was never written for. She loved him more than she found bearable and surely there'd be a more appropriate time to tell him she would never be able to bear him a child.

## 42

# CORNWALL, MAY 1990

## VANESSA

Vanessa had scant respect for most men and, if she used her charms to get what she wanted, it hardly bothered her. It had taken her some time and several late-night visits to bars she'd rather not frequent to find the person who could confirm her suspicions.

What she learned in Söller had led her to here, and the library's records verified what she already believed to be true. She was sad. It was the end of that particular journey, but knowing Henry as she did, she found consolation.

She read again the newspaper cutting, a review of a concert at The Royal Albert Hall, that she'd carried around with her for the last three years. She imagined the scene it depicted as she had done so many times before and then tore it in two before dropping it in the wastepaper basket.

Her train back to London left in an hour. She loved Malissa and Henry, appreciated how happy they were and realised she had already decided telling either of them of her discovery would serve no purpose. She would see them, and their new baby daughter, tomorrow as planned.

## 43

# MAJORCA, AUGUST 1999

## TEN YEARS AFTER THE VILLA'S COMPLETION

Lewis was frustrated. His younger sister was quickly approaching his time of two minutes twelve. Although they had both joined the swimming club back home at similar ages, Millie was by far and away the keener of the two, Lewis preferring to spend as much of his free time as possible honing his talent for music.

Millie, who qualified for the National Championships last year, was more technically correct, and this largely negated her brother's additional strength. They clearly loved each other but she'd tease him, saying that by the end of the holiday a girl would have beaten him, and Malissa was unable to convince him to ignore her remarks.

Henry thought it was amusing, said it was unimportant and if it were a music competition there'd be no contest. "Millie likes swimming and you like music, it's as simple as that." Lewis had returned to the villa to console himself on the piano, but Millie stayed on the beach with her parents, probably because she knew it would make her brother wonder whether she was practicing even harder.

Henry and Malissa sat on deck chairs. They had been talking about The Fenner Agency and considering the company's options following Brian's decision to retire at the end of the year. He was happy to let

Malissa continue to run it or, if she preferred, they could sell. There were several potential buyers.

Malissa and Henry loved the time they spent alone with their children, especially here at the villa. Like so many previous summers, friends would be arriving tomorrow. Holidays here were special.

"I recall, Mr Ovmeister," said Malissa, "a certain young man being rather concerned about a younger French lady threatening to beat him. Was your reaction so dissimilar to Lewis's?"

"Hmm."

She wondered whether he would *ever* stop saying 'hmm' whenever he perceived something was challenging his wisdom.

"I recall something of that nature, Miss Keats." Only once, in 15 years of marriage, could Malissa ever recall him addressing her as 'Mrs Ovmeister'. "But, of course, if I remember, that was in the early days when co-ordination, which improves with experience, counted more than one's swimming ability. I also believe I had a cold. The record books do not lie."

She smiled. Sometimes she wondered if he would ever truly grow up. "What are you writing?"

"I'm writing a poem, Miss Keats."

"What about?"

"I don't know yet, business I think."

"Ah, not love then?"

"It could be construed as love. Love and business need not be so dissimilar."

"Read it to me." Malissa loved hearing him read his poems. She often said he chose her purely because of her surname and his secret desire to have married a poet.

"Well, you know I'm not fond of New Year?"

"Yes, Henry, everyone knows that."

"Exactly, so as we approach, not only a new year but a new millennium, I look at the way the world is going, the way we communicate, the internet, mobile communications, materialism, and what people seem to strive for, and I wonder if it is progress. To me, I see people searching for happiness in the wrong places. So, I'm writing about that."

"How profound. Can I hear?"

He picked up his papers and cleared his throat.

*"Mobile this, throw away that, the internet, credit, and now. Instant gratification, without pontification, I ponder and furrow my brow.* Hmm, pontification..." He crossed out the word and continued. *"I contemplate where we're heading and wonder if, at the start, we're being programmed to follow what we are told, and not to follow our heart..."*

"I can see a certain philosophy there, Henry," Malissa said when he had finished reading. "But I wonder if there isn't just a hint of hypocrisy? After all, it could be argued that Ovmeister Communications had no small part in bringing such terrible technology to these shores and, as for mortgages and questioning an Englishman's Castle, would I not be correct in suggesting you own more properties than could be considered necessary? I suppose you could close your technical development offices in LA, you know, to ensure no more of these technological evils find their way into the world. Perhaps you should talk to Brad tomorrow?"

It was the bones of a good poem and Henry's businesses were run with the ethics that reflected his own philanthropy, but she loved this banter with him. She laughed. "I would love to see that debate, you suggesting closing LA."

Henry's reply was as expected. A simple, "Hmm," and he picked up his pen, returning his concentration to the poem.

Malissa sighed and looked around. The palms they'd planted had flourished and she wondered whether they were now strong enough to support the hammock Henry had bought some years ago. She looked at the old hooter on Blackpool glistening in the sunshine and smiled to herself. If the palms weren't quite up to it, perhaps she could get Juan to fix some suitable fixings into the rocks around the beach. She felt totally content and again found herself contemplating the feasibility of making this their more permanent family home.

"Have I told you I love you lately, Henry?" she asked softly.

He put down his pen and slipped his arm around her shoulder.

"I'm not sure you have, Miss Keats. Not lately."

"Not last night, when you suggested I should be a little quieter?"

"Hmm."

"I have calculated, Henry, that I tell you I love you 17 times more than you tell me."

In the water, Millie embarked on another lap.

"Malissa, I loved you the moment I saw you. I loved you even more in Dubai. When we won the Oaks I was ecstatic that you were there with me, and when we got married I fell in love all over again. When Lewis was born, I didn't think I could love you more, but then Millie came along and scuppered that belief. As our children have grown and we have become a family I find I love you even more than I thought possible, and today I love you more than life itself. If love were measured in numbers then what started out as a 70, perhaps a little more, has accumulated to the 95 I love you today..."

"Not 100 then?"

"There must always be room for improvement."

"Then maybe we should spend tonight in the farmhouse to see if I can get you to reach that magical figure?"

"Malissa, sometimes I wonder if you believe your sheer physical beauty alone can be used to seduce me. You make me very happy." He kissed her.

Malissa rested her head on Henry's shoulder. She almost 40, Henry approaching 50 with successful businesses, beautiful children, friends and the most wonderful home in the world.

Over recent years, life had slowed to a more sedate pace and out here, at the villa they'd built, Malissa couldn't be happier. The decade that was ending belonged to them. She got up and gathered the towels. She looked at her husband, his pen in his mouth, and wondered if he would ever consider publishing his work. Maybe he'd even give up business altogether and concentrate on writing.

He was still the man who had kidnapped her at Goodwood, the man who saw her blow up her nose and dared to say hello. What she didn't know at the time was that she would still be under his spell 16 years later. She called to Millie. It was time for lunch.

# 44

## MAJORCA, 28 DECEMBER 1999

Their villa had become synonymous with gatherings and was the obvious venue to see in the new millennium. They expected upwards of 100 guests, many of them from England who were due to arrive over the next two days and would be accommodated in the Söller hotels. Like so many previous years, Malissa and Henry had spent Christmas at the villa with family and friends, but this evening they were dining at The Söller Grand.

Brad and Julie had married earlier in the year. Julie first visited Söller, when she and Brad came out for a week in the summer two years ago. She was most impressed to learn of her husband's investment in the town at a time when its potential as a vacation centre could have been questioned.

Sitting at the circular table were Henry and Malissa, Brad and Julie, Alice and Charlie, Vanessa, and Malissa's parents. Other than their children, this was, as far as Malissa was concerned, the nearest Henry had known to family, and if Bobby was there too it would have been complete. Henry stood up halfway through dinner and tapped a spoon on the table.

"Oh no, a speech," giggled Alice, putting down her cutlery to ensure she gave Henry her full attention.

"I'm afraid so Alice," he smiled.

"Malissa…" he said, touching her arm. "Friends. Family. We all take journeys. Life is a journey…"

"It's the millennium," Brad said to Julie. "He hates New Year and this one he's been seriously dreading."

"Tis true, my friend," Henry continued. "I have always said the turn of the year, from one number to another, is very indicative of the time we spend here, and yes, Brad, a change of century for someone like me..."

"There's no one like you, Henry," interjected Alice who then said, "Oops," realising she aired her thoughts aloud.

He smiled and carried on. "For someone like me, it brings home certain realisations, certain feelings, and gives me great cause for reflection.

"We do not always have the opportunity to be together or to express how we feel or to say, 'thank you'. Or indeed 'I love you'. Sometimes we're simply too busy.

"Malissa informed me in the summer that she said 'I love you' at a ratio of 17 to 1 compared to the number of times I say it. I disagreed, of course, but I do wonder if we forget to say some things sometimes. I didn't intend to stand up and say anything…"

"We all know how you hate making speeches, Henry," interrupted his wife, then felt a pang of regret for interrupting him. He was being serious. He smiled at her and continued.

"I was looking around the table and realised how so very dear the people around it are to me. Time passes us all by. As can life, if we are not careful.

"Sometimes life can deliver cruel blows and sometimes it can deliver magic, and the greatest magic is love, and around this table this evening is love. Is magic.

"It surely is what life is about. About moments, about moments like this that make memories, and as those moments roll into more moments, they become your journey. A journey through life with those you love, and I cannot think of another man who has been so blessed to have had such wonderful companions with whom to share his journey. And on behalf of Malissa and I, I thank you for being here with us."

He sat down. Malissa put her hand on his thigh, which he found and squeezed. Alice was smiling broadly, a tear in her eye.

Brad stood up. It was apt he replied. "I remember a time in Denmark, my dear friend, when observing tradition on a Viking night we could hardly walk after the speeches and the toasting, but I assure you we shall not follow that Scandinavian custom tonight.

"Your impromptu announcement, however, warrants a suitable response. On behalf of us all here, and indeed many others, and some very special people who are unable to be here..." He paused and looked at Henry and Malissa saw, as she had seen so often, that special bond only they shared. "I would like to say that we love you too. Did I just say I loved Henry?" They laughed. "Malissa, Henry, we thank you for asking us to spend this special time with you."

It was too much for Malissa's mum. With handkerchief in hand and wobbly legs she went to stand up, felt her husband's arm restrain her and so simply said, "How lovely," and "cheers," as she polished off her wine.

Henry, Malissa, Brad, Julie, and Vanessa stayed behind after the others had returned to the villa. They were standing at the bar.

"Julie, you really must try the Majorcan wine," suggested Henry. Brad frowned.

Malissa laughed, remembering a time some years ago when they were sitting outside the hotel, her husband fretting about telling Brad of his decision to plough money into the town. She recounted the story to Julie, who was a little disappointed to learn that Brad was not as enthusiastic about this wonderful resort as she had been led to believe.

"That was then," Brad protested. "I'm more mellow now. God, I even said I loved Henry earlier."

"It's taken him 30 years," said Henry. "And it was a 'we' and not an 'I', and a qualified one at that."

They laughed, there was no pleasing Henry.

"Did you ever go back to dancing Vanessa?" asked Julie.

"Not quite," she replied. Her accent had faded over the years but her beauty had not.

"She does dance," said Malissa. "Told you, Ness, you come out here and your ankle will mend."

"And that's taken what, 15 years?" said Brad.

"Well, I dance in Palma sometimes, mostly with the school, but once or twice in the ballet. Only small parts, but not for some time now."

"And the dance school enjoys an enviable reputation, regarded as the best on the island, probably in all of Spain," added Malissa. "I feel a bit guilty sometimes." She made a sad face. "I mean, she was fantastic and maybe if I didn't drag her out here, who knows..."

Vanessa clutched her friend's arm. "I have loved every minute here and the dance school has been a great success. Not quite deserving of the accolade Malissa bestows on it, but several young dancers have found some success. No, as Henry says, life is a journey and sometimes out of adversity or mishap comes something very wonderful. Right, Henry?"

Malissa noticed her husband raise his eyebrow in response to Vanessa's question. Sometimes, just sometimes, she detected something between them she couldn't quite fathom. Perhaps subconsciously they shared an understanding of what it was like to be brought up without parents. She smiled at her friend.

"And, seeing as it seems to be a time for speeches," continued Vanessa, "I have my own announcement to make."

It was most unusual for Vanessa to make an announcement and there was a sudden silence. Malissa thought perhaps she had, at last, seen the light and found herself a man. Or maybe she was pregnant.

"I am opening a dance school in Paris," Vanessa said.

"You're leaving?" Malissa couldn't disguise her concern. She knew Vanessa had talked to her old dance teacher about taking over her school in Paris, but she hadn't mentioned it recently. She had assumed Vanessa would always live in the farmhouse. Realising her comment may have been delivered more harshly than intended, she repeated it, making it sound friendlier. "I mean, you won't be living here? Söller will miss you but its great news."

"Well, yes and no. Francesca will take over the running of this one while I set up, but I expect I'll be back and forth."

Malissa took a deep breath and hugged her, realising it was purely the start of another wonderful adventure and not the end of their great friendship. She still made a sad face, however. Vanessa had probably been dreading telling her.

"I'll guess you'll get to see more of your sister, Ness?" Henry said.

Vanessa turned to him and smiled. "Abigail?" She paused but didn't wait for an answer. "I'm hoping she will work there, maybe in an administrative capacity. She doesn't dance."

"Well, Vanessa, I'm sure you will make it as successful, no, even more successful than this one. Maybe you can teach her to dance too. This calls for a celebration." Henry kissed her on the cheek.

The others talked while Henry ordered champagne. He had felt Vanessa's gaze when he asked about her sister. Like he had felt her gaze so many times before. He could still feel that fleeting caress of her hair when he had kissed her, and the scent of her perfume lingered in his nostrils. Somewhere in his soul it provided such comfort and somewhere else such sadness. He dismissed a ludicrous thought.

The 20th century was ending. An intimate gathering with family and friends before the onslaught of a once in a lifetime celebration. The calm before the storm perhaps.

# IV

# THE REVELATION

*Then could it be you dismantle that memory?*
*Cos the recollection is only of pain*
*Where a butterfly once danced in the meadow*
*Before that meadow was slain*
*So, you carry the angel inside you*
*Alongside the guilt and the blame*
*And bury it deep in another existence*
*Never to surface again*

# 45

## DELAHAY HOUSE, FEBRUARY 2000

### THE REVELATION

It wasn't like Henry not to contact her. The last time she spoke to him was yesterday afternoon, the last communication a text she'd received at 11:45pm which she read when she got up this morning. That was over an hour ago.

*11:45 pm* – ***Malissa, I love you. I don't think I'll be home tonight. I love you xxxxx***

It was not the kind of message he would usually send. She looked at the previous one.

*9:11 pm* – ***Something's come up. Be late DWU***

Don't Wait Up.

She had phoned when she'd received that text but it went to voicemail and now she still hadn't heard from him. It was unusual but not unprecedented. Maybe he was with clients.

When she woke and he wasn't there, she assumed he had spent the night in London and checked her phone for his texted confirmation, but the only messages were those two. She looked at the message before that, the one she received earlier that evening.

*6:17 pm* – ***It's too cold here MK, not conducive to the Human Spirit. When's half term? Should be home by nine. LY xx***

That was a Henry message. When she received it, she had smiled to herself and looked forward to him trying to convince her that the children could just as easily do their holiday assignments in Mauritius or Bora Bora.

The children were still asleep. Whatever *came up,* did so after 6:17pm last night.

She had called Henry's mobile three times already this morning and sent several messages. Something was wrong, something was so wrong, and her stomach churned with worry.

She picked up her mobile to call him again, but it rang just as she did so. It was Brad. "Brad, where's Henry? I'm worried. I haven't heard from him, it's not like him..."

"I'm on my way, Malissa, I'll be ten minutes."

"What's happened, Brad? Is Henry alright?"

"I'll be there in ten."

"Brad, what's happened?"

"I'll explain when I see you."

"Brad. What's wrong? Where's Henry? Is he alright?" Her voice was frantic.

There was a slight pause.

"There's been a fire, Malissa. I'll explain when I get there."

"Fire? At the office? Is he okay?"

Another pause.

"Yes, Malissa, Henry's okay. He's fine but there's been some injuries."

"He's injured?"

"No, he's not. He's perfectly okay."

"But he's not answering his phone."

"Malissa, I'll be there soon, put the kettle on. Henry's fine, I'll explain when I get there."

She pushed End Call and walked into the kitchen, a thousand thoughts swimming through her head. Ten minutes was going to seem an age. She checked on Lewis and Millie; they were still asleep.

She saw Brad pull up and opened the door. He smelled of smoke, his white shirt speckled with soot and his face that of a man who hadn't slept. She flung her arms around him and burst into tears. "I know it's bad, Brad," and he held her until her sobbing stopped.

"Henry's okay, Malissa. He's physically okay and not injured in any way."

"Where is he?"

"He's still there."

"Where? At the fire?"

"Yes, I think so."

"There were people in the office then?"

"Do you mind me sitting here? I'm a bit sooty." He sat down at the table.

"You mentioned injuries. But Henry's okay. God that sounds so selfish. Which office was it?"

"Let's have that tea and I'll explain. Throat's a bit dry. There's no need to panic," Brad said calmly.

She retreated to the kitchen trying to heed his advice. She returned and sat opposite him. "So, there were people in the office. And Henry?"

Brad paused. He wasn't looking at her. He was looking down at his lap.

"It wasn't the office, Malissa," he said glancing up.

"The flat. Oh my God. Is he okay?"

Brad took a deep breath.

"It wasn't the office or the flat. The fire was at Ashbourne House."

Brad watched her, seemingly waiting for the unexpected mention of Ashbourne House to sink in. It didn't make sense. A myriad of tangled thoughts ran through her mind. "Ashbourne House?" she repeated after several seconds.

"Yes."

"Ashbourne House where Henry lived?"

"Yes."

"I don't understand, Brad."

He took another deep breath. "Henry owns Ashbourne House."

She paused. "But it's a children's home."

"It is, Malissa, owned by Henry."

"Owned by Henry. I didn't know. Why didn't I know? I don't understand, Brad. What's Ashbourne House got to do with things?" There was more to this than Brad was telling her.

Brad reached for her hand. "Malissa, Henry is a good man. He's a wonderful man. You know that as well as I do. You know, too, that he would hate to bring any harm to anyone. He loves you and you know that. And I know you love him."

She knew that, of course she did. But his eyes told her there was something more.

"Brad. Why didn't I know? Why don't I know? Why is it relevant? What's wrong with him owning that house? He lived there as a child... What aren't you telling me?"

She wasn't hysterical but there was confusion and a degree of desperation in her voice, and God knows how many more semi-formulated questions in her head.

"Ashbourne House is owned by one of Henry's charities. Ashbourne House is a boarding school. A boarding school for blind children."

"Brad?" She suddenly felt sick.

Brad considered Henry's desperate suggestion that they tell Malissa that The Emma Ovmeister Foundation was set up by Aunt Rose; that the Company was custodian to it, and that Emma was... Emma was what? A blind child who captured her adopted mother's heart?

"Brad?" Malissa pressed him again.

If the fire didn't make the national news, it would warrant front page coverage in the locals. The Emma Ovmeister Foundation would undoubtedly be mentioned and how could that possibly be separated from Henry?

"Emma was blind," he eventually said and could feel himself

coupling links in a chain that could join a series of events that might shatter her world.

"Emma?"

"Emma."

"Blind? I don't understand. What's this got to do with Henry. What do you mean blind?"

"Malissa. You asked me once about Emma."

He saw the name tumbling through her mind.

"Emma. Fourteen-year-old Emma?" A blurred name that had possibly always lurked somewhere deep in her subconscious seemed to gain focus. "Emma?" she repeated.

Brad could feel his heart quickening, but he had to tell her. "Emma Ovmeister," he said.

The surname. Another link in the chain. He waited whilst she absorbed the impact. He could only imagine what thoughts the revelation of the name had roused in her. She looked at him, her eyes wide. She inhaled deeply holding her breath as she digested the information.

"Henry's sister?" she said as she exhaled.

If only it were that simple. For a split second he considered saying, "Yes." But he couldn't. "No. Not his sister, Malissa."

She took several deep breaths. She said nothing for many seconds and he could see she was trying to maintain some sort of composure. He admired her ability to do that and he awaited the obvious question, the response to which he had been mulling over since he left Henry two hours ago.

"His wife?"

Brad sensed her own surprise now that her words were audible. She was struggling to hold back her tears.

"No, not his wife, Malissa. She has the same name because they were both adopted by Gertrude Ovmeister, Aunt Rose, when they were children. They grew up together and later fell in love. She died young.

"I can't begin to tell you the effect it had on Henry and the time it took for him to recover. He forbade people to talk about her, not to mention her and carries some sort of guilt in his heart. Ashbourne House is one of several foundations that Henry has financed over the years. Foundations set up in her memory."

Malissa studied Brad's face. His words were calm, and true, and delivered almost soothingly. She tried to make sense of them, sense of the last five minutes. Why did all this seem so poignant? Why did this revelation shock but not surprise her? Why did that buried memory of a name, that hazy image of a girl which had probably always peaked from behind a door somewhere in the back of her mind, suddenly appear in full view? It was the image of a teenage girl, but as her thoughts materialised the image developed, and the pigtails disappeared. A sickening numbness enveloped her.

She wished she had a cigarette. Brad was mumbling but she had no room in her head to listen. She said nothing and robotically returned to the kitchen. She made more tea and by the time she sat back down, the first stirrings of anger emerged from the numbness she'd been feeling.

The relief she'd felt earlier when learning Henry was okay had deserted her. She felt betrayed and confused – foolish. What was Brad talking about? Why was this Emma so important? What was going on and why wasn't Henry here? Surely it should be him here, not Brad?

"Why isn't Henry telling me Brad?"

"He wanted to."

"Then why isn't he?"

"Because I know him, and I fear for him. And I've seen him vulnerable. And I know talking about Emma, if he could talk about Emma… Well, he would not defend himself or give you any explanation, because of the unfathomable loyalty he would have for her memory.

"He would walk out not feeling deserving of you. But I know he loves you and I know you love him. I may have judged wrongly and, if so, I could regret it forever, but I begged him to let me tell you Malissa. I thought it best I tell you."

She didn't reply. Brad would speak the truth and do so calmly. She could do that too. She knew him and loved him as a friend and knew the feeling was mutual. He would know this would be devastating for her, but she also respected how difficult it must be for him. Was Henry, Henry Ovmeister who would face everything head-on, running away? Getting off lightly?

"It sounds a cop out, Brad." Her trust in the man she adored was evaporating.

"It does, Malissa."

"I trusted him implicitly, Brad. We had no secrets."

"I know."

Would she really have preferred it if Henry was sitting there? She wasn't sure. Brad, so different from him and so matter of fact, was possibly the best person to answer the questions Henry knew she would ask.

"But they were 14." She knew she was clutching at straws.

"Henry was adopted when he was barely six months old. Emma, the same age, shortly after. They grew up together. Henry would always watch out for her. He was her eyes, but he never ever saw her blindness.

"They were great friends and after Aunt Rose died became even closer. As they grew up, they realised the bond between them was more than just friendship and they fell in love. They lived together in Ashbourne House and later in Cornwall. They were in love, just as you and Henry are now. She died aged 25 and Henry was broken. It took him years to find some sort of comfort, and the greatest comfort he ever found was you."

"So, I'm just his comfort blanket?" she was feeling anger building, overriding the other emotions she felt.

"Your heart will tell you if that is true, Malissa."

"But I don't understand. He could have just told me. It's not unusual to have a first love, or even a second. Why so secret?"

"I don't know the answer to that for certain, Malissa."

"What's your opinion?"

She could see how deep the question penetrated and knew he

couldn't answer. They looked at each other without words, his sad eyes telling her a story that somewhere in the back of her mind she perhaps already knew. Brad still had hold of her hands.

"He loved her." She murmured, certain the words completely understated the fact.

"He blames himself for her death," Brad said.

"Morning, Mum. Hi, Brad." It was Lewis, who had appeared at the bottom of the stairs.

"Hi, darling," replied Malissa as he went into the kitchen.

"Where's Dad?" he called.

"He's out, Lewis. He'll be back soon. You can eat your cornflakes in your bedroom and watch TV if you like. I'm just talking to Brad."

Lewis loved that idea and they waited until he had gone back upstairs.

"What do I do, Brad? I don't know what I'm feeling. I'm in shock."

He touched her arm.

"I don't know, Malissa. I don't know where we go from here. As a friend and as someone who loves both of you so much I would hope you could talk about it and try and put it behind you. But because I know Henry, because I know you both, I fear neither of you will find that easy. Maybe..."

He continued talking while Malissa tried to make some sense of the situation, desperately wishing the tightness in her stomach would subside.

"I need to come to terms with this, Brad," she said, interrupting him. "It's deceitful and strange, and I don't know... how can I trust him? I don't know how I feel. I guess it will sink in and..." She paused. She had no idea how she was feeling. "Brad, I just don't know, I've got no idea. I'm so scared."

He stood up and cradled her in his arms as she tried desperately to suppress her sobs for fear of the children hearing. When she gained her composure, they sat back down.

"So, Henry's still there?" she asked. She was trying to shut out any of their conversation about Emma.

"I think he's at the hospital."

"Shit. I forgot you mentioned injuries. Bad?"

He took a deep breath and looked at her.

"There's been a death, Malissa, and some injuries. Two of the children at least."

"Oh my God!" she shouted, and pulled her hands to her face, a thousand indistinct thoughts tearing through her mind.

## 46

# HENRY AT THE HOSPITAL

## THE MORNING AFTER THE FIRE

"She has a sprained ankle, Mr Ovmeister, but nothing broken. And Mathew just some severe bruising, but they'll be okay. Tough kids. They're quite comfortable."

He smiled at the nurse and looked at his phone. Malissa had called and texted several times. He already knew that, but Mathew's parents still hadn't returned his call.

"Thank you," he said and stood up.

He crossed the corridor to the ward and peered through the glass. The children were sitting up in their beds. He considered going in to talk to them again but Daisy's parents, who had been there since the children arrived, seemed to be taking good care of both of them.

"It wasn't your fault you know."

He turned to the nurse, aware of the stench of smoke in his nostrils.

"Look after them," he said. He knew they were in good hands.

He made his way outside, the crisp cold air a welcome intrusion into his lungs. He automatically looked for Paul, wondering where he said he would park, but he must have seen him come out of the hospital because he suddenly appeared. Henry got in.

"Kensington?" Paul asked.

Henry didn't answer but knew Paul would drive him there.

In his mind remained the picture of 20 children standing outside a blazing building, feeling its heat and hearing its crack as they held each other's, and their carer's hands. In his ears the sound of children coughing and the desperate cry of Mrs White. "Where's Donald?"

His phone rang. It wasn't Mathew's parents, so he didn't answer. He was drained and now more aware of the burns on his hands.

He closed his eyes. From the vison of the flames came a familiar face. He knew it would and hoped it would give him comfort and tell him it wasn't his fault. Not this time.

## 47

# FEBRUARY 2000

## MALISSA – THE IMMEDIATE AFTERMATH

Brad stayed two more hours. Her instinct was to ask him to look after the children while she went to the hospital to see, or was it to confront, Henry? Brad understood, he didn't judge, but she heeded his advice to leave it for a while.

A multitude of emotions surged through her, but none would settle. She thought about the fire, about the children, about Henry, but progressively, a girl called Emma invaded every thought she tried to process. Something incomprehensible had been unleashed and she didn't know what the rest of the day held, let alone the future.

When Brad left, she went into the garden to phone Henry. She didn't expect him to answer and wasn't sure what she wanted to say. She left a message, her voice quivering.

"Henry, it's me. Brad's told me about the fire and about Ashbourne House." She had paused at that juncture before adding, "And about Emma. Henry. I don't know what to say. I'm so sorry about the children. I'm so sorry about...Henry, I'm here. I'm here for you and... I'm here, Henry."

She hung up. She'd said only a fraction of what she wanted to say but resisted calling back. She kept her phone with her, desperate for news.

Her mother called and she managed to conduct a normal conversation. She tried hard to prevent Lewis or Millie picking up on her feelings, but after she prepared lunch she contacted Veronica and asked her to come over. She needed to do something. But what?

She had been driving for about ten minutes when Henry's text came through. ***I'm so sorry Malissa. Can you meet me at the cottage at 5?***

It was just after 2pm. The cottage was the place they spent their first week together when they returned from Dubai after getting married and where they sometimes spent weekends. It was an hour's drive from home. She wasn't surprised she was already heading in that direction.

She texted back, '*Yes*' and phoned Veronica who confirmed she could stay the night if necessary. She arrived at the cottage at 3pm somehow managing to pick up milk as well as a packet of cigarettes on the way.

She phoned Brad. She needed to speak to someone. She considered ringing Alice or Charlie, even Bobby Anderson. All would have been party to the secret Henry had harboured and that made her angry. She was struggling to suppress that feeling and the only person who could help her do that was Brad.

"Hi," she said.

"You ok? Silly question."

"Have you seen Henry?"

"I spoke briefly, but he's not speaking, save the little he has to, to the police. I've been speaking to them all afternoon."

Of course. There would be an investigation.

"Is he okay? He's texted me and we're meeting at the cottage. I'm here now."

"I think that's good."

"Brad, I'm angry and I don't think I should be."

"Malissa, you've every right to be angry, and many other things too. Henry will be completely aware of that."

"But Alice would have known. About Emma I mean. About Henry

and Emma. And Bobby, and God knows who else. I feel such a fool. Sorry, it's all sounding about me."

"I understand, Malissa, and I don't know what to say. I can see why you think it was a secret that shouldn't have been."

"But everyone would have known, Brad. Why didn't I?"

"Other than Alice and Charlie, Malissa. And Bobby. I'm not sure many people knew. Some others you may have met possibly would have known about Henry and Emma, but they wouldn't have known much more than that they simply used to be together."

"I didn't even know that, Brad. When did she die?"

"Summer of 1978."

Five years before they met.

"Malissa, you will have many questions and I feel for you. I worry for you. And I worry for Henry."

"But I didn't know, Brad. How could I not know? How could I know him for so long and not know? Why didn't I see?" She was sobbing quietly.

"Because he didn't want anybody to see. It was something, rightly or wrongly, he carried alone. I do know he wanted to tell you. He just couldn't. God, I told him so many times to tell you. As you said, what would it have mattered really? But somehow, he couldn't, and I can't really tell you why."

"Brad, I'm not sure I can do this. It's like I've never known him. He's a stranger. How did I not know?"

Somewhere, in the far corner of her mind, pieces of a chilling jigsaw puzzle kept appearing, showing themselves fleetingly and trying vainly to lock together.

"I understand Malissa. All I can tell you is that when you came along he found what was missing in his life. All I can tell you is that me and Alice love you. Love you and Henry. And to have seen him happy again was wonderful. You brought that to him. He loves you, Malissa, of that I have absolutely no doubt. But this is going to be tough. Talk to Henry. He's still the Henry you met at Goodwood and the man you married in Dubai. What happened to Henry made him into the man you fell in love with."

Had he helped? She wasn't sure.

"Thank you, Brad."

"Malissa, I'm here. Call me anytime. I can't suggest what you say to Henry, I just hope the love you have for each other can get you through."

She attempted a smile.

"Malissa, I mean it. I'm here. I phoned the house earlier and the kids are fine."

"Good old Veronica."

"Yes. Take care and... well, just take care. I'm here."

"Bye Brad."

It was not yet 4pm. She flopped onto the couch feeling the first degrees of warmth from the radiators and went over the last 17 years, wondering how she never knew. Henry would be here in an hour. She had no idea what she would say to him.

48

# THE COTTAGE, THE DAY AFTER THE FIRE

## MALISSA AND HENRY

Malissa probed her memory. She recalled a time when she and Henry stopped outside Ashbourne House but never went in. Maybe if she'd pushed him to write that letter, been more insistent on visiting, they would have done so, but like so much of their life they quickly moved on to the next adventure.

Did he lie to her? He never said he didn't own the place, he never said he sold it, he just said it was a children's home. Which, in a way, it was.

She thought about Cornwall. They had been to Charlie and Alice's many times over the years, but nothing was ever mentioned. Where did they live in Cornwall? Emma and Henry? Brad said they lived there. What, like man and wife? At Feelview Bay? In the farmhouse? Malissa and Henry only stayed at the farmhouse a couple of times even though there was plenty of room. They would usually stay in a hotel in Polperro.

The cottage. She had been there. It was a holiday let but they'd never stayed there, never been inside even though she was sure it was often empty when they visited.

Only once could she recall walking the grounds with Henry. She remembered saying how beautiful the view was. Yes, Henry said, you can *feel* it. Feel it because you couldn't see it, because Emma couldn't see it. *Feel*view Bay. Henry was thinking about Emma when he said it. No wonder he never liked going there. Alice and Charlie's holiday cottage. Of course, they lived there. That sick feeling in her stomach returned as she pictured the cottage, the cliff, the bay and compared it to their own beautiful place in Majorca.

It was ludicrous. If he had told her about Emma, she wouldn't be feeling the resentment she did now. How could he not have told her? She felt a fool and the surges of anger that had been invading since this morning were now more frequent and taking longer to subside.

'"There's been a death," Brad had said. She imagined the terror the children must have gone through and felt so guilty for focusing on her own personal plight.

Should she have a drink to calm herself down or would that make matters worse? She wanted to be rational when Henry arrived. Had he done anything so wrong? He hadn't lied to her, not really, he just hadn't told her the truth. But he had shut her out. God, he was shutting her out now. Surely, she should have been with him at the hospital this morning?

She thought about Henry and Emma. She tried to imagine their relationship. A relationship that, for some reason, her husband needed to keep secret. A relationship that was, that was what? She couldn't imagine it, she couldn't understand. *Be sensible, Mel.* Did it really matter? Of course it fucking mattered!

She was nervous about meeting him. She feared him. *Feared* him! She couldn't rationalise her fear, but it was there. She considered leaving the cottage and going home but that would only postpone the inevitable.

It was 4:30pm and getting dark. The cottage, so quaint and lovely whenever they stayed there, now took on an unfamiliar presence. She wanted to speak to Alice. Dear vulnerable, naïve Alice had kept things secret from her too. For 17 years! Bitch!

She picked up her phone to call her. She wanted to speak to her and... And what? Strip her down? Bring her to her knees, tell her what she thought of her? Malissa could be very intimidating when pressing her point and Alice would be no match for her. But, as hard as she tried, she could not imagine Alice to have a single malicious bone in her body. All she would gain was temporary revenge and she would quickly regret it. She turned on the light and used the landline to call Brad.

"Brad. He'll be here in a minute and I'm feeling so angry. Sorry to call again but alone with my thoughts I'm going crazy. I was thinking of ringing Alice and asking..."

"Asking her why she never said anything?" he interrupted.

"Yes."

"Well, the same reason I never told you Malissa."

"Then why don't I feel angry at you?"

"I'm not sure. I would imagine it's because you're wrongly angry at yourself for not knowing, for not realising, and looking to vent it, but there's no way you would have known unless Henry wanted you to."

"Unless it was me who didn't want to," she said under her breath.

"Sorry?"

"Nothing. I was just..."

"Malissa. Nobody regards this as some kind of *'we know but you don't scenario'*. It was ..."

"Brad, I don't think I know Henry anymore."

A pause. "I understand that."

"Brad, what do I do?"

"I don't know, Malissa. What I can say, and I don't for one minute imagine this will be of any consolation now, but if you saw what I saw all those years ago, you would probably have a better understanding."

"But I wasn't there, Brad. So I didn't see. So I don't know."

Another pause. "I appreciate that, Malissa. I know you love each other, and I just hope that's enough."

Brad was calm, his voice soothing, his concern genuine. She didn't want to vent her anger on him.

"Thanks, Brad." She hung up.

She poured herself a drink. She switched off the main light and turned on the lamp so the room wasn't so bright. It seemed to suit better. She waited, desperately trying to suppress the resentment which was rising inside her.

At 5pm Henry's car pulled into the drive and her heart quickened. She got up from the sofa but made no move to meet him.

He let himself in and, a moment later, stood just inside the doorway to the lounge. He was dishevelled and hadn't slept. She knew his face but couldn't recognise him. No expression, just a pitiful image drained of spirit. This was not Henry. She felt nothing and hated herself for feeling like that.

"I've no idea what to say, Malissa," he eventually said, his voice soft and devoid of emotion.

A strange calmness came over her. She wanted to shout but couldn't. She wanted to hug him but couldn't. Like some princess in a fairy tale she wanted to kiss him and turn him back to the man she kissed on Friday morning. But she couldn't. She felt cold and removed from reality and she imagined he felt the same. Their world somehow shattered because he had loved someone else and neglected to tell her.

Her response was automatic, words forming without thought or feeling. "I don't know you."

He said nothing and just stood there.

She needed emotion from him, any emotion.

"Henry, do you realise what you've done?" Then, she thought of the fire and the injuries and a sickening conflict formed in her stomach.

He stepped into the room, the room in which they had made love in front of the fire but was now just cold, just four walls, an interrogation room in which words needed to be said but in which neither of them may be able to find the right ones to say.

"Why didn't you tell me?" Her words were soft.

No response.

"Henry, for fucks sake, say something." Emotion was returning.

His eyes were red from tiredness and tears, but they looked empty.

"What can I say, Malissa?" Soft words from a worn-out man.

"You could ask if the kids are alright. Fuck me, you could ask how I am!"

She wanted him to say something, to shout, to apologise, to beg forgiveness, even to say to her, *'Why don't you ask about those poor blind children you selfish bitch?'* But he said nothing.

"I loved you, Henry, I loved you and I thought you loved me." She realised she'd used the past tense.

Despite the softness of her words, they seemed to strike him like some great uppercut to a boxer already on the ropes. His face told her he was searching for words, any words that would form a suitable reply, but he couldn't seem to find them. The man she'd often call her bear, her indestructible bear, standing before her like a child in the dark, alone, vulnerable and exposed.

He eventually spoke. His words coming from a place within him she never knew existed. A simple statement that possibly represented all he believed in, and all he longed for. Words he thought had justified so much, but now just manifested doubt. "I fell in love with you, Malissa. I fell in love with you the moment I met you and the love grew. I felt the love between us and I believed such love could overcome everything. Even the devastation of death."

She tried to make sense of what he'd said but was in no place to do so. Perhaps she was seeking reassurance but could any words he spoke provide that? She didn't understand, she couldn't understand, she was just a stranger who walked into his life and become part of the *Repair Henry Ovmeister Brigade*.

"You loved her, Henry. And you didn't tell me. Why didn't you tell me?"

"I couldn't."

"But I'm your wife, the one you are supposed to love."

"I couldn't tell you. I wouldn't have known how."

"But you talk, Henry, you talk for fucking England. God, how we've talked about everything over the years." Her voice was building, volume and velocity spiralling upwards. "We had no secrets. I don't understand the big deal. You fell in love with someone before me and had a relationship. So, fucking, what? That's not unusual, Henry. Why didn't you tell me? I've been a fool for all these years, everyone else knows, except me. Why couldn't you have told me? Tell me now!"

She screamed the last words without having a clue of what she actually wanted him to tell her.

He said nothing. He stood in the doorway his eyes looking at her but seemingly seeing nothing.

Calmer, almost resigned she said. "Henry – we had a life." Past tense again. "It needn't have been an issue."

Tears dripped down his cheeks. He wasn't crying, they just leaked. He made no attempt to wipe them away.

Malissa couldn't cry. Her voice was little more than a whisper. "Why didn't you tell me?" she asked again, begging for the answer that would provide complete justification. Waiting for the answer that could return them to Friday morning but aware she was waiting for an answer that may never come.

"I couldn't," he repeated.

"Henry…" There was such sadness in her voice now. "Henry, I'm not sure I can deal with this."

She gathered her coat. She had to leave. Or did she want him to prevent her from doing so? To shake her up, to rationally explain, to tell her she was over reacting.

He made no attempt to stop her. She kissed him on the cheek, his skin salty and unshaven with the faint smell of ash.

"Goodbye, Henry," she said. And left.

# 49

# DELAHAY HOUSE, FEBRUARY 2000

## MALISSA REFLECTS

The fire happened a week ago. The numbness she felt upon returning home after meeting Henry had remained with her.

She tried to be rational. Henry had loved another woman before her. That was all. But no matter how often she told herself this, she could not quash the resentment that seemed to consume her. Her cosy belief in life and love had been shattered.

She had not spoken to Henry and he hadn't been in contact with the children. It wasn't unusual for him to be absent for a length of time, but it was unusual for him not to telephone. The children would need answers soon.

The fire had been extensively reported in the local papers and, though officially the investigation was on going, Brad had told her it was almost certainly a result of one of the children bumping into a lamp and knocking the shade against a hot bulb. A simple tragic accident. Not all the children were in bed when it broke out otherwise the tragedy could have been so much worse.

Those who were taken to hospital had been discharged without any long-term physical injuries. The man who died was one of the caretakers. He lost his life rescuing two children who were trapped in an upstairs bedroom.

At night when Malissa tried to sleep, she focused her thoughts on the poor children and the carer who lost his life and hated herself when the feelings for her own loss or betrayal encroached upon them. She could not think of Henry as Henry. He had become a stranger. He was living in their Kensington home and, according to Brad, concentrating on nothing except the safety of the other establishments his charity owned.

He had visited the families of all the children and, of course, the widow of the caretaker. Brad said he was functioning on autopilot, shut off, similar in many ways to the man he was in the aftermath of Emma's death. But there was, 'something else.'

"Something else, Brad?" Malissa had asked during one of their many conversations.

"His manner, Malissa. I can't quite put a finger on it, but the look in his eyes when he told me Emma should never have been a secret suggested he was on some kind of mission, like someone preparing to face their demons, like someone..." He had stopped himself at that point and Malissa had asked him if he meant he was considering taking an overdose or something. "I hope not, Malissa," he replied.

She felt for Brad. All this time, regarded as the dispassionate one, the rock, he had suddenly found himself her emotional pillar. He worried for Henry and she sensed his own deep misgivings about keeping the secret of Emma from her. A distraught Alice also sought his counsel. Add to that, his own life, and the business, and the investigation, and she wondered how on earth he coped. If she hadn't already known, she could tell now why this man was so special to so many people and to Henry. Julie was a very lucky woman.

Brad had not flinched at the idea of her meeting with Alice and Charlie, understanding it was completely warranted. He would take her there next week. The past should never have been kept from her and he promised to tell her everything she wanted to know.

When Vanessa had phoned from Paris for one of their weekly chats, Malissa only skirted over the issue. Vanessa knew she was upset but didn't request further details. Unlike her, Vanessa never probed, never judged, and if asked for her opinion, gave careful, some may even say detached, consideration. Malissa would need that in the days ahead and was glad she was coming over the day after tomorrow. She would tell her all then.

# 50

# THE GODDARD'S HOUSE, FEBRUARY 2000

## HENRY

"I'm Henry Ovmeister," he said as the door opened.

Mrs Goddard, her face drained and her eyes still red, observed the man standing at the doorstep. In a tailored grey suit and expensive coat, clean shaven with neatly combed wavy brown hair she had no doubt he had dressed smartly out of respect for her and her late husband. How different from the images printed in the paper last week. He was a man of obvious authority yet his eyes harboured kindness and understanding.

"It's nice to meet you, Mr Ovmeister," she said and invited him in.

He waited in the lounge while she made tea. The walls and mantelpiece were host to many family photographs. Sympathy cards were displayed on anything that offered a surface and several more were still in their envelopes unopened. Vases of flowers adorned the room, and peering out the window he saw more bouquets, unwrapped, laying on the back lawn. Mr and Mrs Goddard were good people.

He would not have protested if she chose to vent her anger and frustration at him, but she remained calm and respectful.

"I thank you for coming, Mr Ovmeister, this must be a terrible time for you." Her words were sincere and somewhat unexpected. "Donald loved working at Ashbourne and would always tell me what a wonderful place it was for the children."

Donald Goddard was one of two full-time caretakers at the children's home. Sixty-three years old he had worked there since it opened and was in one of the outbuildings when the fire broke out. He sacrificed his own life when climbing the stairs of the west wing gathering up the two children trapped in the bedroom and lowering them out of the window to the people below. The window was too small for him to leave in the same way.

"Terrible for so many, Mrs Goddard."

"I just hope Don didn't feel responsible, Mr Ovmeister, that's what's gnawing at me. As caretaker, I mean. He was always so careful about making sure the house was safe."

He took her hand. She continued. "The police seemed satisfied that it was an accident, I think."

Henry had tried to persuade the police that a visit to the dead man's widow would serve only to add to her suffering but conceded it was necessary. By all accounts they were extremely sympathetic and there was no suggestion that her husband was anything other than a hero.

"Mrs Goddard," Henry replied, "many people, including me, will feel they could have done more to prevent this tragedy, but life sometimes throws us a set of circumstances that we can do little about. This was a freak accident, a combination of events that could not have been foreseen." He handed her the photograph. "This is Daisy and Mathew."

She studied the image taken at the hospital.

"They are alive and well, Mrs Goddard, because of your husband. Amongst the emotions you feel, you should make plenty of room for a great deal of pride. These two children live because of Donald."

She held the picture, trying not to cry. She handed it back to Henry.

"Please keep it, Mrs Goddard. In a silver frame it may look nice on the mantelpiece." She wept, and Henry held her.

Brad called him on his mobile while he was being driven back to London. Malissa was as well as could be expected but he should speak to the children. He said he would.

Getting out of the car, he told his driver he wouldn't need him anymore that day. He entered the house he hadn't been in for so long. It felt familiar. There was ice in the freezer and he poured himself a drink. He climbed the stairs, bottle in hand, and unlocked the door to the first bedroom.

Discarding his coat and loosening his tie, he picked up the photograph he once kept in his office and flopped into the chair. He sat for some time. He should have been more truthful, but how could he have been?

He closed his eyes and allowed the gathering gloom of the cold winter afternoon to give way to a warm summer evening in Cornwall, more than 20 years ago.

## 51

# CORNWALL, AUGUST 1978

## EMMA AND HENRY

They had been riding with Alice and Charlie who, at lunch, announced they had booked their wedding for March next year. Emma had already been asked to be bridesmaid but whether Henry would be Charlie's Best Man, giving Alice away, or both, was not discussed.

As usual when Henry was home, Alice was staying with Charlie at the farmhouse. Following their customary stroll around the garden, Emma and Henry sat in the lounge. They were talking about the concert in Truro where Emma would shortly be introducing a couple of her own compositions to the public. Henry thought she was a little sad at lunchtime, but this evening whatever may have been on her mind had clearly passed and she was in a particularly playful mood.

"But the one we can play tonight," she said, "is called Henry and Emma, or The Butterfly and The Sage, and it is just for us."

"Hmm. So, I'm still a butterfly, am I? And 'sage', well, that doesn't sound pretty enough for you."

"Henry, you were born a butterfly, and a field full of flowering sage is beautiful. I picture it often and the sage just happens to be one of the flowers that butterflies love."

"It should be the one they love the most."

"A sage is, of course, also very wise, and the butterfly always returns to the flower he loves."

"Collecting wisdom as well as nectar. I like that."

"You can play piano. There are only two parts and you shouldn't make too much of a hash of it."

"So, I shall be accompanying the greatest violinist of our time. Perhaps we could start our own orchestra, Em? Save all those trips to Dubai, and I do look good in a tux."

Emma showed him the chords he would need to play. "It starts *andante,* builds to *adagietto,* before trailing off *tardo.*"

"Quick, quicker, slow. Got that."

"Sort of, though *andante* is more walking pace."

She demonstrated and within a few minutes she was happy that his accompaniment would be satisfactory.

"You are so beautiful, Emily-Jane," he interrupted as she started to count him in.

"You need to concentrate, Henry. I'll count three. You play two bars and I'll come in. Remember to focus."

"But you are the most beautiful piece of sage in the whole world."

How was it he could be a businessman in Dubai last week, but when here with Emma just some infatuated teenager?

"Concentrate," she reiterated, placing the Capella under her chin. He thought she should have a Stradivarius. Maybe Christmas.

Henry played the first two bars then Emma joined in. The music was delicate and light, and he pictured a butterfly flitting back and forth in a colourful meadow.

He knew he didn't quite get his timing right when she quickened the tempo after a couple of minutes, and when her playing superseded his ability to accompany her, he stopped. They both knew she would be playing alone by this time. He sat there, as he had done on a thousand occasions, mesmerised as he listened. His respect and admiration immense; his love for her total.

She would often close her eyes when she played and, when she did, Henry felt comfortable to gaze upon her beauty. He felt the depth of her concentration as the piece became more demanding. Soon the bow was merely a blur as it scurried back and forth over the strings, the fingers of her left hand constantly reforming on the neck of the instrument. Tiny beads of sweat appeared on her brow.

He had heard her play many pieces at this tempo before but never with this intensity. At points it was almost violent, unsettling Henry as he imagined what was going through her mind. A lock of wet hair fell across her forehead causing her to briefly open her eyes. She didn't see him looking at her and it didn't disrupt her.

Suddenly she paused and took a deep breath. Then she resumed.

This time her music was soft and melancholy. She played so slowly at times you wouldn't have been surprised if the next stroke of the string would have been the last. She was telling a story and Henry was trying to understand. Towards the end, her playing was so gentle anyone much further away than him would have found it difficult to hear.

She had taken him on a journey, at times to places that scared him. In the tenderness of the last few bars he floated back to the meadow and back to the sanctuary of the sage. He took her hand as she put down the violin.

"Well. Top of the Pops?" she asked.

He didn't laugh. "Emma, that was the most emotional piece of music I have ever heard you play."

"Emotional?"

"And dramatic."

"Not beautiful?"

"It threw me, Em, it was full of…"

"Emotion?"

"No life. It was like a story, like you were telling a story." His voice had a little concern.

Emma laughed. "That's the violin for you Henry. I do believe you have been moved." She swept the hair from her forehead and blew up her nose. "In that case, I shall assume you liked it. You stayed in a lot longer than I thought you would. You could yet make a pianist. Maybe Happy Birthday or Roll Out The Barrel down the pub, but the man shows a bit of promise."

He knew she was lightning the mood, so he turned to the piano, playing the opening bars of the Blue Danube perfectly.

*"Je suis trés impressionné, Monsieur Ovmeister."*

"Now, Miss Ovmeister, you know speaking French does certain things to me."

*"Is that so, Henry, then maybe I should refrain from doing so?"* she spoke in French, in which she was fluent. He knew a little, and realised she was teasing him. He loved her accent.

*"Mademoiselle tu est belle,"* said Henry, not grammatically correct but she smiled.

She spoke in French again. Several sentences she would have known to have been beyond his comprehension. She delivered them in her sexiest accent. Henry recognised a few words but wondered if she was deliberately disguising their solemn intent. Her words concerned him just as her music had, and at one point he sensed she was desperately holding back a tear. It was probably just his imagination.

He knew she would expect him to attempt a translation. He dismissed the remnants of any negative thoughts.

"Hmm." *Papillon* he recognised, and she mentioned 'children' and 'always' and of course 'love'.

"I wish I taped that," he said. He found her hands. "So, you think I am wonderful and not only can I play the piano so well, but I am the sexiest man you have ever known and like butterflies we should go out into the garden and make love in the glow of the setting sun?"

She smiled.

He continued. "Oh, and I'm the greatest businessman in the world, and your love for me is immeasurable, and our children will be famous musicians. Oh, and always. You will always love me." His hand squeezed hers.

Emma reverted to English. "I'm impressed. You must have been practicing. I shall have to watch what I say in future."

She moved onto his stool and straddled him, draping her arms around his neck. She kissed him passionately. He closed his eyes, succumbing to the very essence of her. She was the other half of his existence and together they were whole.

~

Henry was in the shower when the phone rang. Emma answered. It was Brad. She chatted with him while Henry dried himself.

"Tell him whatever it is I'm busy and we're going sailing tomorrow," Henry said as he entered the bedroom.

Brad ringing at this time of night was rarely good news. There was a problem in Dubai, meaning his time with Emma would have to be cut short. She understood, of course. She always understood, but they would have a good day tomorrow and Henry could be back in a few days.

"I love you, Henry, you do know that," she whispered as they were drifting off to sleep.

He knew she loved him and words weren't necessary, but she rarely said it. It was invariably Henry who would voice his feelings, even their feelings. As they fell asleep, the story of The Butterfly and The Sage played over and over in his head.

They had breakfast on their beach the next morning, before sailing around the bay. After mooring the boat, they waded back to shore. The beach, when they had first bought the house, had not leant itself to bathing and it took many weeks and several tonnes of sand to construct an area that Henry believed safe for Emma.

A rope led from the beach and formed a square, where at high tide the water would be nearly two metres deep where it was secured 50 metres out. When the tide was halfway in, like now, a large rock in one corner became visible and made a useful diving platform. They lay on their towels for 30 minutes before Henry popped back to the house to get a bottle of wine and some sandwiches.

When he returned, Emma was swimming and he called out to her from the top of the steps to let her know he was there. Henry was the greatest advocate of Emma's independence, but even he felt uneasy when she swam alone. As he descended to the beach, he watched her wade in, ignoring the ropes, using memory and the shallowing of the water to guide her. He smiled to himself, but he still worried.

"No messages?" asked Emma.

"From Brad? Afraid not." It would have been wonderful if Brad had phoned to say not to worry about Dubai.

They sought the shade and had lunch.

"You could come with me?" he suggested but knew she would say no, and for perfectly legitimate reasons.

"And listen to you harping on? I don't think so."

He didn't want to leave. He had seen her just half a dozen days in the last few weeks and was progressively thinking it was here, with her, he belonged.

"When I get back, Em, we should go on holiday."

"Bora Bora?"

They had never been to Bora Bora but Henry had seen images some time ago and always said they should go there.

"Yes, Em, with its little straw huts that extend on jetties from the golden sand, and its turquoise waters and *warm* sea. I like your suggestion. I'll book it when I get back."

She smiled and told him that this was her Bora Bora and the little imaginary island just offshore was fine.

"We need a hammock," said Henry. "We should put a hammock up here and sleep on the beach."

After lunch, they lay on the sand. It was a still, warm day, the only sounds the breaking of little waves and the water that tumbled down from the waterfall. They were sleepy after the wine.

"Why don't you play that new piece at the concert?" He was still thinking about last night.

"Because it's ours, Henry. It's my gift to you."

He cuddled her close.

"I wish Aunt Rose could have heard you play like you do now."

"Maybe she can. Maybe she listens to me and watches over you."

"From Heaven you mean?"

"Where else? Do you ever think about dying, Henry? I mean, not in a bad way, but just sometimes wonder what life's about?"

The question surprised him. He felt her breath on his chest.

"I think about living, Em."

"I know that, Henry, but seriously do you ever think?"

They lay there in a moment's silence. Twin souls.

"Em, if I could choose a moment to die and move on to wherever, I'd choose a moment like this."

"Me too, Henry Ovmeister. I love you."

It was the second time in less than 24 hours she had said that. He pulled her as close as he could, and they slept.

The next morning, he kissed her goodbye and insisted she stay in bed. "I called Alice she'll be here soon."

He stopped at the bedroom door and gazed upon her. Her face so naturally beautiful, her eyes so kind but unable to see the admiration in his. He did not want to leave. "I love you too, Emma," were his parting words.

## 52

# LONDON, MAY 2000

## MALISSA AND BRAD

The only time Malissa had seen Henry in the last three months was when she collected the children from Kensington following a weekend visit a month after the fire. He was a hollow man, unable to interact with anyone, including his family, and she was not surprised when he told her he was going to New York.

She missed him terribly, but her yearning was for the man she once knew, not the stranger he had become. She missed their life. A life shattered because of a secret. He was guilty of hiding the fact he had loved another woman before they met. Hardly grounds for divorce, so why did it weigh so heavily? She felt isolated, and confused, betrayed and, too often, so angry.

Was it the deceit? Was it the disbelief that those she had grown to love and respect, and who were supposed to love her, hadn't told her? Because she was unworthy? Or was it simply because her belief she was Henry's greatest love had been crushed? She could not see a solution.

Establishing the dance school in Paris kept Vanessa busy, but she had managed to visit Malissa in the UK three times since the fire and they talked regularly on the phone.

Their great friendship had been tested when Vanessa, seemingly defending Henry, suggested keeping Emma so secret may have been the only way he felt able to deal with losing her. Malissa loved her friend, respected her candour, and valued her counsel, and any misgivings she may have had soon disappeared. Vanessa was a true friend who, as ever, considered all sides of an argument without pre-judgement. They had arranged to spend some time together in Söller when the dance school closed for the holidays next week, and she looked forward to the respite being with Vanessa would offer.

Malissa appreciated that the fire had triggered Henry's subconsciousness and knew she should feel empathy, but she couldn't. Strangely, apart from Vanessa she regarded Brad, who was as guilty as anyone, as the only person who could offer her a glimmer of understanding. She wondered if staying so close to him meant she was never too far away from Henry.

Brad was taking her to lunch and had promised to tell her all he could. She was ready to hear. She wanted to discover the truth, and hoped by confronting the situation head on she could find some comfort.

Last week, she'd visited Bobby Anderson. Straight talking Bobby, who Malissa knew would not skirt any issues.

"Emma was a beautiful woman, Malissa," she'd said. "And, to tell the truth, I've never seen a relationship like it. Young love maybe, maybe cos Hip loved her tenderness. She was a tender lass, angelic even. Maybe he loved being her eyes and it made him feel needed. Not that I'd frigging know. All blokes are arseholes as far I'm concerned."

"Henry, an arsehole?"

"Yeah, you got me there. Listen, girl, Henry is a lot of things and he's a bit different. Knew that the minute I met him. I didn't really socialise with him and Emma, fuck me I don't socialise with anyone on two legs, but when I did see 'em together it was like looking at a feckin' fairy tale. Like you and him. Like you and Hip when you came up here the first time. Every time. No, Hip's no arsehole, all I've ever received from him is love. Fuck, did I say love?" she laughed.

"I don't know why he kept it such a secret."

"Me neither. We love, we live, we die, we move on. But who knows what goes on in that head of his? All I knew was if ever I mentioned her after she died, he'd go berserk. Remember when we had lunch that first time? Well I nearly said it then, nearly slipped out, him and Emma I mean."

Malissa recalled the conversation they had the first day they met. Bobby had said she was the first woman to *see* Henry's horses and she empathised with her dilemma.

"He wouldn't talk about her," Bobby continued. "I didn't see him for a year after she died. When I did, he was changed. Still lovely but just a little less… well, a little less of what he was. Harder, yeah, less dreamy, if you know what I mean. As time went by he got to being a bit more normal. Well, as normal as Hippy could ever be."

"Or his heart," Malissa said thoughtfully. "Who knows what goes on in his heart?"

"I wouldn't know about that. Me an' affairs of the heart, all shit to me. Look, if it was me, well, if I was you, I'd say, fuck it, so he loved someone else and didn't wanna talk about it? Who the 'ell knows why? He loves me now and life's okay. Maybe ban sex for a month and say don't keep any more feckin' secrets yer bastard."

Malissa could imagine that would be exactly what Bobby would say.

"Yeah and a holiday," she added, "somewhere nice, where I can have a go at you every minute of the day and you can't feckin' escape."

"Bora Bora?" Malissa said quietly, wishing it was as simple as that.

"Who?"

"Never mind, private joke."

"Look, I'm not romantic. You see Jack down there?" Malissa saw one of the stable lads leading out a horse. "Half my age, thick as shit, but hung like a feckin' stallion. I'll shag him now and then, but I'm buggered if I want him to buy me dinner."

Bobby let the horse's leg down. "What I saw with Hip and Emma, I saw with you an' him, and I was happy for him. And for you. You are great people who found love and if it's important to yer both then sort it out. Life's too feckin' short."

Malissa smiled. "You ever thought about a career in counselling or the Samaritans, Bobby?"

Bobby smiled back, threw an arm around her and said, "Come on, let's get you a cup of tea."

She liked Bobby immensely. Now there was someone who would never have a secret. She dealt with all challenges that came her way and despite her pessimistic portrayal of life she was one of the most positive people she knew. Brad would tell her more.

La Romantica in Kensington was now called Puccini's. Brad had spoken to Henry a few times and while Malissa sensed he worried about him, she knew he understood her disbelief that he was able to keep his past so secret. He offered no excuse or defence for his friend, nor did he ask that she should try to understand. They were having coffee.

"As I said, this is where I agreed to work for Henry, just after passing my exams. That was 1973. We sat over there. I was going out with a girl called Suzanne and we met here before going to the theatre."

"Had she always been blind, Brad, from birth I mean?" She had no idea why she thought the question relevant and felt like a journalist using her sources to uncover a politician's past misdemeanours rather than a wife struggling to understand someone she had shared intimacy with for 17 years. She thought she should have a notebook.

"No. It happened when she was very young, maybe three or four, I don't know. I think scarlet fever, but don't quote me on that."

Maybe he too regarded this as an interview for a newspaper.

"You were very fond of her."

"I loved them both. Seems another world away now."

"But not for Henry."

He reached across the table and tried to change the subject. "So, you're off to the villa next week?"

"Yes, I'm meeting Ness there. Why don't you come over? Be different without Henry but you can check up on the hotels..." Malissa paused but couldn't stop herself returning to her line of questioning. "How did she die, Brad? I mean, I know you said she drowned, but you said he blamed himself. I'm just trying to understand. I think I need to know Emma. I think if I know Emma, I'll know Henry. It's difficult to put it into words and it may sound selfish, but I hate this bitterness I feel."

"I do understand, Malissa. He wrote to me. A year after Emma. I was concerned for him."

"Because of the letter?"

"Yes, because of his letter and because of the contact I had with him before I got it."

"He does write good letters."

"He writes a lot."

"He does, I've often said he should let me get him published."

"Yes, he's said that to me. I've never understood why he refused."

"Typical Henry."

He smiled and continued. "He wasn't in a good place. I went out to Majorca to fetch him home."

"Söller?"

"Well, in a bar in Palma, but he had found Söller and loved the place. I've no idea why he ended up there, but it was back in Palma I found him and eventually brought him home. Maybe that's why I felt some kind of resistance to the place, Söller I mean. Too close."

Malissa recalled Brad once telling her he had been to Palma. "I've thought about that too. About the parallels. The house in Cornwall, the villa and other things. Did he and Emma ever go there?"

"To Söller? No, I don't think so. I think Söller was just the end of the line. I guess if he wrote earlier or later I would have found him somewhere else, in Timbuktu perhaps. He was running, or searching..."

"Henry Ovmeister, so strong, so authoritative, so charming and respected, such a businessman, yet he runs from what? His feelings?"

"I don't know, Malissa. Maybe we'll find out one day exactly what it is he runs from. Drink your coffee. If you're up for it, there's something I can show you that might help."

~

Malissa and Henry had only once stayed at the house in Notting Hill. She thought she knew why Brad had brought her here.

"We usually use this place for clients or other visiting guests. I've stayed here on many occasions over the years," he said as they entered.

"Yes, my parents have too."

"This was the first London residence Henry bought."

"And he lived here with Emma?"

"Kensington was bought a little while after, but yes, whenever they stayed in London this was their home."

"Maybe that's why he never talked about it."

Brad smiled. "Come in. There's no ghosts."

"It looks lived in, Brad."

"Whether people stay or not it's serviced weekly, just in case."

"Drink?" Brad offered.

"Am I going to need one?"

He took a bottle of wine from the fridge and they went through to the lounge.

"Does Henry play?" she asked, seeing the piano.

"He does a bit. Or at least did."

"Funny, told me he could play Chop Sticks and Happy Birthday at a push. Another lie?"

"Depends on your point of view. He can be a bit of a perfectionist, so asked if he could play the piano he'd compare himself to those he regarded as more competent than him."

"Emma played piano." She had already discovered Emma loved music.

Brad smiled. "She was a very accomplished musician. Violin was her real forte."

"Brad, am I going to admire this woman?"

He pushed a few keys on the keyboard. "Malissa, to me and you, and everybody else, what she was, what they had, was over 20 years ago."

"What did she look like, Brad? Anything like me?"

"You were both extremely good looking. I mean, you still are, but different I guess."

She knew he was out of his comfort zone but appreciated his candour.

"Well, Henry's a good-looking man, so I guess she would have been a bit of a looker."

Images of Emma and Henry had invaded Malissa's mind ever since the fire. She had thought about asking Alice if she had any photographs, but it was obvious Alice wished to avoid any discussions about Emma.

"She was…" Brad searched for a suitable response. "Tender."

"Bobby said angelic."

"An apt description. It's difficult to tell you, Malissa. You had to see it really. They were so young."

She could tell Brad was struggling with his responses. Malissa had no doubt that Henry had loved Emma and no doubt either that Brad loved the two of them, loved their relationship. How could she expect him to tell her that without him believing he'd be hurting her?

"I don't know how I feel about her being blind, Brad. I mean, I try to imagine them together and when I do I just imagine such an overwhelming…" she paused. "Love. He must have really loved her, Brad."

"Because of her blindness?"

"No. I didn't mean that."

"Malissa," he said gently taking her hand. "He loved her because of who she was."

Suddenly, she was unable to hold back her emotion and burst into tears. Brad comforted her.

"I'm sorry," she said, trying to pull herself together.

"I've thought about this a lot, how best to tell you what I know, Malissa. You know I'm not the most feeling man in the world, so I may be a bit clumsy, but I know you want the truth. The last thing I want to do is add to your pain, but I sense you want as much as I can tell you. I might deliver it wrong but…"

"Brad," her sobbing under control. "You totally underestimate yourself. You are the kindest man I know, and I really appreciate you talking to me. You know I need the truth. You know it's only truth I can deal with."

He handed her a handkerchief. His mobile rang. It was Julie. He talked to her for five minutes, explaining where they were and saying he didn't know what time he would be home. He hung up.

"Julie sends her love," he said.

"Sorry. I'm keeping you."

They refilled their glasses and sat down. Brad talked about Emma and her success as a musician. Once or twice he had witnessed them playing together, but that would invariably have been at a party where they would mess around and maybe get a sing-along going.

As Brad talked, Malissa imagined the young love Emma and Henry shared. It was, as Bobby said, like listening to fairy tale. At times she thought she was being told about someone other than her husband and about a relationship that needn't concern her.

"When did she die, Brad? I mean, what date? Can you remember?"

"12th of August," he replied, quickly. It was obviously etched in his memory.

Malissa searched her mind, trying to recall the past 17 years. Surely Henry would have been reflective on the anniversary of her death?

"You said he blamed himself for her death?"

Brad's manner changed. Hitherto he had been painting a picture of two happy youngsters who found something special. "A week before she died, I phoned him. He was on holiday with Emma in Cornwall. To tell the truth, Cornwall was probably becoming their home by then, well, certainly Emma's, but Henry still needed to be in London. It meant they didn't see each other as much as they had done. Anyway, we had a problem and he had to go to Dubai.

"I didn't want to disturb him, I knew he hadn't been with her as much as we would have liked, but back then if he didn't sort it it might never have got sorted. I met with him the night before he flew out. He hoped he could be there and back in two or three days. He said some things that night that he hadn't said before, things about Emma, about him and Emma, and he asked me to keep an eye on her. He was concerned."

"Concerned?"

"I remember him saying she was talking a bit funny and almost being over loving."

Malissa raised her eyebrows. Having listened to the story she would have thought they told each other how they felt every minute of the day.

"Emma was lovely, and you could see she loved Henry. But it was Henry who was the more demonstrative. I could see he was worried, but he had been called away many times like that before. It was just how it was. I said he should phone and put his mind at rest, so he did. He was glad Alice was there and he felt better. Just his imagination, he said."

Brad's face didn't hide the sadness he was recalling.

"Go on," she said softly.

"Well, whatever went on between them before he went to Dubai made him a bit uneasy. When I talked to him I could tell he couldn't wait to get back. She died, drowned, when he was a couple of hours from Heathrow."

"And that's why he blames himself? He thinks if he got back earlier he would have saved her?"

"Sometimes he hated leaving her but Alice was usually with her. Well, not when she drowned. She was still at the house, Charlie's house up on the farm. It wasn't that unusual for Emma to swim on her own..." He took a deep breath. "The coroner's report said she had taken quite a lot of paracetamol and alcohol before she went swimming that morning and Emma had never really drunk much."

Suddenly, some of the pieces fell into place. Henry's silence about Emma, the unbearable guilt he must have carried all these years. "Suicide?" she could barely force the word from her throat.

"An accident officially, but..." He hung his head and for the first time since the fire, Malissa felt Henry's pain.

She took his hand. Brad looked up. "Later, he discovered that she had, for many months, been going to the doctors who confirmed she would never be able to have a child.

"A couple of nights before she died, Alice and her were drinking and talking about their wedding. Alice told Emma she thought she was pregnant so wouldn't have more than one drink. You know Henry, and you can imagine how he would have enthused about having a child with..."

"The woman he loved. It's okay, Brad."

"I remember him shouting, cursing, blaming himself, saying he'd put too much pressure on her by talking about them having children together. 'We were both fucking adopted, Brad', he'd say. 'Why didn't she talk to me?! We could have adopted hundreds of kids.'"

Malissa let go of his hand and took a large sip of wine. "Do you think she did it?"

"Took her own life?"

She nodded.

"I believe she may well have done, though I've never told Henry I do."

"Why?"

"Why haven't I told him?"

"No, I can understand that. Why do you believe she would have taken her own life?"

"Emma was the most self-effacing human being I have ever met. The most outwardly happy, loving person I have or will ever know. Never once did she hide behind her blindness, or give into it, or look for any special treatment.

"You couldn't help but love her for who she was. A month or so before she died, there was a party at Cornwall. We were about to open the New York office, the stud farm was going well and Emma had finally accepted an invitation to play her own music at a concert. In Truro, I think. Things were really good, hence the celebration. We were talking, me and Emma, and at the time it didn't register but when I look back I wonder."

"What did she say?"

"She joked I had fallen under Henry's spell as much as she had, and we laughed about it. Henry was playing the piano, badly she said, and we were in the kitchen. Before we went back in, she held my arm and said whatever happened I must always tell Henry that she loved him. More than life itself. That she knew he has always loved her and that he should always know that he gave her a life she thought she would never have."

He wiped away the appearance of encroaching tears and finished his wine. "When I asked what she was talking about, she just said, 'promise me, Brad, promise me.' I should have picked up on it, Malissa, talked more, thought about what she said the next day, but I didn't.

"God knows how many times over the years I've told Henry that she was happy. Maybe I had drunk too much. I never thought about it until after. Anyway, she chucked Henry off the piano and we all had a sing-song. 'I'm Getting Married in the Morning' and 'New York, New York'. Funny the things you remember. As strange as it may sound, if you knew her I know you would have loved her too."

She had been listening to a love story. A tragic one. "Thank you," she whispered touching his hand.

They sat quietly for a few minutes. It was getting dark. "Do you have any pictures of her?" she asked.

He smiled as if he knew the question would be coming. He went to the kitchen, took a bunch of keys from the drawer and they went upstairs. They stopped at the first door. He searched for the right key.

"It's not the storeroom is it, Brad?" Malissa recalled the time when she asked Henry why the door was locked.

She felt she was in a film and that behind the door there'd be a room untouched since somebody's death. A shrine where everything had been left as it was, like some sacred memorial. That feeling of betrayal began to rise in her and she didn't like it. Brad opened the door.

It was a bedroom but there was no bed. There was an armchair, a couple of brooms and a hoover, some tins of paint and several card-board boxes on the floor. An antique dresser which would have looked more at home in a farmhouse kitchen stretched across one wall and four violin cases, lent against another.

Malissa was relieved the contents were not as chilling as she expected. On the dresser were two framed photographs. She approached, knowing they would be of Emma, or of Emma and

Henry. She picked up the largest one and immediately thought she knew the woman who stared back at her.

She was naturally beautiful. If she was wearing makeup it was difficult to detect. She was looking slightly right rather than full on, her grey-green eyes exuding uncanny compassion and looking directly at the camera. Her cheeks were slightly flushed with one or two moles, her nose perfect. Her auburn hair wasn't brushed and cascaded to her shoulders, most behind but some in front of her ears, just touching her cheek and framing a face whose beauty was matched only by the kindness it promised.

She handed the photograph to Brad and searched for words.

"How don't those eyes see?" he said, interpreting her thoughts.

"She was beautiful, Brad."

She examined the other photograph, again of Emma. She walked around the room trailing her hand across the violin cases. The dresser drawers were locked but the stack of cardboard boxes on the floor unsealed. She drew out a photo album and flicked through the images. When she turned to Brad she had tears in her eyes.

"Maybe you'll find some answers in here," he said.

"It's funny. I wanted to know. I'm here where Emma must have stood a hundred times. In those cases, the instruments she serenaded Henry with. In these photographs, not only her beauty but a kindness I can only imagine. I feel their love, Brad, and I don't know how I should feel about that. I feel I'm prying, touching something I've no right to touch, something beyond me, beyond my understanding and I've no idea how I should feel."

For the second time she found herself sobbing gently into his chest. Her anger had subsided, displaced by sadness and a strange empathy. She didn't doubt Henry loved this woman and didn't doubt he tried to love her. But she or no one else could ever replace Emma.

"He loves you, Malissa."

She tried to smile.

"I can't say he didn't love Emma, and I think you know that, but I know he loves you. Maybe we should go now. You can have these." He handed her the keys.

She looked at them. "Maybe Henry was right. Maybe some things are perhaps best left in the past."

They left the bedroom. She locked the door. "You know, Brad. The more I discover, the less I realise I know. It's like I'm looking at someone else, someone other than Henry."

"It was a long time ago."

"Henry creates many things and brings so much to people. It's almost as if he creates his own world. In business too. You and I know he's not motivated by money and it's difficult to imagine what he would actually regard as a success. It's like he creates this fantasy and invites everybody in and they love it. I've seen Henry's softness and Emma just reflects it, like she represented his idea of how the world should be."

"I sort of get where you're going."

"Maybe he creates and believes and sees the good and blitzes anything that he thinks might stand in the way of that. Like life, like reality. Maybe it's reality that he fears, maybe it's reality he runs from."

Brad smiled. "He's a complicated man, Malissa. Come on, let's go home."

He would soon be with Julie and she back home with her children. Maybe she would always doubt she was Henry's greatest love, but she would never doubt his ability to love. But, as Bobby Anderson had said, maybe his love would be more at home in a fairy tale.

## 53

# NEW YORK, AUGUST 2000

## HENRY

This city, this paragon of hustle and bustle where, during the day, he could lose himself amongst the suits and ties of businesspeople could, at night, be the loneliest place on the planet. He didn't know why he'd decided to come to New York. He didn't know why he thought he might find answers here. In truth, he didn't even know what questions he had.

He only knew he was running. Running from memories. His head spun and his heart ached for a life he once had. A life shared with Emma or a life shared with Malissa. He didn't, however, deserve either.

He thought work might help. He had visited the New York office, a prestigious building which epitomised the success of his company, and where he was welcomed like royalty. But it offered no solace. He had, like Brad suggested, seen two psychiatrists, the most expensive ones in Manhattan, but they were strangers. They would never understand and so he decided his money would be better spent in the bars where he could buy the medicine that did, at first, help him sleep at night.

He couldn't talk to anyone, certainly not Malissa who he had deceived so badly, and he couldn't talk to Brad. How could he? Brad had seen him like this before and while Henry knew he would offer his support unconditionally, Henry had no intention of imposing on him this time. He knew he had to sort this out himself.

The bottle had proved only a temporary cure and no longer induced sleep, making his nightly conversations with Emma more confusing. He was alone in a city of more than a million people and like the orphan he was, had no mother to offer him comfort.

Mike's Bar wasn't open during the day and as he descended the stairs he realised he no longer looked around wondering whether anyone in his employ was down there. He took up his familiar position at the bar. Arnie – was that his real name? – was telling jokes on the stage. After Arnie it'd be Bill or Fred (their names didn't matter), who would take over, telling jokes or stories, seemingly unconcerned whether anybody listened.

A woman might take up the mic and sing a love song with a sad ending, and last week someone read a poem they had written. Occasionally, Henry witnessed a performance that would not have been out of a place on one of those talent shows on TV, but the performers here had no chance of being discovered. In another time, Henry may have paid more attention, possibly even recognising a talent and revelling in the chance to bring it to the attention of the outside world.

He was at home in this place. Dressed down and in disguise he was one of them. He had several days' stubble which suited the place even better. Perhaps he should grow a full beard? Alcohol was cheap and, like most of the clientele, he had developed a taste for bourbon.

"You alright, John?" It was Ed. Henry was John down here. He knew nothing about Ed, other than he drank as many pints as he could before he switched to bourbon.

"Yeah, good Ed. You?"

"Yeah, good."

It was his stock answer and Henry wondered what represented a bad day for him. Ed bought a drink and returned to his table. People didn't buy rounds down here. He liked that; it epitomised the separation from life he felt.

He was alone. Maybe he was alone when he was a baby, when he was put on a boat in Hamburg, destination unknown. If Aunt Rose hadn't come into his life would he be Ed? Would he like to have been Ed?

He was a successful business and family man who had enjoyed a wonderful life and who was admired by many. He had loved. He had loved so very deeply, and he had lost. But just who was Henry Ovmeister? He ordered another drink, fishing for change in his pocket. He hoped he had removed the $100-dollar bills from his wallet should he need to call on the tens in there when he exhausted his supply of coins.

He was glad he found this place. It was the 14th August, two days after the anniversary of Emma's death, but this year it had little impact. He had been talking to her every day since the fire.

He looked around. Maybe 30 people, all with a story to tell. He wondered if there was another chief executive of a multimillion-dollar company in the room. He doubted it. Were there any other orphans? That seemed more likely. He thought about the time he first discovered the identity of his own mother. That day in September when he called on his best friend's father to take custody of the papers Aunt Rose had set aside for him. Twenty-two years ago, but today, despite the fog of the alcohol, he remembered it like yesterday.

"This is all the information you asked for, Henry," Charles said, handing him a wad of files. "I'm not sure of the contents of these envelopes," he handed them to him separately, "but if there is anything you believe I may be able to elaborate on, please don't hesitate to come and see me."

"And you've set up the trust?"

"Of course."

"Thank you."

"Henry…" Charles called after him as he went to leave. "You are a good man and your aunt would be so proud of you."

He knew Charles wanted to say sorry about Emma. He knew he wanted to help. But Charles Carmichael's belief that he was worthy of such consideration was misplaced.

In his flat he had sat on the bed he and Emma shared. The papers concerning the disbursement of the remainder of Aunt Rose's finances were in nothing but the best of order and he had no need to check them.

It was the letters he wanted to see – the one's his aunt had left him. He held the sealed envelope marked *Read This First* for many minutes before carefully opening it, and he held the papers within for several more before unfolding them.

*"Dearest Henry,*

*Dearest, dearest Henry. I would hope you are reading this letter when you are as old as me and from a happy place, but maybe you are not and if not I can but guess the circumstances that have led you here.*

*I've told you many times about my life in Germany and the family fortune. You know of my great love for Arthur and the loss I felt following his death. You know I fled my homeland to take up residence in England."*

He skipped the rest of the page and the next, he could read them later… Who was his mother? Who was his father?

*"Your Mother was a beautiful woman,"* he read. "Was" – that means she's dead. He skipped a bit more.

*"Her name was Delores. I believe that was her correct name, but the surname she used was Delahay and whilst I've no reason to believe this was incorrect, it was not uncommon for those in the resistance to use false names, or indeed several names, such were the times. I believe she was born in France..."*

He skipped more, not sure what he sought.

*"There is a letter from your Mother that I have kept which will explain more, in her words, about how you came to be with me..."*

*"Your father was a German officer..."*

The last paragraph.

*"Henry, like so many, I owe my life to your Mother. Part of you will remember her and her wonderful qualities will always be with you. It would have broken her heart to have had to let you go. You were conceived from a love in loveless time and out of two people who should have been enemies but found love with one another. I have tried to raise you as your mother would have done and I'm so very proud to have counted you as my own son."*

"Hello, handsome..." He was brought back to the present by a woman half his age. "Hello..." she repeated.

She was chewing gum. He wondered if she had come here to drink, sing, or purely on business. "You wanna buy me a drink?" she said when she thought she had gained his attention.

"Sure," said Henry, and she ordered a large bourbon.

"So, what brings you here?"

"I guess the same reason as so many."

"Ah, an Englishman. An Englishman in New York. How romantic."

Henry offered a wry smile, unsure if he wanted to continue the conversation.

"I'm Cindy," she said, offering her hand.

Henry didn't for one moment believe her name was Cindy, but it suited her and it didn't matter.

"John," he lied.

There was a ripple of laughter from the tables, which pleased the man on stage who was probably surprised that anyone was listening.

"So, what does bring you here?" Cindy continued. "I mean, I've never seen you here, not that I come here that often, but you don't seem the usual type. And I don't even mean cos you're English."

Henry had never held a conversation greater than an exchange of pleasantries in this bar before and would have to be rude to end this one. He saw no harm in talking. She was pretty and in her twenties. Had fate dealt her a different hand he could imagine her having a half decent job, engaged to a respectable fellow, looking forward to getting married and being at home preparing for Thanksgiving. Instead, she was here. He was judging but suspected she was on a soliciting mission.

"I come here from time to time," he said. "And you? What brings you here?"

"You know, John, something tells me you already know that." She had a nice smile.

Whether she finished her drink and said 'thank you' or carried on talking to him, he didn't really mind, but he thought he should set the record straight.

"It's the sort of place you can have a drink without anybody bothering you." It was a little harsh.

"And I'm bothering you?" It was a statement as opposed to a question. "Well, if you want to be alone, that's fine, but I'm off duty, so to speak, and something tells me you're not looking for what I may have been offering anyway."

He smiled. He liked her directness. He expected her to go but she didn't. "So, John. What does bring you here?"

It was the third time she had asked. Harmless conversation. Ships that pass in the night and so on. She was a survivor and not unintelligent. He wondered if his own mother would have been similar, needing to survive on her wits and her ability to be whoever she needed to be. He wondered fleetingly whether he'd had to too. There was something about her and he realised he would have been disappointed had she left.

"That's a very good question and one to which I am not entirely convinced I have the answer." He thought he might be speaking a little too well for the establishment, more Henry than John.

"Well, is it wife trouble? Work? I reckon you have a decent job. Is it being alone in a big city?"

Henry thought. The recollections of Aunt Rose's letters still fresh in his mind. "You want my life story, Cindy?"

"Be more interesting than mine."

"I wonder if it would?"

"I think you could tell me mine and you'd know you'd be right. Go on, I'm a good listener and you never know."

He smiled and ordered two more drinks. He was pleased he had removed the hundreds from his wallet.

"I guess I'm here because I'm thinking. Not least of thinking how I got here."

"Yellow cab?" she smiled. He warmed to her.

"Quite."

"Let me tell you your story John, and you see if I'm right: Born in England. Obviously. Parents rich. Had all the privileges of education, married a woman you didn't love, rebelled, spent a load of money, got disowned, cut out of the will and came down here to drink yourself silly."

It was a shot in the dark, but it made Henry laugh, something he couldn't recall having done for several months.

"That's not a bad guess." he said

"Completely wrong?"

He smiled.

"And what's your story, Cindy?"

"You think that suits me, John? Cindy, I mean."

"As a pseudonym, yes."

"Well, mine's the usual. Abandoned as a child, brought up by whoever in the Bronx, no family…"

"You're an orphan?" Henry interrupted

"Well, I do know my mother now, not that I'd ever call her Mom. And my dad? Could be any one of three or four apparently…"

He interrupted her again. "You hungry?"

"John, I'm always hungry."

"And you're off duty?"

"Well, that depends. I can always be on duty."

"Hmm," he heard himself say and thought about Malissa. "I'd like you to be off duty and eat with me."

"Sounds like on duty to me," she smiled, but seemed to know he wasn't proposing the usual.

They left Mike's and hailed a cab.

"I'm not familiar with the restaurants around here," he said as he opened the door for her. It was 1:30am.

Cindy laughed. "You wanna eat?"

"Of course."

"There's a place I know…" and she gave the driver the details.

They drove for less than five minutes and were soon sitting in a booth of a restaurant with perhaps half a dozen other customers.

They ordered coffee and Cindy studied the menu, ordering for them both when the waitress returned with their drinks.

"I'm an orphan too," Henry announced, not entirely sure why he was telling her.

"Shit, no rich parents, never mind."

"My mother was," he hesitated., "she was a resistance fighter in the Second World War. I never knew her."

"Sounds fascinating. Except you must be older than I thought."

"I was brought up by an aunt in England. A lovely, kind woman."

"But not your mom." Her words were matter of fact, no judgement, no nothing, but they carried utter empathy.

"No," he said softly. "She wasn't my mother."

"Well, John, that's probably why you were at Mike's. People with real mothers, or ones that give a damn, rare as rocking horse shit down there. And as for fathers, well, they're probably non-existent. They just do the deed and piss off."

She was obviously recalling her own situation.

"My mother cared," he said, almost protesting.

She looked at him and for a second, he saw concern in her eyes. They sat quietly for a moment, Henry wondering why on earth he had invited this woman to have dinner with him.

"You're very pretty," he said eventually.

"No need for that, John. Nice, but no need."

"I'm sorry, I didn't mean anything by that other than you are a very pretty woman."

"Helps in my business. Why you ask me here, John?"

He paused. "Do you know I've no idea."

"Maybe you wanted to tell me your life story after all? I get the feeling you know you don't belong here. And certainly not in Mike's."

Another pause while two steaks were delivered to the table.

"When I was young," Henry continued, "I fell in love."

"Well, that can happen."

"When I say, 'in love', this girl, Emma, was my life."

"That's deep."

"Everything I did, I realise I did it for me and Emma, even though I might not have known it at the time. She was my…" He paused. "Motivation. My…"

"Reason?" Cindy interrupted, "reason to live?"

It was a statement from the most unexpected source, but it resonated with Henry.

"She died. Many years ago, and something of me died with her."

"John," she said. "While I'm quite happy to negotiate the price of a blow job, when it comes to counselling, well I know some people who pay 50 an hour."

She saw the remark may have been insensitive and reached across the table, clasping his wrist and smiling. "I'm only joking, sorry. I haven't had steak in ages and was getting carried away. Tell me. I won't have any answers but sometimes when someone you don't know listens, it's like telling yourself and you can find your own."

This woman was half his age but possibly knew more about people, about people largely outside Henry's life, than he could ever do. He wanted to talk to her.

"I loved Emma," he continued, "and everything was wonderful. Well as far as I could see it was. When she died, I thought I would never be happy again. Certainly not love again."

"But then you met someone else?"

"Yes, I did, and we found love too. A great love. Different to me and Emma but…"

She waited.

"But…" he repeated.

"But what? You loved one girl, she died, and you found another one? That's very fortunate, you should be grateful. Not many people find one love let alone two."

Henry smiled, realising the situation in which he'd found himself was slightly absurd: a millionaire and a prostitute, two orphans given completely contrasting opportunities, talking about life. Cindy had never been given a chance and went about her business with no great expectations. Steak and chips might even be the highlight of her week and Henry suddenly felt ungrateful and loathed his own self-pity.

"And you, Cindy? Have you ever had love?"

She laughed. "Once, when I was 13, I thought this boy loved me, but no, John, I can't say I've ever found love. Not like you tell it."

"That's sad." He paused, wondering why he felt a sudden compulsion to help. "Everyone should know love. Love is the only thing worthwhile. We all show it in different ways, but maybe understand it differently too."

"Well, there's survival too. Great steak. You should eat, not talk."

"Do you see your parents?" he asked.

"My Mom was, well, *is,* a resistance fighter of a different sort. I see her, she lives in Queens with the most obnoxious man you'd ever meet. She's not happy but survives. Tracked her down when I was 16. She had me when she was 15. We get on okay."

"Who brought you up?"

"The establishment. Hey, you're deep for a Mike's Bar junkie."

"And what do you want from life?" The waitress appeared with her dessert.

She looked at him as if the question was completely extraneous. "John. What I want right now is this knickerbocker glory. I'll worry about life tomorrow." He knew she wouldn't.

"So, why do you go to Mike's?" she asked taking a spoonful of the ice cream.

"Because I'm an orphan?" he ventured.

"Nope, don't buy that. You should have had one. Here, taste." She offered him a spoonful of the dessert. He liked her.

"So, what about this second love of yours?" Cindy didn't let eating get in the way of conversation. "Is she your wife? Do you still love her?"

"Yes, she is my wife. We haven't seen each other for a while and, yes, I love her."

"And she loves you?"

He realised he didn't have the answer to that question. "I never told her about Emma."

"And she got jealous? I assume she found out. But you said Emma died. That's the trouble sometimes, you romantics can jump from one relationship to another without breathing. My guess is you were still in love with Emma and it was too soon."

"I met her five years after Emma."

Cindy had finished her dessert. "John, I'm no counsellor and to be honest I can't really see your issue - unless your wife's a jealous bitch and doesn't think you should have had a past?"

"I kept it secret."

"Secret?"

"The depth of my feelings for Emma. Nobody was allowed to talk about it."

She was confused, and he couldn't blame her, and she was certainly in no position to provide answers or a cure to the sadness he felt. And how could he expect her to understand when, in her world, his issues would seem so trivial?

"I'm good at whispering in ears, John, and making men feel they're Casanova. Sometimes I don't mind what I do cos it brings a little bit of joy into a man's life. But if I had a great love, and then another one, I'd sing it from the roof tops and be happy to share it. Not sure I'd want to keep it secret. Unless he was married of course, but then I've never had that kind of love, so what do I know?"

"I guess I sang to myself," he muttered thoughtfully. "Selfish when you think about it..." and as the words left his lips he wondered if he had discovered the beginnings of the answers he sought.

It was 3:30am when Henry said they should be going. They shared a taxi, dropping her off first.

As Cindy approached her front door and reached in her jacket pocket for her house key, she retrieved a wad of bank notes folded under a plastic paper clip. Each was a hundred bill, and there were more than ten of them.

## 54

# NEW YORK, NOVEMBER 2000

## BRAD VISITS HENRY

Cindy had said she was not a regular at Mike's so Henry shouldn't have been surprised he hadn't seen her there since they met in the summer. Ships in the night, he reminded himself. Mike had, however, given him the note she left for him a few days after their encounter.

*Dear John,*

*I'm not sure whether you'll get this note. Part of me hopes not because it means you haven't come here again. You and Emma had a love in another time and it must have been wonderful. Your wife loves you now and I hope you find a way to live that love once more. Park your love for Emma and be happy about it and move on. You have a lot to offer this world.*

*I took my Mom to O'Neill's last night and she had two knickerbocker glories. You should have one some time.*

*Thank you, Henry. (The paper clip.)*

*Thank you xx*

*Rachel aka Cindy xxx*

He continued to frequent Mike's Bar two or three nights a week. One evening he told Mike he had won big on the horses in England

and would like to buy everybody a drink. Since then he noticed a subtle change and one or two people bought a few drinks rather than just their own. He knew many names, but little about the life that accompanied them. There was a strange sense of community.

Last month he played the piano and was pleasantly surprised when several of the customers gathered round and sang a couple of old songs. He finished the session with three minutes of the Blue Danube. Any mistakes would have only been noticed by an accomplished musician and he received a generous round of applause. Maybe one day he would recite one of the poems he had written about the place. He had discovered no other orphans and was certain no other millionaires went there.

There was a children's home in Queens and two in the Bronx, located in neighbourhoods which had taken some time to lose their threat. Several times he thought about calling on them to see if he could help. He spent most days wandering the streets and the nights either alone in his Madison Avenue apartment or at Mike's. He no longer visited the Ovmeister–Carmichael offices on 5th.

The fire at Ashbourne House had thrown him back to a past life from which he couldn't escape, and he carried Emma with him always. Sometimes the image of Malissa eclipsed her memory and caused him great confusion and guilt, and he would have to reassure Emma that his love for her would never die.

He still talked to her most nights and lay awake awaiting her answers, but his questions just hung in the dark. He thought it positive he no longer drank during the daytime and, although each day passed slowly, he considered time had flown by when he thought about how long he had been away from his family. He was a successful and respected man, intelligent and personable, but every day he wondered if people knew who he really was. He wondered if he knew.

He had spoken to Malissa and the children when he felt able but thought he was imposing. He had written to her several times, hoping she was okay, and in each letter repeated his apologies for not being more forthcoming about Emma. He understood if she wanted a divorce.

She'd reply saying she was fine and update him on their children's welfare. He kept her letters and often re-read them looking for clues that might tell him she'd forgiven him. He realised all he wanted to read was, *I love you, Henry.*

He talked to Brad but couldn't quite tell him his deepest fears. Not this time. He was visiting today and had come straight to the apartment from their New York office. They had been talking for some time.

"And you're looking a bit thin," Brad said.

"You think I'm working out too much?"

"And I remember when you last grew a beard."

Brad was referring to the time he came out to Palma, finding Henry slumped across a table in a nightclub surrounded by champagne and scantily clad women and their boyfriends. Then, he was mourning the loss of Emma. This time, Henry had little idea of exactly what is was, he was trying to come to terms with.

"I think it suits me," he replied, again trying to steer the discussion away from his well-being.

Brad brought the subject back to the psychiatrist Henry had told him he'd been seeing and reminded him, as he had done on so many previous occasions, that he wasn't responsible for Emma's death. Henry appreciated his friend was concerned so repeated that "taking time out and coming to terms with his adoption" was the advice he was paying a fortune for. "It's not just Emma, Brad," he said.

"You talked to Malissa this week?" Brad asked.

"Yeah, I think she's okay."

"She said she asked if you were coming back. To see the children."

"I know I should, Brad. And I will. Of course, I will."

"You've got to face this Henry."

"I know. How are they?"

"Can't you talk to her? About Emma."

His eyes told him he couldn't.

"Henry, do you want her to hate you? Is that it? Is that the punishment you need?"

Henry remained silent.

"Emma's gone Henry. She went 20 years ago. You can't blame yourself and I'm sure if you spoke to Malissa you could..."

"Forget her?" he exclaimed, standing and walking away. "I'm trying. I really am."

They looked at each other for a few moments. Henry hoped he would drop the subject and sensed Brad knew that too. He sat back down.

Brad broke the silence. "The network goes live next week."

Henry picked up his glass. "To Ovmeister–Carmichael," he proposed, as though he was toasting a dead friend.

"I still think Carmichael–Ovmeister would have sounded better."

Henry knew Brad was heeding his wish to change the subject and to lighten the situation, but he also appreciated how much of a better man than he his friend was. Instead of his usual retort he looked at him earnestly.

"The company would not have been born without the greatest brain I have ever had the privilege to have known. And the greatest friend. I agree. We should change it."

"Well, I'm glad you recognise that, Henry. Great idea. But that's one hell of a lot of paperwork, not to mention the expense. I'll leave it in your capable hands."

Henry thought Brad should have sounded surprised, even delighted by his announcement and greeted it with a degree of enthusiasm, but Brad showed little reaction and placed his briefcase on the table.

"I got some information," he said. "It's not complete, and they tell me there's more to come." Brad retrieved a large envelope from the case and placed it in front of Henry.

Henry picked it up. On it was typed *Ms Delores Delahay,* and he wondered what comfort, if any, he would find inside. He looked at it for a few seconds before placing it back down on the table. "Thank you," he said, pondering whether he would ever have been able to run a business without him. "Bedtime reading, I think. Now, my friend. I hope you've brought some clothes without a Saville Row label cos there's a place I'd like to take you. Have you tried bourbon?"

Brad looked at him quizzically.

Henry smiled. "Come on, get changed. You'll love it."

Henry cleared the glasses and put the envelope away. It had been sometime since he had seen Brad and he desperately wanted to share an enjoyable evening with him. He knew he wouldn't immediately take to Mike's, but it would be an experience and they could always adjourn to one of the restaurants nearby if he thought it too terrible. It was good to see his friend and he felt his mood lightening.

"Are you paying rent to the company for this gaff?" Brad shouted from the bedroom. "If not, you should be. In fact, it should be deducted from your wages. Incidentally, I wanted to talk to you about that. It does appear you are taking rather an inordinate amount of holiday."

Henry smiled to himself, wishing Brad wasn't going home tomorrow and walked across to the bedroom. He peered in. "May I remind my dear friend, you are employed by Ovmeister–Carmichael, not Carmichael–Ovmeister. And I strongly suggest you remember that."

# 55

## NEW YORK, DECEMBER 2000

### HENRY

After Emma's death in 1978, Henry took the first tentative steps on the road to discovering his mother. He quickly abandoned the project, however, failing to see what comfort it would bring. But the fire had triggered memories and, unable to ignore the calling this time, he had appointed a specialist to find out as much as possible about the woman he knew as Delores Delahay.

The documents Brad had brought confirmed she was indeed part of the Resistance in Germany and there were several testaments to her bravery and selflessness in Occupied Europe. It was almost certain she was born Francesca De Hay in Paris, the only child of a baker and his wife who lost their lives when France was invaded. The identity of his father would for the time being remain a mystery.

She most likely died in a spate of vengeance killings in East Berlin in the winter of 1952, about the same time Aunt Rose was rescuing Henry from the London orphanage. No death certificate existed, nor did any official record of Henry's birth in Germany.

He peered out of his apartment window. It was snowing and the street was busy with early evening shoppers. Fathers with young children were carrying Christmas Trees. Why was he here? Why wasn't he at home with *his* children? Had he abandoned them like his mother had him?

He studied the letter from Aunt Rose like he had studied it so many times before. It was the only thing he possessed that leant legitimacy to his existence. He wanted to believe the image he held in his heart; that image of his mother formed out of a yearning and augmented by words written so long ago.

When he was young, he had Aunt Rose and Emma and didn't need his mother, and with Malissa he felt he belonged. Now he felt a void and that emptiness could surely be filled if he could know his mother.

He pictured himself as a baby, cradled in her arms, being showered with affection, and wondered just what drove her to abandon him. He needed to believe he was loved, loved by her. But what did he know of love?

He felt the familiar knots in the pit of his stomach tighten as the doubts and regrets that haunted him, and the questions he couldn't answer, took hold. Why had he hidden Emma? Why was it so important that he, and he alone, could wallow in her death? Was Malissa right? Was she, like she had said to Brad, just a replacement, part of the 'Repair Henry Ovmeister Brigade'?

Emma's blindness. Malissa's fragility. Henry's instinct to protect, to nurture, to find joy in knowing his existence was worthwhile, was that love or just some self-centred gratification? No one questioned his ability to love so why did he? Did Emma question it? He would never have hurt her, never, but he had, and he would never forgive himself.

In loving another, Henry had betrayed her. In keeping Emma a secret, he had betrayed Malissa. No, he didn't know love. Love doesn't leave such devastation in its wake. *Thank God Malissa is strong.*

He hated where he was going. He was spiralling down, this time deeper than he had 22 years ago. This time he was questioning his very nature and he felt alone. So very alone and despised by those he loved.

He needed confirmation that he was a good man and could think of no source to get it. He needed answers, he needed reassurance. He needed to be the butterfly returning to the sage. He needed Emma to tell him she didn't flee this world because of him. He needed Malissa to say she understood and that she still loved him.

He needed, he needed, he needed. How fucking selfish! Did people know how selfish he was? Emma – a love so young, so pure, so innocent, so tragic. Malissa – a love so wonderful, so strong, and so right. How could he, who could not love, have deserved the love of two of the most beautiful people he had ever known?

He wanted to be six months old and with his mother. To be sleeping in her arms and protected from the harshness and reality of this world. And from himself.

# 56

## NOTTING HILL, DECEMBER 2000

### MALISSA

The room was much as Malissa had found it when she came here with Brad. She sat on the chair, holding the photograph and feeling her heart pumping in her chest. The cardboard boxes contained pictures of Emma and Henry from a life long ago. There would be documents and letters and God knows what else. She needed to be calm.

She still adored the man who proposed to her in a coffee shop in Dubai but that man, the man no other could ever replace, was dead. Her anger had dissipated and been replaced by a void. Seventeen years they were together, seventeen wonderful years, but those years seemed to belong to another existence, to a dream.

She had not seen Henry for nearly ten months. It was as if time was standing still, waiting for something to happen. But what, what could happen to either end their relationship or bring them back together?

When Brad had given her the keys she imagined she would have returned much sooner but had put it off. Perhaps she needed to be sure she was ready. She hoped she was.

She opened one of the violin cases and took out the instrument.

She rested it under her chin and drew the bow across the strings. It screeched. She was touching what Emma had touched and realised it was once in the hands of someone so much more proficient than her. She shuddered when she considered the same scenario could have applied to the handling of her husband.

She sifted through the boxes. Younger versions of the people she had grown to love were dotted amongst the photographs in the albums. The kindly old woman must have been Aunt Rose and she could make educated guesses about the identity of many others.

She recognised places she had been with Henry and had to supress the intermittent flare of resentment that ran through her. She found herself pausing longer and longer to look at the images of Emma and Henry. By the time she had closed the album she saw them in another time, as two young people who shared love, and her resentment abated.

She found poems, many of which were about Emma, or Emma and Henry, or just love. Some were truly beautiful and she tried to shut out the image of him reading them to her. It was impossible for Malissa to know exactly how she felt and what she believed.

In one of the boxes there was music. Sheets of it. Some handwritten, some typed. Brad said Emma had composed music and maybe these were her compositions. To Malissa they were dots and shapes on a grid. She felt guilty taking some and putting them in her handbag. She would return them but wanted to hear the music they represented. Maybe Lewis could bring them to life.

She picked up a thicker pad of type. The title on the first page read 'Aunt Rose and Arthur'. She read a little and thought she had read something like it before.

As she read she felt a sickness welling in her stomach. Pieces locked into place like a jigsaw and she realised just where she had read this before. With an audible gasp, she stopped reading and, as if she had picked up a hot coal, suddenly threw the wad of paper to the other side of the room. 'Aunt Rose and Arthur' was a book that she had published many years ago under the title of 'An English Rose', written by the non-existent Jack Dexter. It was the book that launched her career at Fenner's. Anger and embarrassment surged through her veins. Who the fuck did he think he was? Who was Henry Ovmeister? Who had she been living with these past 17 years?

57

## CHRISTMAS DAY, NEW YORK, 2000

### HENRY

Henry could hardly blame Brad for allowing Malissa access to his past life with Emma. He should have done that himself, years ago. The possibility of being with his family at Christmas had been crushed because of a book he wrote. Because of another secret he thought he needed to keep.

Malissa's discovery of the Arthur and Rose story had been the final nail in the coffin. He would not fight her request for a divorce, neither would he appoint a lawyer to do anything other than draw up the papers, yielding to whatever requests she made.

He had been invited to spend Christmas with both Brad and Alice, but he assured them he was okay. He'd be happy to spend it in New York with friends.

He walked the deserted snow-covered streets of Manhattan. He thought about the first Christmas he'd spent without Emma and the darkness of that day and it scared him. He walked aimlessly, like his life. He had run out of cigarettes by the time he reached Brooklyn Bridge. His bottle of bourbon was empty too.

He was cold, but it didn't matter. He stopped halfway along the bridge, wondering just how many had made this journey before.

There was no one about. He looked through the grating and focussed on the cold, grey water below.

"Emmaaaaa," he hollered, his voice as alone as the grey dank day. "Emma," he called again, this time with so much more desperation. "Why? Why, Emma?" He repeated her name until it was merely a whimper and tears rolled down his cheeks.

He had shed tears before, he had wept, but not like this; this was uncontrollable. He was sobbing and finding it difficult to breathe, and with each fraught intake of freezing air a memory appeared, a memory of her laughing, of dancing, of playing the violin. Memories of her beautiful face and the touch of her lips.

Then the vision of her lying face down in the water, motionless, her spark extinguished. "I'm so sorry, Emma!" he shouted into the emptiness. "I'm so sorry..." his words stretched from the bridge and splintered into nothing.

He shouted her name, he called for her, but she didn't answer. He was reliving the nightmare of 22 years ago but this time he was calling to her, calling to the other half of himself that he lost so long ago.

Exhausted, he stopped, his sobbing now no more than a series of snivels. He closed his eyes and saw her face. The cold disappeared as he held her in his arms on a little beach in Cornwall, her head on his chest, the salted scent of her hair filling his nostrils. Where was she? He needed her. Surely, after so long, she could forgive him. He never meant to hurt her. He only wanted to protect her, to love her, to make her happy. Why did she leave him?

"Have you ever thought about dying, Henry?" Her soft voice filled his spinning head. This time he replied, "Yes, Em. Yes, I have thought about that," and the solution to his misery became clear.

The icy wind stung his face like the summer sun and it felt so good. Soon he would be with her. Soon like Emma, he'd feel the sweet saltwater filling his lungs, stifling his ability to take in the air that anchored him to this world; a world in which she no longer existed.

He put a foot on the rail of the barrier and stretched up, his hands trying to get a grip on the mesh that imprisoned him. His coat restricted his reach. Stepping back down, he searched for the buttons of his cashmere. A distant chime encroached upon the noise in his head and he became aware of a humming over his heart.

His numb fingers detected a vibration and as the chimes collected into a sound he recognised, he reached inside his pocket. He pushed the green button and held the phone to his ear. "Happy Christmas, Daddy!" It was Lewis. He dropped the phone, which bounced, before tumbling into the dark water. He fell to his knees. He was still alive. And his son loved him.

# 58

# DELAHAY HOUSE, MARCH 2001

## MALISSA DIVORCES HENRY

Malissa wondered what she would ever do without Vanessa. Over the last year their friendship had become even deeper. She was possibly the person she trusted most in the world and was comfortable to share her every thought and feeling. Although they had often disagreed about Henry, Malissa always felt her friend was helping her to explore her own emotions and open her mind to possibilities she may have otherwise never considered.

Vanessa had endured a difficult upbringing, far removed from Malissa's suburban, middle class one. She rarely discussed her past and Malissa had learned not to probe. She was a lesbian, Malissa heterosexual, but that difference had no impact on the love they shared. Their instinctive responses to many situations were very different but they listened and learned from one another. It was as though each possessed something the other lacked and they had often joked that between them they could make the perfect woman. They had been friends for 15 years and it was difficult to imagine the circumstances that would cause a rift between them.

One day Vanessa may tell her more about her younger days and her life in France. No doubt she had her own secrets and every right to keep them that way. Vanessa did not judge Henry as Malissa did, and although she questioned Malissa's decision to divorce him, she didn't judge that either.

"But the book, Ness. How could he?"

"Because he wanted to help you?"

"But he didn't tell me."

"Henry loves you."

"And I love Henry, but I'm not divorcing Henry, I'm divorcing someone else."

"Maybe he'll see it the same way."

"I hope so."

# 59

## KENSINGTON, MAY 2001

"Thank you," he called from the doorstep as she opened the door to get in the car. The comment surprised her.

"Thank you?"

"For looking after our children and for trying to understand. I'm so sorry."

He smiled, and Malissa saw genuine remorse in his eyes and a glimmer of the Henry she once knew. She wanted to hold him.

She smiled back. "Take care, Henry," she said as she got into the car.

She slipped the papers he had signed into her handbag and started the engine. Should she get out and talk to him? But say what? She still saw only the shadow of the man she married and could not imagine any conversation that could return them to the life they once enjoyed.

He'd be returning to New York tomorrow. Did she believe this was the end? She didn't know. Maybe only time could provide that answer.

She pulled away. Lewis and Millie were talking about the weekend they had just spent with their father. She was pleased some of the damage had been repaired.

# 60

## NEW YORK, SEPTEMBER 2001

### HENRY'S RECOVERY

Henry had slightly mixed feelings about the changes to Mike's Bar. He half expected an announcement of a dress code or a hike in the price of the drinks. When Mike had told him he was thinking of closing the bar, Henry had intervened, suggesting that with one or two improvements he may attract more customers.

"More down-and-outs John? Present company excepted."

"Maybe," Henry replied, "but they are loyal, they respect you and there is rarely any trouble. And I believe you have something quite unique here."

"Unique? A bar cum credit facility. That's bloody unique."

"But they always pay when they're paid. You know that. No, it's the fact they get on the stage and perform."

"They perform alright," he laughed. "Getting them off the stage is the problem. Present company excepted, once again, John. It's funny, they actually listen to your poems. I mean, not funny, they listen. You are a poet, even I can tell that."

Henry accepted the degree of talent could at best be described as variable but was surprised how he liked being referred to as a poet and smiled.

"I have a friend…" Henry paused. Was he about to create another secret?

"You have a friend?" Mike prompted.

"You sound surprised, Mike. I'm quite a guy really." They laughed. Mike continued to dry the glasses. Henry carried on speaking. "The open mic idea is fantastic. The bar has potential for improvement, enlargement, maybe better tables, bit more lighting, but it's the open mic scenario that's already established. There's karaoke bars but nothing with the room of this place. You even have a grand piano, out of tune admittedly, but it's there."

"That old thing? I'd chuck it out if I could."

"Better lighting over the stage, an improved sound system. God, some of these singers might even sound good then." Henry's brain had engaged for the first time in what felt like forever. "Maybe Monday to Friday could be rehearsal nights, weekends the chance for the best of them to perform. You never know, we might discover a star and it'll make us rich. I see it Mike, it could be really something." He realised he'd said 'we', but if Mike picked up on it he didn't say. "You could change the name to Open Mike's!"

Mike put down the tea towel. Was his interest kindled? The sudden pause in the conversation reminded Henry of long past exchanges with Brad. Only he and Henry were in the bar. Mike poured two drinks and Henry waited for a response.

"You paint an intriguing picture, John, but that costs money and while I might be Rockefeller compared to those I serve down here, I don't have that kind of dosh."

"I have," said Henry, pleased he had told the truth. "I mean, I have some savings, not a great deal but enough and I'd be delighted to go into some sort of partnership with you. I like this place, Mike."

"Then you can buy it," he joked.

Henry could, but he smiled. "But I like you too, and from what I know about business, Open Mike's would work so much better with a Mike in charge."

Mike thought again. "You got that kind of money?"

"Yes."

"And you'd invest in here?"

He wanted to say he had invested in far worse but resisted and just nodded.

"I've always wondered what a man like you was doing down here. Tell me your idea again."

An hour later they had hatched a plan. Just before he left, Henry turned to Mike. "Incidentally, my real name's Henry."

Mike smiled. "You're John to me. But I *am* Mike, by the way"

"I gathered that."

That conversation had taken place three months ago. It would take several years to recoup the money he and Mike had put in, but they were both pleased with their investment. Last week Henry noticed another bar for sale 200 metres from his apartment and wondered if replicating Mike's in a more salubrious part of the city would be viable.

As well as Mike's Bar, he would always call it that, he had busied himself at the Children's Home in Queens. There, he felt a little uneasy about using the pseudonym of 'John Delahay', and was known as Henry, the New York representative of Carmichael's, the trading name of Carmichael–Ovmeister; a trust set up to assist orphans and disadvantaged children.

Brad had been his usual exasperated self when Henry told him what he had done, but Henry was sure he secretly liked the fact his name came first in the new company. He also detected Brad was pleased he was at last finding the energy to do something positive.

He talked to Malissa and the children regularly and had been home several times, staying in his Kensington flat. His conversations with his ex-wife were becoming warmer and she no longer asked him questions to which he had no answers, or certainly not answers she would easily understand. He missed his family and looked forward to Lewis coming over next month but he knew things would never be as they were.

When Malissa told him she was dating he was unable to ask any further details but was pleased he managed to keep his feelings in check. She was a wonderful woman who had shown him nothing but love and she deserved to be happy. He missed her desperately but hadn't told Emma just how much.

Today, Henry was having lunch with the management of Ovmeister–Carmichael. He had nothing specific on his mind, but it had been nearly a year since his last visit. He felt a little nervous about visiting the company that he first set up more than 20 years ago and which now employed over 300 people. The chief executive was Bill Cavanagh, who had been with the company since the outset, but he was abroad so today he would be hosted by the general manager, Dan Johnson, who had recently transferred from OC Communications Inc. in LA.

He walked in through the revolving doors and saw a sign in the lobby. *'Today we welcome Mr Henry Ovmeister.'* Typically American. He smiled and was pleased with the way he was greeted and was soon discussing business with Dan and several others in the boardroom.

He was a little out of touch with developments but soon felt comfortable. He had nothing to prove and little to contribute. In truth, he was much more useful at Mike's, but he felt a sense of pride, something that had deserted him entirely 18 months ago.

Before lunch he was offered a tour of the offices. Ovmeister–Carmichael occupied the top eight floors of the 22-storey building. Henry still found it incredible that he and Brad owned such prime real estate. He remembered as a 15- year-old sinking every penny he had into a two-up two-down rundown building in West London and turning it into a record shop. He wondered if they still owned it.

The administrative headquarters for the Dubai operation was on the 15th floor, the last they would visit before lunch. Henry retained a particular affection for their operations in Dubai and he thought of Malissa. The employees stood to attention as he was introduced to them. As he greeted each one, he wanted to tell them he felt just as uncomfortable as they did. But this was business protocol, so he maintained the charade of asking appropriate questions and thanking them for their endeavours.

The post trolley blocked the route between the banks of desks as they headed to the exit. They heard a girl's voice as they approached. "In your dreams, Justin." The post girl had just dropped off some mail.

On seeing Dan Johnson, Justin's jaw dropped as he searched for something to say. Aware of her colleague's sudden change in attitude, the post girl turned to see the cause of his embarrassment.

The look on Mr Johnson's face was one of *'I'll deal with you later, young man',* but Henry couldn't even imagine the look on his own. The girl, confident and getting on with her job, the girl he first met in a bar when she called herself Cindy, simply said, "Sorry, Mr Johnson, I'll move this," and as she manoeuvred the trolley out of the way she looked at Henry. "Mr Ovmeister, it's a pleasure to meet you."

"Thank you, Rachel," Dan Johnson said and, as they walked towards the door added, "she really should have a better position than post girl. Italian for lunch, if that's okay with you Henry?"

"Italian? My favourite, Dan," he replied stealing a look back over his shoulder.

## 61

# NEW YORK, NOVEMBER 2001

## HENRY AND RACHEL

The letter Aunt Rose received from his mother was apparently one of several she had written. It was dated 27th September 1952.

*My Dearest Gertrude,*

*This is one of many letters I have written and I pray that this or some others reach you. I am in desperate trouble and I fear it is only a matter of time before we are discovered. I gave birth to my beautiful son, Henri, six months ago but he is not safe here, and by the time you receive this communication I hope he will be safe and sleeping in England and in the care of St Mary's Orphanage.*

*This place is not safe for me but nor can I easily flee. I have no family and appeal to your good nature to take care of him. I do not know what will become of me. Please tell him I love him dearly and so wish things could have been different. I have enclosed a photograph of my beautiful little boy. He has a birth mark on his right ankle, almost in the shape of a heart. It is very dangerous here and I know no other to turn to. He would never be safe in this Godforsaken country.*

*The oak tree where we first met still stands so proud, but that woman you once called Löwenherz now finds it broken.*

*With love,*

*D*

The letter was devoid of an address and the reference to lionheart was to verify, to Aunt Rose, her identity. It was delivered to Ashbourne House in October that year, probably passing through several hands to reach her.

St Mary's had long since closed but the researchers were adamant that records existed somewhere. Henry was thankful for that little heart-shaped birth mark. He wondered which day in March he was actually born. He saw the irony of being the son of parents who lived a necessarily secretive life.

One day he might also trace the origins of the little girl who lay next him in the cot the day Aunt Rose first went to the orphanage. A pretty little girl who would lose her ability to see and become such a significant part of his life.

When Lewis visited last month, he played at Mike's Bar. Seeing him play encouraged Henry to purchase the other premises on Madison Avenue. Mike had given him a sly look when Henry said he would lend him the money for his share of the premises and the set-up costs but, wasn't entirely surprised when Henry revealed his true identity. 'Mike's Too' would open in the new year, but Mike would always call Henry, John.

He had thought about Rachel ever since their unexpected encounter at the office and could no longer ignore the nagging desire to see her again. They had arranged to meet for dinner tonight. Not this time as the young girl offering her services and the millionaire in disguise, but as the post girl and her boss. He wasn't sure why she intrigued him, but the meeting called for more secrecy of course.

He was already at the table when she entered, just as pretty as the day he met her but better dressed. He liked her confidence as she approached him.

"Mr Ovmeister," she said shaking his hand.

Henry smiled. "Rachel, it's nice to see you."

She sat down and they ordered a drink. The money he had left in her pocket had been clasped in a plastic paper clip with his company's logo. She had investigated, and it hadn't taken long to find a photograph of him. When a job came up in the post room, she applied. The rest was history. It was as simple as that.

"Well, congratulations. I hope they treat you well."

"It's a good company, Henry. Can I call you Henry? It would be Mr Ovmeister if I ever see you in the office or if there's anyone else around, and it's so much nicer than John."

Henry smiled. He instinctively trusted this woman.

"Of course, if they didn't offer me the job," she continued, "I would have just said I knew Henry Ovmeister from Mike's and that I was sure he'd give me a pretty a good reference." She smiled.

He loved her positivity. It reminded him of himself when he was even younger than her. "So, you enjoy it?" he asked.

"Post girl was okay, but HR, now that's something I'm really getting my teeth into."

"HR?"

"Human Recourses. They promoted me last month. Nineteen K."

"Well, more congratulations. Human Resources sounds very interesting."

"It is. My boss is a bit up herself but it's great."

Henry could only guess why firms had Human Recourses departments. Probably another American quirk, but her gregariousness and experience of many aspects of humanity should serve her well.

"And, no." She lowered her voice and leant across the table, "I'm not on the game anymore." She seemed to be a step ahead of him. He was glad they had met again.

The waiter asked for their order. Rachel enquired about one or two of the dishes with a surety that impressed Henry. He wondered what the waiter made of this oddly matched couple.

"Anyway, I'm Rachel Mayr - M-A-Y-R. That's my mother's name. I'm 27 and I live with my mother in a small apartment downtown. I'm a Cancerian, smoke occasionally, do not do drugs, but probably drink a little more than I should. I'm not keen on sports but I do enjoy running. I've lived in New York all my life. I like all types of music but

Luther's my fave… My favourite treat is getting my nails done and my favourite food is lobster thermidor, which I shall order because it's the most expensive thing on the menu and I assume I'm not paying. There. That's me. In a nutshell."

"I thought knickerbocker glory was your favourite?"

"It's not even on this menu, Henry. What kind of place have you brought me to?" She raised her wine glass. "It's nice to see you again."

They clinked glasses. "Some introduction," he said. "Well, I'm Henry Ovmeister. I'm…" he hesitated, "I'm 50 next year."

"That's it?"

"And I too am ordering lobster in order to demonstrate to my guest how one should consume it."

"You are a gentleman."

They talked very easily throughout dinner. This girl, almost half his age, did not need rescuing. He had no intentions, or at least he told himself that he had no intentions, of starting a relationship with her. They talked about New York and her life there and as they did he felt safe, he felt comfortable, and he felt drawn to her energy.

It was just gone ten when she said she should be going. He was disappointed, he thought it early and he wanted to talk more.

"I have to be in work tomorrow, Mr Ovmeister," she smiled. "But tomorrow is Friday. Pay day in fact and if you're free I could buy you dinner. But hot dogs, not lobster."

They agreed to meet and Henry hailed a cab. She kissed him on the cheek and he walked back home.

That night, he talked to Emma, apologising that he hadn't done so for a few days. He told her he had met someone who's outlook on life intrigued him. She was not much older than Emma had been when she died, but he assured her they were only friends. From very different backgrounds but possibly with much to learn from one and other.

The place Rachel suggested they met comprised two floors. Most people gathered downstairs at the main bar and the clientele was diverse, from youngsters who looked as though they had left their skateboards outside to businessmen still dressed in suits. Henry wondered if there were any Ovmeister–Carmichael workers there. It was some distance from the office, so he hoped not. The upstairs bar where they met was quieter and had a restaurant.

Rachel insisted on buying the first round. He couldn't remember a woman buying him a drink before. He hoped she didn't regard him as her boss and was surprised how comfortable he felt about being so much older than her. It seemed to suit the relationship.

"Most OC workers drink in the bars on Lower East on a Friday," she said. "We could go down there if you like, you know, to show them what comes with success."

Henry became serious. "Rachel, it's not like that at all. I just thought…"

"Henry, I'm kidding, I may be young but I do know a thing or two."

He didn't doubt that. "What I mean," he said, "is that when I'm with you it's like I'm the man from Mike's Bar, you know, an ordinary guy just trying to make sense of it all."

She smiled again. "Last time I looked, Mike's had gone a bit upmarket. Got another shareholder I heard…"

"Hmm." He couldn't remember the last time he said 'Hmm' and so much of his old self came flooding in. An image of Vanessa popped into his head and memories of a conversation they once had. That was it, it was Vanessa she reminded him of, and through Vanessa that tentative link to a sixth sense and the wonders of Emma. "Mayr. That's German right?"

"Austrian. My mother said her great grandad was related to the king of Austria. My mom's full of shit."

"I found out a little more about my mother." He was resuming the conversation they'd had at O'Neill's.

He told her what he had discovered and when he finished he told her Emma was adopted too. He told her about Malissa and the love he found with her. He hadn't planned to tell her these things, but it felt good to share them. He needed to be truthful to someone.

He was on a journey, but the road ahead was long and devoid of signs. It wasn't so uphill now, but he wondered what was at the end. And as he wondered, he knew it was Malissa, and his children, and the villa in Majorca that he yearned for. How to get there was the issue. Rachel listened intently.

"You got a boyfriend?" Henry asked casually, then wondered why he had.

"You know, Henry, for the first time in my life I'm waiting for Mr Right."

Henry suddenly realised he was single and talking intimately with an attractive woman who he had invited to dinner. She read his mind.

"Don't worry, as attractive as you are, I know your heart is elsewhere. Besides, you're old enough to be my father. At the moment I'm not looking for a boyfriend. It's my round."

Henry loved the fact that New York never closed. It was gone eleven by the time they sat down to eat and they would by no means be amongst the last of the diners.

"Emma was blind, "Henry suddenly said when they had been sitting down for ten or fifteen minutes. The revelation surprised Rachel, but it would have surprised anyone. He wanted to talk about her and so carried on. "I don't know why that's relevant, but it is unusual, so I thought I'd tell you. She was beautiful too. I mean, you wouldn't look at her and think anything other than she was a beautiful woman."

"She was the girl you loved."

"Yes, she was," he smiled and continued to tell Rachel about Emma.

As he talked, he became aware he was talking to a relative stranger, moreover, one who would be the recipient of information known by very few people including those who held her career prospects in their hands. But he trusted her. As he told the story, he wished he was back in a coffee shop in Dubai and the woman sitting opposite him listening was Malissa.

"So that's me, that's Henry Ovmeister. I've already told you I'll be 50 soon."

Rachel looked at him thoughtfully and said nothing for a few seconds as she digested the story he'd just relayed. "Henry, I will never say this again.

I know you are a special man with some struggles. I know you are a successful man with power over so many. I don't know love like you know it, but I thank God I have learned that gentleness and compassion can create a power that most people believe belongs only in the hands of self-centred arrogant tyrants. I see nothing wrong with your take on love, Henry. Nothing wrong at all. And those who have been lucky enough to feel it, will never forget."

Her speech surprised him. Or did it? He had instinctively chosen this girl to… to what? To help him?

"You think I need professional help?"

"Mr Ovmeister, I work in HR at one of the most respected firms in New York. In our employ are several psychiatrists and counsellors who make themselves available to staff who believe they have issues. I'm sure I could get you a discount, but my previous occupation tells me you need professional help of another kind."

He laughed. He really liked Rachel.

"So, you talk to Emma at night… but she doesn't answer you?" Rachel asked.

"Daft eh?"

"And you want her to say, 'Henry, go find love. Go and love Malissa…'?"

He smiled.

"You say you feel responsible for her death?"

"Yes, I do."

"Do you also take credit for the wonderful life she had? A life I imagine in her wildest dreams she never thought she'd have. I think, Henry Ovmeister, you should talk to her tonight. I believe I know what she would say, and I'd be happy to interpret so you can understand. All part of the service we offer at OC Human Resources. And no charge." She smiled, and Henry knew he would introduce her to Emma that night.

~

Rachel was in the kitchen when Henry woke, wearing one of his shirts. She was making coffee and searching the fridge and the cupboards to make something for breakfast.

"Good morning," he said.

"You people might be rich, but don't you ever stock up on the essentials?"

He looked at her. "Rachel?" he said, but again she was a step ahead.

"Henry, before you get any big ideas and think just because you're a rich powerful guy that you can entice pretty young girls into your bed willy-nilly, I'd like to tell you life's not like that. I shall make you breakfast in exchange for the taxi fare home. If you ever need another appointment I suggest you contact OC Human Recourses. You'll find the number in the phone book. Do you have sugar?"

Henry smiled and went for a shower. When he returned, Rachel was dressed and sitting at the table, a concoction of eggs and bread and tomatoes waiting.

They ate and discussed nothing more in-depth than the weather. When she went to leave, she kissed him. "You are a very special man Henry, and it's a privilege knowing you."

"And you, Rachel, are a very special lady."

She smiled, her eyes displaying a message he understood, and she left. He heard the elevator arrive and descend and he realised he had not given her the taxi fare home.

It was 10:30am, 3:30pm in the UK. He phoned Brad asking him to clear out the Notting Hill flat, find suitable homes for the violins, and dispose of the papers as he felt necessary. He would also like to sell the house.

## 62

# DELAHAY HOUSE, SPRING 2002

## MALISSA AND VANESSA

"They're really written for the violin, as I said, Ness, but they are beautiful."

Vanessa agreed.

"Play one more, Lewis, then I must take Vanessa to lunch."

Her son selected another sheet. "I could play this on guitar," he said, picking up the instrument and turning around on the piano stool.

Before Christmas Brad had told her Henry wished to sell the Notting Hill property and get rid of the physical memory of Emma. "Part of the healing process, I guess." Malissa hadn't talked to Henry about it, and though she detected a definite lightening of his mood over recent months neither of them seemed able to discuss Emma. Their conversations were, however, civil and warm and his relationship with the children with whom he spoke frequently solid. They had recently discussed the possibility of having a family holiday in Majorca this coming summer.

Malissa wasn't exactly sure why she couldn't let Emma's artefacts be disposed of, but before the house was sold, she had decided to remove them. The music Lewis had been playing this morning was Emma's, those pieces written on the papers she had taken from the Notting Flat when she visited there 18 months ago. She took Vanessa to Puccini's, it seemed fitting.

"Thing is, Ness," she said as they drank coffee, "I feel absolutely no malice towards Emma. I've no malice towards Henry and Emma. In fact, I can imagine how they were and it must have been beautiful. It's just the fact I didn't know. Is that stupid?"

"No," her friend replied. "It's not. I think it's wonderful you feel that. From what you have told me, Emma was a lovely girl, a lovely woman and it's good you're coming to terms with it all."

"I used to get angry, but not anymore. Sometimes it's like I'm just an observer, just looking at some romantic love story between two young people. In some ways it was a tragedy. I mean, it was a tragedy. And when I think like that I'm ok. When I think like that, it's not my Henry I picture. Although that Henry was lovely too."

"Another life, another time."

"Yes. And another woman," she smiled. "I could never compete with that love, Ness, and I think that's what causes me so much..."

"Pain?"

"Yes, pain, but confusion and a concern that he never really loved me. That I was just some kind of substitute."

"Would it have been better if he never loved again?"

"I'm selfish, I know." Henry had shown her nothing but love, a love she believed in, and a love they had lived happily in for 17 years. "I divorced Henry on grounds of unreasonable behaviour. He didn't object. The option to divorce on the grounds that he loved someone else before we met, oh, and that he wrote a book so I could get it published and boost my career, wasn't an option, funnily enough."

They laughed.

"But he deceived you." Malissa wasn't sure if Vanessa was making a statement or posing a question.

"Or I deceived myself. Brad told me Henry's been trying to find out about his mother. Did you know she was known as Delores Delahay?"

"Yes, you told me."

"Funny. I don't resent that cover up. Guess his mother was no threat. Maybe it's because I never thought of him as an orphan. Well, I did sometimes, but generally it was never mentioned. I mean he got on so well with everyone. I couldn't fault him as a father and he loved my parents."

Vanessa was not an orphan but was effectively abandoned by her mother when she was very young, and Malissa thought this gave her a certain amount of natural empathy with Henry. Perhaps that's why she listened so intently to her opinions.

"Maybe you did?" said Vanessa. "Maybe you had a subconscious awareness of it, thought 'how sad' and therefore understood why he didn't talk about it."

Malissa thought of the possible duplicity. His mother and Emma. Two people whose loss had caused him so much pain; pain he'd rather not share. She was completely okay he felt unable to talk about one, but not the other. "Yeah, funny," she said. "Don't burden me with your orphan story but tell me about the other things that hurt you."

Vanessa smiled. "That's being a bit hard on yourself."

"Sorry, Ness, sometimes I get embroiled in myself. I mean, you couldn't have had a more typical, cosy family upbringing than I had."

"It's possibly why I judge a bit less than you. Sometimes, even though you're with friends and even those who become family, there's always a void. Loss can be a terrible thing and we all have to try and deal with it the best we can."

"By ignoring it and keeping it secret you mean?" Malissa sometimes wished she could be as understanding and as compassionate as her friend.

"Something like that."

"Ness, as much as I resent not knowing, I love Henry." She realised she hadn't used the past tense lately and paused before continuing. "And as much as I would have liked this to have never happened, or in some ways, never been..."

"Discovered? To have remained a secret?"

"Maybe. But as much as it hurt me, I cannot let Henry destroy the love he had for her. I can't let him dispose of those things that connect him to her. Is that strange?"

"No. It's not strange. I believe it's love. A greater love."

Malissa smiled. Vanessa was a font of wisdom.

"I wonder if I did know. I mean, if Henry had told me the truth, I wonder if I would have been jealous. I wonder if he had shown me the photographs of them together and told me about their life together whether I would have thought I could ever have lived up to her?"

"Like you feel now?"

"I don't know. It's possible I would always have questioned him. I mean, you know me Ness. Could I have handled that? Would our relationship have ever got off the ground?"

Since divorcing Henry, Malissa was aware that she had certainly developed a greater sense of empathy. Vanessa smiled.

"And being blind," Malissa continued. "It haunts me. It's so difficult to imagine. She was truly beautiful. And her eyes. Ness, they oozed compassion and softness. Imagine a love like that?"

Vanessa paused before posing the question. "Do you really have to *imagine* that, Malissa?"

Malissa knew what she meant. She had felt Henry's love. "But keeping it so secret. Do I understand that? Then again, do I really resent it?"

"Malissa." Vanessa took her hand.

Malissa squeezed it and before her friend could say what she wanted to say, she interrupted. "Ness, I was raised in a family home. I wasn't exposed to knowing what longing for something was like. Maybe keeping things to yourself, things that could jeopardise your future happiness is taking responsibility for them. I love Henry, Ness, I always will. I guess I'm just trying to understand. Maybe some things are best left unsaid." She finished her coffee.

"Kept secret?" Vanessa ventured.

"Possibly," Malissa replied. "Sorry, I interrupted you, as ever. What were you going to say?"

"Nothing," she replied.

Malissa let go of her hand and rose from the table. "You are the greatest friend a woman could ever have, Vanessa Cozzette. Come on, we've got some violins to collect."

"Malissa we all have secrets," Vanessa said as she got up.

Malissa smiled and asked for the bill. Maybe one day Vanessa would feel safe enough to tell her all about her childhood.

## 63

# NEW YORK, AUGUST 2003

## HENRY READS A POEM

Although Lewis had visited his father several times, Malissa thought Millie was too young to travel to New York without her. They had arrived Thursday and were sharing an apartment with Brad and Julie and their daughter Jess.

Lewis only stayed the first night, preferring to spend the remainder of their holiday at Henry's apartment which was near the club he owned and where Lewis played piano. Malissa hadn't been there but had heard about it. "One or two people who could do with a bit of PR there, Mum. You should go", Lewis had said. It was the first time Malissa had been to New York since the divorce.

Millie was in the apartment with Jess. Malissa, Brad and Julie were just finishing dinner in a local restaurant.

"So how is Henry?" asked Malissa. Although she had phoned him last week, Brad had been in New York since Monday and she assumed he would have seen him.

"He's getting there I think," Brad replied.

"Yeah, Lewis says he seems to be in a better place now."

"Is Lewis playing piano tonight?" asked Julie.

"I'm not sure. I think so. He keeps saying I should go there. Perhaps over the weekend."

"It's a good place," said Brad. "Getting quite a reputation. More up market than the first bar he bought, though from what I see I think Henry still has a soft spot for the old one."

Malissa listened as Brad elaborated on Henry's involvement in the two bars. She knew much, but the detail Brad provided always gave her more of an understanding of the trouble Henry had been going through these last three and a half years. It was obvious the development of the new business, as well as his involvement in the children's homes, had helped him.

"Well, I imagine he'll be there tonight," he said when Malissa asked about the original bar.

"Shall we go?" she asked.

Although Millie was nearly 14 and a perfectly responsible babysitter, Julie thought it best she returned to the apartment, but suggested Brad take Malissa. "From what Brad says, it's not the sort of neighbourhood a woman should wander alone."

"Well, we're probably suitably dressed," he said.

For some time now Brad had sensed a softening in Malissa's attitude towards the secret of Emma, and she and Henry certainly talked more warmly these days. He wondered how much of Malissa's desire to go to Mike's Bar was curiosity and how much concern but also whether he detected the beginnings of a reconciliation between them.

He was aware that Malissa had been on one or two dates and Julie had told him she had recently met a Frenchman who seemed very keen on her, but on those occasions when he saw them together he was sure he witnessed that questioning look in their eyes. He believed that if either of them made a first move, the other would respond positively. Or was it just his imagination, just what he hoped for?

It was nearing the anniversary of Emma's death and Malissa had chosen this time to visit New York, to visit Henry. Brad thought it notable too that Henry had booked a table at Smolenski's, which was once Malissa's and Henry's favourite restaurant for the night of the 12th. Time would tell he guessed.

They dropped off Julie and soon found themselves descending the stairs to Mike's. Brad was surprised how busy it was and as they made their way to the bar they heard a familiar voice from the stage. Henry was just delivering the punch line of a poem and the appreciative audience laughed.

"Thank you," said Henry.

The spotlight softened on him. "I call this, 'The Butterfly and The Bear'," he said.

Even from where they stood, they could see a solemnity in his eyes. For a moment, Brad regretted bringing Malissa. Henry started to recite the poem…

*She said he was born a butterfly,*
*To bloom where the buddleia grows.*
*And nurtured and nourished, with tenderness flourished.*
*In the love of compassionate Rose.*
*His world was a meadow of ranunculus fields*
*Of orange and crimson and gold,*
*A world in which he could flit freely,*
*One in which he need never grow old...*

He was remembering Emma. The crowd fell silent as he took them on a journey. Towards the middle Henry's manner changed, almost becoming enraged as he read the words describing the demolition of a young love as the butterfly crashed to the ground. He paused towards the end and his audience remained respectfully quiet. Then he delivered the last few verses, giving the listeners the happy ending they longed for.

*...With her he took to the skies again*
*His heart as light as the air*
*Reliving the life of that butterfly*
*But not flying too far from the bear.*

There was a moment's hush when he finished before someone clapped, initiating a generous round of applause.

Only Brad and Malissa understood the story Henry had just told. The poem clearly reflected the conflict in his heart. They hadn't ordered a drink, but Malissa suggested it was time to go. Brad wondered if Malissa appreciated that the poem's ending demonstrated the longing he had for her. They hardly talked in the cab and Brad wasn't sure if taking her there was a good thing or not.

## 64

## SÖLLER OLD TOWN, OCTOBER 2003

### VANESSA AND HENRY

"Hi," she said. "May I?"

"Of course. What are you doing here?" Henry looked pleased to see her.

"Thought you could use some company."

He closed the pad he had been writing on. "They get away okay?"

"Delayed an hour, but they should be home now."

He took Vanessa's hand. "It's good to see you."

Henry was always subdued when he said goodbye to his family, but this time Vanessa sensed its impact was a little more severe. No doubt, she thought, because he knew Malissa was spending the rest of her holiday with Robert in England.

She sat down and ordered a coffee. "I remember sitting here once with you and Lewis. Seems a lifetime ago."

"Yeah, a lot of things changed since then."

"You miss her a lot, Henry."

"Yes. I do. But life goes on. Hey, you should come out to New York."

"Is that an invitation?"

"Most certainly. You eaten?" She hadn't.

"How about we finish our drink, go and get pizza, and then get drunk?"

"Haven't you got to get up early tomorrow?"

"Well, a bit tipsy then. We can put the world to rights and you can tell me about Paris."

"I think it'd take more than a couple of drinks to put the world to rights, Henry. But yeah, why not. How's your book going?"

Although she was Malissa's best friend, Vanessa knew he felt able to talk to her. She even believed her sexuality meant he was even more comfortable with their relationship. Like her, he rarely judged such things and they shared some kind of unspoken empathy. They made their way to the pizza bar in the square and sat outside sharing a bottle of wine. It was 7pm and the evening was just starting to cool.

"Robert's a good man," Henry said, possibly seeking Vanessa's opinion about something.

"Yes, he is. And French."

"Hmm."

Vanessa laughed and took his hand. "Henry, Malissa will never love him like she loved you. I doubt she'll ever love anyone like she loved you. Do you ever think you could get back together?"

"I think about it and I think, you know, I would like that, but I don't see how."

"You still think about Emma?"

Henry paused. "Yes, I do. Not as I used to, and certainly not in the way I did a couple of years ago. That fire really brought back some memories. The pain will always be there but it gets easier. Think I'm finally coming to terms with it. I should have done so a long time ago of course." He smiled. He *did* seem more at ease these days.

"Malissa knows you loved her, Emma I mean, but I think she's become okay with that."

"But not about me keeping it so secret. And I understand that."

"Maybe she will one day. So, how's New York? Malissa said you were getting some work published?"

As they ate, they spoke about Henry's life in New York. About work, the children's charity, the bars he owned and the journey he had been on since the fire at Ashbourne House. He told her about his writing and how he had been approached by the New York Times to write a weekly column. They talked about Vanessa and Paris and the dance school there and the one here in Söller.

"I miss England," he said, "and here of course, but I try and keep busy. And you, Ness, got someone special yet?"

She smiled. "I've got many special people in my life."

"What a terrible waste," he joked.

"I'll take that as a compliment Henry."

"So, you think it's serious then, with Robert?"

"She's very fond of him. I think because she doesn't have to see him much." She laughed.

"He's a good man. Even though he's French."

"Henry, do you remember when we sat at the patio table and didn't need the sangria?"

He smiled. "I remember."

"You looked at me sometimes as though I reminded you of someone and I think I know who that may have been."

"I believe you do. Same hair of course, but there was something else. Couldn't tell you what, but it was there."

"And not now?"

He took her hand and looked into her eyes. Observers would have assumed they were lovers. "Maybe I've got used to you. Now, back to Paris and the dance school. Malissa said you've over 200 pupils which must be good."

"A hundred and ten, but yes, it's going well, thank you. I thought you were coming to Paris? To find out more about your mother?"

"I will do. Funny, I do feel I know her now, well certainly more than I did. Never met her, and as yet I've never seen a picture of her, Ness, but I miss her. Is that strange?"

"I knew my mother, talked to her and touched her, but never really had a mother and I will always miss her. Is that stranger?"

"Monique?" A local interrupted their conversation.

"Mikel," Vanessa replied hiding her surprise.

He looked at Henry.

"This is my husband, Robert," she said suddenly.

The men nodded. Mikel looked puzzled and was about to say something when Vanessa interrupted his thoughts. "It's good to see you, Mikel, but I really have no time to talk now." Vanessa smiled but her tone suggested the Spaniard's intrusion was not welcome.

Henry took her hand and smiled. "Well, my love we really should be getting back." He finished his wine. "Nice to meet you, Mikel. Come on, darling, don't want to keep the babysitter waiting."

Mikel looked at Vanessa. "Yeah. Okay. I just pass and see you, I not know..."

"Don't let us keep you," she said standing up.

Mikel was obviously a little drunk and quite confused. He glanced at Henry and then back at Vanessa. She smiled, raised her eyebrows and nodded, strongly suggestion that their conversation was over.

"Si. Nice to see you again," he said and shuffled away awkwardly. He looked back over his shoulder after walking 20 metres.

"You can be very frightening, Miss Cozzette," said Henry. "I think he wanted a drink in here."

"Thanks for helping me out," she said.

"Something tells me you'd never need helping out. Monique? Suits you. Should we go? Or are we safe from any more admirers for the time being?"

Mikel had disappeared.

"We could move indoors. Getting a little chilly out here," she suggested.

Henry smiled. They moved inside.

"So where were we?" Henry said when they were seated. "No, I don't think it's strange. I think when your mother is not there, for whatever reason, it must leave its mark. I met a woman called Rachel a couple of years ago. She reminded me of you somewhat."

He told her the story. Vanessa listened and as she did, she warmed to Rachel and could see why Henry made the connection between the two of them. She was relieved he made no mention of Mikel; he obviously hadn't recognised him.

"So, she helped you?"

"Yes, I think she did. Funny, I thought she would help me regarding my mother, but more so I think she helped me to come more to terms with Emma."

"And you have come to terms with Emma?"

"I think so. She will always be with me, but it gets easier. I shut her out, I refused to face the memory of her before the fire and I think it all caught up with me. Even the children's homes in New York, that was different. Yes, sure the memory of Emma was there, but this time it was so much more for the plight of the children, because *they* didn't have parents, not because Emma was an orphan. You understand?"

She nodded.

"No, these days I'm afraid it's the image of Malissa that haunts me, but not in the same way. I miss her, but I do understand why we're not together."

"Henry..." Vanessa had become suddenly more serious. "Emma was..." She paused and took a sip of her wine. "Emma was... You and Emma grew up together. Your love would have been different. Do you still see Rachel?"

Henry smiled. "No. Well, not in that way. She's doing really well at work and I heard she has a decent man now."

They chatted some more and made tentative plans to meet up in New York or Paris. It was nearly midnight when they got in the taxi to take them back to the villa.

They kissed good night and held each other for a while. "Yes, Miss Cozzette," he smiled as he broke their embrace and looked at her, "beauty beyond the reach of man. Such a waste."

For a moment, Vanessa considered how he would respond if she suggested he spend the night with her. She would have loved to talk more. She kissed him on the cheek. "Goodnight, Henry. Have a pleasant flight tomorrow." She smiled and went inside. Henry walked up to the farmhouse.

Vanessa lay in her bed. She loved Henry and she loved Malissa and maybe one day they would overcome the obstacle that kept them apart.

Henry hadn't recognised Mikel, the fisherman who he once told his story to and who was only too happy to relay it to her over a few drinks some 12 years later. She saw him looking at Henry, trying to recall just where he had seen him before, but thankfully time and no doubt a few beers had clouded his memory. One day she would tell Henry the truth. Perhaps when she went to New York.

# V

# THE LATER YEARS

*Events come and go and with the passage of time*
*Love melts to a memory we carry inside*
*So heals a heart broken, its pain to disguise*
*But love knows only asleep cos love never dies.*

# 65

## NEW YORK, JUNE 2005

### HENRY OVMEISTER

Henry visited the Ovmeister-Carmichael offices in Los Angeles every six months. His visits to their New York office were more frequent and though his input was minimal, it kept him in touch with developments. He loved the pictures, painted by the children from the children homes, which adorned the corridor walls. "Much can be learned from a child's uncontaminated portrayal of business," he'd say.

It was the ethical approach to business which he held so dear. His columns in the New York Times were, at first, received with some alarm but most of the correspondence he received these days was positive and encouraging. It was, after all, very difficult for the traditional businessman to argue that the Ovmeister–Carmichael way of running a business was in any way flawed. Balance sheets didn't lie.

He held great affection for Rachel Mayr and was delighted her career had blossomed. She naturally empathised with the philosophy of the business, and as head of HR now sat in on board meetings. Remembering the Jack Dexter novel, and the misunderstanding his desire to help had caused with Malissa, he was pleased he never intervened to give Rachel any kind of assistance. He had told Brad how happy he was that she had done so well in their Company - so deserved.

"But you did suggest the Human Resources Department deserved greater recognition Henry. I saw the memo," Brad had said. "Hmm," Henry replied detecting a degree of unjustified cynicism in his partner's observation and changed the subject.

Henry had spent every Christmas since the Brooklyn Bridge incident with Malissa and their children. They also spent holidays together at the villa. Lewis would often come over to stay with him and on several occasions Malissa had also brought Millie. He returned to England regularly.

On his 51st birthday, Malissa and he had talked about Emma and, although the conversation held little depth, it was a breakthrough. Henry didn't feel the children were their only bond and whenever he said goodbye to her, he did so with a heavy heart.

Majorca remained a special place, and when they were all together there it was as though they had never been apart. Many nights he would lay awake in the farmhouse wishing Malissa would come through the door.

They talked at least weekly. The ghost of Emma would almost certainly remain with him, but it no longer haunted him. He could only assume it still haunted Malissa. He believed she loved the Henry she knew in Dubai but perhaps not the one who had deceived her.

When he learned about Robert, he had spent many sleepless nights trying to come to terms with the fact Malissa had moved on. He wished things were different, that they were still together, but he concealed his feelings. He wanted her to be happy, to be as happy as they once were but he knew his yearning for her would never go.

But he should be grateful. He enjoyed a fantastic relationship with his children and in some ways his time with Malissa was now even more precious to him. After all, she could have quite justifiably shut him out of her life, and he wasn't sure he would have been able to cope with that.

Although he spent most of his time in New York and had made

many friends and had commitments that demanded much of his time, in his heart his home was still England. He knew he should be happy and maybe one day he would, but for now he remained grateful for those moments that ignited those memories of bliss he had enjoyed when he was married.

On the second Saturday of every month, Open Mike's hosted 'Poets Night'. Henry enjoyed these evenings and would often open proceedings with a topical piece he had written. He had been a published poet for over a year using the pseudonym John Carmichael.

Open Mike's Too on Madison was more sophisticated, but Henry retained an affinity for this place; an establishment he'd always call Mike's Bar. Most of the clientele were different to those he met five years ago, but many of the old regulars still came. They had to dress a little smarter these days, but they didn't seem to mind, and their gold membership entitled them to half price drinks.

Despite many knowing his identity, he was still often called John down here and he liked that. It reminded him of a time when Mike's Bar was the closest thing to a home he knew.

He hadn't seen Brad for two months and was pleased when he called to say he would stop by on his way back from LA. He had a key to the apartment, had let himself in and would be here soon.

Brad arrived later than expected but still managed to take in the last of the acts. He was surprised at the changes and at the quality of the performers, but Henry thought he seemed subdued. Something was nagging him.

Mike's Bar now had an official closing time and people had been filing out steadily since the end of the stage show. "What's troubling you, Braddon Carmichael?" Henry asked as they took a seat at the bar.

"Have another drink, Henry."

"That serious uh? Well, let's see, I can't imagine it to be business. You don't look unwell. You're too young to retire and I can't believe you'd want to leave the company. Julie is pregnant again? But you love children. It's another woman. Braddon, I'm surprised at you."

Brad let out an ironic laugh and downed his scotch. He fixed his eyes on Henry's as he had done so many times before when he had something serious to say. "I had sex with Malissa."

No response.

"I had sex with Malissa. Your Malissa," he repeated. "We've never had secrets Henry and that's why I'm–"

Henry's fist caught him full on the jaw, toppling him to the floor.

Brad wasn't surprised Henry had hit him before storming out of the bar. Neither was he surprised he wasn't at the apartment when he let himself in nearly two hours ago. He knew he would be considering how to respond to the revelation. They had argued before and both knew the rules, and Henry would be searching for the compromise that would allow them to put the situation behind them.

This, however, was not business and Henry would be struggling. It could not be negotiated or solved, neither could it easily be left behind. He knew Henry loved Malissa. He also knew Henry loved him.

He would be in a bar now, trying to understand, questioning his worthiness of being loved. The feeling that he had been betrayed would be bombarding his thoughts and he would be trying to push it aside, telling himself he had no right to feel so hard done by.

He'd be trying to convince himself his love for Malissa was irrelevant, that she was a free agent. Brad was the one who had been unfaithful and in normal circumstances he would feel it his duty to be there for him in any capacity Brad wanted. Henry would be stacking up these facts and trying to smother his emotions. While he waited his return, Brad wondered whether it was indeed wise to have told him. He started to write down the circumstances that led to the incident.

. . .

It had happened in Söller. It had just... happened. He and Malissa talked about Emma, something they hadn't done for some time. Malissa had needed a shoulder, as she had many times before, and as he held her it just happened. It wasn't passion, it wasn't desire, but it was perhaps inevitable. They didn't even undress and it was over in a matter of minutes.

As she left to go back to the villa, she'd had tears in her eyes. "What have we done, Brad? What have we done?"

The next morning, he had phoned her. They agreed it should never have happened, would never happen again, and they needn't talk about it anymore. No one else needed to know and he needn't tell Henry.

He heard the key turn. His chin still ached, and he wondered whether it would have to accept another blow. Henry walked straight into the kitchen and poured himself a drink. He hesitated, then retrieved another glass, poured a second for Brad and handed it to him.

Neither said anything for a full minute. Brad instinctively knew it was Henry's turn to speak.

"Do you love her?" he eventually asked.

Brad almost spat out his whisky. "Of course I fuckin' love her. I've loved her since I met her."

Henry frowned. "What about Julie?"

Henry would not have been this calm a couple of hours ago.

"What about her, Henry?"

"You gonna tell her?"

Brad knew where this was going. Brad knew Henry. Brad knew him like he knew himself. Whenever something challenged the love he felt for someone, he would analyse the situation and come up with the worst scenario. In this case it was one where Brad would divorce Julie, paying her God knows how many millions in a settlement, leave the company, set up on his own, steal the business, marry Malissa, steal his children, and live happily ever after. Probably in their villa in Majorca.

"No Henry. I'm not. I love Julie. Julie is the woman I want to spend the rest of my life with."

"And just shag my wife every now and again?"

Brad wanted to laugh. Many times, in business, when things didn't quite go his way Henry would sulk like a two-year-old. It was a sulk easily remedied by a metaphoric cuddle. Brad trusted his own judgement believing Henry sought a real hug. He stood up, walked over to him, and cradled his head on his shoulder.

He whispered in his ear. "It just happened, Henry, it never should have done and Malissa is as devastated as me that it did. It just happened. Five minutes of something neither of us planned or understood and so deeply regret. It was not love, not lust, It just happened Henry. And it never should have. We are both so sorry."

Henry broke away and refilled their glasses. Brad felt his turmoil. The anger had subsided but the confusion and conflict remained.

"Rachel." Henry muttered.

Brad heard but said nothing, guessing Henry was somehow relating the situation to his encounter with the woman he had often talked about.

"I still love Malissa, Brad."

"I know that."

"I mean, not like you love her, that's fine, I mean I love her."

"I think, Henry, you'll find you are *in love* with Malissa. Always have been, always will be."

"She knows you told me?"

"No, she has said it should never be mentioned. And I think she needs that. I promised her I wouldn't tell you."

"Then why tell me?"

Brad needn't reply.

"So she will have a secret?" Henry continued.

"It may do her good."

"Then if I sleep with Julie, we can be equal?"

"Only if we're divorced."

"Hmm. But you never slept with Emma."

"For fuck's sake Henry, if I didn't know you..."

"But you do know me, Brad" he interrupted, "and I thank you for being honest. You deserved the punch though."

Brad rubbed his chin. "That's reason enough not to go there again," he joked, and Henry feigned to giving him another right hander.

## 66

## MAJORCA, JULY 2005

### MALISSA AND VANESSA

Malissa had not seen Vanessa for several weeks. Lewis was in New York and Millie was on a school trip. Robert wasn't due until the weekend which meant she would enjoy the best part of a week with her friend.

Robert had called on her mobile, but she hadn't answered. She wondered if she would have done if it had been Henry. She missed Henry. Gradually, over the last few years, their relationship had eased into something comfortable – a word she was sure neither of them would have ever thought they'd have used to describe their life together.

He slept in the farmhouse whenever he came out here and many nights she had lay in her bed in the villa wishing he was next to her. She wondered if he ever wished the same.

Some time ago Malissa had taken Emma's compositions to a friend in the music business who was keen to bring them to life, but Malissa hesitated. Last year, however, following a visit to the theatre in Palma, Vanessa and she discussed the possibility of using the music in a ballet of their own, and for the last couple of months Vanessa had been choreographing appropriate routines whilst Malissa looked for a suitable story.

Lewis was a natural musician and Malissa wondered about mysterious forces that had delivered the gift of music to him. She had often thought about asking him to play Emma's music again, but he was unaware of its origin and enlightening him would surely put him in an awkward position.

She thought about Henry. She thought about her last visit to New York when she and Millie visited his bar on Madison where Lewis was playing piano. She remembered how they talked and recalled her thoughts of how natural it would have been for them to have continued the evening; to have adjourned to a restaurant and then returned to his apartment. They had been through much but their underlying love for one another remained and that made her smile.

When Fenner's was sold, Malissa remained on the board for a while in a non-executive capacity. She had made many friends over the years and attending functions where her presence would be beneficial was rarely a chore. It was at one of these functions she'd met Robert.

She looked forward to catching up with Vanessa; to discussing everything and learning about the dance schools which thrived under her stewardship. They met as often as their schedules allowed, once or twice in Paris and sometimes in England, but it was here at the villa that their get togethers were so special. She went for a quick swim and couldn't resist pressing the hooter before getting out and heading back to the villa.

Vanessa arrived late afternoon. Malissa prepared supper while Vanessa showered, and soon they were sitting by the pool eating tapas, drinking sangria, and talking. Later in the year Henry was going to Paris and Vanessa was going to give him a tour of the streets where his mother was raised.

Malissa was pleased Henry and Vanessa were friends. It mirrored the relationship she valued with Brad.

Henry had told Malissa that his father was a German officer, who defected during the Second World War and joined the French Resistance. Later he, like his mother, spied for the West, and it was almost certain the two of them were assassinated in Berlin before Henry was one year old.

She was glad Henry talked to her about his mother, and though she detected his discomfort in sharing those emotions she hoped there would come a day when he would naturally feel able to confide in her about everything. And then she'd remember she was marrying Robert.

Talking with Vanessa helped her understand Henry. She always provided a degree of balance whenever they discussed him, or more specifically discussed him and Emma. Right now, they were talking about Robert.

"But then again, Ness, what is my idea of love?" She laughed.

Vanessa laughed too. Malissa had taken some time to accept Robert's proposal.

"Have you told Henry?"

"Not yet. But I'll think he'll understand."

"Would you want him to?" Vanessa could ask searching questions. Malissa didn't answer and changed the subject. "Do you think I should tell Henry I have Emma's music?"

"I think sometimes, Malissa, that you want to tell him. And then I ask myself why. I've seen you look at Henry's past, firstly with horror and disbelief, and anger, but over the years I've seen you look at it differently. Perhaps you are trying to find a way of telling him so many things."

Vanessa's words resonated with her, but she kept the subject to Emma's music. "How's it going? The music and the ballet?"

"Emma's music." Vanessa said softly. Then added. "Musique qui soulève les secrets de notre âme"

Malissa wrinkled her brow.

"It's an old French saying about how music can stir the secrets in our soul."

Malissa smiled.

Vanessa confirmed she had been using the music in both dance schools and had talked to the manager of the theatre in Palma who seemed open to the idea of staging the ballet there.

Malissa wasn't exactly sure why she felt the creation of the ballet was important, but it made her feel warm inside. "And Jenny," she said, "you know the writer I told you about? She's come up with a story about a bear looking for his long-lost family in the forest. She's going to fax it through. Maybe I should tell Henry. I think he believes it's all been destroyed. It surprised me he could let it all go so easily."

"I doubt it was easy."

Malissa knew that was true. She had also detected there was something troubling Vanessa, something on her mind. Vanessa would share whatever that was, if anything, when she was ready.

"So, I shouldn't tell him?" Malissa asked, aware that she was trying to get Vanessa to make the decision for her.

"I don't know. I think he has really tried to put Emma's memory to one side, to somewhere it belongs, and maybe reminding him wouldn't be wise. I don't know."

"Brad said he's never asked. Just accepted the house was sold. I wouldn't want it to drag up more memories. Well, I guess we'll keep it secret for now."

Vanessa raised her eyebrows and smiled. "A secret?"

"That not *that* kind of secret," Malissa protested.

"And Brad?" asked Vanessa.

"That was wrong, Ness," Malissa said with authority. "Me and Brad both know that and it's in the past. End of. It didn't happen. That's a secret that could do nothing but hurt innocent people if it was known. It was a mistake and something I'll have to learn to live with."

Vanessa gave her that look that always compelled Malissa to question herself and consider any deeper meaning. "So, they're my secrets too," she said. "I mean, Brad, *and* Emma's music are also my secrets now."

"Because we're friends, Ness. God, I have to tell somebody!"

Vanessa laughed but Malissa still felt as though there was something else on her mind.

There was a pause in the conversation, after which Vanessa

reached across the table and took Malissa's hand. The gentleness of her touch surprised Malissa. "And I have secrets too," Vanessa said seriously. "Something I've been wanting to share for a long time."

"Ness," Malissa interrupted, "as much as I love you, and believe me I do, I don't think I could show you love in that way. You are beautiful and..."

Vanessa laughed out loud. "Sweet lovely, Malissa. I love you dearly too. But no, Malissa. A desire to sleep with you is not the secret I'm referring to."

Malissa smiled and squeezed her hand. "Well, it nearly happened once." They had from time to time over the years joked about the night they spent on the farmhouse lawn.

"You are a very special woman, Malissa. You have shown me nothing but kindness and you are the best friend a woman could ever have had. But that is not my secret." She held Malissa's hand tightly before letting go. "I have something to tell you, Malissa, that you will find difficult to understand. I have thought so many times about telling you, about telling anybody, but on balance believed keeping it a secret would be the best thing."

"You've slept with Henry?"

"No, Malissa, I have not slept with Henry. Wrong gender remember?"

"Funny, Ness, if you had said you had, it would have made me feel better I think. About Brad, I mean. And do you know, in some funny way I wouldn't have regarded that as deceit. How strange is that? I mean, I used to be, I don't know, jealous. That might be the wrong word. In awe maybe, of Emma and Henry. But I could never have replaced the love he had for her. And she for him. It was a beautiful story, Ness. I used to think he used me to mend his broken heart and it upset me cos I thought, I don't know, thought I was being used. But not once did I ever *fee*l used. I know Henry loved me and if I repaired his heart and brought happiness back, then I'm proud of that. That's love right?"

"And very profound."

"Even with Brad," Malissa continued, "I regret it and it was over in a second, but it sort of got something out the way. Like our friendship is stronger because we know we never want to be like that. Do you know what I mean?"

Vanessa smiled and took a deep breath, the seriousness in her eyes making Malissa sit up a little straighter in her chair. What was it she needed to tell her?

"I have had relationships with men," Vanessa said. "I was… raped… when I was 14, two boys. To get by and even help my father pay the bills I…" She hesitated. She must have seen the concern in Malissa's eyes.

Malissa reached over the table, finding her hand. "I didn't know, I'm sorry. I know so little about your past, Ness, but I do know it wasn't easy."

Malissa mentally kicked herself. 'Wasn't easy' was hardly empathy for being raped.

Vanessa continued. "When something like that happens, you lose any kind of self-worth. You certainly lose your childhood, your innocence. I had no mother, not really, and as much as I wanted to believe my father loved me, I quickly realised I was either in the way, or when it suited, simply his best asset."

Malissa could only imagine what she meant but saw a look in her eyes she had not seen before.

"They would think they could use me," Vanessa continued, "and they did. But I learned I could use them too, stealing money while they slept or threatening that I'd tell their wives."

"I'm so sorry, Ness."

"Mademoiselle Lauren wasn't much better than those bastards but at least she was gentle. And she taught me to dance. When my mother died, I didn't cry. I had hit the jackpot with Etienne, a politician's son who's pay off meant I could choose if I wanted to sleep with anyone. Fuck me, it even gave me the money to get to England and without that…" She paused again. "Well, without that I think I would have ended up… I've no idea where I would have ended up, but without that pay off I would never have met you, never had the dance schools...Never have been sitting here."

She poured more wine. Malissa said nothing. Vanessa drew her hand away.

"Just before my father died, I came to England. I was searching. I was searching for someone. Someone my mother had told me about."

Malissa had never seen her friend like this. Vanessa was practically shaking.

"I didn't know what I would find, but the person I sought was no longer there…" Vanessa took another sip of her wine. Malissa hoped she knew that whatever she told her would, in no way, change her feelings for her.

"What I did discover," Vanessa continued, "led me inevitably to you. To us. To our friendship which I have always cherished so deeply. When you took me in and looked after me it was the first time anyone had shown they cared. Really cared. I felt loved. It led me to you." She paused. "It led me to you because I was looking for Henry."

The flickering light from the candle picked out the tears forming in Vanessa's eyes. She was indeed beautiful and in that light with her auburn hair framing her face, Malissa thought she saw for the first time why her husband had looked at her the way he had. Previous half-finished conversations raced through Malissa's mind. "I love you Ness. And whatever it is, I'll understand."

Vanessa made no attempt to wipe away the tears that seeped down her cheeks. Her words were choked as she struggled to maintain a degree of composure.

"I wanted to go back to France. I had found what I needed to find. I had discovered it was no longer there. Telling anybody why I came to England seemed pointless. Sharing my discovery couldn't change things, wouldn't have done any good.

"But I didn't go back, and we became friends. And after a while it didn't seem so important. Then you asked me to come out here with you and I felt I belonged; felt in some way I had found what I had come looking for. I found comfort and love, and the secret I had seemed best to remain just that. A secret. And I am so sorry if I was wrong. I am so sorry, Malissa."

Tears were steaming down Vanessa's cheeks now. She bit her lip, reached for Malissa and squeezed her hand tightly. Her words struggled against the sobbing that was now overwhelming her. "No, Malissa, I never slept with Henry," she said. "But my sister did."

"Gabrielle?" Even as Malissa asked the question, she knew Vanessa wasn't referring to her younger sister.

"No, Malissa, not Gabrielle. I never met my sister who slept with Henry. She… She was blind and beautiful, and died so very, very young."

## 67

## DELAHAY HOUSE, JULY 2005

### MALISSA FINDS ENLIGHTENMENT

Henry had phoned earlier and spoken to the children. Malissa wanted to talk to him too but Robert, who was unable to come to Majorca last week because of work commitments, was there. Now he had returned to his hotel she considered ringing. It was 01:30 pm, 6:30pm in New York.

She sat down considering what she wanted to say and wondering why it felt so important to ring. She had been home five days.

Vanessa had been distraught after divulging she was Emma's sister. Malissa had known her for 20 years. Known her, like so many had, as a strong independent woman who would quietly deal with everything thrown her way. Last week she saw a vulnerability and pain she had never shared.

Anna, Vanessa's mother, had given birth to Emma in London when she was 15. The baby's father was one of two sons of a wealthy landowner for whom Anna's mother, who had died the previous year, kept house.

Emma was a secret from birth and was handed over to the authorities before she was a week old. Anna never saw or held her daughter, and when she eventually escaped the clutches of the family that had treated her so cruelly she discovered, through a liaison with a porter who worked at the orphanage, that Emma had been adopted.

Vanessa's father first told her the story, and just before she died Anna confirmed it, sharing all the information she had gathered about the daughter she never knew. Vanessa was 19 when she came to England in search of Emma. Ovmeister was hardly a common name and Vanessa was a dancer looking for work. Her meeting with Malissa was inevitable; their subsequent friendship maybe fate.

Somehow the shock of Vanessa's revelation dissipated almost immediately. As she told her story it was as though she was merely adding detail to the outline of one already embedded in Malissa's subconscious.

Malissa truly empathised with her friend's plight and understood the impossible position she had found herself in when discovering Emma was so much more than the teenage crush Malissa had initially assumed. These were circumstances that put her in a position she could hardly have wished for and Malissa thought hard about how *she* would have reacted had she been Vanessa.

Many times over the years Malissa believed Vanessa wanted to tell her something. She recalled those early months they spent together, long before Vanessa met her husband. "Does Henry have a sister?" she had asked. "No, Ness, Henry's an orphan."

"You were so happy, Malissa," Vanessa had said. "When I first found about Emma, I thought she must have been Henry's sister, or stepsister or something. It was only later I found out more. How could I tell you? What good would it have done? In Söller someone told me about Henry, about how he was distraught, running away because he had lost Emma. Millie had just been born when I discovered the truth. How could I tell you? You were both so in love."

They had sat up talking until dawn. When the sun came up they were even firmer friends and as the light lit up the plateau, so it illuminated an understanding of love that had hitherto laid buried in the shadows.

Love is forgiveness, compassion, and kindness. An appreciation of our differences, our strengths and weaknesses. We judge from our own experiences and beliefs, from inherent senses of right and wrong. She would judge from an upbringing of stability, security, and trust. Vanessa on the other hand would instinctively judge from her own upbringing, one so far removed from Malissa's.

And Henry. How would he judge? What early experiences built his world? Would he recall being abandoned as a baby? Did he feel abandoned when Aunt Rose died? Malissa could only imagine the sense of loss he must have felt with Emma.

When Vanessa was distraught and crying on her shoulder, Malissa held her and her very welfare in her hands. She could vent her anger, renounce the love that they shared and cast their friendship aside, maybe as she had cast aside her marriage? Or…she could forgive and comfort her and allow compassion and understanding to overrule the negative and possibly more natural feelings of betrayal.

But she had felt no anger. She just felt an overwhelming feeling of empathy. They spent the following three days on the plateau, talking about everything and sleeping together at night, comforted by a love only they understood.

Malissa no longer held any resentment regarding Henry's relationship with Emma. Far from it, she regarded it as perfect and beautiful, soft, almost make believe; a relationship that re-wrote the rules of love.

The overwhelming burden of betrayal she once felt no longer plagued her. Maybe it would have faded naturally over the years, but by appreciating the world they shared and empathising with the loss Henry must have felt, compassion had driven such feelings from her heart. She was starting to understand why he would have believed it would have been impossible to tell her.

She knew she could never love Robert how she had loved Henry, and when these feelings surfaced they reinforced her belief that Henry could never love her like he had loved Emma. Henry could never love anyone like he loved Emma. But she knew too, that nobody could ever love her like her husband had.

A more profound feeling came over her when she considered whether Emma took her own life. Lewis and Millie were the product of the love Malissa and Henry shared. Lewis and Millie. Henry's children. Children he would never have had if Emma hadn't died. Henry's children, the product of Emma's love for him. How precious the gift of children.

Vanessa once vowed never to have children, scared they would experience what she had, but her attitude had changed. Changed because she had seen the wonder of Lewis and Millie, changed because she had seen love, and Malissa knew that Vanessa would make a wonderful mother.

Malissa sat in the front room and looked at the telephone. What did she want to say to Henry? Did she want to tell him Vanessa was Emma's half-sister? Or did she simply want to tell him she understood?

She had a secret. Like Vanessa had, maybe like Henry had when they first met. She had knowledge. Knowledge that in itself would have no profound effect on her life but could so easily destabilise another's.

She was aware too, that she had come to terms with the secret of Emma and strangely, this woman she had never met, this woman who she used to believe had shattered her life, held a position in her heart she could never have imagined.

She didn't phone Henry. Instead she went to bed with an enlightened heart and a feeling of contentment she had never known.

# 68

## FEELVIEW BAY, 12 AUGUST 2005

### MALISSA AND HENRY

In her heart Malissa knew Henry still loved her, she felt it. And she loved him. The last five years had been a journey. At first it was a painful one but more recently it was one of enlightenment and self-awareness.

She and Vanessa had talked much over recent weeks and agreed Henry needed to be told the truth; that Vanessa was Emma's half-sister. When and how to break the news they weren't sure, but both thought it best he was told by Vanessa.

Malissa and Henry were no longer married; they no longer spoke or saw each other every day and no longer shared a bed. But they shared something and that something was so much more than their children.

Henry lived mostly in New York, she in England and although they often discussed each other's daily life that part of their existence remained separate. Time spent with Henry, especially Henry and their children, was like a holiday; it was special, and derailing their new-found relationship was something Malissa didn't want to do. She wasn't sure what the future held but couldn't imagine them being out of one another's lives.

She was driving to Feelview Bay. She thought about Robert, her and Robert. Yes, she loved him too. Not as she had loved Henry, not with that intensity but she was happy, and their relationship was comfortable. He had asked her to marry him and she wondered how much of her hesitation was concern for its impact on her relationship with Henry.

When Robert proposed he told her he loved her, even though he appreciated she could never love him like she had loved Henry. The comment surprised Malissa, and though she tried to make light of it, she saw a seriousness in his eyes and a sincerity in his smile when he said he completely understood. Did it mirror her belief that Henry could never love anyone as much as he'd loved Emma?

Maybe she would never feel the passion for Robert she'd felt for Henry, but she was older now, wiser, and her welfare was not dependent on a close relationship with a man. Like her, Robert had his own commitments, a life outside their relationship and perhaps that suited them both.

Robert's secondment to the Seychelles was expected to last 18 months in total. She would spend the first three months with him, taking Millie who could continue her studies there. Lewis was happy to stay at home or in New York with his father.

She had spent the last few days with Robert in Looe. Next week they were going to Brittany to meet his family. They had agreed to postpone any official announcement of their engagement until Robert returned from the Seychelles.

Although she didn't tell him why she was visiting Henry today, she was pleased he didn't object. He was a good man. In fact, she often thought he deserved better than her.

Last year on this day she and Henry were in Majorca. The year before, New York. She knew he would be thinking of Emma and she did not want him to feel he was alone.

She parked behind his car and walked the shady path with a strange sense of calm. She noticed the little raised kerbs and tried to imagine the beautiful blind girl who once felt her way up there. She reached the gate. To her right, the cottage, majestic in its humbleness. In front the colourful garden with its white picket fencing, and beyond, a wave of grassy meadow that sloped gently to the cliff edge and the sea.

Malissa had been here before, but this was the first time she could recall comparing the scene to their home in Söller. Did she have this image in mind when she first saw that peninsular? She paused, letting a feeling that she may be trespassing dissipate.

Entering the garden, she stepped quietly, avoiding the gravel. She thought Henry would be on the beach and was crossing the garden when she heard his voice. He was at the back of the house. She stopped. He was talking to Emma.

She wanted to stay. She wanted to listen. Or would she be intruding? Should she turn around and go? Most of all, however, she wanted Henry to know he had done nothing wrong by loving Emma. She quietly retreated to the gate, banging it loudly and calling to Henry as she strode purposefully back to where she had been standing.

Henry answered, surprise in his voice. "How wonderful to see you," he smiled, kissing her gently as they met on the front lawn. "What are you doing here?"

That was not an easy question to answer. "It's the 12th, I thought you could do with some company."

Their eyes met. In Malissa's, concern and love. In Henry's, momentary confusion, but a genuine joy to see her.

"The 12th," he repeated softly.

"I hope I'm not intruding?"

"No, not at all. It's so good to see you. It's... wonderful."

She knew he wasn't certain what to say.

"You sit at the back?"

Henry looked over his shoulder and then back at Malissa. She knew he wanted to say the right thing but didn't have a clue what the right thing was. "Yeah. Sometimes I sit there, it's…"

Malissa took his hand. "I imagine you and Emma sat there many times."

Her voice was soft and comforting. Henry smiled gently. They walked around to the back of the house and sat on the bench he must have been sitting on when she first arrived. A bench she imagined he had sat at many times with Emma.

"I thought you and Robert were in London. Aren't you meant to be on holiday?" His voice had regained some composure. Malissa wished he would cry onto her shoulder.

"We were. We came down here for a few days. Robert's never been to Cornwall. Think he believes they're a bit anti-Europe."

"He's not wrong there."

Malissa sensed he didn't like hearing too much about the man she would soon be telling him she was marrying. "Brad said you scattered her ashes here."

"Yeah."

She wondered if he would talk about her.

He thought for a moment. "Emma always imagined an island out in the bay. I think she would have loved to have lived there, on the Island. If it was there, of course. Seemed fitting."

Malissa was holding his arm. She wanted to nestle into him but resisted.

He continued. "I mean, the stream, down to the sea, you know, her ashes would have..."

"I know," she said, squeezing his arm. "I know, Henry. And I think she would have liked that."

They sat in silence for a minute. Malissa broke it. "Hey, I read your book. Very good."

"Thank you."

"You writing another?"

"Poems?"

"Whatever. Thought you might write a novel."

"Now there's an idea."

They both smiled.

"Well, if you ever need any promotion."

She closed her eyes for a moment listening to the little stream as it bubbled down gently over its pebbly bed.

"I really do appreciate you coming," Henry said quietly. "And I'm really sorry I didn't..."

"Shh." She felt his vulnerability and wished she could have sat here with him many years ago.

He smiled, a hint of a tear in his eye, and Malissa knew they didn't appear solely because of the memory of Emma. He looked away briefly, so she wouldn't see. They were holding hands, the tenderness between them as soft as the summer day.

Her phone rang. She squeezed his hand stood up and talked to Robert.

"Would you like tea or anything before you go?" Henry asked when she'd hung up.

"No. I'll grab a coffee on the way back."

They walked around to the front garden.

"Are you staying over?" she asked.

"Just tomorrow. Millie wants to go riding."

"Delores?"

"Yeah, poor old lady, she's getting too old for all that now, but you know Millie. Only the best will do."

"Where is she?"

"Alice has taken her into town. We're meeting for dinner. Why don't you join us? You and Robert."

She knew Robert was an afterthought and that he would hate the idea of sharing her with him. "You'd like that?" she asked

His "Hmm," was music to her ears and she laughed out loud.

"Malissa?" Henry said, stopping just before the gate. There was a pause while both wondered what he was about to say. "Thank you for coming. It means a lot."

They kissed at the gate and she wanted it to last longer. She remembered wanting to kiss him at the cottage after the fire, to turn him back to the man she once knew. Their eyes exchanged a message. Neither could be sure of its exact meaning, but both knew their love for one another would never die.

She went through the gate. "When are you going back to New York?" she asked.

"Week after next I think."

"Söller next month?"

"Of course."

"And Lewis." Lewis was in New York

"Yes, and Lewis. Maybe his girlfriend too."

"He's got a girlfriend?"

"I'll let him tell you about that. She's a singer down at Mike's. Looks set for a bit of stardom, I believe."

"He never tells me anything." Malissa sensed her comment suggested secrecy and impacted a little on him. "I guess he will when he feels it's right." Her words had a double meaning. "Bye, Henry, take care."

She walked down the path.

When she had taken ten steps, she heard his voice from behind.

"Enjoy your afternoon, Malissa."

She turned. Standing at the gate was the man she first set eyes on outside a phone booth at Goodwood. "Did I ever tell you, you have a wonderful smile, Henry?"

"Never, Malissa," he grinned. "Give my regards to Robert."

She left wondering whether he would ever call her 'Miss Keats' again.

# 69

## PARIS, DECEMBER 2005

### VANESSA AND HENRY

They had spent the morning visiting the area around the bakery where Henry's mother was born and the afternoon at the dance school. It was the first time he had met Gabrielle, Vanessa's sister. She was in her late twenties. She had longer hair and softer features than her sister, but you could not mistake they were related. When she looked over her shoulder to greet them, she reminded him of Emma.

"Do I not have the prettiest sister in the world, Henry?"

"With that, Vanessa, I could not argue. But I believe I would have been asked that same question if Gabrielle had made the introductions."

Vanessa smiled. "Henry, if only you were a woman."

He loved Vanessa the way he guessed Malissa loved Brad. Everyone should have a best friend of the opposite sex. He hadn't seen Malissa since their autumn break at the villa and hadn't spoken to her for more than a week. She was abroad with Robert and though he genuinely wished them well, her absence served to remind him he would always have that pang in his heart.

The last time he had spoken to the ghost of Emma was over four months ago. Her gentleness and beauty were within him now, part of his soul, and he no longer felt compelled to consciously rekindle her memory. It was only the image of Malissa that invaded his thoughts these days, and he often recalled the vision of her sitting next to him by that little stream in Cornwall where he used to sit with Emma.

Sometimes when he spoke to his ex-wife he was sure she felt the same way, and he longed to say something. But Robert was a decent man and Malissa deserved the best. He couldn't interfere. He had arranged to meet Vanessa later that evening for dinner.

They met at a little restaurant in the city, in an avenue bejewelled with festive fairy lights. It was cold and there was a light covering of snow. At dinner they talked about the dance schools and Henry's life in New York. It wasn't much past 8pm when they were having coffee and Henry didn't want the night to end.

"Malissa tells me you and Gabrielle are coming for Christmas," he said.

"Yes, and her husband. Pascal's never been to England."

"Yeah, Majorca would be warmer. Bit of a shock to her system when she arrives, Malissa I mean."

Malissa was in the Seychelles with Robert.

"Strange she chooses to spend Christmas with you."

Robert was spending Christmas in France.

"I think, Vanessa, you'll find she regards Christmas as family time. I am, after all, the father of her children, there by default maybe."

Apart from the year of the fire, Malissa and Henry had spent every Christmas as a family.

"So, that's the end of your search?"

"I think so," replied Henry. "It was good to see that she led at least some of her life in a kinder environment." They were talking about the area where his mother grew up.

"I imagine she was a wonderful woman."

"I think she was. I've heard so many good stories. My father didn't turn out too bad either."

"And I know you are a good man, Henry."

Henry raised an eyebrow. She rarely put good and man together in the same sentence.

"And Emma?" she ventured

"Emma?"

"You must have thought about tracing her parents."

Since Henry's arrival in Paris Vanessa had been searching for the right moment to tell Henry the truth about her relationship to Emma. Was she testing the water?

"I've thought about that many times over the years. Did you know *her* mother was French too? Or so I believe. I found that out after she died. Probably why you used to remind me of her, the French connection I mean. I loved it when Emma spoke French. Didn't always understand what she said, but maybe it was always part of her."

Although she always knew why he looked at her, it was the first time he had alluded so directly to the resemblance. Maybe this was the time to tell him. "That's interesting," she said.

"But other than that, I never dug further, though a couple of years ago I thought about using the same people who tracked down my mother to look into it. But, Vanessa, some things are perhaps left alone. Emma was Emma and that's it I guess."

"So, she was born in France?"

"Emma? No, I'm sure she was born in London. She was certainly rescued from St Mary's and she wouldn't have been more than six months old. I imagine it's a strange story and maybe a sad one. I don't know. Who knows - one day perhaps?"

"Like you?"

"Like me?"

"Found in St Mary's."

He smiled. "My aunt often told me she first saw us in a cot together. Cuddling under a blanket she said, two peas in a pod."

Vanessa was touched by the vision of the two babies lying side by side and saw that the memory of Emma had invaded his thoughts. She sensed, however, it was one of fondness and that he was okay to continue talking.

"What happened to her mother? Is she still alive?"

"I doubt it. I don't know why exactly but something tells me not. The orphanage wouldn't disclose any details. Once, not long after Emma died, I burst in there, drunk and demanding to know about Emma. I was arrested and held in a cell overnight.

"But I did meet someone who knew someone who had worked there and had apparently met her mother. Said she was very young. Anyway, it seemed she just disappeared. Maybe I could have asked him more, but back then I wasn't really in a fit state to do anything. I was just… I was just angry, heartbroken I guess. No, one day I might try and find out more but, to tell the truth, I'd be pretty scared."

"And your Aunt. Did she ever say anything else?"

"No, she didn't… and I've always regretted not asking more. She left quite a lot of letters for me after she died. Remember the ones I showed you in New York?"

Vanessa nodded.

He took a sip of his coffee, a brief solemnness creeping over his face as he replaced the cup on the table. "I was surprised none made a mention of Emma. Sometimes I worry she felt she never existed."

Vanessa reached across the table and took his hand. "She existed Henry. She had love."

They sat in silence for a minute.

"Tell me about her," Vanessa said softly. "About you and her. I don't mean to pry but it does sound like a fairy tale."

"No, it's fine. I should have talked about her long before now. To Malissa, to other people. She should never have been a secret."

She squeezed his hand and gently let go.

He continued, his mood suddenly lighter. "We were young. They say love is for the young and if that's the case I had love in spades. She was the most wonderful human being I had ever known, and pretty. God, she was beautiful, and clever, and you should have heard her play the violin. Or the piano, or any other instrument for that matter."

Vanessa was always aware that Henry could feel he was being too effusive when he talked about Emma in this way, that what he was saying might make its way back to Malissa, but she reassured him. "Malissa knows you adored her."

"I loved Malissa too. I still love Malissa. I always will. They are not that dissimilar, both sort of… innocent, believers in love. Or something like that."

"I think Emma believed she was truly loved."

"Yes, I loved her. We were happy. If I had died with her I could easily have said I had as much happiness as a man could ever expect. And she was happy too." His manner was momentarily more reflective.

Through his eyes she saw the goodness in his heart, saw his love, saw why Malissa and Emma would have loved him.

Her mind flashed back to that night spent outside the villa with Malissa after she had told her she was Emma's sister. She recalled their conversations and Malissa's absurd suggestion that Vanessa could bear the child Emma could never have. An absurd suggestion that had over the subsequent days lost its incredulity and which right now seemed so right. Her heart skipped a beat.

"But you didn't die with her. You found happiness again with Malissa."

"Yes, I did."

"Malissa is a wonderful woman Henry. I've talked to her so much these last couple of years and shared some…." She paused. "Some wonderful moments."

Henry looked at her. She wondered what he was thinking. Remembering her sexuality, she laughed in case his thoughts were heading that way.

"I'm talking about talking to her, Henry, exchanging feelings and stories of our past lives. About secrets. And I don't just mean about Brad."

Henry looked into her eyes. He would have known Malissa would have confided in her about Brad, and she knew Brad would have told him. Before he could reply, she decided it was time to change the subject. She didn't feel it right to reveal she was Emma's sister just yet, and they'd surely discuss the Brad episode later. "I was thinking I should take you to the ballet tonight."

"Ballet?"

"Henry, I will show you ballet that I'm sure you will appreciate. And tomorrow I will show you *my* Paris."

## 70

## THE SEYCHELLES, DECEMBER 2005

### MALISSA

Malissa studied herself in the mirror, thinking how strange it was that this evening would be the second time she'd be attending a dinner at a golf club in a hot country far from home in December. This time, however, it would be with Robert and upwards of 100 guests, and she was pretty sure he would not be surprising their host with the news that they intended to marry the day after tomorrow.

She missed England and would be returning home the week after next. She loved Christmas and spending it at Delahay House would present a good old-fashioned family get together. Lewis had only been able to come out to the Seychelles for a week and that was in October. Malissa couldn't wait to see him, and possibly his new girl-friend too, though Lewis had said she'd probably be spending the festive period with her family in the States. She and Robert would celebrate an early Christmas here and then catch up in France or in England in the new year before he had to return.

Millie made no secret of the fact that she was homesick. It seemed even she had become fed up with white sandy beaches, coconut palms, endless sunshine and people at her beck and call.

Vanessa had been in regular contact and had phoned at lunchtime confirming she was with Henry in Paris. She checked her watch; they'd probably be at the dance school now. She smiled to herself, momentarily thinking of Henry. Yes, there was a little apprehension, even a tinge of jealousy, but certainly no malice or resentment. Vanessa and Henry were two people entwined in her life; two people she loved dearly.

She fastened the necklace Robert had bought her. They would have an enjoyable evening. Maybe a bit too stuffy for her liking but it would be okay. She would have deeper, more meaningful discussions with Vanessa when she returned home.

Robert called from downstairs. Their car was waiting. A final check in the mirror and she descended the stairs, wondering whether Henry would actually be surprised by what Vanessa would surely be telling him soon.

# 71

## PARIS, DECEMBER 2005

### HENRY AND VANESSA

Henry liked Paris. Like New York, it rarely slept but the bars and cafes were more intimate and romantic, especially at this time of year. Both he and Vanessa were beginning to feel the effects of a long day, and after a quick drink at one of the bars by the theatre they headed back to Henry's hotel for a night cap.

"Now, Miss Cozzette. We have recently watched naked women performing on the stage. And, I have to say, as you quite rightly surmised, that it was a take on ballet I enjoyed."

"And no tap dancing."

"Quite. But was that for my benefit or for yours?"

"Henry, that is such a typical remark from a non-typical man and I am surprised you ask."

"Hmm."

She looked at her watch. She didn't want the evening to end, she wanted to tell Henry she was Emma's sister. "I guess I'd better start thinking about ordering a taxi."

She could see Henry didn't want her to go either. "Well, you're welcome to my bed Vanessa. I do have a rather palatial couch in the room."

"I'm surprised you didn't ask me to share your bed, Henry, considering your last homophobic remark."

"You must remember, Vanessa, I am still a man and you a beautiful woman. I share your preference for women, that was joke not a homophobic remark by the way, so for my sanity at least I would be only too happy on my couch."

They giggled, realising the barman had been listening to their conversation. Henry's phone rang. It was Lewis, calling from New York. He apologised for ringing so late but wanted to tell his father that Anna had just been offered a recording contract.

"He has a gift, Henry," she said after he relayed the message to her.

Henry smiled and asked the barman to top up their glasses.

"He phoned me once before when I didn't expect it," he said thoughtfully. "I owe him a lot."

Vanessa wasn't exactly sure what he meant, but something told her he was ready to hear.

"Children are wonderful," she said. "You must be very proud. Music is in his heart. Part of his soul. A gift from heaven."

"Yes, they are. And with Lewis I wonder just where that gift came from. It certainly wasn't from me."

"But you play piano well."

"Nowhere near as well as some."

She smiled. "Malissa has talked to me about that."

"About my ability to play the piano?"

She laughed, trying to keep the subject light but remained determined to tell him what he needed to know.

"About mysterious forces. About how something of Emma, through you, lives in Lewis."

He looked at her. "Emma couldn't have children," he said softly.

She caught his gaze. She felt her heart quicken and realised now was the time to tell him. "I know, Henry. Me and Malissa have discussed that too. How wonderful it would be if something of Emma lived in another human being."

"Malissa talks about Emma like that?"

"You'd be surprised Henry."

His mouth opened as if trying to find the question he wanted to ask, but the moment was suddenly broken as a group of people came noisily into the room.

She took his hand and smiled. "Tomorrow, Henry, I shall show you where I lived. I shall tell you all about my mother and my upbringing and why I came to England. But it's been a long day and if you're serious about that bed, I think it's time we slept."

The people who had just came in said 'hello' and perched themselves on the stools next to them and ordered some drinks.

Henry was lying on the couch when Vanessa emerged from the bathroom. The room was dimly lit and they looked at one another for several seconds. She smiled, walked over and sat down beside him. From the pocket of her bathrobe she retrieved the envelope Malissa had given her a couple of months ago.

"Malissa is a very special woman, Henry," she said, and handed the envelope to him.

He looked at it. And then at her. "From Malissa?" He would have recognised the handwriting.

She touched his arm and looked into his eyes. "She wrote it shortly after I told her about my sister," she said slowly. "She said I should give it to you when I thought the time was right."

It was as though she had handed him a key to unlock a dormant thought locked so deep inside him. He said nothing as he digested the words, but Vanessa could almost hear the whirring in his mind. His moist, piercing eyes fixed on hers, looking into her heart, gradually gathering the confirmation they sought.

"Your…" He paused and swallowed, struggling to form his words. "Your… older sister."

It wasn't a question.

"Yes," she whispered, and as the tears began to seep from his eyes she cradled his head to her chest.

# VI

# A WEDDING IN MAJORCA

*...I've no idea where this journey leads or where, if ever, it ends. I only know that each of us can impact on another's life – especially those we are so close to and with a soft and open heart and true understanding of those we love, we can impact so beautifully.*

## 72

# MAJORCA, JUNE 2007

## MALISSA AND VANESSA

"She's sleeping." Vanessa said sitting down at the table with Malissa, who had been reflective ever since Lewis left. "Regrets?" she asked.

Malissa smiled. "No, Ness. *Je ne regrette rien.* Well, no recent ones. I wonder how many times we've sat out here over the years?"

"Or at the villa," Vanessa replied.

"She's got her father's eyes."

"I do think she has."

"I was just thinking about the time we first came out here, Ness. The old generator, the villa being built. It's different now, but still the same, especially when it's just me and you. Lewis was a toddler then, not much older than Fifi really."

"He sung her to sleep the other night."

"Oranges and Lemons?"

"He calls it Juan and Theresa. Fifi seemed to appreciate it."

"He said 'hmm' the other day when we were talking about her. Said his mission was to make sure she grows up normal and doesn't inherit his other sister's more unfathomable traits."

"Poor Millie," smiled Vanessa and reached across the table taking Malissa's hand. "You miss him, Malissa. And I know he misses you."

Malissa knew she was referring to Henry. She squeezed her hand. She did miss Henry. Fifi somehow reflected all that was good in this world and was a symbol of reparation; of mending broken hearts. Her birth should have brought closure, but Malissa's heart still yearned.

"Do you ever think about how strange life is, Ness? About love, about friendship, about what we do during our short time here. Whether we really make a difference?"

"You really *do* miss him." She got up and returned to the kitchen to fetch the tea.

Malissa changed the subject. "Me and Robert were talking about where we should live."

"Naturally," Vanessa called from the kitchen.

Of course it was natural thought Malissa. It was the most obvious consideration of two people looking forward to getting married and contemplating a new beginning. "I've been thinking about it for a while now, Ness. Trouble is my heart is here."

Vanessa came out from the kitchen, smiled at Malissa and sat down. "Could you not live here? At least sometimes?"

Both knew this place belonged to her and Henry.

"We've had so many good times here, Ness. It feels like home. It is my home. I obviously couldn't sell it, but I don't know. God where would *we* meet up if not here. I mean, yes, of course, me and Robert should live together, I'm just not sure where. France, I guess, but why not England? We talk about it, but well, you know…"

"He travels a lot. Perhaps live here when he's away?"

She smiled. "I'm sure he'd be okay with that – it isn't as if we've got any kids to consider, or other ties really. He says he feels a little awkward when he stays here though."

"That's understandable."

"When Henry's here it's like home again. We must have had 20 holidays here together since we split up. And in those times, it's like nothing ever changed. Do you know what I mean? He sleeps here and I sleep in the villa, but I still sort of regard it as…"

"Your place," interrupted Vanessa. "Yours and Henry's."

"Yes, I guess so. Lewis asked me if Henry had said anything about us marrying here. He hasn't, but maybe it's not the best idea in the world."

Vanessa looked at her the way she had done so many times over the years, listening and saying nothing but compelling Malissa to consider any deeper sentiment behind her statement.

"Anyway," she said picking up her tea. "I've still got a few months to sort it all out. So, how's the ballet coming along? Are we going down there tomorrow?"

"Well, that was the plan."

"I think I really need to tell Henry about Emma's music. God, Ness, how many years is that?"

"You're thinking about Henry, Malissa. I think you have been thinking a lot over the past few months and I see how you are together. Even closer than usual."

"Yes, we do get on well now and I'd never want that to go. I hope he's happy, Ness. He seems to be. I just have to sort a few things out."

"Talk to him, Malissa."

"Robert?"

"You know I mean Henry. Talk to Henry."

"We talk all the time, Ness."

"Do you still love him?"

She didn't have to answer.

"Talk to him. I mean *really* talk to him Malissa. Talk from your heart, tell him your fears, tell him how you feel. He loves you, of that I have absolutely no doubt and I don't think you doubt it either. Let him know it was okay to have loved Emma as well as you, because I fear he is the one who feels he's unable to accept that. He won't make the first move."

Malissa wanted to do as Vanessa said. She wanted so badly to talk to Henry. The realisation that she would soon be marrying Robert had unsettled her. It represented the end of a journey; a journey she felt unready to end.

"Despite his strength and belief in love," Vanessa continued, "somewhere he will feel he is not deserving of you. I know that feeling. It's the abandonment thing and it's deeply embedded in him. He's probably not even aware of it. He thinks you *can't* love him, believes himself unworthy. He'll be telling himself you love Robert so much more and he won't let his own feelings override that."

"Did I abandon him?"

"No, you didn't. He thinks you would have been justified to do so though. Do you remember how he wouldn't say anything? At the beginning, when you first found out? That's because he thought he deserved to be abandoned, punished perhaps. He can handle that because that's what he knows. He blames only himself. He believes he lost you because he didn't let go of his feelings for Emma."

"He should never have to let go of those feelings, Ness."

"In a way, he has let them go. He already had really, he just thought it would have been wrong to."

"I would never have left him if he'd told me. He just needed to talk to me. I would have understood. I would have come to terms with it. I just needed… Well, I don't know what I needed, really, but I'm sure I could have got over it."

"You have, Malissa. You did some years ago. It's Henry who hasn't. If it's Henry you want, the Henry you loved, let him be him, don't block him, allow him to love. Open that door again, let him know you are there, let him in and let him know you will never abandon him."

Malissa looked down at the villa and wondered what would be going through her mind when she said 'I do'. She wondered what would be going through Henry's. A butterfly landed on the lawn. Malissa watch it. It was joined by another before both flew off. If Millie was there, she would surely have told her mother they had landed on the very spot she was conceived.

# 73

## NEW YORK, JUNE 2007

### HENRY AND RACHEL

"He's very like you, Henry. You should be very proud," Rachel said as Lewis left them.

Henry smiled. "Well, I hope it's the good points he's picked up on. There are some underlying conditions that I hope never darken his doorstep."

Tuesdays at Mike's Too was set aside for the romantics; those who preferred a quiet dinner for two in intimate surroundings. Lewis was only too happy to serenade them on the piano whenever he was in town.

Henry had been surprised when Rachel asked if he would step in for her non-existent father and give her away on her wedding day. Surprised and honoured - humbled even. Like so many in his life she was a special person who deserved to be happy, and he was thrilled her life seemed so much more settled these days. They often had lunch together, but this was the first time they had dined here.

Rachel's natural empathy and willingness to consider all views of an argument had given her almost chairman like status in her professional life and she was often called upon to arbitrate in company politics. Her success did not surprise Henry; after all weren't those the very attributes that also made it so natural for him to have often sought her valuable counsel?

She had met Vanessa on a few of occasions but not yet Malissa or Millie. Henry wasn't in the least bit surprised that Vanessa and her bonded instantly; it must have been like looking in the mirror when they met. When Vanessa announced she was pregnant Rachel showed genuine and unabated joy at the news. If they didn't live 3,000 miles apart, he was sure they would be great friends. She'd be great friend with Malissa too.

Lewis had immediately warmed to Rachel. He was not aware of his father's original connection to her, but Henry didn't doubt he would have realised she was very special to him. Lewis had recently returned from Majorca. He had asked Henry what he thought of his mother marrying again. Henry had told him Robert was a good man and his mother deserved to be happy. Furthermore, he needn't concern himself too much; his parents enjoyed a wonderful relationship and would, in their own way, always love each other.

"Have *you* ever thought about marrying again, Dad?" he had asked. Henry laughed at the question and hoped Lewis believed he was happy.

In three weeks' time, they would be returning to Majorca for another holiday. Lewis, like Henry, knew it may well be the last time they'd spend a holiday there as a family – Malissa marrying Robert would surely change that particular dynamic.

Henry lived in New York, but for the past couple of years had yearned to return home. Bobby had phoned him last week, talking about horses, telling him she had found one that he should certainly buy if he still wanted to win the Derby. Bobby kept in regular contact but at the end of that conversation she too asked how he felt about Malissa marrying. He gave her the stock answer. He wondered if she believed him.

When Brad came over last month they got drunk and reminisced. They talked about Brad's father, Aunt Rose, their business and of course Emma. With regards to Vanessa and Fifi Brad conceded, "That love my friend, is beyond my comprehension," but added that little surprised him these days. Brad's own family kept him busy, but he too missed the old days. Henry had asked if he and Julie would come out to Majorca in July. He was considering it.

"I think Mr Ovmeister, your thoughts are elsewhere," Rachel smiled. She had been speaking about Lewis and Mike's Too and whether it would be an appropriate venue for the office's summer party.

"Sorry, Rachel. I was just thinking. Do you think I should tell the chef he should have knickerbocker glories on the menu?"

"I think Henry, that would be the icing on the cake. So, Malissa's getting married and you wish her well?"

It was another one of her statements designed to provoke thought.

"Yes, Robert's a good man. Even thinks I should go and work for the EU. Couldn't think of anything worse really. Anyway, let's talk about your marriage and Tom. I'm certain he's not good enough for you."

"But you'll give me away anyway - to someone you think is undeserving?"

"Hmm"

She smiled and took his hand across the table. "And who would be deserving of me? I can think of only man. Charming, handsome, runs a great big company, owns a rather lovely bar in Manhattan, well two really, and writes in the New York Times. But I think his heart will always lie somewhere else and I know I could never compete. Plus, he's old enough to be my dad."

Henry smiled. "You're very special, Rachel. I'm so happy you're happy."

"I am, Henry. And if that father figure I love so much could ever put his ghosts to rest, realise that sometimes feeling he needs something is okay, and realising too that sometimes people are only too pleased to fulfil that need, I'd be over the moon."

He laughed. "You ever been to Majorca, Rachel?" He knew she hadn't but wanted to divert the subject. "You should go there with Tom. There's a little place I know that when you're there everything, and I mean everything, is alright with the world. By the way, do you swim?"

She looked at him, probably appreciating he wanted to keep their discussions light-hearted. "Sometimes Henry, no matter how far out of your reach they seem, you should try and grab hold of your dreams. "

For a moment she looked like the woman he first talked to in a late-night burger bar seven years ago. "Dreams?"

"I met a man once, who by some strange quirk of fate changed the direction of my life. He was a troubled man, a deep thinker, but I detected he would never let anything stand in the way of a dream. His only problem was he was unsure if it was somebody else's dream too. He seemed afraid to ask. Funny when you considered how he'd tackle everything else in life so head on." She let go of his hand. She loved dessert. "Well, the fudge brownies are a reasonable substitute, so perhaps best not to upset the chef too much."

Henry smiled and raised his eyebrows. No wonder she had excelled in business. The soft notes from the piano filled the restaurant. Henry loved hearing his son's rendition of Fleur De Lys.

# 74

## MAJORCA, JULY 2007

### MALISSA

Millie had gone to Palma with Vanessa and Fifi. Henry was arriving on the afternoon flight, and Brad, Julie, and their children would arrive over the weekend. Lewis wouldn't be here until Monday. This would be the third year in a row they had all spent this particular week together at the villa.

When she told Henry she was marrying Robert she wondered if she wanted him to protest. To declare his love for her. She had detected a distinct change in his voice and knew he struggled with the news, but he congratulated her and wished her well. She was sure the Henry she knew in Dubai would have seen Robert as an obstacle to his love for her and have tried to remove it. Henry now pushed that instinct away and accepted it was her choice. Vanessa's words weighed heavily on her.

"So, you loved Henry?"

"With all my heart."

"You don't resent his relationship with Emma?"

"No, it was a beautiful love."

"But you resent him not telling you?"

"I don't know."

"Do you understand why he didn't want it to get in the way of your relationship?"

"It wouldn't have." Was she sure of that?

"Do you think it would have for Henry?"

"Possibly."

"Do you believe he loved you?"

"Yes."

"Do you think he should have tried to love again after Emma?"

"Yes"

"Who is the man who has made you most happy?"

"Henry. But, the saddest too."

"Can you imagine him out of your life?"

"No, I would hate that."

"Do you still love him?"

"Yes."

The memory of Emma was no longer a threat to Malissa. Was it to Henry?

## 75

# MAJORCA, JULY 2007

## MALISSA AND HENRY

It wasn't often Malissa and Henry were alone. They were sipping wine outside the villa. It was seven o'clock in the evening.

"Tell me about Emma, Henry." Her request was soft but she sensed it took him by surprise. She would have loved to have heard a 'hmm' but this subject was too close to his heart.

"You know about her," he replied, shuffling a little in his chair.

She reached for his hand. "It's okay, Henry, please just tell me. Trust me."

"It was a long time ago, Malissa." She wanted him to call her 'Miss Keats'.

"I know you love me Henry and I know you loved Emma too... and that's okay. She was a very beautiful woman. In every way."

Henry looked at her. She could sense him trying to suppress the feelings in his heart as he searched to find a response that she'd believe was appropriate.

"I do," he said after a moment, "love you."

It was the first time he had told her he loved her since they broke up.

~

He had little idea what, if anything, lay behind her question, but sensed it was nothing remotely approaching malice. He looked at her. He saw the girl he first met at Goodwood.

He had learned that talking about Emma was okay and if it were Vanessa or Rachel sitting opposite him he could deal with it. If it were Brad he would know what to say. But asking the question now was the person he loved most and he wasn't sure how to respond.

"Where should I start?" His voice was quivery.

"Why didn't you tell me about her?" She was asking the same question she had asked so many times in the past, first in the cottage the day after the fire. Surely, she knew why? Everybody would have known why. It dawned on him, however, that he had never actually voiced the reason. Maybe she needed to hear it from him – or maybe he needed to hear himself saying it? Why didn't he tell her? Why couldn't he talk about her? He waited for the image of Emma to appear. It didn't.

He tightened his grip on her hand and looked into her eyes. He had considered how he could respond to this question a thousand times but any words he may have mentally rehearsed had deserted him. He wanted to answer. Her knowing eyes peered into his very depths, pulling the words from deep inside him. He spoke slowly without thought, allowing the words to form their own unequivocal meaning.

"I couldn't tell you because I felt like I would have betrayed her. I couldn't tell you because... because. I couldn't tell you because I would have lied about the love I had for her. How could I have found that love again with someone else? But I did Malissa I found it with you... and ..."

She interrupted him softly. "Do you think you made her happy Henry?"

He realised the question she was asking was one that had haunted him for nearly 30 years. She could have asked if he believed Emma took her own life, took her own life because of him. To Henry, these were the same question. Images of a previous existence scurried through his mind, finding their way to his throat and choking his ability to respond. He felt the squeeze on his hand allaying the fear that she may have let go, and saw the compassion in her eyes as she answered the question he couldn't.

"I have felt your love, Henry," she said. "I have felt the tenderness of it. It's a beautiful feeling to be the recipient of such love. I don't doubt for one minute that you made her happy. She knew you loved her. She died knowing a love so very few people would have known. If she died as a result of fate, it was a fate that had also given her such love. If she died because she chose to, she did so because of love.

"I have no doubt she was happy, Henry. I know this because I have felt your love and the wonder it brings. She was a very special woman who found love with a very special man."

In the 17 years of their marriage, and the seven since they had separated, it was the first time Malissa had seen him cry. She walked around the table. He stood up and pulled her to him and they held each other tightly. Empathy, kindness, and love flowed through her. Remnants of any past bitterness, jealousy, or deceit were swamped by something so powerful and pure. She shared the strength and depth of her love, a love that had purpose and meaning. A love made up of everything good in this world, and she held him until his crying stopped.

"I've something to show you," she said.

They entered the villa. In the third bedroom was a cupboard and in that cupboard were four violins and several cardboard boxes.

"I couldn't let them go," she said.

When they slept that night, they did so in each other's arms in the farmhouse. Much of the ghost of the past had been laid to rest. Malissa had talked to him.

## 76

# MAJORCA, JULY 2007

## MALISSA AND HENRY

They'd woken up as they had done so many times before, her head on his chest and his arm around her. But it had been more than seven years since they greeted a new day like that. They had not made love, just held each other throughout the night.

The rising sun had filtered through the window where the blind was just half drawn. She hadn't wanted to move, she would have laid there forever. If only it was that simple. She left early so she would be in the villa when Millie arrived.

She recalled the conversations they'd had last night They talked of Emma, his past life with her and their own 17 years of marriage. They talked about Lewis and Millie and Fifi, the child Emma could never have. When they talked about life, life and death, she had jokingly asked him that if there was a heaven and he found himself up there with her and Emma, who would he choose.

As soon as the words had left her lips, she realised their insensitivity – realised he wouldn't have taken them as lightly as she intended. She apologised profusely, desperately trying to withdraw them, but he lay still, not answering for many seconds, seemingly digesting them as though they represented the very essence of a question that had haunted him for years. His soft solemn words were fresh in her memory.

"Emma was blind. I was her eyes. We grew up together and maybe it was inevitable that we would be bound together. I ask myself whether I *ever* chose, it was just what I knew. You blew up your nose at Goodwood and the pain I had held onto melted. I had seen a million women since her death and I chose no one until I saw you. Never did I think I would love again, never would I be able to choose, but I chose..."

She had interrupted him, re-iterating the question was asked in jest and changed the subject to their daughter who had gone shopping in Palma to buy him a hat. She brought their conversation back to the present, and about them, and they eventually fell asleep.

"Morning, Mum" said Millie, interrupting her thoughts.

Malissa smiled and kissed her daughter.

"I'll take a couple up to Dad," she said, grabbing two croissants. "Beautiful morning to go sailing. Why don't you come?" she added, before heading back out the door excited to see her Father.

Henry stood in the garden and sipped his coffee. He looked down at the villa. Malissa was probably in the kitchen preparing breakfast. Soon Millie would come bounding up the hill, brandishing some monstrosity of a sailor's hat she'd bought him in Palma yesterday and holding a plan of the route they'd be taking today. He loved sailing with her but wondered if her mother would be accompanying them too.

He thought about last night, about the conversations they'd had and about how right it felt as she lay on his chest. He thought about Emma and a life he once shared with her and smiled to himself, grateful for that time. But his thoughts this morning were mainly of Malissa; Malissa and a family life they once shared.

He knew she regretted the question she'd asked him. She believed it a thoughtless, spontaneous and irrelevant remark, but was it really so much out of context? Perhaps it reminded him of a question Emma once asked him on a little beach in Cornwall, a question back then, he certainly didn't want to consider. Perhaps it encompassed the conflict he had always held in his heart and as he tried to answer he realised he was finally reassuring himself. If he had answered straight away would she now be reconsidering marrying Robert?

He would love them to get back together and didn't doubt Malissa loved him. But she loved Robert too and he understood. Whatever the future held, he felt in his heart that he and Malissa would always love one another, and while he did struggle to suppress some of the hurt he was grateful that so much of what they had once shared had been salvaged. He would always be there for her. He hoped Robert appreciated just what a wonderful woman Malissa was.

Millie waved to him as she ran into the villa. He waved back. She'd be here soon. He had not seen his *Estrellas* for many weeks and looked forward to catching up and listening to her telling him how to sail a boat properly.

# 77

## MAJORCA

### THE DAY BEFORE THE WEDDING

Malissa was happy with arrangements. The bar was adequately stocked and the refrigerators working satisfactorily. The flowers would be delivered this evening and she had checked with the caterers. All guests that should have arrived by now had done so, most she imagined spending the day sunning themselves in Söller.

The villa garden was an abundance of colour, as was the surrounding plateau which had erupted in a carpet of white and pink and yellow following the recent rain. The orange trees had lost their blossom, but the sweet fragrance of the orchard still hung in the air. She loved this time of year. Warm but not yet hot, and she would be happy to spend the rest of her life here with her new husband.

Robert, as cordial as ever, had visited this morning before checking into The Grand. She was pleased he would be enjoying a drink with Henry this evening, though hoped they would go easy on the Majorcan wine.

She looked up to the farmhouse. Vanessa and Fifi were in the garden. It was approaching midday, little more than 24 hours before the wedding, and after the hustle of the last few days Malissa suddenly found she had nothing to do.

Fifi greeted her in French. *"En anglais, Fifi,"* Vanessa instructed and her daughter repeated the greeting in English. She always knew Vanessa would make a wonderful mother and to seeing her with Fifi always made her smile.

She paused as she shut the garden gate. Was it really almost 20 years ago that she and Vanessa first stood there together? Nowadays there was no dodgy generator or questionable structures to worry about and no longer was it the temporary home which had served them so well while the villa was being built. Yet, despite the wi-fi and mod cons, *Casa de La Colina,* the house on the hill, remained the most wonderful little farmhouse in the world.

"All seems in order, Ness."

"I don't think anything could ever be more so," her friend replied.

Malissa picked up Fifi and followed Vanessa into the kitchen. "I think I'd like a hen night."

"Well, that is traditional, but we'd better arrange it quickly."

"I have," she said. "I will make sangria and we can drink it on the lawn and look at the stars."

"Will the Great Bear be out tonight?"

"I expect so, Ness". They heard a faint honk from below. Lewis and Millie and several others were on the beach.

"You want one last go as a single woman?" Vanessa asked. "It's just twomseconds to make up, you know."

It had been several years since she last attempted to beat Vanessa's long-standing record. "I think maybe, Ness, we should restructure the rules to accommodate the over forties. Are those garlic prawns I smell?"

"Yes, they are, but maybe they'll taste better with sangria in the cool of the evening. I say we lunch on the beach with some cheese and a bottle of wine and talk about how beautiful you will look tomorrow."

"Sounds good to me."

Malissa took Fifi into the garden and helped her water the plants. Fifi was a product of love of a special kind, one that so few people would ever understand. She wondered what life had in store for her but recalling her cameo performance at the ballet yesterday didn't doubt that music and theatre would play a significant part in it. Perhaps she'd be a famous dancer.

She thought about the farm girl who used to live here and about life and love. She thought about the journey we each go through, about the twists and turns and the impact we have on one another, and those moments that stay with us and accumulate to form the pattern of our lives. She thought about tomorrow.

She called to Vanessa. "I wonder, Ness, how often a mother and daughter have been bridesmaids at the same wedding?"

"I wouldn't have thought many," Vanessa said bringing her a glass.

"No, me neither," she smiled. "Well, I guess I'll never get that traditional wedding I was brought up to believe in."

"I think your mum's come to terms with it."

Malissa smiled. "Have I ever told you I love you, Ness?"

"Only when you were completely satisfied it was safe to do so."

"You would have loved mine and Henry's wedding."

"Which one?"

She smiled. "Dubai was a more impromptu event. I like to think of that as an engagement. No, I was referring to our one in England, just after Delores won the Oaks."

# 78

## JULY 1984

## THE ENGLISH WEDDING

While Malissa often thought Henry lived in another world, sometimes she wondered just what galaxy her mother was from. As the cars arrived, and with her father out of earshot, her mother adjusted her daughter's veil. "Henry is a man, Malissa," she said earnestly. "A good man, and your father and I love him like a son. But men expect certain things on their wedding night and you should not be alarmed. It's completely natural, so just go along with things and all will be fine. There. You look gorgeous."

Malissa managed to prevent herself from bursting out laughing and, slipping in beside her father, caught the more knowledgeable look in his eye. What a wonderful marriage they shared and what a beautiful upbringing they had given her. She looked out the window. Her mother was beaming. She was a beautiful woman.

She and her father travelled in the ruby and white Rolls-Royce. Her mother, her brother and his wife followed in the silver one. She was married already, but this felt like the real thing; the traditional occasion she was brought up to believe in. The sun was shining as requested and the drive to the church was about 30 minutes through leafy lanes. She was excited and nervous.

They stopped just short of the church, allowing the other guests time to assemble. She would be the customary five minutes late.

She took her father's hand. He had a tear in his eye, something she had never seen. She smiled, knowing he wanted to say something but knew words were not his forte. She knew he would be nervous about making his speech. He clasped his hand on hers.

"Malissa, I have loved you from the second you were born. You know I am not a man of words, and your mother does most of the talking, but I want you to know just how very proud I am of you and just how beautiful you are. Inside and out. Henry is a wonderful man, but today he takes over custody of the most precious thing I have ever held in my arms. If he loves you like I love your mother, then I know you are in safe keeping. I love you so very much." He pulled a handkerchief from his breast pocket. "This will be a wonderful day."

"Thank you, Daddy," she said and, as they resumed their journey, she thought about Henry and the fact he had no parents or family to be so proud of him.

Sam, her bridesmaid, looked lovely in pink and matched the church. She picked up the train of her dress and Malissa took her father's arm. They ascended the steps and the doors to the chapel opened. They were greeted by Reverend Eduardo, his smile as lovely as she remembered. She looked at his pink socks.

"I thought you'd like them after all," he whispered. She did.

It was the most beautiful building she had ever set foot in. Sunlight streamed in through the windows, creating a glow as warm as the one in her heart. Flowers as fragrant as they were colourful adorned the walls and every vacant space on the floor. The scene belonged in a fairy tale, as did she, and she couldn't recall having ever been so happy.

The music started and the congregation stood, all faces turning towards her. Familiar faces, their joy just for her, as she walked slowly towards Henry who was standing at the far end of the chapel with Brad, his handsome face wearing a warm and wonderful smile.

The music stopped when she reached him. He took her hand and she wondered whether everybody could hear her heart beating in the sudden silence. The reverend came to the rescue. "Dearly Beloved," he commenced, his voice rich and soulful and happy. "I welcome you to this joyous occasion to celebrate the joining of this man," a look at Henry, "and this woman," a look towards her, "in holy matrimony."

The change to the wording was subtle with 'celebrate' replacing 'witness', and he continued his address in much the same vein. He talked about Jesus being a guest at a wedding in Galilee (normal) and he talked about God being Love, quoting verses from Corinthians that were more akin to a *renewal* of your wedding vows. Otherwise, his welcome was just as conventional as you would witness at any traditional wedding. He delivered his address with a charm and a love that surely touched everyone as it touched her.

"Who hath given this woman?" A slight variation, but her father stood up in acknowledgement.

"And if there exist any objections to why these two beautiful people should not be lawfully married, they should speak now." For one moment she thought Brad might butt in and say, 'Well, actually Ed, they're already married.' But he didn't.

The oaths were always going to be the biggest obstacle, but his switch to another language where necessary just added to the mystique. They exchanged rings, the ones from Hatton Garden not Dubai, and then they kissed.

The ceremony lasted 45 minutes but it seemed like two. They left the chapel a more bona fide Mr and Mrs Ovmeister.

As they gathered on the lawns for the photographs, Malissa could hear her mother eulogising over the ceremony which everyone found as wonderful as the chapel. Delores Delahay, a surprise guest, her mane interwoven with pink and white, made a wonderful centrepiece for several photographs, before Bobby cried, "Enough!" and sent her back home.

It was as traditional an English wedding as you could have imagined. The uniqueness of the chapel and the Reverend Eduardo simply added something so very special to the occasion.

Malissa went to the bathroom before the speeches. On her return, she paused at the door. Twelve tables of eight and a top table. Malissa's family, many she hadn't seen for a long time and several she had never met, occupied more than half of them. Colleagues from work and some friends from the theatre or school occupied others.

Alice and Charlie sat at the top table and Henry's friends filled the rest. Again, she was reminded he was an orphan. She returned to the table and kissed him. She would give him the family he deserved.

When it came to the speeches, her father surprised her. He was witty and warm, causing both her and her mother to shed a tear. Maybe she would have thought Henry would be in his element but when he stood up he simply thanked everyone for coming and read a poem which moved everybody as well as her:

When you think you're blessed with everything,
A man could ever need.
When you've read the text of every book
So there's nothing left to read.
When you accept the sun will rise each morn
And set each day the same
When you stick, or pass, contented that
You're happy with your game.

When ambition no longer motivates,
So you needn't question why,
Nor have cause to wonder whether
A chance has passed you by.
When happiness is moments
And you think you've had them all,
Someone comes along to show you,
You've not had much at all.

So, if I thought that I had happiness
Was it really real?
Because when I met you, Malissa,
I again began to feel,

The sun on my face and the taste of the rain
And the wind that ruffled my hair.
The sky became bluer, the stars they shone bright,
And flowers sweetened the air.
And life took on a new meaning,
My heart so overjoyed,
To beat next to another, a best friend and lover
Not beat on its own in a void.

And where there was okay there's now wonder,
Where there was doubt now there's sure.
I know why the sun rises each morning
I didn't, Malissa, before.
And the road we're now taking's forever,
Each day we will find something new.
And discovering love as we travel this lifetime,
Is a journey I will relish with you.

Brad's Best Man's speech was very funny, recounting some of the less successful business ventures he and Henry had undertaken. He referred to their antics as youngsters, recounting several of the stories he told Malissa earlier that year. And when he mentioned racehorses, an investment he would never understand, it naturally solicited several colourful interventions from Bobby Anderson, necessitating Malissa to explain to her mother that 'feckin" was a traditional and much revered old Irish adjective.

Never one to forgo an opportunity Brian Fenner stood up, singing Malissa's praises and as a wedding gift gave her a promotion, making her second in command. "So that she can't take over the whole bloody business so easily," he laughed. And, as a present for Henry, he promised he would buy one of his yearlings. Apparently, he had been promising that for years.

To finish, Brad read several cards and telegrams from well-wishers including one from Rod North which included a parcel. Brad opened it to find a pair of black trousers and a bewildering note saying, 'Just in case'. The traditional toasts were followed by the cutting of the cake, the bride and groom figures on top holding hands in front of a marzipan telephone booth.

Reverend Eduardo appeared in the evening. Her mother was surprised by his sudden change of costume and a little confused over his wellbeing when she asked how he was. "I'm boom diggitty, thank you, Mrs Keats, absolutely boom boom diggitty doo." A camera would have been wonderful to have recorded the expression on her mother's face, but when Eduardo took to the dance floor and 'got on up' to James Brown, many photos were taken, and these would always remind her.

She and Henry heard her mother explaining to her Aunt Cybil and Mrs Banbridge from the WI that James Brown was, in fact, Reverend James Brown and he and the Reverend Eduardo were of the same order. By this time, her mother had consumed two glasses of wine and didn't care.

They danced to the same song they had in Dubai, and as darkness fell they went outside for a fireworks display. Henry had hired the whole place and no doubt was breaking several house rules. She thought Matthew Bailey may have suggested several of the outbuildings needed new roofs too.

As custom dictated, they left before proceedings concluded. New York, New York played as they said goodbye to their guests who had formed the traditional circle.

She didn't want to leave. She hugged her mother, who she half expected to whisper the virtues of oral sex to her as parting words of marital advice. She found it incredibly difficult to pull herself away from her father who said little but in doing so said so much.

Alice eventually let go of Henry and then it was just the two of them in the back of the car. To cheers and wishes of good luck they headed for Gatwick, a short stay in the hotel and then an early flight to Majorca.

She had been surrounded by her family and friends and the day belonged to her. Her wedding day was everything she'd ever dreamed.

She kissed her husband. “Thank you, Henry,” she whispered as she cuddled up to him.

“Miss Keats,” he replied, “have I told you just how very beautiful you look today?” He had, about a hundred times, but she had her answer. He would probably always call her Miss Keats.

79

# EARLY SUMMER 2008

## A WEDDING IN MAJORCA

"You know, Ness. This is effectively the third time I'll shall be marrying. The first, secretly in Dubai with a vicar in Y-fronts, the second a little fairy tale in a little pink chapel with a reverend who worshipped James Brown, and now in my own back garden. So much for tradition, eh?"

"And now in paradise. Utopia by the sea. Would you rather it be at a church?"

Malissa smiled, knowing that this place was the perfect setting for the occasion. "Seems a little unfair we have to stay here whilst the others are enjoying themselves though."

"That is tradition. The Bride always makes an entrance."

Vanessa was tending her hair and from the farmhouse window Malissa looked out over the plateau. The villa, the marquee, the rows of chairs and the little stage under the gazebo where the ceremony would take place, were bathed in sunshine and sitting on a colourful piece of land that jutted out to a beautiful clear blue sea.

People had been arriving for the last hour or so and were gathered below her, drinks in hand and chatting. Children were running about. Women in colourful dresses and men in suits. She loved the little

Pimm's kiosk Henry had arranged. Perhaps he planned to whisk her away from a conversation and have a drink with her there.

She saw him talking to Robert. Strange? It seemed nothing was strange in the Henry and Malissa world as far as affairs of the heart were concerned. She was pleased Robert had been so understanding and pleased they got on so well; her ex-husband and the man she was going to marry. In an hour or so she'd be beginning another new chapter in her life.

"You're looking very lovely, Bobby," said Henry, offering her a glass of champagne.

"Frigging too warm for me," she replied.

Brad joined them. "Hi, Bobby."

"Hi Brad, how's things?"

Things were good but Brad was a little out of his depth as the other two talked about racehorses. Brian Fenner appeared. He was well into his seventies now but had three horses in training with Bobby Anderson, one of which was due to run next week. He asked after their welfare and about Delboy, the first offspring of Delores Delahay, who had finished third in the Derby 20 years ago.

As the guests mingled, Henry looked up to the farmhouse knowing Malissa was there. He saw her briefly yesterday but stayed the night at The Söller Grand with Brad where they drank Majorcan wine and reminisced. Like Malissa, he too knew that today represented a completion of a journey that belonged in a book. He wondered if he would write it one day.

"You okay?" asked Brad

"Yes, my friend. I'm okay. I love weddings."

"I brought you a present."

"A present? For me?"

"Don't sound so surprised. I often think about getting a present for you."

"Yes, my friend. And you always say it's the thought that counts."

Brad ignored his cynicism and produced a little gift box. "Open it," he said handing it to Henry.

Henry did. Printed on the silk lining was a simple message: *For my friend,* and underneath, *With love*. In the box was a silver dollar coin.

Henry looked at him. He had seen the coin before.

"My father gave me that coin was I was seven years old. His father gave it to him."

"An heirloom," said Henry. He knew this was a poignant moment.

"Whenever you have doubt and must make a decision between two scenarios, allocate one decision to one side of the coin, and the alternative to the other. Flip the coin and your decision becomes clearer."

Charles Carmichael had been a special man. At his funeral Henry realised he was the nearest thing he had known to a father. Brad knew that too. His father had looked out for him when he was young and, of course, facilitated the great friendship Henry shared with his son. He knew Brad would have held this coin in his hand and his father's memory in his heart when considering gifting it to him. Brad had no brother and was six months older than Henry.

"You see, if you allocate heads," Brad continued, "and it comes down heads, and you smile, you know that was always the decision you harboured in your heart. It was the one you always felt was right."

"Hmm," said Henry catching his friend's eye and exchanging that understanding they'd always shared. He didn't need to tell Brad he knew the significance of the gift. "That doesn't sound like good business. That doesn't sound like a Braddon Carmichael method of working."

"But that's where you are wrong. You see, if you allocate heads and it comes down tails and you still feel uneasy, it's almost certainly because, deep down, you know the other scenario was the correct choice."

Henry could see the logic in that. "And this is how you've run the company for the last 35 years?"

Brad laughed. "You'd be surprised how many times I have used it."

They looked at one and other, their unspoken love and respect understood by them and them alone.

"Then it's a very precious thing to you," Henry said.

"And so are you." Brad was not going to say he loved him.

"Hmm," said Henry, thinking one day he might just say the words. "But won't you make all the wrong decisions from now on?"

"I'll use a ten pence piece."

Henry held the coin and considered tossing it. He didn't. He knew this coin was very special to the man he had known and loved for 40 years.

"Thank you," he said and hugged him.

"Once I had to toss it five times before I felt I had the right answer," Brad added.

"Five times?" That seemed to contradict its usefulness.

"Yes, five times. Heads I take the job with Hollis and Hills, tails I go work for you. Four heads in a row came up."

"It took you five times? Five spins? And there's me all these years thinking you had no doubt, that we had something special, that you were as enthusiastic as me. Bloody hell, I wouldn't have needed a coin, I would have just known!"

Brad was laughing at his protestations.

"Five times. I can't believe that. I'm truly hurt, Brad."

Henry was laughing now too. He turned to Bobby and interrupted the conversation she was having. "Bobby, did you ever doubt working with me?"

"I doubt that decision every frigging day, Hip," she retorted, and resumed her conversation with Brian Fenner.

"Hmm."

Brad laughed. "You should have tossed that coin to see who you should have asked. Bobby was certainly not the one to give you the answer you wanted. You see its usefulness, Henry?"

Henry thought. Then he smiled. "You know something my friend?" he said. "I don't think there would be many people who would have loved me so much they would have ignored *four* consecutive wrong tosses of coin."

Brad shook his head. "Henry…" he said, seemingly searching for a suitable response. "Henry…" he repeated. Then probably resigning himself to the fact that Henry had succeeded in having the last word, slipped an arm around his shoulder. "Come on my friend. One more to steady the nerves, then we've got a wedding to attend."

The makeshift church seated 40 on each side and the congregation stood as Malissa approached. Lewis played the piano, his own composition which, if you listened closely, resembled a slower and cushioned version of Oranges and Lemons.

With her father at her side and Vanessa, Millie and Fifi behind, she walked between the two rows of standing people to meet up with her husband-to-be. She passed Alice and Charlie and their children, and Rod who had flown in from Dubai and wore a brand-new linen suit. Like in the little pink chapel, so many faces that greeted her were familiar. Older now, hopefully wiser, but so recognisable as those who had touched her life. New faces too, and children of parents who would have been children themselves the last time she walked down the aisle.

In the front row stood her mother. More beautiful than ever, Malissa didn't doubt she was delighted at last, to be witnessing the legal betrothal of her daughter. And holding her mother's hand, a retired clergyman who was almost ninety, beamed the kindest, most infectious smile Malissa had ever seen. He was dressed in pink.

And at the end of the aisle waiting for her, the most wonderful man she had ever known. Greyer now but still so handsome, the look in his eyes as disarming as the day she first fell in love with him outside a drinks kiosk on a little green lawn at Goodwood. The man who loved her and the man with whom she would be spending the rest of her life.

She hoped the DJ had some James Brown.

# EPILOGUE

## A BALLET IN MAJORCA, TWO DAYS BEFORE THE WEDDING

The theatre in Palma was a truly magnificent building capable of seating almost 2,000 people. It was full. Vanessa booked the performance two years ago and ever since had been readying her pupils from both Söller and Paris for the occasion. While only a supporting act of 45 minutes, it would be far and away her company's biggest production.

Henry was nervous for her but Malissa, who had witnessed its development, remained confident. They had seats on the balcony, just right of the stage.

The lights changed and hushed the audience. The curtains opened and Henry took Malissa's hand. On stage were a dozen dancers dressed as flowers and when the music started six small children, accompanied by Vanessa, appeared.

"That's Fifi," Henry said with surprise. He wasn't aware she would be one of the performers. Not even two, she was the youngest of those on the stage.

"This is your wedding gift, Henry." She pulled him close.

The young children dressed as butterflies skipped about the stage, zig zagging between the flowers that swayed to the music. After a couple of minutes, the young performers exited with Vanessa to much applause.

The lights dimmed and you could hear the scuffling as the scene was changed. When it was quiet, a solitary piano started playing and when the lights came back on there were more than 25 dancers on the stage. Butterflies, flowers, and a bear.

Percussion joined the piano and the dancing began. Henry smiled. The music sounded vaguely familiar. He was not surprised by the quality of the dancing and it occurred to him he had not, in all the years he had known her, seen Vanessa dance. Maybe she would make an appearance.

When the violins came in he felt Malissa's hand tighten. He smiled at her and then found his focus drifting from the stage to the orchestra pit and eventually to the three violinists. That vague familiarity of the tune was developing into something he undoubtedly recognised. Momentarily stunned as if something had stirred his very soul, his gaze flittered from the dancers to the musicians, from butterfly to bear, to Fifi holding Vanessa's hand in the wings, and then to Malissa.

Tears welled in his eyes, tears of joy as he slowly realised the music they were playing was Emma's. Music he had heard so often. Music he thought was lost. Music rescued, just as he had been by a woman who knew no ill.

He looked at her. Her kind knowing eyes full of love.

"Her music lives, Henry. As she does in our hearts," she said softly.

This woman holding his hand was showing love no man had the right to expect. Tears rolled down his face, not for Emma but because of love. Holding his hand was love, and in holding his hand he knew for sure, that she would forever hold his heart.

# ABOUT THE AUTHOR

I've always enjoyed writing. I promised myself that one day I would write a novel. And so I have – *The Butterfly and the Bear*. The first, I hope, of many more novels.

I remember the enjoyment I got from writing at school. I loved the stories you could create using just pen, paper, and a little imagination, but I would always veer off the subject slightly, trying to add another angle. Poetry too, or ditties, I found could tell a story. They could be written quickly, incorporate humour or something more poignant and deliver a message in a more entertaining way. On a personal level, I have often found comfort in writing to myself – discharging feelings onto paper in order to better understand them, airing them and moving them out into the open.

After school, I worked in the City. It was there I found a position within a shipping company. The original idea was to travel the world but several years later I found myself running a shipping agency, something I'm still associated with today and which employs a small number of dedicated and happy staff.

Like so many, I have always thought about writing a book. Indeed, over the years I have had several ideas and even written the opening chapters. I started writing The Butterfly and the Bear whilst on holiday in Majorca. I had little idea where the novel was going but the story unfolded much motivated by the characters I had created. Deciding to publish was a hesitant process but once sure I'd like to, the question was how.

A little research suggested a form of self-publishing would suit best. With any book, any new idea, the challenge is to 'get it out there'. I have never been an avid user of social media, but a few chats with those more savvy about these things (my children!) encouraged me to give it a try.

And so, Little Bear Publications was born. My hope is to use this fledgling company to publish both my novels and some of the poems I have written over the years. I very much hope you'll join me on this exciting journey and I'm always happy to hear from my readers, so please do get in touch and follow me on the fancy social media account my children helped to set up!

Facebook @littlebearpublications
www.littlebearpublications.co.uk

Join my mailing list to receive a free book of poems, written by Henry Ovmeister himself.

You'll also get the chance to be part of my Advanced Reader Team and receive freebies, exclusives, and lots more.

**www.littlebearpublications.co.uk**

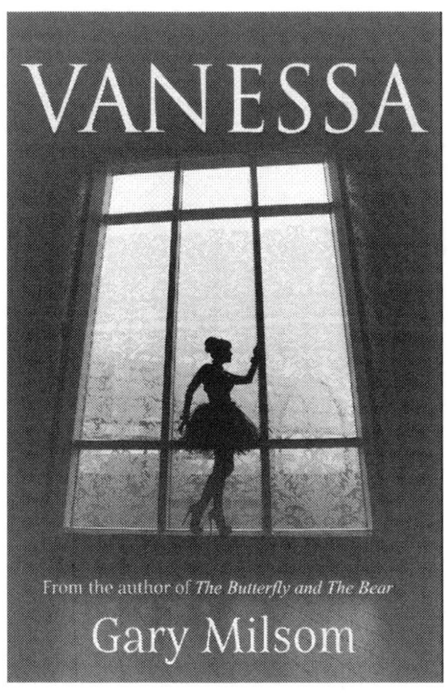

VANESSA
From the author of The Butterfly and The Bear
Gary Milsom


**PROLOGUE**

*OFFICES OF THE CORNISH TIMES MAY 1990*

Vanessa had scant respect for most men and, if she used her charms to get what she wanted, it hardly bothered her. It had taken her some time and several late-night visits to bars she'd rather not frequent to find the person who could confirm her suspicions.

What she learned in Soller had led her here, and the library's records verified what she already believed to be true. She was sad. It was the end of that particular journey, but knowing Henry as she did, she found consolation.

She read again the newspaper cutting, a review of a concert at The Royal Albert Hall, that she'd carried around with her for the last few years. She imagined the scene it depicted as she had done so many times before and then tore it in two before dropping it in the wastepaper basket.

Her train back to London left in an hour. She loved Malissa and

Henry, appreciated how happy they were and realised she had already decided that telling either of them of her discovery would serve no purpose. She would see them, and their new baby daughter, tomorrow as planned. New day, new beginning.

*Delve into Vanessa's captivating past with Gary's provocative and gripping follow up to The Butterfly and The Bear.*

***VANESSA***

*Available Summer 2020.*

# ACKNOWLEDGMENTS

From idea, through process, to  novel.
I'd like to thank Sandra Cooper and Cara Thurlbourn for encouraging me to turn an aspiration into a reality.

Printed in Great Britain
by Amazon